"十三五"江苏省高等学校重点教材

编号：2017-2-013

Classical Western Short Stories

西方经典短篇小说阅读教程

主　编　左　进　李利红
编　者　郁　敏　王春梅　张明兰
　　　　张秀娟　徐耀云　吕晓棠

本书更多资源，请扫描

南京大学出版社

图书在版编目(CIP)数据

西方经典短篇小说阅读教程 / 左进，李利红主编.
— 南京：南京大学出版社，2018.2(2023.2重印)
ISBN 978-7-305-19780-2

Ⅰ.①西… Ⅱ.①左… ②李… Ⅲ.①短篇小说-小说集-世界 Ⅳ.①I14

中国版本图书馆CIP数据核字(2017)第321406号

出版发行　南京大学出版社
社　　址　南京市汉口路22号　　邮　编　210093
出 版 人　金鑫荣

书　　名　西方经典短篇小说阅读教程
主　　编　左进　李利红
责任编辑　裴维维　　　　　　　　编辑热线　025-83592123

照　　排　南京南琳图文制作有限公司
印　　刷　广东虎彩云印刷有限公司
开　　本　787×1092　1/16　印张16　字数467千
版　　次　2018年2月第1版　2023年2月第3次印刷
ISBN 978-7-305-19780-2
定　　价　39.00元

网址：http://www.njupco.com
官方微博：http://weibo.com/njupco
官方微信号：njupress
销售咨询热线：(025) 83594756

* 版权所有，侵权必究
* 凡购买南大版图书，如有印装质量问题，请与所购
　图书销售部门联系调换

前　言

《大学英语教学指南》(2020版)(以下简称《教学指南》)作为高等学校人才培养质量国家标准,是新时代普通高等学校制定大学英语教学大纲、进行大学英语课程建设、开展大学英语课程评价的最新依据。

《教学指南》提出:大学英语的教学目标是"培养学生的英语应用能力,增强跨文化交际意识和交际能力,同时发展自主学习能力,提高综合文化素养",还指出:"根据我国现阶段基础教育、高等教育和社会发展的条件现状,大学英语教学目标分为基础、提高、发展三个等级。"根据最新的《教学指南》,现行三个级别的大学英语教学目标都对学生英语的阅读理解能力作出了明确的要求。只有多阅读,不断增加英语语言知识的输入,逐步加大阅读量,拓展阅读的广度和深度,方能不断提高英语听、说、读、写、译的综合应用能力。我们根据该文件的精神编写了大学英语拓展类高级阅读教材《西方经典短篇小说阅读教程》。

《西方经典短篇小说阅读教程》的编写符合教育部各文件对大学英语教学目标的要求,有三点特色:(1)阅读课程的最终目的应是让学生享受阅读,这也是目前诸多阅读教材难以实现的目的。本教材所选篇章用词准确、语句优美,蕴含丰富的文化知识,使学生在阅读的同时,感受英语字词的生动运用和含义丰富的句意表达。学生可在增加词汇量的同时,又能提高英语学习的技能。(2)本书所述英文原版短篇小说的文学性、趣味性更强,文化传达更完整,思维导向更清晰;同时又避免了碎片化的阅读,有益于学生思辨力的培养。(3)学生在阅读和欣赏经典美文的同时,也能够深刻了解西方有关伦理、道德、习俗等其他方面的知识,还能在阅读中领略西方文化的方方面面,感受经典篇章带给人的震撼力,从而提升自己跨文化交际的能力,提高自己的文学素养。

本教材按照有利于教师教学、有利于学生学习的思路进行编写。本书每单元后配备的习题既对学生的阅读有启发,又能发挥学生的主观能动性,启发学生思考,以达到师生互动。

全书共14个单元,每个单元分为 Part A 和 Part B 两个部分,具体安排如下:每个单元每部分都以导入练习(Lead-in Questions)为引子,导入相关小说的话题,以激发学生对后面篇章阅读的兴趣,也给学生提供了练习英语口语的机会;Questions about the Author and the Story 的目的是帮助学生顺利阅读篇章;主篇章均为精选的西方经典的短篇小说原文,易懂意深;篇章后的 Questions for Discussion 的目的是检查学生对篇章主题、重要细节等内容的掌握情况,此部分有助于学生深度理解篇章,为学生的思维提供更广阔的空间。

本教程主题丰富,引发学生思考的维度亦不同。按照设定,Part A 部分为精讲部分,Part B 部分为学生课后扩充阅读的部分。为确保完成阅读任务,需要采取课内与课外相结合的方式,加强对学生课外自主学习的指导,使学生充分利用课内外的时间,提高英语阅读能力,提升对英语的运用能力。

为适应信息化教学的需要,我们在各单元的 Part A 和 Part B 最后都提供了相关网址,以便学生自主学习时利用网上资源;有些篇幅较长的小说,为了学生阅读方便,省略了部分段落并辅以二维码供学生扫码阅读。在书中无法呈现的配套资源,读者也可扫描扉页二维码处获得。

本教材主编左进、李利红负责全书的策划、选材、设计和审校,李利红、郁敏、王春梅、张明兰、张秀娟、徐耀云和吕晓棠负责各章节的编写工作。本教材供高等学校非英语专业已完成大学英语基础阶段学习且已达到大学英语教学要求中"提高"或"发展"层级的学生使用,也可以供具有相当英语水平的英语学习者和研究人员使用。

本教材获批江苏省 2017 重点教材建设立项,感谢江苏省教育厅的支持;感谢淮阴工学院教务处的支持;感谢淮阴工学院历届公选课学生的试用及给出的反馈意见;在教材出版准备过程中,南京大学出版社提出了建设性的意见。在此,谨一并致谢。

限于编者水平,难免存在疏漏错讹,敬请广大师生批评指正。

《西方经典短篇小说阅读教程》编写组
2021 年 12 月

Contents

Chapter One 1
   Part A Hills like White Elephants 1
   Part B Indian Camp 7

Chapter Two 13
   Part A A Worn Path 13
   Part B A Rose for Emily 21

Chapter Three 32
   Part A A Native Child 32
   Part B The Egg 46

Chapter Four 52
   Part A The Interlopers 52
   Part B Before the Law 58

Chapter Five 62
   Part A The Chink and the Child 62
   Part B Tape-Measure Murder 73

Chapter Six 85
   Part A God Sees the Truth, but Waits 85
   Part B The Christmas Tree and the Wedding 93

Chapter Seven 101
   Part A The Bet 101
   Part B The Lottery Ticket 108

Chapter Eight 114
   Part A After Twenty Years 114

Part B	The Cop and the Anthem	118

Chapter Nine — 125
Part A	The White Silence	125
Part B	The Law of Life	134

Chapter Ten — 141
Part A	The Philosopher in the Apple Orchard	141
Part B	The Signal-Man	149

Chapter Eleven — 162
Part A	The Monkey's Paw	162
Part B	A Cup of Tea	173

Chapter Twelve — 181
Part A	Is He Living or Is He Dead?	181
Part B	The Mark on the Wall	189

Chapter Thirteen — 198
Part A	The End of the Flight	198
Part B	The Necklace	204

Chapter Fourteen — 213
Part A	Letter from an Unknown Woman	213
Part B	The Bear Came Over the Mountain	240

Chapter One

Hills Like White Elephants

By Ernest Hemingway

Ernest Hemingway (1899—1961) was one of the best-known American authors of the 20th century. Hemingway was born in Oak Park, Illinois. After high school, he worked as a newspaper reporter and then went overseas to take part in World War Ⅰ as an ambulance driver and infantryman with the Italian army. He was badly wounded at the age of eighteen. Also, he took an active part in the anti-Fascist struggle in the Spanish Civil War and in World War Ⅱ, and served as a war correspondent in both. Emotional breakdowns that proceeded from his frustrations about writing well in addition to physical ailments resulting from war wounds and heavy drinking finally led to his suicide in 1961.

Hemingway's main works include *In Our Time* (1925), *The Sun Also Rises* (1926), *A Farewell to Arms* (1929), and *The Old Man and the Sea* (1952) which won the Pulitzer Prize (1953) and the Nobel Prize in Literature (1954). His fiction usually focuses on people's living essential and dangerous lives—soldiers, fishermen, athletes, bullfighters, who meet the pain and difficulty of their existence with stoic courage. This code may be summed up in his phrase "grace under pressure." His style is characterized by the understatement, the suppression of emotion, the almost indifferent handling of the extraordinary, and the deceptive economy in expression. This is known as the "iceberg technique." What's more, he is distinguished for his skill in developing the plot through casual conversations rather than action. His best known stories *Hills like White Elephants* and *Indian Camp* are good examples to present his themes and writing styles.

Lead-in Questions
1. Why is Hemingway called the spokesman of the Lost Generation?
2. How is the Iceberg Theory embodied in Hemingway's works?

Questions about the Author and the Story
1. The girl's name Jig is mentioned in the story, but the man's name is not. Why might Hemingway have done so?
   A. Because the man is not important to the story.
   B. Because the man isn't the one thinking of having an operation.
   C. Because the girl is the one who talked about hills like white elephants.
   D. Because the man could represent any man, anywhere in the world.
2. Where does the story take place?
   A. In Barcelona.   B. In a bar.
   C. At a train station.   D. In a hotel.
3. The girl told the man that the Anis del Toro tasted like licorice, and then said: "Everything tastes of licorice." Why did she say that?
   A. Licorice is a spice used in many Spanish dishes.
   B. Spanish water has a slight licorice taste.
   C. Licorice is common in Spain. She thinks that all new things become boring after a while.
   D. She loves licorice and loves their life of traveling and trying new things.
4. Further on in the conversation he says, "I think it's the best thing to do. But I don't want you to do it if you don't really want to." What does he really mean?
   A. He is not sure if the operation is safe, but he doesn't want to scare her.
   B. He doesn't mind whether she has the operation or not.
   C. He doesn't want her to have the operation, but she can if she wants to.
   D. He wants her to have the operation, but also wants her to take responsibility for the decision.
5. Towards the end of the story the man says, "We can have the world." The girl answers: "No, we can't. It isn't ours any more. ... And once they take it away, you never get it back." What might the girl's answer mean?
   A. She is worried that if she has the operation, they may not be able to travel any more.
   B. No one can own the world. It can't belong to any one.
   C. She is scared that she might die if she has the operation.
   D. She is worried that if she has the operation, she might lose the most important thing in the world.

The hills across the valley of the Ebro① were long and white. On this side there was no shade and no trees and the station was between two lines of rails in the sun. Close against the side of the station there was the warm shadow of the building and a curtain, made of strings of bamboo beads, hung across the open door into the bar, to keep out flies. The American and the girl with him sat at a table in the shade, outside the building. It was very hot and the express from Barcelona would come in forty minutes. It stopped at this junction for two minutes and went on to Madrid.

"What should we drink?" the girl asked. She had taken off her hat and put it on the table.

"It's pretty hot," the man said.

"Let's drink beer."

"Dos cervezas②," the man said into the curtain.

"Big ones?" a woman asked from the doorway.

"Yes. Two big ones."

The woman brought two glasses of beer and two felt pads. She put the felt pads and the beer glasses on the table and looked at the man and the girl. The girl was looking off at the line of hills. They were white in the sun and the country was brown and dry.

"They look like white elephants," she said.

"I've never seen one," the man drank his beer.

"No, you wouldn't have."

"I might have," the man said. "Just because you say I wouldn't have doesn't prove anything."

The girl looked at the bead curtain. "They've painted something on it," she said. "What does it say?"

"Anis del Toro③. It's a drink."

"Could we try it?"

The man called "Listen" through the curtain. The woman came out from the bar. "Four reales④."

"We want two Anis del Toro."

"With water?"

"Do you want it with water?"

"I don't know," the girl said. "Is it good with water?"

---

① the Ebro: the river that goes through the north of Spain into the Mediterranean;埃布罗河,流经西班牙北部,注入地中海

② Dos cervezas:[Spanish] two beers;[西班牙语]来两杯啤酒

③ Anis del Toro:[Spanish] an alcoholic drink that is dark in color and tastes like licorice;[西班牙语]茴香酒,味道像甘草的绿色酒

④ reales: a coin used in Spain in the old days;里亚尔,昔时西班牙使用的货币

"It's all right."

"You want them with water?" asked the woman.

"Yes, with water."

"It tastes like licorice," the girl said and put the glass down.

"That's the way with everything."

"Yes," said the girl. "Everything tastes of licorice. Especially all the things you've waited so long for, like absinthe①."

"Oh, cut it out."

"You started it," the girl said. "I was being amused. I was having a fine time."

"Well, let's try and have a fine time."

"All right. I was trying. I said the mountains looked like white elephants. Wasn't that bright?"

"That was bright."

"I wanted to try this new drink. That's all we do, isn't it—look at things and try new drinks?"

"I guess so."

The girl looked across at the hills.

"They're lovely hills," she said. "They don't really look like white elephants. I just meant the coloring of their skin through the trees."

"Should we have another drink?"

"All right."

The warm wind blew the bead curtain against the table.

"The beer's nice and cool," the man said.

"It's lovely," the girl said.

"It's really an awfully simple operation, Jig," the man said. "It's not really an operation at all."

The girl looked at the ground the table legs rested on.

"I know you wouldn't mind it, Jig. It's really not anything. It's just to let the air in."

The girl did not say anything.

"I'll go with you and I'll stay with you all the time. They just let the air in and then it's all perfectly natural."

"Then what will we do afterward?"

"We'll be fine afterward. Just like we were before."

"What makes you think so?"

"That's the only thing that bothers us. It's the only thing that's made us unhappy."

The girl looked at the bead curtain, put her hand out and took hold of two of the

---

① absinthe: a bitter and green alcoholic drink made with herds; 艾酒,艾叶制作的味苦的绿色酒

strings of beads.

"And you think then we'll be all right and be happy."

"I know we will. You don't have to be afraid. I've known lots of people that have done it."

"So have I," said the girl. "And afterward they were all so happy."

"Well," the man said, "if you don't want to you don't have to. I wouldn't have you do it if you didn't want to. But I know it's perfectly simple."

"And you really want to?"

"I think it's the best thing to do. But I don't want you to do it if you don't really want to."

"And if I do it you'll be happy and things will be like they were and you'll love me?"

"I love you now. You know I love you."

"I know. But if I do it, then it will be nice again if I say things are like white elephants, and you'll like it?"

"I'll love it. I love it now but I just can't think about it. You know how I get when I worry."

"If I do it you won't ever worry?"

"I won't worry about that because it's perfectly simple."

"Then I'll do it. Because I don't care about me."

"What do you mean?"

"I don't care about me."

"Well, I care about you."

"Oh, yes. But I don't care about me. And I'll do it and then everything will be fine."

"I don't want you to do it if you feel that way."

The girl stood up and walked to the end of the station. Across, on the other side, were fields of grain and trees along the banks of the Ebro. Far away, beyond the river, were mountains. The shadow of a cloud moved across the field of grain and she saw the river through the trees.

"And we could have all this," she said. "And we could have everything and every day we make it more impossible."

"What did you say?"

"I said we could have everything."

"We can have everything."

"No, we can't."

"We can have the whole world."

"No, we can't."

"We can go everywhere."

"No, we can't. It isn't ours any more."

"It's ours."

"No, it isn't. And once they take it away, you never get it back."

"But they haven't taken it away."

"We'll wait and see."

"Come on back in the shade," he said. "You mustn't feel that way."

"I don't feel any way," the girl said. "I just know things."

"I don't want you to do anything that you don't want to do—"

"Nor that isn't good for me," she said. "I know. Could we have another beer?"

"All right. But you've got to realize—"

"I realize," the girl said. "Can't we maybe stop talking?"

They sat down at the table and the girl looked across at the hills on the dry side of the valley and the man looked at her and at the table.

"You've got to realize," he said, "that I don't want you to do it if you don't want to. I'm perfectly willing to go through with it if it means anything to you."

"Doesn't it mean anything to you? We could get along."

"Of course it does. But I don't want anybody but you. I don't want any one else. And I know it's perfectly simple."

"Yes, you know it's perfectly simple."

"It's all right for you to say that, but I do know it."

"Would you do something for me now?"

"I'd do anything for you."

"Would you please please please please please please please stop talking."

He did not say anything but looked at the bags against the wall of the station. There were labels on them from all the hotels where they had spent nights.

"But I don't want you to," he said, "I don't care anything about it."

"I'll scream," the girl said.

The woman came out through the curtains with two glasses of beer and put them down on the damp felt pads.

"The train comes in five minutes," she said.

"What did she say?" asked the girl.

"That the train is coming in five minutes."

The girl smiled brightly at the woman, to thank her.

"I'd better take the bags over to the other side of the station," the man said. She smiled at him.

"All right. Then come back and we'll finish the beer."

He picked up the two heavy bags and carried them around the station to the other tracks. He looked up the tracks but could not see the train. Coming back, he walked through the barroom, where people waiting for the train were drinking. He drank an Anis at the bar and looked at the people. They were all waiting reasonably for the train.

He went out through the bead curtain. She was sitting at the table and smiled at him.

"Do you feel better?" he asked.

"I feel fine," she said. "There's nothing wrong with me. I feel fine."

Questions for Discussion

1. What's the real problem with the two characters? Has the man tried to understand the woman? Do they understand each other?
2. What's the significance of the setting in this novel?
3. Why does the author use the title "Hills like White Elephant"?

Links

1. https://en.wikipedia.org/wiki/Ernest_Hemingway
   关于海明威生平及创作的详细介绍。
2. http://genius.com/Ernest-hemingway-hills-like-white-elephants-annotated
   关于海明威的小说《白象似的群山》的细读资料。

Indian Camp

By Ernest Hemingway

Lead-in Questions

1. What are the characteristics of Hemingway's Code Hero?
2. How much do you know about the theme and the style of Ernest Hemingway's writing?

Questions about the Author and the Story

1. In *Indian Camp*, Nick, the main character, witnesses _____.
   A. a tragic killing of the Indians by the white men
   B. the real friendship between the white men and the Indians
   C. a senseless killing of each other
   D. the terrible scenes of birth and death
2. What is Nick's father's reaction after Nick witnesses the Indian man's suicide?
   A. Angry.   B. Apologetic.   C. Confused.   D. Pleased.
3. What did Nick's father compare the operation to immediately?
   A. Football player after a game.   B. Politician after a speech.

C. Student after a test.   D. Soldier after a battle.
4. Which of the following lines convinces you of Nick's innocence?
   A. "Where are we going, Dad?"
   B. "Oh, Daddy, can't you give her something to make her stop screaming?"
   C. "Nick didn't look at it."
   D. All of the above.
5. In *Indian Camp*, Nick's night trip to the Indian village and his experience inside the hut can be taken as _____.
   A. an essential lesson about Indian tribes
   B. a confrontation to the harshness of life
   C. an initiation to the harshness of life
   D. a leading process in human relationship

At the lake shore there was another rowboat drawn up. The two Indians stood waiting.

Nick and his father got in the stern of the boat and the Indians shoved it off and one of them got in to row. Uncle George sat in the stern of the camp rowboat. The young Indian shoved the camp boat off and got in to row Uncle George.

The two boats started off in the dark. Nick heard the oarlocks of the other boat quite a way ahead of them in the mist. The Indians rowed with quick choppy strokes. Nick lay back with his father's arm around him. It was cold on the water. The Indian who was rowing them was working very hard, but the other boat moved farther ahead in the mist all the time.

"Where are we going, Dad?" Nick asked.

"Over to the Indian camp. There is an Indian lady very sick."

"Oh," said Nick.

Across the bay they found the other boat beached. Uncle George was smoking a cigar in the dark. The young Indian pulled the boat way up the beach. Uncle George gave both the Indians cigars.

They walked up from the beach through a meadow that was soaking wet① with dew, following the young Indian who carried a lantern. Then they went into the woods and followed a trail that led to the logging road that ran back into the hills. It was much lighter on the logging road as the timber was cut away on both sides. The young Indian stopped and blew out his lantern and they all walked on along the road.

They came around a bend and a dog came out barking. Ahead were the lights of the

---

① soaking wet: very wet; 湿透

shanties where the Indian bark peelers① lived. More dogs rushed out at them. The two Indians sent them back to the shanties. In the shanty nearest the road there was a light in the window. An old woman stood in the doorway holding a lamp.

Inside on a wooden bunk lay a young Indian woman. She had been trying to have her baby for two days. All the old women in the camp had been helping her. The men had moved off up the road to sit in the dark and smoke out of range of the noise she made. She screamed just as Nick and the two Indians followed his father and Uncle George into the shanty. She lay in the lower bunk, very big under a quilt. Her head was turned to one side. In the upper bunk was her husband. He had cut his foot very badly with an ax three days before. He was smoking a pipe. The room smelled very bad.

Nick's father ordered some water to be put on the stove, and while it was heating he spoke to Nick.

"This lady is going to have a baby, Nick," he said.

"I know," said Nick.

"You don't know," said his father. "Listen to me. What she is going through is called being in labor. The baby wants to be born and she wants it to be born. All her muscles are trying to get the baby born. That is what is happening when she screams."

"I see," Nick said.

Just then the woman cried out.

"Oh, Daddy, can't you give her something to make her stop screaming?" asked Nick.

"No. I haven't any anesthetic," his father said. "But her screams are not important. I don't hear them because they are not important."

The husband in the upper bunk rolled over against the wall.

The woman in the kitchen motioned to the doctor that the water was hot. Nick's father went into the kitchen and poured about half of the water out of the big kettle into a basin. Into the water left in the kettle he put several things he unwrapped from a handkerchief.

"Those must boil," he said, and began to scrub his hands in the basin of hot water with a cake of soap he had brought from the camp. Nick watched his father's hands scrubbing each other with the soap. While his father washed his hands very carefully and thoroughly, he talked.

"You see, Nick, babies are supposed to be born head first but sometimes they're not. When they're not they make a lot of trouble for everybody. Maybe I'll have to operate on this lady. We'll know in a little while."

When he was satisfied with his hands he went in and went to work.

"Pull back that quilt, will you, George?" he said. "I'd rather not touch it."

---

① bark peelers: those people who take the skin on boughs and trunks off a tree; 剥树皮的土著人

Later when he started to operate Uncle George and three Indian men held the woman still. She bit Uncle George on the arm and Uncle George said, "Damn squaw① bitch!" and the young Indian who had rowed Uncle George over laughed at him. Nick held the basin for his father. It all took a long time.

His father picked the baby up and slapped it to make it breathe and handed it to the old woman.

"See, it's a boy, Nick," he said. "How do you like being an internee?"

Nick said, "All right." He was looking away so as not to see what his father was doing.

"There. That gets it," said his father and put something into the basin.

Nick didn't look at it.

"Now," his father said, "there's some stitches to put in. You can watch this or not, Nick, just as you like. I'm going to sew up the incision I made."

Nick did not watch. His curiosity had been gone for a long time.

His father finished and stood up. Uncle George and the three Indian men stood up. Nick put the basin out in the kitchen.

Uncle George looked at his arm. The young Indian smiled reminiscently.

"I'll put some peroxide on that, George," the doctor said.

He bent over the Indian woman. She was quiet now and her eyes were closed. She looked very pale. She did not know what had become of the baby or anything.

"I'll be back in the morning," the doctor said, standing up. "The nurse should be here from St. Ignace by noon and she'll bring everything we need."

He was feeling exalted and talkative as football players are in the dressing room after a game.

"That's one for the medical journal, George," he said. "Doing a Caesarian with a jackknife② and sewing it up with nine-foot, tapered gut leaders."

Uncle George was standing against the wall, looking at his arm.

"Oh, you're a great man, all right," he said.

"Ought to have a look at the proud father. They're usually the worst sufferers in these little affairs," the doctor said. "I must say he took it all pretty quietly."

He pulled back the blanket from the Indian's head. His hand came away wet. He mounted on the edge of the lower bunk with the lamp in one hand and looked in. The Indian lay with his face toward the wall. His throat had been cut from ear to ear. The blood had flowed down into a pool where his body sagged the bunk. His head rested on his left arm. The open razor lay, edge up, in the blankets.

"Take Nick out of the shanty, George," the doctor said.

---

① squaw: American Indian woman; 美国印第安妇女
② jackknife: large pocket-knife with a folding blade; 大折刀

There was no need of that. Nick standing in the door of the kitchen, had a good view of the upper bunk when his father, the lamp in one hand, tipped the Indian's head back.

It was just beginning to be daylight when they walked along the logging road back toward the lake.

"I'm terribly sorry I brought you along, Nickie," said his father, all his postoperative exhilaration gone. "It was an awful mess to put you through."

"Do ladies always have such a hard time having babies?" Nick asked.

"No, that was very, very exceptional."

"Why did he kill himself, Daddy?"

"I don't know, Nick. He couldn't stand things, I guess."

"Do many men kill themselves, Daddy?"

"Not very many, Nick."

"Do many women?"

"Hardly ever."

"Don't they ever?"

"Oh, yes. They do sometimes."

"Daddy?"

"Yes."

"Where did Uncle George go?"

"He'll turn up all right."

"Is dying hard, Daddy?"

"No, I think it's pretty easy, Nick. It all depends."

They were seated in the boat, Nick in the stern, his father rowing. The sun was coming up over the hills. A bass① jumped, making a circle in the water. Nick trailed his hand in the water. It felt warm in the sharp chill of the morning.

In the early morning on the lake sitting in the stern of the boat with his father rowing, he felt quite sure that he would never die.

❈ Questions for Discussion

1. What happened to the woman who was having a baby in the story?
2. What happened to the new father? How do you understand him? Is he brave or cowardly?
3. In *Indian Camp*, what is the effect of the young husband's death on Nick Adams?

---

① bass: a kind of fish; 欧洲鲈鱼

Links

1. https：//en.wikipedia.org/wiki/Ernest_Hemingway
   关于海明威生平及创作的详细介绍。
2. http：//www.chinadmd.com/file/poiooxppwzpous6xivoeravu_2.html
   关于海明威的小说《印第安营寨》的细读资料。

Chapter Two

Part A

A Worn Path

By Eudora Welty

Eudora Welty (1909—2001) is widely considered one of the most important contemporary fiction writers in America. Welty was born in Jackson Mississippi, where she spent nearly all her life peacefully. She was educated at the Mississippi State College for Women and the University of Wisconsin. In 1941, she published her first collection of stories, *A Curtain of Green and Other Stories*, and won, for *A Worn Path*, the first of her six O. Henry Memorial Contest Awards. During the World War Ⅱ, she was a staff member of *The New York Times Book Review*. In 1943, her second book of stories, *The Wide Net and Other Stories* came out. In 1972, her novel *The Optimist's Daughter* won the Pulitzer Prize. In 1980, her 41 stories were collected and published under the title *The Collected Stories of Eudora Welty*. She has written several novels, but it is her command of the short story as art form that makes her a master. Her works, especially the short stories, are considered the treasure of southern literature.

As a promising young writer of Southern Renaissance, Welty inherited traditions of southern literature, and developed the artistic style and writing techniques of Modernism. In her stories, she uses the perspectives of temperaments, ironic distance and the method of drawing back to frame a picture. More importantly, she dramatizes something out of the seeming nothingness of human situations with an insightful feminine sensitivity. The story *A Worn Path* is a detailed account of an old black woman—Phoenix Jackson's journeys on foot through rough terrain to obtain medicine for her grandson. There is no apparent sympathy and even admiration in the vivid description of this old lady.

Lead-in Questions

1. How much do you know about the race relations in Mississippi during the 1940s, and how are the same beliefs and ideas represented in Welty's *A Worn Path*?
2. Why did Welty name the main character Phoenix? What does the main character's name mean?

Questions about the Author and the Story

1. What motivates Phoenix to make the long journey time and again?
   A. Love for her grandson.
   B. The need to find work.
   C. Interest in the city's cultural life.
   D. A penchant for people to watch.
2. What does Phoenix Jackson think she sees when she rests by the riverbank?
   A. An alligator.
   B. A singing bird.
   C. A boy offering a piece of cake.
   D. A scarecrow.
3. Why did NOT Phoenix ever go to school?
   A. She was too old by the time black children were allowed to attend.
   B. She had no interest in attending school.
   C. There were no schools near her.
   D. Her parents forbade her from attending.
4. What, in the city, does Phoenix seem to be ashamed of?
   A. Her lack of money.
   B. Her religious views.
   C. Her lack of education.
   D. Her mismatched socks.
5. What's the nurse's attitude towards Phoenix?
   A. Contemptuous.   B. Friendly.
   C. Indifferent.   D. Impolite.

It was December—a bright frozen day in the early morning. Far out in the country there was an old Negro woman with her head tied in a red rag, coming along a path through the pinewoods. Her name was Phoenix① Jackson. She was very old and small

---

① A phoenix is an imaginary bird which, according to ancient stories, burns itself to ashes every five hundred years and is then born again; 凤凰, 长生鸟, 根据远古传说, 凤凰可活五百年, 然后自焚为灰而再生

and she walked slowly in the dark pine shadows, moving a little from side to side in her steps, with the balanced heaviness and lightness of a pendulum in a grandfather clock. She carried a thin, small cane made from an umbrella, and with this she kept tapping the frozen earth in front of her. This made a grave and persistent noise in the still air, that seemed meditative, like the chirping of a solitary little bird.

She wore a dark striped dress reaching down to her shoe tops, and an equally long apron of bleached sugar sacks, with a full pocket: all neat and tidy, but every time she took a step she might have fallen over her shoelaces, which dragged from her unlaced shoes. She looked straight ahead. Her eyes were blue with age. Her skin had a pattern all its own of numberless branching wrinkles and as though a whole little tree stood in the middle of her forehead, but a golden color ran underneath, and the two knobs of her cheeks were illumined by a yellow burning under the dark. Under the red rag her hair came down on her neck in the frailest of ringlets, still black, and with an odor like copper.

Now and then there was a quivering in the thicket. Old Phoenix said, "Out of my way, all you foxes, owls, beetles, jack rabbits, coons and wild animals! ... Keep out from under these feet, little bob-whites ... Keep the big wild hogs out of my path. Don't let none of those come running my direction. I got a long way." Under her small black-freckled hand her cane, limber as a buggy whip, would switch at the brush as if to rouse up any hiding things.

On she went. The woods were deep and still. The sun made the pine needles almost too bright to look at, up where the wind rocked. The cones dropped as light as feathers. Down in the hollow was the mourning dove—it was not too late for him.

The path ran up a hill. "Seem like there is chains about my feet, time I get this far," she said, in the voice of argument old people keep to use with themselves. "Something always take a hold of me on this hill—pleads I should stay."

After she got to the top, she turned and gave a full, severe look behind her where she had come. "Up through pines," she said at length. "Now down through oaks."

Her eyes opened their widest, and she started down gently. But before she got to the bottom of the hill a bush caught her dress.

Her fingers were busy and intent, but her skirts were full and long, so that before she could pull them free in one place they were caught in another. It was not possible to allow the dress to tear. "I in the thorny bush," she said. "Thorns, you doing your appointed work. Never want to let folks pass, no sir. Old eyes thought you was a pretty little *green* bush."

Finally, trembling all over, she stood free, and after a moment dared to stoop for her cane.

"Sun so high!" she cried, leaning back and looking, while the thick tears went over her eyes. "The time getting all gone here."

At the foot of this hill was a place where a log was laid across the creek.

"Now comes the trial," said Phoenix.

Putting her right foot out, she mounted the log and shut her eyes. Lifting her skirt, leveling her cane fiercely before her, like a festival figure in some parade, she began to march across. Then she opened her eyes and she was safe on the other side.

"I wasn't as old as I thought," she said.

But she sat down to rest. She spread her skirts on the bank around her and folded her hands over her knees. Up above her was a tree in a pearly cloud of mistletoe. She did not dare to close her eyes, and when a little boy brought her a plate with a slice of marble-cake on it she spoke to him. "That would be acceptable," she said. But when she went to take it there was just her own hand in the air.

So she left that tree, and had to go through a barbed-wire fence. There she had to creep and crawl, spreading her knees and stretching her fingers like a baby trying to climb the steps. But she talked loudly to herself: she could not let her dress be torn now, so late in the day, and she could not pay for having her arm or her leg sawed off if she got caught fast where she was.

At last she was safe through the fence and risen up out in the clearing. Big dead trees, like black men with one arm, were standing in the purple stalks of the withered cotton field. There sat a buzzard.

"Who you watching?"

In the furrow she made her way along.

"Glad this not the season for bulls," she said, looking sideways, "and the good Lord made his snakes to curl up and sleep in the winter. A pleasure I don't see no two-headed snake coming around that tree, where it come once. It took a while to get by him, back in the summer."

She passed through the old cotton and went into a field of dead corn. It whispered and shook, and was taller than her head. "Through the maze now," she said, for there was no path.

Then there was something tall, black, and skinny there, moving before her.

At first she took it for a man. It could have been a man dancing in the field. But she stood still and listened, and it did not make a sound. It was as silent as a ghost.

"Ghost," she said sharply, "who be you the ghost of? For I have heard of nary death close by."

But there was no answer, only the ragged dancing in the wind.

She shut her eyes, reached out her hand, and touched a sleeve. She found a coat and inside that an emptiness, cold as ice.

"You scarecrow," she said. Her face lighted. "I ought to be shut up for good," she said with laughter. "My senses is gone. I too old. I the oldest people I ever know. Dance, old scarecrow," she said, "while I dancing with you."

Chapter Two

She kicked her foot over the furrow, and with mouth drawn down shook her head once or twice in a little strutting way. Some husks blew down and whirled in streamers about her skirts.

Then she went on, parting her way from side to side with the cane, through the whispering field. At last she came to the end, to a wagon track where the silver grass blew between the red ruts. The quail were walking around like pullets, seeming all dainty and unseen.

"Walk pretty," she said. "This the easy place. This the easy going."

She followed the track, swaying through the quiet bare fields, through the little strings of trees silver in their dead leaves, past cabins silver from weather, with the doors and windows boarded shut, all like old women under a spell sitting there. "I walking in their sleep," she said, nodding her head vigorously.

In a ravine she went where a spring was silently flowing through a hollow log. Old Phoenix bent and drank. "Sweet gum makes the water sweet," she said, and drank more. "Nobody know who made this well, for it was here when I was born."

The track crossed a swampy part where the moss hung as white as lace from every limb. "Sleep on, alligators, and blow your bubbles." Then the track went into the road.

Deep, deep it went down between the high green-colored banks. Overhead the live oaks met, and it was as dark as a cave.

A big black dog with a lolling tongue came up out of the weeds by the ditch. She was meditating, and not ready, and when he came at her she only hit him a little with her cane. Over she went in the ditch, like a little puff of milkweed.

Down there, her senses drifted away. A dream visited her, and she reached her hand up, but nothing reached down and gave her a pull. So she lay there and presently went to talking. "Old woman," she said to herself, "that black dog come up out of the weeds to stall you off, and now there he sitting on his fine tail, smiling at you."

A white man finally came along and found her—a hunter, a young man, with his dog on a chain.

"Well, Granny!" he laughed. "What are you doing there?"

"Lying on my back like a June-bug waiting to be turned over, mister," she said, reaching up her hand.

He lifted her up, gave her a swing in the air, and set her down. "Anything broken, Granny?"

"No sir, the old dead weeds is springy enough," said Phoenix, when she had got her breath. "I thank you for your trouble."

"Where do you live, Granny?" he asked, while the two dogs were growling at each other.

"Away back yonder, sir, behind the ridge. You can't even see it from here."

"On your way home?"

"No sir, I going to town."

"Why, that's too far! That's as far as I walk when I come out myself, and I get something for my trouble." He patted the stuffed bag he carried, and there hung down a little closed claw. It was one of the bob-whites, with its beak hooked bitterly to show it was dead. "Now you go on home, Granny!"

"I bound to go to town, mister," said Phoenix. "The time come around."

He gave another laugh, filling the whole landscape. "I know you old colored people! Wouldn't miss going to town to see Santa Claus!"

But something held Old Phoenix very still. The deep lines in her face went into a fierce and different radiation. Without warning, she had seen with her own eyes a flashing nickel fall out of the man's pocket onto the ground.

"How old are you, Granny?" he was saying.

"There is no telling, mister," she said, "no telling."

Then she gave a little cry and clapped her hands and said, "Git on away from here, dog! Look! Look at that dog!" She laughed as if in admiration. "He ain't scared of nobody. He a big black dog." She whispered, "Sic him!"

"Watch me get rid of that cur," said the man. "Sic him, Pete! Sic him!"

Phoenix heard the dogs fighting, and heard the man running and throwing sticks. She even heard a gunshot. But she was slowly bending forward by that time, further and further forward, the lids stretched down over her eyes, as if she were doing this in her sleep. Her chin was lowered almost to her knees. The yellow palm of her hand came out from the fold of her apron. Her fingers slid down and along the ground under the piece of money with the grace and care they would have in lifting an egg from under a setting hen. Then she slowly straightened up; she stood erect, and the nickel was in her apron pocket. A bird flew by. Her lips moved. "God watching me the whole time. I come to stealing."

The man came back, and his own dog panted about them. "Well, I scared him off that time," he said, and then he laughed and lifted his gun and pointed it at Phoenix.

She stood straight and faced him.

"Doesn't the gun scare you?" he said, still pointing it.

"No, sir, I seen plenty go off closer by, in my day, and for less than what I done," she said, holding utterly still.

He smiled, and shouldered the gun. "Well, Granny," he said, "you must be a hundred years old, and scared of nothing. I'd give you a dime if I had any money with me. But you take my advice and stay home, and nothing will happen to you."

"I bound to go on my way, mister," said Phoenix. She inclined her head in the red rag. Then they went in different directions, but she could hear the gun shooting again and again over the hill.

She walked on. The shadows hung from the oak trees to the road like curtains.

Then she smelled wood smoke, and smelled the river, and she saw a steeple and the cabins on their steep steps. Dozens of little black children whirled around her. There ahead was Natchez shining. Bells were ringing. She walked on.

In the paved city it was Christmas time. There were red and green electric lights strung and crisscrossed everywhere, and all turned on in the daytime. Old Phoenix would have been lost if she had not distrusted her eyesight and depended on her feet to know where to take her.

She paused quietly on the sidewalk, where people were passing by. A lady came along in the crowd, carrying an armful of red-, green-, and silver-wrapped presents; she gave off perfume like the red roses in hot summer, and Phoenix stopped her.

"Please, missy, will you lace up my shoe?" She held up her foot.

"What do you want, Grandma?"

"See my shoe," said Phoenix. "Do all right for out in the country, but wouldn't look right to go in a big building."

"Stand still then, Grandma," said the lady. She put her packages down on the sidewalk beside her and laced and tied both shoes tightly.

"Can't lace'em with a cane," said Phoenix. "Thank you, missy. I doesn't mind asking a nice lady to tie up my shoe, when I gets out on the street."

Moving slowly and from side to side, she went into the big building, and into a tower of steps, where she walked up and around and around until her feet knew to stop.

She entered a door, and there she saw nailed up on the wall the document that had been stamped with the gold seal and framed in the gold frame, which matched the dream that was hung up in her head.

"Here I be," she said. There was a fixed and ceremonial stiffness over her body.

"A charity case, I suppose," said an attendant who sat at the desk before her.

But Phoenix only looked above her head. There was sweat on her face, the wrinkles in her skin shone like a bright net.

"Speak up, Grandma," the woman said. "What's your name? We must have your history, you know. Have you been here before? What seems to be the trouble with you?"

Old Phoenix only gave a twitch to her face as if a fly were bothering her.

"Are you deaf?" cried the attendant.

But then the nurse came in.

"Oh, that's just old Aunt Phoenix," she said. "She doesn't come for herself—she has a little grandson. She makes these trips just as regular as clockwork. She lives away back off the Old Natchez Trace." She bent down. "Well, Aunt Phoenix, why don't you just take a seat? We won't keep you standing after your long trip." She pointed.

The old woman sat down, bolt upright in the chair.

"Now, how is the boy?" asked the nurse.

Old Phoenix did not speak.

"I said, how is the boy?"

But Phoenix only waited and stared straight ahead, her face very solemn and withdrawn into rigidity.

"Is his throat any better?" asked the nurse. "Aunt Phoenix, don't you hear me? Is your grandson's throat any better since the last time you came for the medicine?"

With her hands on her knees, the old woman waited, silent, erect and motionless, just as if she were in armor.

"You mustn't take up our time this way, Aunt Phoenix," the nurse said. "Tell us quickly about your grandson, and get it over. He isn't dead, is he?"

At last there came a flicker and then a flame of comprehension across her face, and she spoke.

"My grandson. It was my memory had left me. There I sat and forgot why I made my long trip."

"Forgot?" The nurse frowned. "After you came so far?"

Then Phoenix was like an old woman begging a dignified forgiveness for waking up frightened in the night. "I never did go to school, I was too old at the Surrender," she said in a soft voice. "I'm an old woman without an education. It was my memory fail me. My little grandson, he is just the same, and I forgot it in the coming."

"Throat never heals, does it?" said the nurse, speaking in a loud, sure voice to Old Phoenix. By now she had a card with something written on it, a little list. "Yes. Swallowed lye. When was it? —January—two—three years ago—"

Phoenix spoke unasked now. "No, missy, he not dead, he just the same. Every little while his throat begin to close up again, and he not able to swallow. He not get his breath. He not able to help himself. So the time come around, and I go on another trip for the soothing-medicine."

"All right. The doctor said as long as you came to get it, you could have it," said the nurse. "But it's an obstinate case."

"My little grandson, he sit up there in the house all wrapped up, waiting by himself," Phoenix went on. "We is the only two left in the world. He suffer and it don't seem to put him back at all. He got a sweet look. He going to last. He wear a little patch quilt and peep out holding his mouth open like a little bird. I remembers so plain now. I not going to forget him again, no, the whole enduring time. I could tell him from all the others in creation."

"All right." The nurse was trying to hush her now. She brought her a bottle of medicine. "Charity," she said, making a check mark in a book.

Old Phoenix held the bottle close to her eyes, and then carefully put it into her pocket.

"I thank you," she said.

"It's Christmas time, Grandma," said the attendant. "Could I give you a few pennies out of my purse?"

"Five pennies is a nickel," said Phoenix stiffly.

"Here's a nickel," said the attendant.

Phoenix rose carefully and held out her hand. She received the nickel and then fished the other nickel out of her pocket and laid it beside the new one. She stared at her palm closely, with her head on one side.

Then she gave a tap with her cane on the floor.

"This is what come to me to do," she said. "I going to the store and buy my child a little windmill they sells, made out of paper. He going to find it hard to believe there such a thing in the world. I'll march myself back where he waiting, holding it straight up in this hand."

She lifted her free hand, gave a little nod, turned around, and walked out of the doctor's office. Then her slow step began on the stairs, going down.

Questions for Discussion

1. What deterrents did the old woman encounter on her trip to town?
2. Is the grandson, in the story *A Worn Path*, dead or alive? Give your reasons.
3. What positive human qualities does the old black woman represent if this is a story about human dignity? How does she struggle to maintain her dignity?

Links

1. https://en.wikipedia.org/wiki/Eudora_Welty
   关于尤多拉·韦尔蒂生平及创作的详细介绍。
2. http://xroads.virginia.edu/~drbr/ew_path.html
   关于尤多拉·韦尔蒂的小说《熟路》的细读资料。

A Rose for Emily

By William Faulkner

William Faulkner (1897—1962) is one of the great American writers of the 20th century. Born in New Albany, Mississippi, and raised in nearby Oxford, Faulkner lived there almost all his life. Most of Faulkner's novels are set in Yoknapatawpha County, an imagery area in Mississippi with a colorful history and a richly varied population. The county is a microcosm of the South as a whole, and Faulkner's novels examine the effects of the dissolution of traditional values and authority on all levels of southern society.

Faulkner wrote altogether 19 novels, among which the best-known ones are *The Sound and the Fury* (1929), *As I Lay Dying* (1930), *Sanctuary* (1931), *Light in August* (1932), *Absalom, Absalom!* (1936), *The Hamlet* (1940), *Intruder in the Dust* (1948). In addition to novels, Faulkner published several volumes of short stories including *These 13* (1931), *Go Down, Moses* (1942), *Knight's Gambit* (1949), and *Big Woods* (1955); and collections of poems and essays.

Faulkner has always been regarded as a man with great might of invention and experimentation. The most characteristic way of structuring his stories is to fragment the chronological time. The modern stream-of-consciousness technique and multiple points of view were also frequently and skillfully exploited by Faulkner. The other narrative techniques Faulkner used to construct his stories include symbolism and mythological and biblical allusion. Faulkner was awarded the 1949 Nobel Prize in Literature. *A Rose for Emily* is a tragic story which is typically Faulknerian both in terms of subject matter and narrative techniques. *A Rose for Emily* has been read variously as a Gothic horror tale, a study in abnormal psychology, an allegory of the relations between North and South, a meditation on the nature of time, and a tragedy with Emily as a sort of tragic heroine.

Lead-in Questions

1. What is Gothic literature, and how is it related to Gothic art, architecture, and culture?
2. What's the Old Southern Ethic and how did it affect women at that time?
3. What's the setting of Faulkner's novels?

Questions about the Author and the Story

1. Which of the following is depicted as the mythical county in William Faulkner's novels?
   A. Cambridge. B. Oxford.
   C. Mississippi. D. Yoknapatawpha.
2. The narrator implies that Miss Emily's father tended to do all of the following EXCEPT _____.
   A. trust her B. spoil her
   C. control her D. overprotect her
3. When the smell developed around Miss Emily's house, the older aldermen were reluctant to ask her about it because they _____.
   A. were afraid of her temper
   B. were afraid of what they might discover

C. didn't want to embarrass or humiliate a lady with such a question
D. knew she would be too ill to do anything about it

4. In the setting of this story, it is assumed that the ultimate goal of a young woman such as Miss Emily is to _____.
   A. marry
   B. become wealthy
   C. serve the community
   D. gain fame in a profession

5. Which of the following words BEST describes Emily?
   A. Cheerful.   B. Cooperative.   C. Lively.   D. Creepy.

When Miss Emily Grierson died, our whole town went to her funeral: the men through a sort of respectful affection for a fallen monument①, the women mostly out of curiosity to see the inside of her house, which no one save an old manservant—a combined gardener and cook—had seen in at least ten years.

It was a big, squarish frame house that had once been white, decorated with cupolas and spires and scrolled balconies② in the heavily lightsome style of the seventies, set on what had once been our most select street. But garages and cotton gins had encroached and obliterated even the august names of that neighborhood; only Miss Emily's house was left, lifting its stubborn and coquettish decay above the cotton wagons and the gasoline pumps—an eyesore among eyesores③. And now Miss Emily had gone to join the representatives of those august names where they lay in the cedar-bemused cemetery among the ranked and anonymous graves of Union and Confederate soldiers who fell at the battle of Jefferson.

Alive, Miss Emily had been a tradition, a duty, and a care; a sort of hereditary obligation upon the town, dating from that day in 1894 when Colonel Sartoris, the mayor—he who fathered the edict that no Negro woman should appear on the streets without an apron—remitted her taxes, the dispensation dating from the death of her father on into perpetuity. Not that Miss Emily would have accepted charity. Colonel Sartoris invented an involved tale to the effect that Miss Emily's father had loaned money to the town, which the town, as a matter of business, preferred this way of repaying. Only a man of Colonel Sartoris' generation and thought could have invented it, and only a woman could have believed it.

---

① a fallen monument: Here the author implies that Emily is the symbol of an old tradition and certain values. Her death is like a monument fallen to the ground. 此处作者将艾米丽的死亡比作倒下的纪念碑,暗示艾米丽是旧传统、旧价值观的化身。

② cupolas and spires and scrolled balconies: This is a typical western-style building; 带圆形屋顶、尖塔和涡形花纹的阳台,一种比较典型的西方建筑

③ an eyesore among eyesores: 丑中之丑

When the next generation, with its more modern ideas, became mayors and aldermen①, this arrangement created some little dissatisfaction. On the first of the year they mailed her a tax notice. February came, and there was no reply. They wrote her a formal letter, asking her to call at the sheriff's office at her convenience. A week later the mayor wrote her himself, offering to call or to send his car for her, and received in reply a note on paper of an archaic shape, in a thin, flowing calligraphy in faded ink, to the effect that she no longer went out at all. The tax notice was also enclosed, without comment.

They called a special meeting of the Board of Aldermen. A deputation waited upon her, knocked at the door through which no visitor had passed since she ceased giving china-painting lessons eight or ten years earlier. They were admitted by the old Negro into a dim hall from which a stairway mounted into still more shadow. It smelled of dust and disuse—a close, dank smell. The Negro led them into the parlor. It was furnished in heavy, leather-covered furniture. When the Negro opened the blinds of one window, they could see that the leather was cracked; and when they sat down, a faint dust rose sluggishly about their thighs, spinning with slow motes in the single sun-ray. On a tarnished gilt easel before the fireplace stood a crayon portrait of Miss Emily's father.

They rose when she entered—a small, fat woman in black, with a thin gold chain descending to her waist and vanishing into her belt, leaning on an ebony cane with a tarnished gold head. Her skeleton was small and spare; perhaps that was why what would have been merely plumpness in another was obesity in her. She looked bloated, like a body long submerged in motionless water, and of that pallid hue. Her eyes, lost in the fatty ridges of her face, looked like two small pieces of coal pressed into a lump of dough as they moved from one face to another while the visitors stated their errand.

She did not ask them to sit. She just stood in the door and listened quietly until the spokesman came to a stumbling halt. Then they could hear the invisible watch ticking at the end of the gold chain.

Her voice was dry and cold. "I have no taxes in Jefferson. Colonel Sartoris explained it to me. Perhaps one of you can gain access to the city records and satisfy yourselves."

"But we have. We are the city authorities, Miss Emily. Didn't you get a notice from the sheriff②, signed by him?"

"I received a paper, yes," Miss Emily said. "Perhaps he considers himself the sheriff ... I have no taxes in Jefferson."

"But there is nothing on the books to show that, you see. We must go by the—"

---

① alderman: a member of the governing council of a city; 市参议员

② sheriff: the chief law enforcement officer for the courts in a US country; 县治安官,美国县级法院的主要的执法官员

"See Colonel Sartoris. I have no taxes in Jefferson."

"But, Miss Emily—"

"See Colonel Sartoris." (Colonel Sartoris had been dead almost ten years.) "I have no taxes in Jefferson. Tobe!" The Negro appeared. "Show these gentlemen out."

So she vanquished them, horse and foot①, just as she had vanquished their fathers thirty years before about the smell. That was two years after her father's death and a short time after her sweetheart—the one we believed would marry her—had deserted her. After her father's death she went out very little; after her sweetheart went away, people hardly saw her at all. A few of the ladies had the temerity to call, but were not received, and the only sign of life about the place was the Negro man—a young man then—going in and out with a market basket.

"Just as if a man—any man—could keep a kitchen properly," the ladies said; so they were not surprised when the smell developed. It was another link between the gross, teeming world and the high and mighty Griersons.

A neighbor, a woman, complained to the mayor, Judge Stevens, eighty years old.

"But what will you have me do about it, madam?" he said.

"Why, send her word to stop it," the woman said. "Isn't there a law?"

"I'm sure that won't be necessary," Judge Stevens said. "It's probably just a snake or a rat that nigger② of hers killed in the yard. I'll speak to him about it."

The next day he received two more complaints, one from a man who came in diffident deprecation. "We really must do something about it, Judge. I'd be the last one in the world to bother Miss Emily, but we've got to do something." That night the Board of Aldermen met—three gray-beards and one younger man, a member of the rising generation.

"It's simple enough," he said. "Send her word to have her place cleaned up. Give her a certain time to do it in, and if she don't ..."

"Dammit, sir," Judge Stevens said, "will you accuse a lady to her face of smelling bad?"

So the next night, after midnight, four men crossed Miss Emily's lawn and slunk about the house like burglars, sniffing along the base of the brickwork and at the cellar openings while one of them performed a regular sowing motion with his hand out of a sack slung from his shoulder. They broke open the cellar door and sprinkled lime there, and in all the outbuildings. As they recrossed the lawn, a window that had been dark was lighted and Miss Emily sat in it, the light behind her, and her upright torso motionless as that of an idol. They crept quietly across the lawn and into the shadow of

---

① horse and foot: with great effort; 全力以赴
② nigger: a disparaging term for a black person; 黑鬼,是对黑人的侮辱性的称呼

the locusts that lined the street. After a week or two the smell went away.

That was when people had begun to feel really sorry for her. People in our town, remembering how old lady Wyatt, her great-aunt, had gone completely crazy at last, believed that the Griersons held themselves a little too high for what they really were. None of the young men were quite good enough for Miss Emily and such. We had long thought of them as a tableau①, Miss Emily a slender figure in white in the background, her father a straddled silhouette in the foreground, his back to her and clutching a horsewhip②, the two of them framed by the back-flung front door. So when she got to be thirty and was still single, we were not pleased exactly, but vindicated; even with insanity in the family she wouldn't have turned down all of her chances if they had really materialized.

When her father died, it got about that the house was all that was left to her; and in a way, people were glad. At last they could pity Miss Emily. Being left alone, and a pauper, she had become humanized. Now she too would know the old thrill and the old despair of a penny more or less.

The day after his death all the ladies prepared to call at the house and offer condolence and aid, as is our custom. Miss Emily met them at the door, dressed as usual and with no trace of grief on her face. She told them that her father was not dead. She did that for three days, with the ministers calling on her, and the doctors, trying to persuade her to let them dispose of the body. Just as they were about to resort to law and force, she broke down, and they buried her father quickly.

We did not say she was crazy then. We believed she had to do that. We remembered all the young men her father had driven away, and we knew that with nothing left, she would have to cling to that which had robbed her, as people will.

She was sick for a long time. When we saw her again, her hair was cut short, making her look like a girl, with a vague resemblance to those angels in colored church windows—sort of tragic and serene.

The town had just let the contracts for paving the sidewalks, and in the summer after her father's death they began the work. The construction company came with riggers and mules and machinery, and a foreman named Homer Barron, a Yankee—a big, dark, ready man, with a big voice and eyes lighter than his face. The little boys would follow in groups to hear him cuss the niggers, and the niggers singing in time to

---

① tableau: a group of people who do not speak or move, arranged on stage to show a famous event; 舞台造型,一群人在舞台上塑造静态画面,以表现著名事件

② horsewhip: a whip used to control a horse; the legendary weapon used by American fathers to protect their daughters from unwelcoming suitors; 马鞭,美国传说中父亲用来赶走女儿那些不受欢迎的追求者的武器

the rise and fall of picks. Pretty soon he knew everybody in town. Whenever you heard a lot of laughing anywhere about the square, Homer Barron would be in the center of the group. Presently we began to see him and Miss Emily on Sunday afternoons driving in the yellow-wheeled buggy and the matched team of bays① from the livery stable.

At first we were glad that Miss Emily would have an interest, because the ladies all said, "Of course a Grierson would not think seriously of a Northerner, a day laborer." But there were still others, older people, who said that even grief could not cause a real lady to forget *noblesse oblige*②—without calling it *noblesse oblige*. They just said, "Poor Emily. Her kinsfolk should come to her." She had some kin in Alabama; but years ago her father had fallen out with them over the estate of old lady Wyatt, the crazy woman, and there was no communication between the two families. They had not even been represented at the funeral.

And as soon as the old people said, "Poor Emily," the whispering began. "Do you suppose it's really so?" they said to one another. "Of course it is. What else could ... " This behind their hands; rustling of craned silk and satin behind jalousies closed upon the sun of Sunday afternoon as the thin, swift clop-clop-clop of the matched team passed: "Poor Emily."

She carried her head high enough—even when we believed that she was fallen. It was as if she demanded more than ever the recognition of her dignity as the last Grierson; as if it had wanted that touch of earthiness to reaffirm her imperviousness. Like when she bought the rat poison, the arsenic③. That was over a year after they had begun to say "Poor Emily," and while the two female cousins were visiting her.

"I want some poison," she said to the druggist. She was over thirty then, still a slight woman, though thinner than usual, with cold, haughty black eyes in a face the flesh of which was strained across the temples and about the eye sockets as you imagine a lighthouse-keeper's face ought to look. "I want some poison," she said.

"Yes, Miss Emily. What kind? For rats and such? I'd recom—"

"I want the best you have. I don't care what kind."

The druggist named several. "They'll kill anything up to an elephant. But what you want is—"

"Arsenic," Miss Emily said. "Is that a good one?"

"Is ... arsenic? Yes, ma'am. But what you want—"

"I want arsenic."

---

① matched teams of bays: two reddish-brown horses similar in size and appearance; 配成对的枣红马,体形及外表都相似

② noblesse oblige: [French] noble obligation expected of people of high social position; [法语]应有的高贵

③ arsenic: a violent poison; 砒霜

The druggist looked down at her. She looked back at him, erect, her face like a strained flag. "Why, of course," the druggist said. "If that's what you want. But the law requires you to tell what you are going to use it for."

Miss Emily just stared at him, her head tilted back in order to look him eye for eye, until he looked away and went and got the arsenic and wrapped it up. The Negro delivery boy brought her the package; the druggist didn't come back. When she opened the package at home there was written on the box, under the skull and bones: "For rats."

So the next day we all said, "She will kill herself"; and we said it would be the best thing. When she had first begun to be seen with Homer Barron, we had said, "She will marry him." Then we said, "She will persuade him yet," because Homer himself had remarked—he liked men, and it was known that he drank with the younger men in the Elks' Club①—that he was not a marrying man. Later we said, "Poor Emily" behind the jalousies as they passed on Sunday afternoon in the glittering buggy, Miss Emily with her head high and Homer Barron with his hat cocked and a cigar in his teeth, reins and whip in a yellow glove.

Then some of the ladies began to say that it was a disgrace to the town and a bad example to the young people. The men did not want to interfere, but at last the ladies forced the Baptist② minister—Miss Emily's people③ were Episcopal—to call upon her. He would never divulge what happened during that interview, but he refused to go back again. The next Sunday they again drove about the streets, and the following day the minister's wife wrote to Miss Emily's relations in Alabama.

So she had blood-kin④ under her roof again and we sat back to watch developments. At first nothing happened. Then we were sure that they were to be married. We learned that Miss Emily had been to the jeweler's and ordered a man's toilet set in silver, with the letters H. B. on each piece. Two days later we learned that she had bought a complete outfit of men's clothing, including a nightshirt, and we said, "They are married." We were really glad. We were glad because the two female cousins were even more Grierson than Miss Emily had ever been.

So we were not surprised when Homer Barron—the streets had been finished some time since—was gone. We were a little disappointed that there was not a public blowing-off, but we believed that he had gone on to prepare for Miss Emily's coming, or to give her a chance to get rid of the cousins. (By that time it was a cabal, and we were all Miss

---

① Elks' Club:麋鹿俱乐部
② Baptist: an American religious group; 浸礼会
③ Emily's people: Emily's families
④ blood-kin:close-relations; 近亲

Emily's allies to help circumvent the cousins.) Sure enough, after another week they departed. And, as we had expected all along, within three days Homer Barron was back in town. A neighbor saw the Negro man admit him at the kitchen door at dusk one evening.

And that was the last we saw of Homer Barron. And of Miss Emily for some time. The Negro man went in and out with the market basket, but the front door remained closed. Now and then we would see her at a window for a moment, as the men did that night when they sprinkled the lime, but for almost six months she did not appear on the streets. Then we knew that this was to be expected too; as if that quality of her father which had thwarted her woman's life so many times had been too virulent and too furious to die.

When we next saw Miss Emily, she had grown fat and her hair was turning gray. During the next few years it grew grayer and grayer until it attained an even pepper-and-salt① iron-gray, when it ceased turning. Up to the day of her death at seventy-four it was still that vigorous iron-gray, like the hair of an active man.

From that time on her front door remained closed, save for a period of six or seven years, when she was about forty, during which she gave lessons in china-painting. She fitted up a studio in one of the downstairs rooms, where the daughters and granddaughters of Colonel Sartoris' contemporaries were sent to her with the same regularity and in the same spirit that they were sent to church on Sundays with a twenty-five-cent piece for the collection plate②. Meanwhile her taxes had been remitted.

Then the newer generation became the backbone and the spirit of the town, and the painting pupils grew up and fell away and did not send their children to her with boxes of color and tedious brushes and pictures cut from the ladies' magazines. The front door closed upon the last one and remained closed for good. When the town got free postal delivery, Miss Emily alone refused to let them fasten the metal numbers above her door and attach a mailbox to it. She would not listen to them.

Daily, monthly, yearly we watched the Negro grow grayer and more stooped, going in and out with the market basket. Each December we sent her a tax notice, which would be returned by the post office a week later, unclaimed. Now and then we would see her in one of the downstairs windows—she had evidently shut up the top floor of the house—like the carven torso of an idol in a niche, looking or not looking at us, we could never tell which. Thus she passed from generation to generation—dear, inescapable, impervious, tranquil, and perverse.

And so she died. Fell ill in the house filled with dust and shadows, with only a

---

① pepper-and-salt: with small dark and light dots; 黑白相间的
② collection plate: the plate used to collect money during church services; 教堂里做礼拜时用来募捐的盘子

doddering Negro man to wait on her. We did not even know she was sick; we had long since given up trying to get any information from the Negro. He talked to no one, probably not even to her, for his voice had grown harsh and rusty, as if from disuse.

She died in one of the downstairs rooms, in a heavy walnut bed with a curtain, her gray head propped on a pillow yellow and moldy with age and lack of sunlight.

The Negro met the first of the ladies at the front door and let them in, with their hushed, sibilant voices and their quick, curious glances, and then he disappeared. He walked right through the house and out the back and was not seen again.

The two female cousins came at once. They held the funeral on the second day, with the town coming to look at Miss Emily beneath a mass of bought flowers, with the crayon face of her father musing profoundly above the bier① and the ladies sibilant and macabre②; and the very old men—some in their brushed Confederate uniforms—on the porch and the lawn, talking of Miss Emily as if she had been a contemporary of theirs, believing that they had danced with her and courted her perhaps, confusing time with its mathematical progression, as the old do, to whom all the past is not a diminishing road but, instead, a huge meadow which no winter ever quite touches, divided from them now by the narrow bottleneck of the most recent decade of years.

Already we knew that there was one room in that region above stairs which no one had seen in forty years, and which would have to be forced. They waited until Miss Emily was decently in the ground before they opened it.

The violence of breaking down the door seemed to fill this room with pervading dust. A thin, acrid pall as of the tomb seemed to lie everywhere upon this room decked and furnished as for a bridal: upon the valance curtains of faded rose color, upon the rose-shaded lights, upon the dressing table, upon the delicate array of crystal and the man's toilet things backed with tarnished silver, silver so tarnished that the monogram was obscured. Among them lay a collar and tie, as if they had just been removed, which, lifted, left upon the surface a pale crescent in the dust. Upon a chair hung the suit, carefully folded; beneath it the two mute shoes and the discarded socks.

The man himself lay in the bed.

For a long while we just stood there, looking down at the profound and fleshless grin. The body had apparently once lain in the attitude of an embrace, but now the long sleep that outlasts love, that conquers even the grimace of love③, had cuckolded④ him.

---

① bier: a coffin; 棺材
② the ladies sibilant and macabre: the ladies whispering and gossiping about the death; 妇女们悄声地谈论着死亡
③ grimace of love: the imitation of love; 爱情的嘲弄
④ cuckold: make another cuckold by seducing his wife; 使……戴绿帽子

What was left of him, rotted beneath what was left of the nightshirt, had become inextricable from the bed in which he lay; and upon him and upon the pillow beside him lay that even coating of the patient and biding dust.

Then we noticed that in the second pillow was the indentation of a head. One of us lifted something from it, and leaning forward, that faint and invisible dust dry and acrid in the nostrils, we saw a long strand of iron-gray hair.

 Questions for Discussion
1. Why did Miss Emily kill Homer Baron?
2. What kind of woman do you think Emily is?
3. What are the symbolic meaning of "rose" and the significance of the title?

 Links
1. https://en.wikipedia.org/wiki/William_Faulkner
   关于威廉姆·福克纳生平及创作的详细介绍。
2. http://xroads.virginia.edu/~drbr/wf_rose.html
   关于威廉姆·福克纳的小说《献给艾米丽的一朵玫瑰花》的细读资料。

Chapter Three

A Native Child

By Isak Dinesen

Isak Dinesen (1885—1962), the pen name of Karen Blixen, is a Danish writer, twice nominated for the Nobel Prize. Her first book, *Seven Gothic Tales*, was completed in 1933. In 1938, her second book, an exciting new work now the best known of her works, *Out of Africa*, was published and its success firmly established her reputation as an author. *Out of Africa* described the author's life on a coffee farm in Kenya, artfully related her efforts to running a coffee farm in East Africa between 1914 and 1931. She described her love for Africans and for farming and her tragic loss of the farm in the Great Depression.

Isak Dinesen's story is notable for its lyrical description of Africa and the larger-than-life friends she made there. In 1985, based on the autobiographical book *Out of Africa* and the additional material from Dinesen's book *Shadows on the Grass* and also other sources, the American epic romantic drama film *Out of Africa* was directed and produced by Sydney Pollack and starred Robert Redford and Meryl Streep.

 Lead-in Questions
1. What is Africa like in your mind?
2. Do you have any idea of the native people's life in Kenya, Eastern Africa?
3. How did Westerners colonize Africans? Does the influence of colonization on the Africans still exist?

 Questions about the Author and the Story
1. Which of the following is Isak Dinesen's real name?
   A. Pierre Andrezel.　　　　　　B. Karen Blixen.

C. Olive Schreiner. D. Doris Lessing.
2. What is grown on the author's farm?
   A. Sugarcane. B. Coffee. C. Bananas. D. Maize.
3. Who is the author's original chef?
   A. Juma. B. Esa. C. Wamai. D. Old Knudsen.
4. What does Kamante fear less after he becomes a Christian?
   A. Dead people. B. God. C. Satan. D. Lions.
5. Which one is INCORRECT about Kamante in the following statements?
   A. He later became the chef in the author's kitchen.
   B. He was shrewd in money matters, and he did a number of wise deals with the other Kikuyu in goats.
   C. He strongly wanted to contact the world around him.
   D. He realized his separation from the great souls and he learned secretly when the author teaches the children.

Kamante was a small Kikuyu boy, the son of one of my squatters. I used to know my squatter children well, for they both worked for me on the farm, and used to be up round my house herding their goats on the lawn, in the faith that here something of interest might always occur. But Kamante must have lived on the farm for some years before I ever met him; I suppose that he had been leading a seclusive existence like a sick animal.

I came upon him for the first time one day when I was riding across the plain of the farm, and he was herding his people's goats there. He was the most pitiful object that you could set eyes on. His head was big and his body terribly small and thin, the elbows and knees stood out like knots on a stick and both his legs were covered with deep running sores from the thigh to the heel. Here on the plain he looked extraordinarily small, so that it struck you as a strange thing that so much suffering could be condensed into a single point. When I stopped and spoke to him, he did not answer, and hardly appeared to see me. In his flat, angular, harassed, and infinitely patient face, the eyes were without glance, dim like the eyes of a dead person. He looked as if he could not have more than a few weeks to live in, and you expected to see the vultures, which are never far away from death on the plain, high up in the pale burning air over his head. I told him to come round to my house the next morning, so that I could try to cure him.

I was a doctor to the people on the farm most mornings from nine to ten, and like all great quacks I had a large circle of patients, and generally between two and a dozen sick people up by my house then.

The Kikuyu are adjusted for the unforeseen and accustomed to the unexpected. Here they differ from the white men, of whom the majority strive to insure themselves against the unknown and the assaults of fate. The Negro is on friendly terms with destiny, having been in her hands all his time; she is to him, in a way, his home, the familiar darkness of the hut, deep mould for his roots. He faces any change in life with great calm. Amongst the qualities that he will be looking for in a master or a doctor or in God, imagination, I believe, comes high up in the list. It may be on the strength of such a taste that the Caliph Haroun al Raschid Maintains, to the hearts of Africa and Arabia, his position as an ideal ruler; with him nobody knew what to expect next, and you did not know where you had him. When the Africans speak of the personality of God they speak like the Arabian Nights or like the last chapters of the book of Job; it is the same quality, the infinite power of imagination, with which they are impressed.

To this characteristic in my people I myself owed my popularity, or my fame, as a doctor. When I first came out to Africa I travelled on the boat with a great German scientist, who was going out, for the twenty-third time, to experiment with cures for sleeping-sickness①, and who had over a hundred rats and guinea-pigs on the boat with him. He told me that his difficulty with the Native patients had never been any lack of courage in them—in the face of pain or of a great operation they generally showed little fear—but it was their deep dislike of regularity, of any repeated treatment or the systematization of the whole; and this the great German doctor could not understand. But when I myself got to know the Natives, this quality in them was one of the things that I liked best. They had real courage: the unadulterated liking of danger—the true answer to the creation to the announcement of their lot—the echo from the earth when heaven had spoken. I sometimes thought that what, at the bottom of their hearts, they feared from us was pedantry. In the hands of a pedant they die of grief.

My patients waited on a paved terrace outside my house. Here they squatted—the old skeletons of men with tearing coughs and running eyes, the young slim smooth brawlers with black eyes and bruised mouths, and the mothers with their feverish children, like little dry flowers, hanging upon their necks. I often had bad burns to treat, for the Kikuyu at night sleep round the fires in their huts, and the piles of burning wood or charcoal may collapse and slide down on them—when at times I had run out of my store of medicine, I found that honey was not a bad ointment for burns. The atmosphere of the terrace was animated, electric, like the atmosphere of the casinos in Europe. The low lively flow of talk would stop when I came out, but the silence was pregnant with possibilities, now the moment had come when anything might happen. They did, however, always wait for me myself to choose my first patient.

---

① sleeping-sickness: disease caused by the tsetse-fly; it results in weakening of the mental powers and usually death. 睡眠症,昏睡病,又名"非洲锥虫病",是一种寄生虫病。锥虫通过采采蝇的叮咬,入侵人类神经系统,病人会不断陷入昏睡状态,直至永远醒不过来,死亡率近百分之百。昏睡症只发生在南撒哈拉非洲。

Chapter Three

I knew little of doctoring, just what you learn at a first-aid course. But my renown as a doctor had been spread by a few chance lucky cures, and had not been decreased by the catastrophic mistakes that I had made.

If now I had been able to guarantee my patients a recovery in each single case, who knows but that their circle might have thinned out? I should then have attained a professional prestige—here evidently was a highly efficient doctor from Volaia①—but would they still have been sure that the Lord was with me? For of the Lord they knew from the great years of droughts, from the lions on the plains at night, and the leopards near the houses when the children were alone there, and from the swarms of grasshoppers that would come on to the land, nobody knew where from, and leave not a leaf of grass where they had passed. They knew him, too, from the unbelievable hours of happiness when the swarm passed over the maizefield and did not settle, or when in spring the rains would come early and plentiful, and make all the fields and plains flower and give rich crops. So that this highly capable doctor from Volaia might be after all a sort of outsider where the real great things in life were concerned.

Kamante to my surprise turned up at my house the morning after our first meeting. He stood there, a little away from the three or four other sick people present, erect, with his half-dead face, as if after all he had some feeling of attachment to life, and had now made up his mind to try this last chance of holding on to it.

He showed himself with time to be an excellent patient. He came when he was ordered to come, without fault, and he could keep account of time when he was told to come back every third or fourth day, which is an unusual thing with the Natives. He bore the hard treatment of his sores with a stoicism that I have not known the like of. In all these respects I might have held him up as a model to the others, but I did not do so, for at the same time he caused me much uneasiness of mind.

Rarely, rarely, have I met such a wild creature, a human being who was so utterly isolated from the world, and, by a sort of firm, deadly resignation, completely closed to all surrounding life. I could make him answer when I questioned him, but he never volunteered a word and never looked at me. He had no pity whatever in him, and kept a little scornful laughter of contempt, and of knowing better, for the tears of the other sick children, when they were washed and bandaged, but he never looked at them either. He had no wish for any sort of contact with the world round him, the contacts that he had known of had been too cruel for that. His fortitude of soul in the face of pain was the fortitude of an old warrior. A thing could never be so bad as to surprise him; he was, by his career and his philosophy, prepared for the worst.

---

① Volaia：古希腊地名，当地名医盛会，现在意大利境内。

All this was in the grand manner, and recalled the declaration of faith of Prometheus①: "Pain is my element as hate is thine. Ye rend me now: I care not." And, "Ay, do thy worst. Thou art omnipotent." But in a person of his size it was uncomfortable, a thing to make you lose heart. And what will God think—I thought—confronted with this attitude in a small human being?

I remember well the first time that he ever looked at me and spoke to me of his own accord. This must have been some time along in our acquaintance, for I had given up my first mode of treatment, and was trying a new thing, a hot poultice that I had looked up in my books. In my eagerness to do the thing thoroughly, I made it too hot, and as I put it on his leg and clapped the dressing on top of it Kamante spoke: "Masbu"②, he said, and gave me a great glance. The Natives use this Indian word when they address white women, but they pronounce it a little differently, and change it into an African word, with a diverging ring to it. In Kamante's mouth now it was a cry for help, but also a word of warning, such as a loyal friend might give you, to stop you in a proceeding unworthy of you. I thought of it with hope afterwards. I had ambition as a doctor, and I was sorry to have put on the poultice too hot, but I was glad all the same, for this was the first glimpse of an understanding between the wild child and myself. The stark sufferer, who expected nothing but suffering, did not expect it from me.

As far as my doctoring of him went, things did not, however, look hopeful. For a long time I kept on washing and bandaging his leg, but the disease was beyond me. From time to time he would grow a little better, and then the sores would break out in new places. In the end I made up my mind to take him to the hospital of the Scotch Mission③.

This decision of mine for once was sufficiently fatal, and had in it enough possibilities, to make an impression on Kamante—he did not want to go. He was prevented by his career and his philosophy from protesting much against anything, but when I drove him to the mission, and delivered him there in the long hospital building, in surroundings entirely foreign and mysterious to him, he trembled.

I had the Church of Scotland Mission as a neighbor twelve miles to the north-west,

---

① Prometheus: In Greek mythology, Prometheus is a Titan, culture hero, who defies the gods and gives fire to humanity, an act that enabled progress and civilization. 普罗米修斯,希腊神明,曾为人间窃取火种,触怒宙斯,被锁在高加索山上,每天被神鹰啄食肝脏。
② Masbu: 姆萨布。印度语和斯瓦希里语中的敬语,意为"夫人"。
③ Scotch Mission: 苏格兰长老会。基督东正教的一派,起源可追溯到苏格兰宗教改革。多分布于英国以前的殖民地,如美国、加拿大、澳洲、新西兰和印度等。

five hundred feet higher than the farm; and the French Roman Catholic① Mission ten miles to the east, on the flatter land, and five hundred feet lower. I did not sympathize with the missions, but personally I was on friendly terms with them both, and regretted that between themselves they should live in a state of hostility.

The French Fathers were my best friends, I used to ride over with Farah, to hear Mass with them on Sunday morning, partly in order to speak French again, and partly because it was a lovely ride to the mission. For a long way the road ran through the Forest Department's old wattle plantation, and the virile, fresh pinaceous scent of the wattle trees was sweet and cheering in the mornings.

It was an extraordinary thing to see how the Church of Rome was carrying her atmosphere with her wherevers she went. The Fathers had planned and built their church themselves, with the assistance of their Native congregation, and they were with reason very proud of it. There was here a fine big grey church with a bell-tower on it; it was laid out on a broad courtyard, above terraces and stairs, in the midst of their coffee-plantation, which was the oldest in the colony and very skillfully run. On the two other sides of the court were the arcaded refectory and the convent buildings, with the school and the mill down by the river, and to get into the drive up to the church you had to ride over an arched bridge. It was all built in grey stone, and as you came riding down upon it, it looked neat and impressive in the landscape, and might have been lying in a southern canton of Switzerland, or in the north of Italy.

The friendly fathers lay in wait for me at the church door, when Mass was over, to invite me to *un petit verre de vin*, across the courtyard in the roomy and cool refectory; there it was wonderful to hear how they knew of everything that was going on in the colony, even to the remotest corners of it. They would also, under the disguise of a sweet and benevolent conversation, draw from you any sort of news that you might possibly have in you, like a small lively group of brown, furry bees—for they all grew long, thick beards—hanging on to a flower for its store of honey. But while they were so interested in the life of the colony, they were all the time in their own French way exiles, patient and cheerful obeisants to some higher orders of a mysterious nature. If it had not been for the unknown authority that kept them in the place, you felt they would not be there, neither would the church of grey stone with the tall bell-tower, nor the arcades, the school, or any other part of their neat plantation and mission station. For when the word of relief had been given, all of these would leave the affairs of the colony

---

① Roman Catholic: a term sometimes used to differentiate members of the Catholic Church in full communion with the Pope in Rome from other Christians, especially those who also self-identify as "Catholic", such as Anglo-Catholics and Independent Catholics. 罗马天主教。正式名称为"罗马天主教会"或"罗马公教会",即由罗马教宗领导的教会。天主教一词用于信奉罗马天主教理论体系,包括道德、圣餐仪式以及教条,并完全服从圣座的基督宗教信徒。

to themselves and take a beeline back to Paris.

Farah, who had been holding the two ponies while I had been to church, and to the refectory, on the way back to the farm would notice my cheerful spirits—he was himself a pious Mohammedan and did not touch alcohol, but he took the Mass and the wine as co-ordinant rites of my religion.

The French Fathers sometimes rode on their motor-bicycles to the farm and lunched there; they quoted the fables of La Fontaine① to me and gave me good advice on my coffee-plantation.

The Scotch Mission I did not know so well. There was a splendid view, from up there, over all the surrounding Kikuyu country, but all the same the mission station gave me an impression of blindness, as if it could see nothing itself. The Church of Scotland was working hard to put the Natives into European clothes, which, I thought, did them no good from any point of view. But they had a very good hospital at the mission, and at the time when I was there, it was in the charge of a philanthropic, clever head-doctor, Dr. Arthur. They saved the life of many of the people from the farm.

At the Scotch Mission they kept Kamante for three months. During that time I saw him once. I came riding past the mission on my way to the Kikuyu railway station, and the road here for a while runs along the hospital grounds. I caught sight of Kamante in the grounds; he was standing by himself at a little distance from the groups of other convalescents. By this time he was already so much better that he could run. When he trotted along, on his side of the fence, like a foal in a paddock when you pass it on horseback, and kept his eyes on my pony, but he did not say a word. At the corner of the hospital grounds he had to stop, and when, as I rode on, I looked back, I saw him standing stock still, with his head up in the air and staring after me, in the exact manner of a foal when you ride away from it. I waved my hand to him a couple of times; the first time he did not react at all, then suddenly his arm went straight up like a pump-spear, but he did not do it more than once.

Kamante came back to my house on the morning of Easter Sunday②, and handed me a letter from the hospital people who declared that he was much better and that they thought him cured for good. He must have known something of its contents, for he watched my face attentively while I was reading it, but he did not want to discuss it, he had greater things in his mind. Kamante always carried himself with much collected or restrained dignity, but this time he shone with repressed triumph as well.

All Natives have a strong sense for dramatic effects. Kamante had carefully tied old bandages round his legs all the way up to the knee, to arrange a surprise for me. It was

---

① La Fontaine：拉·封丹。17世纪法国古典文学代表作家之一，著名的寓言诗人。
② Easter Sunday：复活节。西方的重要节日，在每年春分月圆之后的首个星期日。

clear that he saw the vital importance of the moment, not in his own good luck, but, unselfishly, in the pleasure that he was to give me. He probably remembered the times when he had seen me all upset by the continual failure of my cures with him, and he knew that the result of the hospital's treatment was an astounding thing. As slowly, slowly, he unwound the bandages from his knee to his heel there appeared, underneath them, a pair of whole smooth legs, only slightly marked by grey scars.

When Kamante had thoroughly, and in his calm grand manner, enjoyed my astonishment and pleasure, he again renewed the impression by stating that he was now a Christian. "I am like you," he said. He added that he thought that I might give him a rupee① because Christ had risen on this same day.

He went away to call on his own people. His mother was a widow, and lived a long way away on the farm. From what I heard from her later I believe that he did upon this day make a digression from his habit and unloaded his heart to her of the impressions of strange people and ways that he had received at the hospital. But after his visit to his mother's hut, he came back to my house as if he took it for granted that now he belonged there. He was then in my service from this time till the time that I left the country—for about twelve years.

Kamante when I first met him looked as if he were six years old, but he had a brother who looked about eight, and both brothers agreed that Kamante was the eldest of them, so I suppose he must have been set back in growth by his long illness; he was probably then nine years old. He grew up now, but he always made the impression of being a dwarf, or in some way deformed, although you could not put your finger on the precise spot that made him look so. His angular face was rounded with time, he walked and moved easily, and I myself did not think him bad-looking, but I may have looked upon him with something of a creator's eyes. His legs remained forever as thin as sticks. A fantastic figure he always was, half of fun and half of diabolism; with a very slight alteration, he might have sat and started down, on the top of the cathedral of Norte Dame in Paris. He had in him something bright and live; in a painting he would have made a spot of unusually intense coloring; with this he gave a stroke of picturesqueness to my household. He was never quite right in the head, or at least he was always what, in a white person, you would have called highly eccentric.

He was a thoughtful person. Perhaps the long years of suffering that he had lived through had developed in him a tendency to reflect upon things, and to draw his own conclusions from everything he saw. He was all his life, in his own way, an isolated figure. Even when he did the same things as other people he would do them in a different way.

I had an evening school for the people of the farm, with a Native schoolmaster to

---

① rupee: 卢比。英属殖民地使用的货币,当时肯尼亚、埃塞俄比亚、印度等国都使用。

teach them. I got my schoolmasters from one of the missions, and in my time I have had all three—Roman Catholic, Church of England①, and Church of Scotland schoolmasters. For the Native education of the country is run rigorously on religious lines; so far as I know, there are no other books translated into Swaheli than the Bible and the hymnbooks. I myself, during all my time in Africa, was planning to translate Aesop's fables, for the benefit of the Natives, but I never found time to carry my plan through. Still, such as it was, my school was to me a favorite place on the farm, the center of our spiritual life, and I spent many pleasant evening hours in the long old store-house of corrugated iron in which it was kept.

Kamante would then come with me, but he would not join the children on the school-benches, he would stand a little away from them, as if consciously closing his ears to the learning, and exulting in the simplicity of those who consented to be taken in, and to listen. But in the privacy of my kitchen, I have seen him copying from memory, very slowly and preposterously, those same letters and figures that he had observed on the blackboard in the school. I do not think that he could have come in with other people If he had wanted to; early in his life something in him had been twisted or locked out, and now it was, so to say, to him the normal thing to be out of the normal. He was aware of this separateness of his, himself, with the arrogant greatness of soul of the real dwarf, who, when he finds himself at a difference with the whole world, holds the world to be crooked.

Kamante was shewed in money matters; he spent little, and did a number of wise deals with the other Kikuyu in goats. He married at an early age, and marriage in the Kikuyu world is an expensive undertaking. At the same time I have heard him philosophizing, secondly and originally, upon the worthlessness of money. He stood in a peculiar relation to existence on the whole; he mastered it, but he had no high opinion of it.

He had no gift whatever for admiration. He might acknowledge, and think well of the wisdom of animals, but there was, during all the time that I knew him, only one human being of whose good sense I heard him speak approvingly; it was a young Somali woman who some years later came to live on the farm. He had a little mocking laughter, of which he made use in all circumstances, but chiefly towards any self-confidence or grandiloquence in other people. All Natives have in them a strong strain of malice, a shrill delight in things going wrong, which in itself is hurting and revolting to Europeans. Kamante brought this characteristic to a rare perfection, even to special self-irony, that made him take pleasure in his own disappointments and disasters, nearly exactly as in those of other people.

---

① Church of England：英格兰圣公会。英王亨利八世因为不满意教皇不批准他离婚，在英国发起宗教改革，令英国教会脱离罗马教会，成为英格兰圣公会。

I have met with the same kind of mentality in the old Native women have been roasted over many fires, who have mixed blood with Fate, and recognized her irony, wherever they meet it, with sympathy, as if it were that of a sister. On the farm I used to let my houseboys deal out snuff—*tombacco* the Natives say—to the old women on Sunday mornings, while I myself was still in bed. On this account I had a queer lot of customers round my house on Sundays, like a very old, rumpled, bald and bony poultry yard; and their low cackling—for the Natives will very rarely speak up loudly—made its way through the open widows of my bedroom. On one particular Sunday morning, the gently lively flow of Kikuyu communications suddenly rose to ripples and cascades of mirth; some highly humorous incident was taking place out there, and I called in Farah to tell me about it. Farah did not like to tell me, for the matter was that he had forgotten to buy snuff, so that to-day the old women had come a long way, as they say themselves, boori—for nothing. This happening was later on a source of amusement to the old Kikuyu women. Sometimes, when I met one of them on a path in a maizefield, she would stand still in front of me, poke a crooked bony finger at me, and, with her old dark face dissolving into laughter, so that all the wrinkles of it were drawn and folded together as by one single secret string being pulled, she would remind me of the Sunday when she and her sisters in the snuff had walked and walked up to my house, only to find that I had forgotten to get it, and that there was not a grain there—Ha ha Msabu!

The white people often say of the Kikuyu that they know nothing of gratitude. Kamante in any case was not ungrateful, he even gave words to his feeling of an obligation. A number of times, many years after our first meeting, he went out of his way to do me a service for which I had not asked him, and when I asked him why he had done it, he said that if it had not been for me he would have been dead a long time ago. He showed his gratitude in another manner as well, in a particular kind of benevolent, helpful, or perhaps the right word is forbearing, attitude towards me. It may be that he kept in mind that he and I were of the same religion. In a world of fools, I was, I think, to him one of the greater fools. From the day when he came into my service and attached his fate to mine, I felt his watchful penetrating eyes on me, and my whole *modus vivendi* subject to a clear unbiased criticism; I believe that, from the beginning, he looked upon the trouble that I had taken to get him cured as upon a piece of hopeless eccentricity. But he showed me all the time great interest and sympathy, and he laid himself out to guide my great ignorance. On some occasions I found that he had given time and thought to the problem, and that he meant to prepare and illustrate his instructions, in order that they should be easier for me to understand.

Kamante began his life in my house as a dog-toto; later he became a medical assistant to me. There I found out what good hands he had, although you would not have thought so from the look of them, and I sent him into the kitchen to be a cook's boy, a marmiton, under my old cook Esa, who was murdered. After Esa's death he succeeded to him, and he was now my chef all the time that he was with me.

Natives have usually very little feeling for animals, but Kamante differed from type here, as in other things. He was an authoritative dog-boy, and he identified himself with the dogs, and would come and communicate to me what they wished, or missed, or generally thought of things. He kept the dogs free of fleas, which are a pest in Africa, and many times in the middle of the night, he and I, called by the howls of the dogs, have, by the light of a hurricane-lamp, picked off them, one by one, the murderous big ants, the *Siafu*, which march alone and eat up everything on their way.

He must also have used his eyes at the time when he had been in the mission hospital—even if it had been, as was ever the case with him, without the slightest reverence or prepossession—for he was a thoughtful, inventive doctor's assistant. After he had left this office, he would at times appear from the kitchen to interfere in a case of sickness, and give me very sound advice.

But as a chef he was a different thing, and precluded classification. Nature had here taken a leap and cut away from the order of precedence of faculties and talents; the thing now became mystic and inexplicable, as ever where you are dealing with genius. In the kitchen, in the culinary world, Kamante had all the attributes of genius, even to that doom of genius—the individual's powerlessness in the face of his own powers. If Kamante had been born in Europe, and had fallen into the hands of a clever teacher, he might have become famous, and would have cut a droll figure in history. And out here in Africa he made himself a name, his attitude to his art was that of a master.

I was much interested in cookery myself, and on my first visit back to Europe, I took lessons from a French chef at a celebrated restaurant, because I thought it would be an amusing thing to be able to make good food in Africa. The chef, Monsieur Perrochet, at that time made me an offer to come in with him in his business of the restaurant, for the sake of my devotion to the art. Now when I found Kamante at hand, as a familiar spirit to cook with, this devotion again took hold of me. There was to me a great perspective in our working together. Nothing, I thought, could be more mysterious than this natural instinct in a savage for our culinary art. It made me take another view of our civilization; after all it might be in some way divine and predestined. I felt like the man who had regained his faith in God because a phrenologist[①] showed him the seat in the human brain of theological eloquence: if the existence of theological eloquence could be proved, the existence of theology itself was proved with it, and in the end, God's existence.

---

① phrenologist：颅相学者，颅相学家。颅相学是18世纪提出的一种认为人的心理与特质能够根据头颅形状确定的心理学假说。目前已被证实是伪科学。

Chapter Three

Kamante, in all cooking matters, had a surprising manual adroitness. The great tricks and *tour-de-force* of the kitchen were child's play to his dark crooked hands; they knew on special gift for making things light, as in the legend the infant Christ forms birds out of clay and tells them to fly. He scorned all complicated tools, as if impatient of too much independence in them, and when I gave him a machine for beating eggs he set it aside to rust, and beat whites of egg with a weeding knife that I had had to weed the lawn with, and his whites of eggs towered up like light clouds. As a cook he had a penetrating, inspired eye, and would pick the fattest chicken out of a whole poultry-yard, and he gravely weighed an egg in his hand, and knew when it had been laid. He thought out schemes for improvement of table, and by some means of communication, from a friend who was working for a doctor far away in the country, he got me seed of a really excellent sort of lettuce, such as I had myself for many years looked for in vain.

He had a great memory for recipes. He could not read and he knew no English, so that cookery books were of no use to him, but he must have held all that was ever taught stored up in his ungraceful head, according to some systematization of his own, which I should never know. He had named the dished after some event which had taken place on the day they had been shown to him, and he spoke of the sauce of the lightning that struck the tree, and of the sauce of the grey horse that died. But he did not confound any two of these things. There was only one point that tried to impress upon him without any success: that was the order of the course within a meal. It became necessary to me, when I had guests for dinner, to draw up for my chef as it were a pictorial menu: first a soup-plate, then a fish, then a partridge, or an artichoke. I did not quite believe this shortcoming in him to be due to a faulty memory, but he did, I think, in his own heart, maintain that there is a limit to everything and that upon anything so completely immaterial, he would not waste his time.

It is a moving thing to work together with a demon. Norminally the kitchen was mine, but in the course of our co-operation, I felt not only the kitchen, but the whole world in which we were co-operating, pass over into Kamante's hands. For here he understood to perfection what I wished of him, and sometimes he carried out my wishes even before I had told him of them; but as to me I could not make clear to myself how or indeed why he worked as he did. It seemed to me a strange thing that anyone could be so great in an art of which he did not understand the real meaning, and for which he felt nothing but contempt.

Kamante could have no idea as to how a dish of ours ought to taste, and he was, in spite of his conversion, and his connection with civilization, at heart an arrant Kikuyu, rooted in the traditions of his tribe and in his faith in them, as in the only way of living worthy of a human being. He did at times taste the food that he cooked, but then with a distrustful face, like a witch who takes a sip out of her cauldron. He stuck to the maize-cobs of his fathers. Here even his intelligence sometimes failed him, and he came and offered me a Kikuyu delicacy—a roasted sweet potato or a lump of sleep's fat—as even a civilized dog, that has lived for a long time with people, will place a bone on the floor before you, as a present. In his heart he did, I feel, all the time, look upon the trouble that we give ourselves about our food, as upon a lunacy. I sometimes tried to extract from him his views upon these things, but although he spoke with great frankness on many subjects, on others he was very close, so that we worked side by side in the kitchen, leaving one another's ideas on the importance of cooking alone.

  I sent Kamante into the Muthaiga Club to learn, and to the cooks of my friends in Nairobi, when I had had a new good dish in their house, and by the time that he had served his apprenticeship, my own house became famous in the colony for its table. This was a great pleasure to me. I longed to have an audience for my art, and I was glad when my friends came out to dine with me; but Kamante cared for the praise of no one. All the same he remembered the individual taste of those of my friends who came most often to the farm. "I shall cook the fish in white wine for Bwana Berkeley Cole," he said, gravely, as if he were speaking of a demented person. "He sends you out white wine himself to cook fish in." To get the opinion of an authority, I asked my old friend, Mr. Charles Bulpett of Nairobi, out to dine with me. Mr Bulpett was a great traveller of the former generation, themselves a generation away from Phineas Fogg[①]; he had been all over the world and had tasted everywhere the best it had to offer, and he had not cared to secure his future so long as he would enjoy the present moment. The books about sport and mountaineering, of fifty years ago, tell of his exploits as an athlete, and of his mountain climbings in Switzerland and Mexico, and there is a book of famous bets called *Light Come Light Go*, in which you can read of how for a bet he swam the Thames in evening clothes and a high hat—but later on, and more romantically, he swam the Hellespont[②] like Leander[③] and Lord Byron[④]. I was happy when he came out to the farm for a *tete-a-tete* dinner; there is a particular happiness in giving a man whom you like very much, good food that you have cooked yourself. In return he gave me his ideas on food, and on many other things in the world, and told me that he had nowhere dined better.

---

  ① Phineas Fogg:费尼斯·福格。《八十天环游地球》里的男主人公,沉默寡言,不爱与人交往,因为在俱乐部里打赌,从而在八十天里环游了地球。

  ② Hellespont:赫勒斯滂。现称为恰纳卡莱海峡,是连接马尔马拉海和爱琴海的海峡,属土耳其内海。

  ③ Leander:利安德。希腊神话里,女祭司赫罗与青年利安德认识并相爱。他每夜泅过赫勒斯滂与她相会,她在塔楼上高擎火把为他引路。一个暴风雨之夜火把熄灭了,利安德溺水而死。赫罗看到他的尸体悲痛万分,跳水自杀身亡。

  ④ Lord Byron:拜伦勋爵。英国著名浪漫主义诗人,在一八一零年横渡赫勒斯滂,揭开了近代横渡海峡史的第一页。

The Prince of Wales① did me the great honor to come and dine at the farm, and to compliment me on a Cumberland sauce②. This is the only time that I have seen Kamante listening with deep interest when I repeated the praise of his cooking to him, for Natives have very great ideas of kings and like to talk about them. Many months after, he felt a longing to hear it once more, and suddenly asked me, like a French reading-book, "Did the son of the Sultan③ like the sauce of the pig? Did he eat it all?"

Kamante showed his good will towards me outside the kitchen as well. He wanted to help me, in accordance with his own ideas of the advantages and dangers in life.

One night, after midnight, he suddenly walked into my bedroom with a hurricane-lamp in his hand, silent, as if on duty. It must have been only a short time after he first came into my house, for he was very small; he stood by my bedside like a dark bat that had strayed into the room, with very big spreading ears, or like a small African Will-o'-the-wisp, with his lamp in his hand. He spoke to me very solemnly. "Msabu," he said, "I think you had better get up." I sat up in bed bewildered; I thought that if anything serious had happened, it would have been Farah who would have come to fetch me, but I told Kamante to go away again, he did not move. "Msabu," he said again, "I think that you had better get up. I think that God is coming." When I heard this, I did get up, and asked him why he thought so. He gravely led me into the dining-room which looked west, towards the hills. From the door-windows I now saw a strange phenomenon. There was a big grass-fire going on, out in the hills, and the grass was burning all the way from the hill top to the plain; when seen from the house it was a nearly vertical line. It did indeed look as if some gigantic figure was moving and coming towards us. I stood for some time and looked at it, with Kamante watching by my side; then I began to explain the thing to him. I meant to quiet him, for I thought that he had been terribly frightened. But the explanation did not seem to make much impression on him one way or the other; he clearly took his mission to have been fulfilled when he had called me. "Well, yes," he said, "it may be so. But I thought that you had better get up in case it was God coming."

Questions for Discussion

1. How will you comment on the narrator's stand over the issue of colonialism?
2. Isak Dinesen states that the African natives preserve "a knowledge that was lost to us by our first parents." What "knowledge" does she refer to according to this story?

---

① The Prince of Wales:威尔士亲王,后来的英王爱德华八世(1894—1972),但在位时间不长,因要娶离过婚的辛普森夫人而自愿退位,成为温莎公爵。
② Cumberland sauce:英国坎伯兰郡名产,用柠檬、橘子、葡萄干、芥末和酒等调制而成。
③ Sultan:苏丹(某些伊斯兰国家统治者的称号)。此处指威尔士亲王。

3. What kind of image is the native boy Kamante in the story?

Links

1. https://en.wikipedia.org/wiki/Karen_Blixen
   关于伊萨克·丹尼森生平及创作的详细介绍。
2. http://www.sparknotes.com/lit/africa/context.html
   关于伊萨克·丹尼森的小说《走出非洲》的细读资料。

Part B

The Egg

By Andy Weir

Andy Weir (1972—), born and raised in California, was the only child of an accelerator physicist father and an electrical-engineer mother who divorced when he was eight. Weir grew up reading classic science fiction such as the works of Arthur C. Clarke and Isaac Asimov. At the age of 15, he began working as a computer programmer for Sandia National Laboratories and has been working as a software engineer ever since. He studied computer science at UC San Diego, although he did not graduate. He worked as a programmer for several software companies, including AOL, Palm, MobileIron and Blizzard. He is also a lifelong space nerd and a devoted hobbyist of subjects like relativistic physics, orbital mechanics, and the history of manned spaceflight.

Weir began writing science fiction in his 20's and published works on his website for years. He also authored a humour web comic called *Casey and Andy* from 2001 to 2008; he also briefly worked on another comic called *Chesire Crossing*. The attention these gained him has been attributed as later helping launch his writing career. Weir is best known for his first published novel, *The Martian*. In 2016, Weir released *The Principles of Uncertainty*—collection of short stories on the TAPAS App platform. His first work which gained significant attention is *The Egg*, a 2009 short story that has been translated into over 30 languages by readers and adapted into a number of YouTube videos and a one-act play and it was also adapted for a short film in 2012.

Lead-in Questions

1. It is said that *The Egg* makes people question life. What, in your opinion, is the meaning of life?
2. Who is the narrator of *The Egg*? What point of view is the narration presented from?

Questions about the Author and the Story

1. What was Andy's background before becoming a writer?
   A. An engineer.　　　　　　　　B. A potato farmer.
   C. A teacher.　　　　　　　　　D. A computer programmer.
2. What do you think contributes to the great popularity of the *The Egg*?
   A. Its plot.　　　　　　　　　　B. Its characterization.
   C. Its style.　　　　　　　　　　D. Its inspiring feature.
3. Which of the following is the dialogue in the story probably set in?
   A. A transitional stage between life and death.
   B. A transitional stage between the paradise and hell.
   C. A transitional stage between this life and future life.
   D. A transitional stage between human and nature.
4. As John Lennon once wrote, "I am he as you are he as you are me and we are all together". Which of the following can express best the underlying concept of the story?
   A. Oneness.　　B. Confidence.　　C. Optimism.　　D. Negativeness.
5. Which of the following summarizes best the story?
   A. A story about the universe.　　B. A story about life.
   C. A story about love.　　　　　　D. A story about friendship.

You were on your way home when you died.

It was a car accident. Nothing particularly remarkable, but fatal nonetheless. You left behind a wife and two children. It was a painless death. The EMTs① tried their best to save you, but to no avail②. Your body was so utterly shattered you were better off, trust me.

And that's when you met me.

"What ... what happened?" You asked. "Where am I?"

"You died," I said, matter-of-factly. No point in mincing words.

---

① EMT: Emergency Medical Technician; 紧急医疗救护技术员
② no avail: useless; 无用的

"There was a ... a truck and it was skidding ... "

"Yup," I said.

"I ... I died?"

"Yup. But don't feel bad about it. Everyone dies," I said.

You looked around. There was nothingness. Just you and me. "What is this place?" You asked. "Is this the afterlife?"

"More or less," I said.

"Are you god?" You asked.

"Yup," I replied. "I'm God."

"My kids ... my wife," you said.

"What about them?"

"Will they be all right?"

"That's what I like to see," I said. "You just died and your main concern is for your family. That's good stuff right there."

You looked at me with fascination. To you, I didn't look like God. I just looked like some man. Or possibly a woman. Some vague authority figure, maybe. More of a grammar school teacher than the almighty.

"Don't worry," I said. "They'll be fine. Your kids will remember you as perfect in every way. They didn't have time to grow contempt for you. Your wife will cry on the outside, but will be secretly relieved. To be fair, your marriage was falling apart. If it's any consolation, she'll feel very guilty for feeling relieved."

"Oh," you said. "So what happens now? Do I go to heaven or hell or something?"

"Neither," I said. "You'll be reincarnated[①]."

"Ah," you said. "So the Hindus were right."

"All religions are right in their own way," I said. "Walk with me."

You followed along as we strode through the void. "Where are we going?"

"Nowhere in particular," I said. "It's just nice to walk while we talk."

"So what's the point, then?" You asked. "When I get reborn, I'll just be a blank slate, right? A baby. So all my experiences and everything I did in this life won't matter."

"Not so!" I said. "You have within you all the knowledge and experiences of all your past lives. You just don't remember them right now."

I stopped walking and took you by the shoulders. "Your soul is more magnificent, beautiful, and gigantic than you can possibly imagine. A human mind can only contain a tiny fraction of what you are. It's like sticking your finger in a glass of water to see if it's hot or cold. You put a tiny part of yourself into the vessel, and when you bring it back out, you've gained all the experiences it had."

"You've been in a human for the last 48 years, so you haven't stretched out yet and

---

① reincarnated: to be born again in another body after you have died; 转世

felt the rest of your immense consciousness. If we hung out here for long enough, you'd start remembering everything. But there's no point to doing that between each life."

"How many times have I been reincarnated, then?"

"Oh lots. Lots and lots. An in to lots of different lives." I said. "This time around, you'll be a Chinese peasant girl in 540 A.D."

"Wait, what?" You stammered. "You're sending me back in time?"

"Well, I guess technically. Time, as you know it, only exists in your universe. Things are different where I come from."

"Where you come from?" You said.

"Oh sure," I explained. "I come from somewhere. Somewhere else. And there are others like me. I know you'll want to know what it's like there, but honestly you wouldn't understand."

"Oh," you said, a little let down. "But wait. If I get reincarnated to other places in time, I could have interacted with myself at some point."

"Sure. Happens all the time. And with both lives only aware of their own lifespan you don't even know it's happening."

"So what's the point of it all?"

"Seriously?" I asked. "Seriously? You're asking me for the meaning of life? Isn't that a little stereotypical?"

"Well it's a reasonable question," you persisted.

I looked you in the eye. "The meaning of life, the reason I made this whole universe, is for you to mature."

"You mean mankind? You want us to mature?"

"No, just you. I made this whole universe for you. With each new life you grow and mature and become a larger and greater intellect."

"Just me? What about everyone else?"

"There is no one else," I said. "In this universe, there's just you and me." You stared blankly at me. "But all the people on earth ..."

"All you. Different incarnations of you."

"Wait. I'm everyone!?"

"Now you're getting it," I said, with a congratulatory slap on the back.

"I'm every human being who ever lived?"

"Or who will ever live, yes."

"I'm Abraham Lincoln[①]?"

"And you're John Wilkes Booth[②], too," I added.

"I'm Hitler?" You said, appalled.

---

① Abraham Lincoln:亚伯拉罕·林肯,美国第十六任总统
② John Wilkes Booth:约翰·威克斯·布思,刺杀美国总统林肯的刺客

"And you're the millions he killed."

"I'm Jesus①?"

"And you're everyone who followed him."

You fell silent.

"Every time you victimized someone," I said, "you were victimizing yourself. Every act of kindness you've done, you've done to yourself. Every happy and sad moment ever experienced by any human was, or will be, experienced by you."

You thought for a long time.

"Why?" You asked me. "Why do all this?"

"Because someday, you will become like me. Because that's what you are. You're one of my kind. You're my child."

"Whoa," you said, incredulous. "You mean I'm a god?"

"No. Not yet. You're a fetus②. You're still growing. Once you've lived every human life throughout all time, you will have grown enough to be born."

"So the whole universe," you said, "it's just ..."

"An egg." I answered. "Now it's time for you to move on to your next life."

And I sent you on your way.

✿ Questions for Discussion

1. As to the creation of *The Egg*, Andy Weir once made the remark that: "I wanted to come up with some way to look at the world such that life was fair. A way where everyone came out even in the end. This is what I came up with." How, in your opinion, can we deem life "fair"?

2. How do you view the narration of the story? What effect has this kind of narration achieved?

3. The egg is an important thing in the story. Why do you suppose the story is titled *The Egg*?

4. "Your soul is more magnificent, beautiful, and gigantic than you can possibly imagine. A human mind can only contain a tiny fraction of what you are. It's like sticking your finger in a glass of water to see if it's hot or cold. You put a tiny part of yourself into the vessel, and when you bring it back out, you've gained all the experiences it had." How will you pass a comment on this quotation taken from the story?

---

① Jesus: also referred to as Jesus Christ, was a Jewish preacher and religious leader. He is the central figure of Christianity. Christians believe him to be the Son of God and the awaited Messiah (Christ) prophesied in the Old Testament. 耶稣(上帝之子)

② fetus: an unborn or unhatched vertebrate in the later stages of development showing the main recognizable features of the mature animal; 胎儿

Links

1. http：//andyweirauthor.com/
   关于安迪·韦尔生平及创作的详细介绍。
2. http：//www.topiama.com/r/354/i-am-andy-weir-and-i-wrote-the-egg-ama
   关于安迪·韦尔小说《蛋》的细读资料。

Chapter Four

Part A

The Interlopers

By Saki

Saki (1870—1916), the pen name of Hector Hugh Munro, and also frequently as H. H. Munro, was a British writer whose witty, mischievous and sometimes macabre stories satirize Edwardian society and culture. He is considered a master of the short story, and often compared to O. Henry and Dorothy Parker. Influenced by Oscar Wilde, Lewis Carroll and Rudyard Kipling, he himself influenced other writers.

His best short novels include *The Interlopers*, *Gabriel-Ernest*, *The Toys of Peace*, *The Storyteller*, *The Open Window*, etc.

Many of Saki's works contrast the conventions and hypocrisies of Edwardian England with the ruthless but straightforward life-and-death struggles of nature. *The Interlopers* is one of them. This fable-like story of *The Interlopers* depicts two mortal enemies, Georg Znaeym and Ulrich von Gradwitz, who are pinned under a tree. Trapped, the two have a change of heart and begin calling out to their parties. Unfortunately, their voices attract wolves. Although Saki's design is clearly to draw as much suspense and surprise into as narrow a compass as possible, the story itself nevertheless presents abstract themes of justice in the human world and of the human relationship to the natural world.

Lead-in Questions

1. Imagine that you are in a dark forest on a winter night, hunting an enemy who just happens to be your neighbor, and now suppose that your neighbor is hunting you, too, what would you do?
2. What makes people, who should be friends, become fierce enemies? Who is the

loser in this story's deadly fight?

3. How do you understand the symbolic image of wolf in Saki's works?

Questions about the Author and the Story

1. Which of the following is NOT written by Saki?
   A. *The Open Window*.   B. *The Necklace*.
   C. *The Toys of Peace*.   D. *Gabriel-Ernest*.
2. Who is the story's narrator?
   A. Georg Znaeym.   B. Saki.
   C. Ulrich von Gradwitz.   D. An unnamed, all-knowing storyteller.
3. The narrator tells us the two men _____.
   A. are hunting wolves   B. don't go hunting at night
   C. want to kill each other   D. go to hunting parties together
4. The two men decide to become friends because _____.
   A. their men have ordered them to
   B. they hate their neighbors
   C. they have become tired of being enemies
   D. they hope to save themselves by working together
5. The narrator creates suspense by waiting until the end to _____.
   A. reveal what is approaching the men
   B. tell which man dies first
   C. explain what the men were fighting about
   D. warn readers against hunting at night

In a forest of mixed growth somewhere on the eastern spurs of the Carpathians①, a man stood one winter night watching and listening, as though he waited for some beast of the woods to come within the range of his vision, and, later, of his rifle. But the game for whose presence he kept so keen an outlook was none that figured in the sportsman's calendar as lawful and proper for the chase; Ulrich von Gradwitz patrolled the dark forest in quest of a human enemy.

The forest lands of Gradwitz were of wide extent and well stocked with game; the narrow strip of precipitous woodland that lay on its outskirt was not remarkable for the game it harbored or the shooting it afforded, but it was the most jealously guarded of all its owner's territorial possessions. A famous law suit, in the days of his grandfather, had wrested it from the illegal possession of a neighboring family of petty landowners; the

---

① the Carpathians: (中欧)喀尔巴阡山

dispossessed party had never acquiesced in the judgment of the Courts, and a long series of poaching affrays and similar scandals had embittered the relationships between the families for three generations. The neighbor feud had grown into a personal one since Ulrich had come to be head of his family; if there was a man in the world whom he detested and wished ill to it was Georg Znaeym, the inheritor of the quarrel and the tireless game-snatcher and raider of the disputed border-forest. The feud might, perhaps, have died down or been compromised if the personal ill-will of the two men had not stood in the way; as boys they had thirsted for one another's blood, as men each prayed that misfortune might fall on the other, and this wind-scourged winter night Ulrich had banded together his foresters to watch the dark forest, not in quest of four-footed quarry, but to keep a look-out for the prowling thieves whom he suspected of being afoot from across the land boundary. The roebuck[①], which usually kept in the sheltered hollows during a storm-wind, were running like driven things tonight, and there was movement and unrest among the creatures that were wont to sleep through the dark hours. Assuredly there was a disturbing element in the forest, and Ulrich could guess the quarter from whence it came.

  He strayed away by himself from the watchers whom he had placed in ambush on the crest of the hill, and wandered far down the steep slopes amid the wild tangle of undergrowth, peering through the tree trunks and listening through the whistling and skirling of the wind and the restless beating of the branches for sight and sound of the marauders. If only on this wild night, in this dark, lone spot, he might come across Georg Znaeym, man to man, with none to witness—that was the wish that was uppermost in his thoughts. And as he stepped round the trunk of a huge beech he came face to face with the man he sought.

  The two enemies stood glaring at one another for a long silent moment. Each had a rifle in his hand; each had hate in his heart and murder uppermost in his mind. The chance had come to give full play to the passions of a lifetime. But a man who has been brought up under the code of a restraining civilization cannot easily nerve himself to shoot down his neighbor in cold blood and without word spoken, except for an offence against his hearth and honor. And before the moment of hesitation had given way to action a deed of Nature's own violence overwhelmed them both. A fierce shriek of the storm had been answered by a splitting crash over their heads, and ere they could leap aside a mass of falling beech tree had thundered down on them. Ulrich von Gradwitz found himself stretched on the ground, one arm numb beneath him and the other held almost as helplessly in a tight tangle of forked branches, while both legs were pinned beneath the fallen mass. His heavy shooting-boots had saved his feet from being crushed to pieces, but if his fractures were not as serious as they might have been, at least it was

---

  ① roebuck: 雄獐

Chapter Four

evident that he could not move from his present position till someone came to release him. The descending twig had slashed the skin of his face, and he had to wink away some drops of blood from his eyelashes before he could take in a general view of the disaster. At his side, so near that under ordinary circumstances he could almost have touched him, lay Georg Znaeym, alive and struggling, but obviously as helplessly pinioned down as himself. All round them lay a thick-strewn wreckage of splintered branches and broken twigs.

Relief at being alive and exasperation at his captive plight brought a strange medley of pious thank-offerings and sharp curses to Ulrich's lips. Georg, who was early blinded with the blood which trickled across his eyes, stopped his struggling for a moment to listen, and then gave a short, snarling laugh.

"So you're not killed, as you ought to be, but you're caught, anyway," he cried, "caught fast. Ho, what a jest, Ulrich von Gradwitz snared in his stolen forest. There's real justice for you!"

And he laughed again, mockingly and savagely.

"I'm caught in my own forest-land," retorted Ulrich. "When my men come to release us you will wish, perhaps, that you were in a better plight than caught poaching on a neighbor's land, shame on you."

Georg was silent for a moment; then he answered quietly:

"Are you sure that your men will find much to release? I have men, too, in the forest tonight, close behind me, and they will be here first and do the releasing. When they drag me out from under these damned branches it won't need much clumsiness on their part to roll this mass of trunk right over on the top of you. Your men will find you dead under a fallen beech tree. For form's sake I shall send my condolences to your family."

"It is a useful hint," said Ulrich fiercely. "My men had orders to follow in ten minutes' time, seven of which must have gone by already, and when they get me out—I will remember the hint. Only as you will have met your death poaching on my lands I don't think I can decently send any message of condolence to your family."

"Good," snarled Georg, "good. We fight this quarrel out to the death, you and I and our foresters, with no cursed interlopers to come between us. Death and damnation to you, Ulrich von Gradwitz."

"The same to you, Georg Znaeym, forest-thief, game-snatcher."

Both men spoke with the bitterness of possible defeat before them, for each knew that it might be long before his men would seek him out or find him; it was a bare matter of chance which party would arrive first on the scene.

Both had now given up the useless struggle to free themselves from the mass of wood that held them down; Ulrich limited his endeavours to an effort to bring his one partially free arm near enough to his outer coat-pocket to draw out his wine-flask. Even when he had accomplished that operation it was long before he could manage the unscrewing of the stopper or get any of the liquid down his throat. But what a Heaven-sent draught it seemed! It was an open winter, and little snow had fallen as yet, hence the captives suffered less from the cold than might have been the case at that season of the year; nevertheless, the wine was warming and reviving to the wounded man, and he looked across with something like a throb of pity to where his enemy lay, just keeping the groans of pain and weariness from crossing his lips.

"Could you reach this flask if I threw it over to you?" asked Ulrich suddenly; "there is good wine in it, and one may as well be as comfortable as one can. Let us drink, even if tonight one of us dies."

"No, I can scarcely see anything; there is so much blood caked round my eyes," said Georg, "and in any case I don't drink wine with an enemy."

Ulrich was silent for a few minutes, and lay listening to the weary screeching of the wind. An idea was slowly forming and growing in his brain, an idea that gained strength every time that he looked across at the man who was fighting so grimly against pain and exhaustion. In the pain and languor that Ulrich himself was feeling the old fierce hatred seemed to be dying down.

"Neighbor," he said presently, "do as you please if your men come first. It was a fair compact. But as for me, I've changed my mind. If my men are the first to come you shall be the first to be helped, as though you were my guest. We have quarrelled like devils all our lives over this stupid strip of forest, where the trees can't even stand upright in a breath of wind. Lying here tonight, thinking, I've come to think we've been rather fools; there are better things in life than getting the better of a boundary dispute. Neighbor, if you will help me to bury the old quarrel I—I will ask you to be my friend."

Georg Znaeym was silent for so long that Ulrich thought, perhaps, he had fainted with the pain of his injuries. Then he spoke slowly and in jerks.

"How the whole region would stare and gabble if we rode into the market-square together. No one living can remember seeing a Znaeym and a von Gradwitz talking to one another in friendship. And what peace there would be among the forester folk if we ended our feud tonight. And if we choose to make peace among our people there is none other to interfere, no interlopers from outside ... You would come and keep the Sylvester night beneath my roof, and I would come and feast on some high day at your castle .... I would never fire a shot on your land, save when you invited me as a guest; and you should come and shoot with me down in the marshes where the wildfowl are. In all the countryside there are none that could hinder if we willed to make peace. I never thought to have wanted to do other than hate you all my life, but I think I have changed my mind about things too, this last half-hour. And you offered me your wine-flask ... Ulrich von Gradwitz, I will be your friend."

For a space both men were silent, turning over in their minds the wonderful changes that this dramatic reconciliation would bring about. In the cold, gloomy forest, with the wind tearing in fitful gusts through the naked branches and whistling round the tree-trunks, they lay and waited for the help that would now bring release and succour to both parties. And each prayed a private prayer that his men might be the first to arrive, so that he might be the first to show honourable attention to the enemy that had become a friend.

Presently, as the wind dropped for a moment, Ulrich broke silence.

"Let's shout for help," he said, "in this lull our voices may carry a little way."

"They won't carry far through the trees and undergrowth," said Georg, "but we can try. Together, then."

The two raised their voices in a prolonged hunting call.

"Together again," said Ulrich a few minutes later, after listening in vain for an answering halloo.

"I heard something that time, I think," said Ulrich.

"I heard nothing but the pestilential wind," said Georg hoarsely.

There was silence again for some minutes, and then Ulrich gave a joyful cry.

"I can see figures coming through the wood. They are following in the way I came down the hillside."

Both men raised their voices in as loud a shout as they could muster.

"They hear us! They've stopped. Now they see us. They're running down the hill towards us," cried Ulrich.

"How many of them are there?" asked Georg.

"I can't see distinctly," said Ulrich, "nine or ten,"

"Then they are yours," said Georg, "I had only seven out with me."

"They are making all the speed they can, brave lads," said Ulrich gladly.

"Are they your men?" asked Georg. "Are they your men?" he repeated impatiently as Ulrich did not answer.

"No," said Ulrich with a laugh, the idiotic chattering laugh of a man unstrung with hideous fear.

"Who are they?" asked Georg quickly, straining his eyes to see what the other would gladly not have seen.

"Wolves."

Questions for Discussion

1. Does the narrator reveal the thoughts and feelings of the two men? If yes, what are they?
2. What makes the ending of *The Interlopers* surprising? Has Saki prepared readers for the surprising ending?

3. How would *The Interlopers* be different if it was told from the points of view of Ulrich and Georg? How does the nature seem to get the better of Ulrich and Georg at the story's conclusion?

**Links**

1. https://en.wikipedia.org/wiki/Saki
   关于萨基生平及创作的详细介绍。
2. http://www.anderson.k12.ky.us/Downloads/The%20Interlopers%5B1%5D.pdf
   关于萨基的小说《闯入者》的细读资料。

Part B

Before the Law

By Franz Kafka

Franz Kafka (1883—1924) was a German-language writer of novels and short stories. He was born into a middle-class, German-speaking Jewish family in Prague, the capital of the kingdom Bohemia, then part of the Austro-Hungarian Empire. Kafka learned German as his first language, but he was also almost fluent in Czech. Later, Kafka also acquired some knowledge of French language and culture.

It is generally agreed that Kafka suffered from clinical depression and social anxiety throughout his entire life. He also suffered from migraines, insomnia, constipation, boils, and other ailments, all usually brought on by excessive stresses and strains. He attempted to counteract all of those by a regimen of naturopathic treatments, such as a vegetarian diet. However, Kafka's tuberculosis worsened; he returned to Prague, then went to a sanatorium near Vienna for treatment, where he died on June 3, 1924.

Franz Kafka is widely regarded as one of the major figures of 20th-century literature. His works, which fuse elements of realism and the fantastic, typically feature isolated protagonists faced by bizarre or surrealistic predicaments and incomprehensible social-bureaucratic powers, and have been interpreted as exploring themes of alienation, existential anxiety, guilt, and absurdity. His best known works include *The Metamorphosis*, *The Trial*, and *The Castle*. The term Kafkaesque has entered the English language to describe situations like those in his writings.

Lead-in Questions

1. Have you ever read any parables? If yes, please share one with your classmates.
2. What do you know about Franz Kafka and his writing?

Questions about the Author and the Story

1. Which one is the masterpiece of Franz Kafka?
   A. *The Metamorphosis*.   B. *Ulysses*.
   C. *Waiting for Godot*.   D. *The Waste Land*.
2. Which can best describe the man from the country?
   A. Brave but innocent.   B. Loyal but ridiculous.
   C. Tolerant but stubborn.   D. Trustworthy but childish.
3. Which of the following is TRUE?
   A. The gatekeeper is actually the symbol of responsibility.
   B. All efforts made by the man from the country are in vain.
   C. The man from the country finally gains access into the law.
   D. A close relationship is formed between the gatekeeper and the man.
4. Why is the man from the country eager to have access to the law continuously?
   A. Because he is anxious to explore the nature of law.
   B. Because no one can gain entry into the law except him.
   C. Because the gatekeeper promises his entry into the law.
   D. Because he knows how to take advantage of the gatekeeper.
5. Franz Kafka is one outstanding representative of _____ in the 20th century.
   A. naturalism   B. romanticism   C. modernism   D. realism

Before the law sits a gatekeeper①. To this gatekeeper comes a man from the country who asks to gain entry into the law. But the gatekeeper says that he cannot grant him entry at the moment. The man thinks about it and then asks if he will be allowed to come in later on. "It is possible," says the gatekeeper, "but not now." At the moment the gate to the law stands open, as always, and the gatekeeper walks to the side, so the man bends over in order to see through the gate into the inside. When the gatekeeper notices that, he laughs and says: "If it tempts you so much, try it in spite of my prohibition. But take note: I am powerful. And I am only the most lowly gatekeeper. But from room to room stand gatekeepers, each more powerful than the other. I can't endure even one glimpse of the third." The man from the country has not expected such difficulties; the law should always be accessible for everyone, he thinks, but as he now

---

① gatekeeper: 守门人

looks more closely at the gatekeeper in his fur coat, at his large pointed nose and his long, thin, black Tartar's① beard, he decides that it would be better to wait until he gets permission to go inside. The gatekeeper gives him a stool and allows him to sit down at the side in front of the gate. There he sits for days and years. He makes many attempts to be let in, and he wears the gatekeeper out with his requests. The gatekeeper often interrogates him briefly, questioning him about his homeland and many other things, but they are indifferent questions, the kind great men put, and at the end he always tells him once more that he cannot let him inside yet. The man, who has equipped himself with many things for his journey, spends everything, no matter how valuable, to win over the gatekeeper. The latter takes it all but, as he does so, says, "I am taking this only so that you do not think you have failed to do anything." During the many years the man observes the gatekeeper almost continuously. He forgets the other gatekeepers, and this one seems to him the only obstacle for entry into the law. He curses the unlucky circumstance, in the first years thoughtlessly and out loud, later, as he grows old, he still mumbles to himself. He becomes childish and, since in the long years studying the gatekeeper he has come to know the fleas in his fur collar, he even asks the fleas to help him persuade the gatekeeper. Finally his eyesight grows weak, and he does not know whether things are really darker around him or whether his eyes are merely deceiving him. But he recognizes now in the darkness an illumination which breaks inextinguishably out of the gateway to the law. Now he no longer has much time to live. Before his death he gathers in his head all his experiences of the entire time up into one question which he has not yet put to the gatekeeper. He waves to him, since he can no longer lift up his stiffening body.

The gatekeeper has to bend way down to him, for the great difference has changed things to the disadvantage of the man. "What do you still want to know, then?" asks the gatekeeper. "You are insatiable." "Everyone strives after the law," says the man, "so how is that in these many years no one except me has requested entry?" The gatekeeper sees that the man is already dying and, in order to reach his diminishing sense of hearing, he shouts at him, "Here no one else can gain entry, since this entrance was assigned only to you. I'm going now to close it."

Questions for Discussion

1. How do you understand the metaphor in the story?
2. What is the theme of the story?
3. At the end of the story, the gatekeeper shouted, "Here no one else can gain entry, since this entrance was assigned only to you. I'm going now to close it." What does it mean?

---

① Tartar: 鞑靼人

❀ Links

1. https://en.wikipedia.org/wiki/Franz_Kafka
   关于卡夫卡生平及创作的详细介绍。
2. http://www.dffyw.com/faxuejieti/jd/201109/25080.html
   关于卡夫卡的小说《在法的门前》的细读资料。

Chapter Five

Part A

The Chink and the Child

By Thomas Burke

Thomas Burke (1886—1945) was a British author. He was born in Eltham, London. Burke's father died when he was barely a few months old and he was eventually sent to live with his uncle in Poplar. At the age of ten, he was removed to a home for middle class boys who were "respectably descended but without adequate means to their support." In 1901, he published his first professional written work entitled "The Bellamy Diamonds" in the magazine *Spare Moments*. He also edited some anthologies of children's poetry that were published in 1910—1913.

In 1915, Burke published *Nights in Town: A London Autobiography*, which describes the working-class's nightlife in London. However, it was not until the publication of *Limehouse Nights* in 1916 that he obtained any substantial acclaim as an author, which is a collection of stories centred on life in the poverty-stricken Limehouse district of London. This collection of melodramatic short stories, set in a lower-class environment populated by Chinese immigrants, received marked attention from literary reviewers. *Limehouse Nights* helped to earn Burke a reputation as "the laureate of London's Chinatown". And the short story "The Chink and the Child" from *Limehouse Nights* was used as the basis for a silent film *Broken Blossoms* (1919). Many of Burke's books feature the Chinese character Quong Lee as narrator.

Burke continued to develop his descriptions of London life throughout his later literary works. Burke died in the Homeopathic Hospital in Queens Square, Bloomsbury on 22 September 1945. His short story "The Hands of Ottermole" was later voted the best mystery of all time by the critics in 1949.

Chapter Five

Lead-in Questions

1. Why did many missionaries come to China during the late years of 19th century and the early years of 20th century?
2. Do you know any tales of poverty-stricken people in London at the beginning of 20th century?

Questions about the Author and the Story

1. The followings about the girl's father Battling Burrows are correct EXCEPT _____.
    A. he loves wine, woman and song
    B. he is a boxer, and the pride of Ratcliff, Poplar and Limehouse
    C. he is a very kind and warm father
    D. he is bully and alcoholic
2. Which one is INCORRECT about the girl?
    A. She is always starved and whipped by her brutal father when he drank much.
    B. She wants to escape for love.
    C. She is very beautiful with slender figure and graceful movement.
    D. She dies at last.
3. What is Cheng Huan when the story happens?
    A. He is a poet.   B. He is a sailor.
    C. He is a wanderer.   D. He is a salesclerk.
4. In Cheng Huan's eyes, "the girl seems a poem." Which of the following best illustrates the description?
    A. The girl is very graceful and sentimental.
    B. The girl is good at writing poems.
    C. The girl seems the living interpretation of a Chinese lyric, with the beauty touching his heart like a poem.
    D. The girl is cheerful and birdlike.
5. Which of the following is NOT the cause of the tragedy of their love?
    A. The girl's father's brutality.
    B. The father's prejudice towards the man.
    C. The girl's weakness.
    D. The girl's disobedience to her father.

It is a tale of love and lovers that they tell in the low-lit Causeway that slinks from West India Dock Road to the dark waste of waters beyond. In Pennyfields, too, you

may hear it; and I do not doubt that it is told in faraway Tai-Ping①, in Singapore, in Tokio, in Shanghai, and those other gay-gay-lamped haunts of wonder whither the wandering people of Limehouse② go and whence they return so casually. It is a tale for tears, and should you hear it in the lilied tongue of the yellow men, it would awaken in you all your pity. In our bald speech it must, unhappily, lose its essential fragrance, that quality that will lift an affair of squalor into the loftier spheres of passion and imagination, beauty and sorrow. It will sound unconvincing; a little ... you know ... the kind of thing that is best forgotten. Perhaps.

But listen ...

It is Battling Burrows, the lightning welter-weight of Shadwell, the box o' tricks, the Tetrarch of the ring, who enters first. Battling Burrows, the pride of Ratcliff, Poplar③ and Limehouse, and the despair of his manager and backers. For he loved wine, woman and song; and the boxing world held that he couldn't last long on that. There was any amount of money in him for his parasites if only the damned women could be cut out; but again and again would he disappear from his training quarters on the eve of a big fight, to consort with Molly and Dolly, and to drink other things than barley-water and lemon-juice.

Wherefore Chuck Lightfoot, his manager, forced him to fight on any and every occasion while he was good and a money-maker; for at any moment the collapse might come, and Chuck would be called upon by his creditors to strip off that "shirt" which at every contest he laid upon his man.

Battling was of a type that is too common in the eastern districts of London; a type that upsets all accepted classifications. He wouldn't be classed. He was a curious mixture of athleticism and degeneracy. He could run like a deer, leap like a greyhound, fight like a machine, and drink like a suction-hose. He was a bully; he had the courage of the high hero. He was an open-air sport; he had the vices of a French decadent.

It was one of his love adventures that properly begins this tale; for the girl had come to Battling one night with a recital of terrible happenings, of an angered parent, of a slammed door ... In her arms was a bundle of white rags. Now Battling, like so many sensualists, was also a sentimentalist. He took that bundle of white rags; he paid the girl money to get into the country; and the bundle of white rags had existed in and about his domicile in Peking④ Street, Limehouse, for some eleven years. Her position was

---

① Tai-Ping：太平，地名。
② Limehouse：莱姆豪斯。英格兰伦敦东部区名，旧时为华人聚居区，以贫穷肮脏而著名。
③ Poplar：波普拉区，伦敦的市区。
④ Peking：北京的旧称，现在称 Beijing。

nondescript; to the casual observer it would seem that she was Battling's relief punchball—an unpleasant post for any human creature to occupy, especially if you are a little girl of twelve, and the place be the one-room household of the lightning welter-weight. When Battling was cross with his manager ... well, it is indefensible to strike your manager or to throw chairs at him, if he is a good manager; but to use a dog-whip on a small child is permissible and quite as satisfying at least, he found it so. On these occasions, then, when very cross with his sparring partners, or over-flushed with victory and juice of the grape, he would flog Lucy. But he was reputed by the boys to be a good fellow. He only whipped the child when he was drunk; and he was only drunk for eight months of the year.

For just over twelve years this bruised little body had crept about Poplar and Limehouse. Always the white face was scarred with red, or black-furrowed with tears; always in her steps and in her look was expectation of dread things. Night after night her sleep was broken by the cheerful Battling's brute voice and violent hands; and terrible were the lessons which life taught her in those few years. Yet, for all the starved face and the transfixed air, there was a lurking beauty about her, a something that called you in the soft curve of her cheek that cried for kisses and was fed with blows, and in the splendid mournfulness that grew in eyes and lips. The brown hair chimed against the pale face, like the rounding of a verse. The blue cotton frock and the broken shoes could not break the loveliness of her slender figure or the shy grace of her movements as she flitted about the squalid alleys of the docks; though in all that region of wasted life and toil and decay, there was not one that noticed her, until ...

Now there lived in Chinatown, in one lousy room over Mr. Tai Fu's store in Pennyfields, a wandering yellow man, named Cheng Huan. Cheng Huan was a poet. He did not realize it. He had never been able to understand why he was unpopular; and he died without knowing. But a poet he was, tinged with the materialism of his race, and in his poor listening heart strange echoes would awake of which he himself was barely conscious. He regarded things differently from other sailors; he felt things more passionately, and things which they felt not at all; so he lived alone instead of at one of the lodging-houses. Every evening he would sit at his window and watch the street. Then, a little later, he would take a jolt of opium at the place at the corner of Formosa Street.

He had come to London by devious ways. He had loafed on the Bund at Shanghai. The fateful intervention of a crimp had landed him on a boat. He got to Cardiff, and sojourned in its Chinatown; thence to Liverpool, to Glasgow; thence, by a ticket from the Asiatics' Aid Society[①], to Limehouse, where he remained for two reasons—because it cost him nothing to live there, and because he was too lazy to find a boat to take him

---

① Asiatics' Aid Society: 亚洲人互助会

back to Shanghai.

So he would lounge and smoke cheap cigarettes, and sit at his window, from which point he had many times observed the lyrical Lucy. He noticed her casually. Another day, he observed her, not casually. Later, he looked long at her; later still, he began to watch for her and for that strangely provocative something about the toss of the head and the hang of the little blue skirt as it coyly kissed her knee.

Then that beauty which all Limehouse had missed smote Cheng. Straight to his heart it went, and cried itself into his very blood. Thereafter the spirit of poetry broke her blossoms all about his odorous chamber. Nothing was the same. Pennyfields became a happy-lanterned street, and the monotonous fiddle in the house opposite was the music of his fathers. Bits of old song floated through his mind: little sweet verses of Le Tai-pih①, murmuring of plum blossom, rice-field and stream. Day by day he would moon at his window, or shuffle about the streets, lighting to a flame when Lucy would pass and gravely return his quiet regard; and night after night, too, he would dream of a pale, lily-lovely child.

And now the Fates moved swiftly various pieces on their sinister board, and all that followed happened with a speed and precision that showed direction from higher ways.

It was Wednesday night in Limehouse, and for once clear of mist. Out of the colored darkness of the Causeway stole the muffled wail of reed instruments, and, though every window was closely shuttered, between the joints shot jets of light and stealthy voices, and you could hear the whisper of slippered feet, and the stuttering steps and the sadist. It was to the café in the middle of the Causeway, lit by the pallid blue light that is the symbol of China throughout the world, that Cheng Huan came, to take a dish of noodle and some tea. Thence he moved to another house whose stairs ran straight to the street, and above whose doorway a lamp glowed like an evil eye. At this establishment he mostly took his pipe of "chandu" and a brief chat with the keeper of the house, for, although not popular, and very silent, he liked sometimes to be in the presence of his compatriots. Like a figure of a shadowgraph he slid through the door and up the stairs.

The chamber he entered was a bit of the Orient squatting at the portals of the West. It was a well-kept place where one might play a game of fan-tan② or take a shot or so of li-un, or purchase other varieties of Oriental delight. It was sunk in a purple dusk, though here and there a lantern strung the glooms. Low couches lay around the walls, and strange men decorated them: Chinese, Japs, Malays, Lascars, with one or two white girls; and sleek, noiseless attendants swam from couch to couch. Away in the far corner sprawled a lank figure in brown shirting, its nerveless fingers curled about the

---

① Le Tai-pih: 指唐朝诗人李白

② fan-tan: 番摊, 旧时中国用豆子进行的一种赌博。

stem of a spent pipe. On one of the lounges a scorbutic nigger sat with a Jewess from Shadwell. Squatting on a table in the center, beneath one of the lanterns, was a musician with a reed, blinking upon the company like a sly cat, and making his melody of six repeated notes.

The atmosphere churned. The dirt of years, tobacco of many growings, opium, betel nut, and moist flesh allied themselves in one grand assault against the nostrils.

As Cheng brooded on his insect-ridden cushion, of a sudden the lantern above the musician was caught by the ribbon of his reed. It danced and flung a hazy radiance on a divan in the shadow. He saw—started—half rose. His heart galloped, and the blood pounded in his quiet veins. Then he dropped again, crouched, and stared.

O lily-flowers and plum blossoms! O silver streams and dim-starred skies! O wine and roses, song and laughter! For there, kneeling on a mass of rugs, mazed and big-eyed, but understanding, was Lucy ... his Lucy ... his little maid. Through the dusk she must have felt his intent gaze upon her; for he crouched there, fascinated, staring into the now obscured corner where she knelt.

But the sickness which momentarily gripped him on finding in this place his snowy-breasted pearl passed and gave place to great joy. She was here; he would talk with her. Little English he had, but simple words, those with few gutturals, he had managed to pick up; so he rose, the masterful lover, with feline movements, crossed the nightmare chamber to claim his own.

If you wonder how Lucy came to be in this bagnio, the explanation is simple. Battling was in training. He had flogged her that day before starting work; he had then had a few brandies—not many, some eighteen or nineteen—and had locked the door of his room and taken the key Lucy was, therefore, homeless, and a girl somewhat older than Lucy, so old and so wise, as girls are in that region, saw in her a possible source of revenue. So there they were, and to them appeared Cheng.

From what horrors he saved her that night cannot be told, for her ways were too audaciously childish to hold her long from harm in such a place. What he brought to her was love and death.

For he sat by her. He looked at her—reverently yet passionately. He touched her—wistfully yet eagerly. He locked a finger in her wondrous hair. She did not start away; she did tremble. She knew well what she had to be afraid of in that place; but she was not afraid of Cheng. She pierced the mephitic gloom and scanned his face. No, she was not afraid. His yellow hands, his yellow face, his smooth black hair ... well, he was the first thing that had ever spoken soft words to her; the first thing that had ever laid a hand upon her that was not brutal; the first thing that had deferred in manner towards her as though she, too, had a right to live. She knew his words were sweet, though she did not understand them. Nor can they be set down. Half that he spoke was in village Chinese; the rest in a mangling of English which no distorted spelling could possibly reproduce.

But he drew her back against the cushions and asked her name, and she told him; and he inquired her age, and she told him; and he had then two beautiful words which came easily to his tongue. He repeated them again and again:

"Lucia ... li'l Lucia .... Twelve .... Twelve." Musical phrases they were, dropping from his lips, and to the child who heard her name pronounced so lovingly, they were the lost heights of melody. She clung to him, and he to her. She held his strong arm in both of hers as they crouched on the divan, and nestled her cheek against his coat.

Well ... he took her home to his wretched room.

"Li'l Lucia, come-a-home ... Lucia."

His heart was on fire. As they slipped out of the noisomeness into the night air and crossed the West India Dock Road into Pennyfields, they passed unnoticed. It was late, for one thing, and for another ... well, nobody cared particularly. His blood rang with soft music and the solemnity of drums, for surely he had found now what for many years he had sought—his world's one flower. Wanderer he was, from Tuan-tsen to Shanghai, Shanghai to Glasgow ... Cardiff ... Liverpool ... London. He had dreamed often of the women of his native land; perchance one of them should be his flower. Women, indeed, there had been. Swatow ... he had recollections of certain rose-winged hours in coast cities. At many places to which chance had led him a little bird had perched itself upon his heart but so lightly and for so brief a while as hardly to be felt. But now—now he had found her in this alabaster Cockney child. So that he was glad and had great joy of himself and the blue and silver night, and the harsh flares of the Poplar Hippodrome.

You will observe that he had claimed her, but had not asked himself whether she were of an age for love. The white perfection of the child had captivated every sense. It may be that he forgot that he was in London and not in Tuan-tsen. It may be that he did not care. Of that nothing can be told. All that is known is that his love was a pure and holy thing. Of that we may be sure, for his worst enemies have said it.

Slowly, softly they mounted the stairs to his room, and with almost an obeisance he entered and drew her in. A bank of cloud raced to the east and a full moon thrust a sharp sword of light upon them. Silence lay over all Pennyfields. With a bird-like movement, she looked up at him—her face alight, her tiny hands upon his coat—clinging, wondering, trusting. He took her hand and kissed it; repeated the kiss upon her cheek and lip and little bosom, twirling his fingers in her hair. Docilely and echoing the smile of his lemon lips in a way that thrilled him almost to laughter, she returned his kisses impetuously, gladly.

He clasped the nestling to him. Bruised, tearful, with the love of life almost thrashed out of her, she had fluttered to him out of the evil night.

"O li'l Lucia!" And he put soft hands upon her, and smoothed her and crooned over her many gracious things in his flowered speech. So they stood in the moonlight, while she told him the story of her father, of her beatings, and starvings, and unhappiness.

"O li'l Lucia ... White Blossom ... Twelve ... Twelve years old!"

As he spoke, the clock above the Milwall Docks shot twelve crashing notes across the night. When the last echo died, he moved to a cupboard, and from it he drew strange things ... formless masses of blue and gold, magical things of silk, and a vessel that was surely Aladdin's lamp, and a box of spice. He took these robes, and, with tender, reverent fingers, removed from his White Blossom the besmirched rags that covered her, and robed her again, and led her then to the heap of stuff that was his bed, and bestowed her safely.

For himself, he squatted on the floor before her, holding one grubby little hand. There he crouched all night, under the lyric moon, sleepless, watchful; and sweet content was his. He had fallen into an uncomfortable posture, and his muscles ached intolerably. But she slept, and he dared not move nor release her hand lest he should awaken her. Weary and trustful, she slept, knowing that the yellow man was kind and that she might sleep with no fear of a steel hand smashing the delicate structure of her dreams.

In the morning, when she awoke, still wearing her blue and yellow silk, she gave a cry of amazement. Cheng had been about. Many times had he glided up and down the two flights of stairs, and now at last his room was prepared for his princess. It was swept and garnished, and was an apartment worthy a maid who is loved by a poet-prince. There was a bead curtain. There were muslins of pink and white. There were four bowls of flowers, clean, clear flowers to gladden the white Blossom and set off her sharp beauty. And there was a bowl of water, and a sweet lotion for the bruise on her cheek.

When she had risen, her prince ministered to her with rice and egg and tea. Cleansed and robed and calm, she sat before him, perched on the edge of many cushions as on a throne, with all the grace of the child princess in the story. She was a poem. The beauty hidden by neglect and fatigue shone out now more clearly and vividly, and from the head sunning over with curls to the small white feet, now bathed and sandaled, she seemed the living interpretation of a Chinese lyric. And she was his; her sweet self, and her prattle, and her birdlike ways were all his own.

Oh, beautifully they loved. For two days he held her. Soft caresses from his yellow hands and long, devout kisses were all their demonstration. Each night he would tend her, as might mother to child; and each night he watched and sometimes slumbered at the foot of her couch.

But now there were those that ran to Battling at his training quarters across the river, with the news that his child had gone with a Chink①—a yellow man. And Battling was angry. He discovered parental rights. He discovered indignation. A yellow man after his kid! He'd learn him. Battling did not like men who were not born in the same great country as himself. Particularly he disliked yellow men. His birth and education in Shadwell had taught him that of all creeping things that creep upon the earth the most insidious is the Oriental in the West. And a yellow man and a child. It was ... as you might say ... so ... kind of ... well, wasn't it? He bellowed that it was "unnacherel." The yeller man would go through it. Yeller! It was his supreme condemnation, his final epithet for all conduct of which he disapproved.

There was no doubt that he was extremely annoyed. He went to the Blue Lantern, in what was once Ratcliff Highway, and thumped the bar, and made all his world agree with him. And when they agreed with him he got angrier still. So that when, a few hours later, he climbed through the ropes at the Netherlands to meet Bud Tuffit for ten rounds, it was Bud's fight all the time, and to that bright boy's astonishment he was the victor on points at the end of the ten. Battling slouched out of the ring, still more determined to let the Chink have it where the chicken had the ax. He left the house with two pals and a black man, and a number of really inspired curses from his manager.

On the evening of the third day, then, Cheng slipped sleepily down the stairs to procure more flowers and more rice. The genial Ho Ling, who keeps the Canton store, held him in talk some little while, and he was gone from his room perhaps half-an-hour. Then he glided back, and climbed with happy feet the forty stairs to his temple of wonder.

With a push of a finger he opened the door, and the blood froze on his cheek, the flowers fell from him. The temple was empty and desolate; White Blossom was gone. The muslin hangings were torn down and trampled underfoot. The flowers had been flung from their bowls about the floor, and the bowl slay in fifty fragments. The joss was smashed. The cupboard had been opened. Rice was scattered here and there. The little straight bed had been jumped upon by brute feet. Everything that could be smashed or violated had been so treated, and—horror of all—the blue and yellow silk robe had been rent in pieces, tied in grotesque knots, and slung derisively about the table legs.

I pray devoutly that you may never suffer what Cheng Huan suffered in that moment. The pangs of death, with no dying; the sickness of the soul which longs to escape and cannot; the imprisoned animal within the breast which struggles madly for a voice and finds none; all the agonies of all the ages the agonies of every abandoned lover and lost woman, past and to come—all these things were his in that moment.

Then he found voice and gave a great cry, and men from below came up to him;

---

① Chink: (offensive) used as an insulting and contemptuous term for a person of Chinese birth or descent. "中国佬",是英语俚语,带有种族歧视、贬低的意味。

and they told him how the man who boxed had been there with a black man; how he had torn the robes from his child, and dragged her down the stairs by her hair; and how he had shouted aloud for Cheng and had vowed to return and deal separately with him.

Now a terrible dignity came to Cheng, and the soul of his great fathers swept over him. He closed the door against them, and fell prostrate over what had been the resting place of White Blossom. Those without heard strange sounds as of an animal in its last pains; and it was even so. Cheng was dying. The sacrament of his high and holy passion had been profaned; the last sanctuary of the Oriental—his soul dignity—had been assaulted. The love robes had been torn to ribbons; the veil of his temple cut down. Life was no longer possible; and life without his little lady, his White Blossom, was no longer desirable.

Prostrate he lay for the space of some five minutes. Then, in his face all the pride of accepted destiny, he arose. He drew together the little bed. With reverent hands he took the pieces of blue and yellow silk, kissing them and fondling them and placing them about the pillow. Silently he gathered up the flowers, and the broken earthenware, and burnt some prayer papers and prepared himself for death.

Now it is the custom among those of the sect of Cheng that the dying shall present love-gifts to their enemies; and when he had set all in order, he gathered his brown canvas coat about him, stole from the house, and set out to find Battling Burrows, bearing under the coat his love-gift to Battling. White Blossom he had no hope of finding. He had heard of Burrows many times; and he judged that, now that she was taken from him, never again would he hold those hands or touch that laughing hair. Nor, if he did, could it change things from what they were. Nothing that was not a dog could live in the face of this sacrilege.

As he came before the house in Peking Street, where Battling lived, he murmured gracious prayers. Fortunately, it was a night of thick river mist, and through the enveloping velvet none could observe or challenge him. The main door was open, as are all doors in this district. He writhed across the step, and through to the back room, where again the door yielded to a touch.

Darkness. Darkness and silence, and a sense of frightful things. He peered through it. Then he fumbled under his jacket—found a match—struck it. An inch of candle stood on the mantel-shelf. He lit it. He looked round. No sign of Burrows, but ... almost before he looked he knew what awaited him. But the sense of finality had kindly stunned him; he could suffer nothing more.

On the table lay a dog-whip. In the corner a belt had been flung. Half across the greasy couch lay White Blossom. A few rags of clothing were about her pale, slim body; her hair hung limp as her limbs; her eyes were closed. As Cheng drew nearer and saw the savage red rails that ran across and across the beloved body, he could not scream—he could not think. He dropped beside the couch. He laid gentle hands upon her, and called soft names. She was warm to the touch. The pulse was still.

Softly, oh, so softly, he bent over the little frame that had enclosed his friend-spirit, and his light kisses fell all about her. Then, with the undirected movements of a sleep-walker, he bestowed the rags decently about her, clasped her in strong arms, and crept silently into the night.

From Peking Street to Pennyfields it is but a turn or two, and again he passed unobserved as he bore his tired bird back to her nest. He laid her upon the bed, and covered the lily limbs with the blue and yellow silks and strewed upon her a few of the trampled flowers. Then, with more kisses and prayers, he crouched beside her.

So, in the ghastly Limehouse morning, they were found—the dead child, and the Chink, kneeling beside her, with a sharp knife gripped in a vice-like hand, its blade far between his ribs. Meantime, having vented his wrath on his prodigal daughter, Battling, still cross, had returned to the Blue Lantern, and there he stayed with a brandy tumbler in his fist, forgetful of an appointment at Premierland, whereby he should have been in the ring at ten o'clock sharp. For the space of an hour Chuck Lightfoot was going blasphemously to and fro in Poplar, seeking Battling and not finding him, and murmuring, in tearful tones: "Battling—you dammanblasted Battling—where are yeh?"

His opponent was in his corner sure enough, but there was no fight. For Battling lurched from the Blue Lantern to Peking Street. He lurched into his happy home, and he cursed Lucy, and called for her. And finding no matches, he lurched to where he knew the couch should be, and flopped heavily down.

Now it is a peculiarity of the reptile tribe that its members are impatient of being flopped on without warning. So, when Battling flopped, eighteen inches of writhing gristle upreared itself on the couch, and got home on him as Bud Tuffit had done the night before—one to the ear, one to the throat, and another to the forearm.

❀ Questions for Discussion

1. What roles does Battling Burrows play in this tale?
2. What is the tragic ending of the story?
3. What's the symbolic meaning of "the plum blossom"?

❀ Links

1. https://en.wikipedia.org/wiki/Thomas_Burke_(author)
   关于托马斯·波克生平及创作的详细介绍。
2. https://ebooks.adelaide.edu.au/b/burke/thomas/limehouse_nights/contents.html
   关于托马斯·波克的小说《中国佬和小孩》的细读资料。

Part B

Tape-Measure Murder

By Agatha Christie

Agatha Christie (1890—1976) was an English crime novelist, short story writer and playwright.

Christie was born into a wealthy upper-middle-class family in Torquay, Devon. She was initially an unsuccessful writer with six rejections, but this changed when *The Mysterious Affair at Styles*, featuring Hercule Poirot, was published in 1920. During the Second World War, she worked as a pharmacy assistant at University College Hospital, London, and she acquired a good knowledge of poisons which featured in many of her novels.

She is best known for her 66 detective novels and 14 short story collections, particularly those revolving around her fictional detectives Hercule Poirot and Miss Marple. Among which, *Death on the Nile*, *Appointment with Death*, *The Murder on the Orient Express* are familiar to people. She also wrote the world's longest-running play, a murder mystery, *The Mousetrap*, and six romances under the name Mary Westmacott. In 1971, she was made a Dame for her contributions to literature.

Agatha Christie is known throughout the world as the Queen of Crime, whose works have sold over a billion copies in English with another billion in over 70 foreign languages. She is the most widely published author of all time and in any language, outsold only by the Bible and Shakespeare's works. Guinness World Records lists Christie as the best-selling novelist of all time. According to Index Translationum, she remains the most-translated individual author, and her works have been translated into at least 103 languages. In 1955, Christie was the first recipient of the Mystery Writers of America's highest honor—the Grand Master Award. Most of her books and short stories have been adapted for television, radio, video games and comics, and more than thirty feature films have been based on her work.

❋ Lead-in Questions

1. Have you ever watched the film *Murder on the Orient Express*? What is your imagination of its author?
2. Do you know any famous writers of detective stories worldwide? Have you ever read any works of these writers'? What are they?

Questions about the Author and the Story

1. Which of the following statements about Agatha Christie is TRUE?
   A. She lost both her parents as a child.
   B. She was born into the Royal family.
   C. She studied Literature and Philosophy in Paris.
   D. None of the above.
2. Who is Agatha Christie's most famous sleuth?
   A. Miss Marple.   B. Tommy and Tuppence.
   C. Hercule Poirot.   D. Parker Pyne.
3. According to Miss Marple, who murdered Mrs. Spenlow?
   A. Mr. Spenlow. B. Miss Politt. C. Ted Gerard. D. Miss Hartnell.
4. What is the key clue that contributes to Miss Marple's analysis on the murder?
   A. The pin in Constable Palk's tunic.
   B. The tape measure Miss Politt uses.
   C. The flowers shop Mr. Spenlow and Mrs. Spenlow run.
   D. The fish the fishmonger's boy brought.
5. Which of the following is NOT true of Miss Marple?
   A. She is an elderly spinster living in the village of St. Mary Mead.
   B. She always helps her friends and relatives solve mysterious murders.
   C. She is a police officer working with Mr. Palk.
   D. She hasunparalleled powers of observation.

---

*M*iss Politt took hold of the knocker and rapped politely on the cottage door. After a discreet interval she knocked again. The parcel under her left arm shifted a little as she did so, and she readjusted it. Inside the parcel was Mrs. Spenlow's new green winter dress, ready for fitting. From Miss Politt's left hand dangled a bag of black silk, containing a tape measure, a pin cushion, and a large, practical pair of scissors.

Miss Politt was tall and gaunt, with a sharp nose, pursed lips, and a meager iron-grey hair. She hesitated before using the knocker for the third time. Glancing down the street, she saw a figure rapidly approaching. Miss Hartnell, jolly, weather-beaten, fifty-five, shouted out in her usual loud bass voice, "Good afternoon, Miss Politt!"

The dressmaker answered, "Good afternoon, Miss Hartnell." Her voice was excessively thin and genteel in its accents. She had started life as a lady's maid. "Excuse me," she went on, "but do you happen to know if by any chance Mrs. Spenlow isn't at home?"

"Not the least idea," said Miss Hartnell.

"It's rather awkward, you see. I was to fit on Mrs. Spenlow's new dress this afternoon. Three-thirty," she said.

Miss Hartnell consulted her wrist watch. "It's a little past the half-hour now."

"Yes. I have knocked three times, but there doesn't seem to be any answer, so I was wondering if perhaps Mrs. Spenlow might have gone out and forgotten. She doesn't forget appointments as a rule, and she wants the dress to wear the day after tomorrow."

Miss Hartnell entered the gate and walked up the path to join Miss Politt outside the door of Laburnam Cottage.

"Why doesn't Gladys answer the door?" she demanded. "Oh, no, of course, it's Thursday—Gladys's day out. I expect Mrs. Spenlow has fallen asleep. I don't expect you've made enough noise with this thing."

Seizing the knocker, she executed a deafening rat-a-tat-tat and, in addition, thumped upon the panels of the door. She also called out in a stentorian voice: "What ho, within there!"

There was no response.

Miss Politt murmured, "Oh, I think Mrs. Spenlow must have forgotten and gone out. I'll call round some other time." She began edging away down the path.

"Nonsense," said Miss Hartnell firmly. "She can't have gone out. I'd have met her. I'll just take a look through the windows and see if I can find any signs of life."

She laughed in her usual hearty manner, to indicate that it was a joke, and applied a perfunctory glance to the nearest windowpane—perfunctory because she knew quite well that the front room was seldom used, Mr. and Mrs. Spenlow preferring the small back sitting room.

Perfunctory as it was, though, it succeeded in its object. Miss Hartnell, it is true, saw no signs of life. On the contrary, she saw, through the window, Mrs. Spenlow lying on the hearthrug—dead.

"Of course," said Miss Hartnell, telling the story afterward, "I managed to keep my head. That Politt creature wouldn't have had the least idea of what to do. 'Got to keep our heads,' I said to her. 'You stay here and I'll go for Constable Palk.' She said something about not wanting to be left, but I paid no attention at all. One has to be firm with that sort of person. I've always found they enjoy making a fuss. So I was just going off when, at that very moment, Mr. Spenlow came round the corner of the house."

Here Miss Hartnell made a significant pause. It enabled her audience to ask breathlessly, "Tell me, how did he look?"

Miss Hartnell would then go on: "Frankly, I suspected something at once! He was far too calm. He didn't seem surprised in the least. And you may say what you like, it isn't natural for a man to hear that his wife is dead and display no emotion whatever."

Everybody agreed with this statement.

The police agreed with it too. So suspicious did they consider Mr. Spenlow's detachment that they lost no time in ascertaining how that gentleman was situated as a result of his wife's death. When they discovered that Mrs. Spenlow had the money and partner, and that her money went to her husband under a will made soon after their marriage, they were more suspicious than ever.

Miss Marple, that sweet-faced (and some said vinegar-tongued①) elderly spinster② who lived in the house next to the rectory, was interviewed very early—within half an hour of the discovery of the crime. She was approached by Police Constable Palk, importantly thumbing a notebook. "If you don't mind, ma'am, I've a few questions to ask you."

Miss Marple said, "In connection with the murder of Mrs. Spenlow?"

Palk was startled. "May I ask, madam, how you got to know of it?"

"The fish," said Miss Marple.

The reply was perfectly intelligible to Constable Palk. He assumed correctly that the fishmonger's boy had brought it, together with Miss Marple's evening meal.

Miss Marple continued gently, "Lying on the floor in the sitting room, strangled—possibly by a very narrow belt. But whatever it was, it was taken away."

Palk's face was wrathful. "How that young Fred gets to know everything—"

Miss Marple cut him short adroitly. She said, "There's a pin in your tunic."

Constable Palk looked down, startled. He said, "They do say: 'See a pin and pick it up, all the day you'll have good luck.'"

"I hope that will come true. Now what is it you want me to tell you?"

Constable Palk cleared his throat, looked important, and consulted his notebook. Statement was made to me by Mr. Arthur Spenlow, husband of the deceased. Mr. Spenlow says that at two-thirty, as far as he can say, he was rung up by Miss Marple and asked if he would come over at a quarter past three, as she was anxious to consult him about something.

"Now, ma'am, is that true?"

"Certainly not," said Miss Marple.

"You did not ring up Mr. Spenlow at two-thirty?"

"Neither at two-thirty nor any other time."

"Ah," said Constable Palk, and sucked his moustache with a good deal of satisfaction.

"What else did Mr. Spenlow say?"

"Mr. Spenlow's statement was that he came over here as requested, leaving his own house at ten minutes past three; that on arrival here he was informed by the maidservant that Miss Marple was 'not at home.'"

"That part of it is true," said Miss Marple. "He did come here, but I was at a

---

① vinegar-tongued: 刀子嘴
② spinster: 老姑娘，大龄未婚女性

meeting at the Women's Institute."

"Ah," said Constable Palk again.

Miss Marple exclaimed, "Do tell me, Constable, do you suspect Mr. Spenlow?"

"It's not for me to say at this stage, but it looks to me as though somebody, naming no names, had been trying to be artful."

Miss Marple said thoughtfully, "Mr. Spenlow?"

She liked Mr. Spenlow. He was a small, spare man, stiff and conventional in speech, the acme of respectability. It seemed odd that he should have come to live in the country; he had so clearly lived in towns all his life. To Miss Marple he confided the reason. He said, "I have always intended, ever since I was a small boy, to live in the country someday and have a garden of my own. I have always been very much attached to flowers. My wife, you know, kept a flower shop. That's where I saw her first."

A dry statement, but it opened up a vista of romance. A younger, prettier Mrs. Spenlow, seen against a background off lowers. Mr. Spenlow, however, really knew nothing about flowers. He had no idea of seeds, of cuttings, of bedding out, of annuals or perennials. He had only a vision—a vision of a small cottage garden thickly planted with sweet-smelling, brightly colored blossoms. He had asked, almost pathetically, for instruction and had noted down Miss Marple's replies to questions in a little book.

He was a man of quiet method. It was, perhaps, because of this trait that the police were interested in him when his wife was found murdered. With patience and perseverance they learned a good deal about the late Mrs. Spenlow—and soon all St. Mary Mead knew it too.

The late Mrs. Spenlow had begun life as a between maid[①] in a large house. She had left that position to marry the second gardener and with him had started a flower shop in London. The shop had prospered. Not so the gardener, who before long had sickened and died.

His widow had carried on the shop and enlarged it in an ambitious way. She had continued to prosper. Then she had sold the business at a handsome price and embarked upon matrimony for the second time—with Mr. Spenlow, a middle-aged jeweler who had inherited a small and struggling business. Not long afterward they had sold the business and come down to St. Mary Mead.

Mrs. Spenlow was a well-to-do woman. The profits from her florist's establishment she had invested—"under spirit guidance," as she explained to all and sundry. The spirits had advised her with unexpected acumen.

All her investments had prospered, some in quite a sensational fashion. Instead, however, of this increasing her belief in spiritualism, Mrs. Spenlow basely deserted mediums and sittings and made a brief but wholehearted plunge into an obscure religion

---

① between maid: 打杂的女佣

with Indian affinities which was based on various forms of deep breathing. When, however, she arrived at St. Mary Mead, she had relapsed into a period of orthodox Church-of-England beliefs. She was a good deal at the Vicarage and attended church services with assiduity. She patronized the village shops, took an interest in the local happenings, and played village bridge.

A humdrum①, everyday life. And—suddenly—murder.

Colonel Melchett, the chief constable, had summoned Inspector Slack.

Slack was a positive type of man. When he made up his mind, he was sure. He was quite sure now. "Husband did it, sir," he said.

"You think so?"

"Quite sure of it. You've only got to look at him. Never showed a sign of grief or emotion. He came back to the house knowing she was dead."

"Wouldn't he at least have tried to act the part of the distracted husband?"

"Not him, sir. Too pleased with himself. Some gentlemen can't act. Too stiff. As I see it, he was just fed up with his wife. She'd got the money and, I should say, was a trying woman to live with—always taking up some 'ism' or other. He cold-bloodedly decided to do away with her and live comfortably on his own."

"Yes, that could be the case, I suppose."

"Depend upon it, that was it. Made his plans careful. Pretended to get a phone call—"

Melchett interrupted him: "No call been traced?"

"No, sir. That means either that he lied or that the call was put through from a public telephone booth. The only two public phones in the village are at the station and the post office. Post office it certainly wasn't. Mrs. Blade sees everyone who comes in. Station it might be. Train arrives at two twenty-seven and there's a bit of bustle then. But the main thing is he says it was Miss Marple who called him up, and that certainly isn't true. The call didn't come from her house, and she herself was away at the Institute."

"You're not overlooking the possibility that the husband was deliberately got out of the way—by someone who wanted to murder Mrs. Spenlow?"

"You're thinking of young Ted Gerard, aren't you, sir? I've been working on him—what we're up against there is lack of motive. He doesn't stand to gain anything."

"He's an undesirable character, though. Quite a pretty little spot of embezzlement② to his credit."

"I'm not saying he isn't a wrong 'un. Still, he did go to his boss and own up to that embezzlement. And his employers weren't wise to it."

---

① humdrum: boring; 单调的，无聊的
② embezzlement: 挪用，侵吞

"An Oxford Grouper," said Melchett.

"Yes, sir. Became a convert and went off to do the straight thing and own up to having pinched money. I'm not saying, mind you, that it mayn't have been astuteness—he may have thought he was suspected and decided to gamble on honest repentance."

"You have a skeptical mind, Slack," said Colonel Melchett. "By the way, have you talked to Miss Marple at all?"

"What's she got to do with it, sir?"

"Oh, nothing. But she hears things, you know. Why don't you go and have a chat with her? She's a very sharp old lady."

Slack changed the subject. "One thing I've been meaning to ask you, sir: That domestic-service job where the deceased started her career—Sir Robert Abercrombie's place. That's where that jewel robbery was—emeralds—worth a packet. Never got them. I've been looking it up—must have happened when the Spenlow woman was there, though she'd have been quite a girl at the time. Don't think she was mixed up in it, do you, sir? Spenlow, you know, was one of those little tuppenny-ha'penny jewelers—just the chap for a fence."

Melchett shook his head. "Don't think there's anything in that. She didn't even know Spenlow at the time. I remember the case. Opinion in police circles was that a son of the house was mixed up in it—Jim Abercrombie—awful young waster. Had a pile of debts, and just after the robbery they were all paid off—some rich woman, so they said, but I dont know—old Abercrombie hedged a bit about the case—tried to call the police off."

"It was just an idea, sir," said Slack.

Miss Marple received Inspector Slack with gratification, especially when she heard that he had been sent by Colonel Melchett. "Now, really, that is very kind of Colonel Mechett. I didn't know he remembered me."

"He remembers you, all right. Told me that what you didn't know of what goes on in St. Mary Mead isn't worth knowing." "Too kind of him, but really I don't know anything at all. About this murder, I mean."

"You know what the talk about it is."

"Of course—but it wouldn't do, would it, to repeat just idle talk?"

Slack said, with an attempt at geniality, "This isn't an official conversation, you know. It's in confidence, so to speak."

"You mean you really want to know what people are saying?"

"Whether there's any truth in it or not?"

"That's the idea."

"Well, of course, there's been a great deal of talk and speculation. And there are really two distinct camps, if you understand me. To begin with, there are the people who think that the husband did it. A husband or a wife is, in a way, the natural person to suspect, don't you think so?"

"Maybe," said the inspector cautiously.

"Such close quarters, you know. Then, so often, the money angle. I hear that it was Mrs. Spenlow who had the money and therefore Mr. Spenlow does benefit by her death. In this wicked world I'm afraid the most uncharitable assumptions are often justified."

"He comes into a tidy sum, all right."

"Just so. It would seem quite plausible, wouldn't it, for him to strange her, leave the house by the back, come across the fields to my house, ask for me and pretend he'd had a telephone call from me, then go back and find his wife murdered in his absence—hoping, of course, that the crime would be put down to some tramp or burglar."

The inspector nodded. "What with the money angle—and if they'd been on bad terms lately—"

But Miss Marple interrupted him: "Oh, but they hadn't."

"You know that for a fact?"

"Everyone would have known if they'd quarreled! The maid, Gladys Brent—she'd have soon spread it round the village."

The inspector said feebly, "She mightn't have known," and received a pitying smile in reply.

Miss Marple went on: "And then there's the other school of thought. Ted Gerard. A good-looking young man. I'm afraid, you know, that good looks are inclined to influence one more than they should. Our last curate but one—quite a magical effect! All the girls came to church—evening service as well as morning. And many older women became unusually active in parish work—and the slippers and scarves that were made for him! Quite embarrassing for the poor young man."

"But let me see, where was I? Oh yes, this young man, Ted Gerard. Of course, there has been talk about him. He's come down to see her so often. Though Mrs. Spenlow told me herself that he was a member of what I think they call the Oxford Group. A religious movement. They are quite sincere and very earnest, I believe, and Mrs. Spenlow was impressed by it all."

Miss Marple took a breath and went on: "And I'm sure there was no reason to believe that there was anything more in it than that, but you know what people are. Quite a lot of people are convinced that Mrs. Spenlow was infatuated with the young man and that she'd lent him quite a lot of money. And it's perfectly true that he was actually seen at the station that day."

"In the train—the two twenty-seven down train. But of course it would be quite easy, wouldn't it, to slip out of the other side of the train and go through the cutting and over the fence and round the hedge and never come out of the station entrance at all? So that he need not have been seen going to the cottage. And of course people do think that what Mrs. Spenlow was wearing was rather peculiar."

"Peculiar?"

"A kimono. Not a dress." Miss Marple blushed. "That sort of thing, you know, is perhaps, rather suggestive to some people."

"You think it was suggestive?"

"Oh no, I don't think so. I think it was perfectly natural."

"Under the circumstances, yes." Miss Marple's glance was cool and reflective. Inspector Slack said, "It might give us another motive for the husband. Jealousy."

"Oh no, Mr. Spenlow would never be jealous. He's not the sort of man who notices things. If his wife had gone away and left a note on the pincushion, it would be the first he'd know of anything of that kind."

Inspector Slack was puzzled by the intent way she was looking at him. He had an idea that all her conversation was intended to hint at something he didn't understand. She said now, with some emphasis, "Didn't you find any clues, Inspector—on the spot?"

"People don't leave fingerprints and cigarette ash nowadays, Miss Marple."

"But this, I think," she suggested, "was an old-fashioned crime—" Slack said sharply, "Now what do you mean by that?"

Miss Marple remarked slowly, "I think, you know, that Constable Palk could help you. He was the first person on the—on the 'scene of the crime,' as they say."

Mr. Spenlow was sitting in a deck chair. He looked bewildered. He said, in his thin, precise voice, "I may, of course, be imagining what occurred. My hearing is not as good as it was. But I distinctly think I heard a small boy call after me that he was of the opinion that I had—had killed my dear wife."

Miss Marple, gently snipping off a dead rose head, said, "That was the impression he meant to convey, no doubt."

"But what could possibly have put such an idea into a child's head?"

Miss Marple coughed. "Listening, no doubt, to the opinions of his elders."

"You—you really mean that other people think that also?"

"Quite half the people in St. Mary Mead."

"But, my dear lady, what can possibly have given rise to such an idea? I was sincerely attached to my wife. She did not, alas, take to living in the country as much as I had hoped she would do, but perfect agreement on every subject is an impossible idea. I assure you I feel her loss very keenly."

"Probably. But if you will excuse my saying so, you don't sound as though you do."

Mr. Spenlow drew his meager frame up to its full height. "My dear lady, many years ago I read of a certain Chinese philosopher who, when his dearly loved wife was taken from him, continued calmly to beat a gong in the street—a customary Chinese pastime, I presume—exactly as usual. The people of the city were much impressed by his fortitude."

"But," said Miss Marple, "the people of St. Mary Mead react rather differently. Chinese philosophy does not appeal to them."

"But you understand?"

Miss Marple nodded. "My uncle Henry," she explained, "was a man of an unusual self-control. His motto was 'Never display emotion.' He, too, was very fond of flowers."

"I was thinking," said Mr. Spenlow with something like eagerness, "that I might, perhaps, have a pergola on the west side of the cottage. Pink roses and, perhaps, wisteria. And there is a white starry flower, whose name for the moment escapes me—"

In the tone in which she spoke to her grandnephew, age three, Miss Marple said, "I have a very nice catalogue here, with pictures. Perhaps you would like to look through it—I have to go up to the village."

Leaving Mr. Spenlow sitting happily in the garden with his catalogue, Miss Marple went up to her room, hastily rolled up a dress in a piece of brown paper, and, leaving the house, walked briskly up to the post office. Miss Politt, the dressmaker, lived in rooms over the post office.

But Miss Marple did not at once go through the door and up the stairs. It was just two-thirty, and, a minute late, the Much Benham bus drew up outside the post-office door. It was one of the events of the day in St. Mary Mead. The post-mistress hurried out with parcels, parcels connected with the shop side of her business, for the post office also dealt in sweets, cheap books, and children's toys.

For some four minutes Miss Marple was alone in the post office.

Not till the postmistress returned to her post did Miss Marple go upstairs and explain to Miss Politt that she wanted her own grey crepe altered and made more fashionable if that were possible. Miss Politt promised to see what she could do.

The chief constable was rather astonished when Miss Marple's name was brought to him. She came in with many apologies.

"So sorry—so very sorry to disturb you. You are so busy, I know, but then you have always been so very kind, Colonel Melchett, and I felt I would rather come to you instead of to Inspector Slack. For one thing, you know, I should hate Constable Palk to get into any trouble. Strictly speaking, I suppose he shouldn't have touched anything at all."

Colonel Melchett was slightly bewildered. He said, "Palk? That's the St. Mary Mead constable, isn't it? What has he been doing?"

"He picked up a pin, you know. It was in his tunic. And it occurred to me at the time that it was quite probably he had actually picked it up in Mrs. Spenlow's house."

"Quite, quite. But, after all, you know, what's a pin? Matter off act, he did pick the pin up just by Mrs. Spenlow's body. Came and told Slack about it yesterday—you put him up to that, I gather? Oughtn't to have touched anything, of course, but, as I said, what's a pin? It was only a common pin. Sort of thing any woman might use."

"Oh no, Colonel Melchett, that's where you're wrong. To a man's eye, perhaps, it looked like an ordinary pin, but it wasn't. It was a special pin, a very thin pin, the kind you buy by the box, the kind used mostly by dressmakers."

Melchett stared at her, a faint light of comprehension breading in on him. Miss Marple nodded her head several times eagerly.

"Yes, of course. It seems to me so obvious. She was in her kimono because she was going to try on her new dress, and she went into the front room, and Miss Politt just said something about measurements and put the tape measure round her neck—and then all she'd have to do was to cross it and pull—quite easy, so I've heard. And then of course she'd go outside and pull the door to and stand thee knocking as though she'd just arrived. But the pin shows she'd already been in the house."

"And it was Miss Politt who telephoned to Spenlow?"

"Yes. From the post office at two-thirty—just when the bus comes and the post office would be empty."

Colonel Melchett said, "But, my dear Miss Marple, why? In heaven's name, why? You can't have a murder without a motive."

"Well, I think, you know, Colonel Melchett, from all I've heard, that the crime dates from a long time back. It reminds me, you know, of my two cousins, Antony and Gordon. Whatever Antony did always went right for him, and with poor Gordonin was just the other way about; race horses went lame, and stocks went down, and property depreciated ... As I see it, the two women were in it together."

"In what?"

"The robbery. Long ago. Very valuable emeralds, so I've heard. The lady's maid and the tweeny. Because one thing hasn't been explained—how, when the tweeny married the gardener, did they have enough money to set up a flower shop?

"The answer is, it was her share of the—the swag, I think is the right expression. Everything she did turned out well. Money made money. But the other one, the lady's maid, must have been unlucky. She came down to being just a village dressmaker. Then they met again. Quite all right at first, I expect, until Mr. Ted Gerard came on the scene."

"Mrs. Spenlow, you see, was already suffering from conscience and was inclined to be emotionally religious. This young man no doubt urged her to 'face up' and to 'come clean,' and I dare say she was strung up to do so. But Miss Politt didn't see it that way. All she saw was that she might go to prison for a robbery she had committed years ago. So she made up her mind to put a stop to it all. I'm afraid, you know, that she was always rather a wicked woman. I don't believe she'd have turned a hair if that nice, stupid Mr. Spenlow had been hanged."

Colonel Melchett said slowly, "We can—er—verify your theory—up to a point. The identity of the Politt woman with the lady's maid at the Abercrombies', but—"

Miss Marple reassured him. "It will be all quite easy. She's the kind of woman who will break down at once when she's taxed with the truth. And then, you see, I've got her tape measure. I—er—abstracted it yesterday when I was trying on. When she misses it and thinks the police have got it—well, she's quite an ignorant woman and she'll think it will prove the case against her in some way."

She smiled at him encouragingly. "You'll have no trouble, I can assure you." It was the tone in which his favorite aunt had once assured him that he could not fail to pass his entrance examination into Sandhurst①.

And he passed.

Questions for Discussion

1. What do you suppose makes Agatha Christie's works so popular after you read this story?
2. Is Agatha Christie anything more than a skillful purveyor of pot-boilers?
3. What do you think about the character Miss Marple?

Links

1. https://en.wikipedia.org/wiki/Agatha_Christie
   关于阿加莎·克里斯蒂生平及创作的详细介绍。
2. http://www.agathachristie.com/stories/tape-measure-murder
   关于阿加莎·克里斯蒂的小说《软尺谋杀案》的细读资料。

---

① Sandhurst：桑德赫斯特(英国皇家陆军官校所在地)

Chapter Six

Part A

God Sees the Truth, but Waits

By Leo Tolstoy

Leo Tolstoy (1828—1910) is a Russian novelist and social reformer of world fame, and he is regarded as one of the greatest authors of all time. Born to an aristocratic Russian family in 1828, he is best known for the novels *War and Peace* (1869) and *Anna Karenina* (1877), often cited as pinnacles of realist fiction.

War and Peace is generally thought to be one of the greatest novels ever written, remarkable for its dramatic breadth and unity. Both critics and the public were buzzing about the novel's historical accounts of the Napoleonic Wars, combined with its thoughtful development of realistic yet fictional characters. In 1873, Tolstoy set to work on the second of his best-known novels, *Anna Karenina*. The first sentence of *Anna Karenina* is among the most famous lines of the book: "All happy families resemble one another, each unhappy family is unhappy in its own way."

He continued to write fiction throughout the 1880s and 1890s. One of his most successful later works was *The Death of Ivan Ilyich*, in which the main character struggles to come to grips with his impending death. The title character, Ivan Ilyich, comes to the jarring realization that he has wasted his life on trivial matters, but the realization comes too late.

Over the last 30 years of his life, Tolstoy established himself as a moral and religious leader. His ideas about nonviolent resistance to evil influenced the likes of social leader Mahatma Gandhi. Tolstoy died on November 20, 1910 in Astapovo, Russia. *God Sees the Truth, but Waits* illustrates Tolstoy's favorite theme, the forgiveness of sins, and it is usually considered as the most representative of his short stories.

Lead-in Questions

1. How often do you dream? Would you please describe one of the most memorable dreams?
2. Do you believe that dreams have their particular meanings? Have you heard of two books about dreams, *Zhou Gong Dream Dictionary* and *The Interpretation of Dreams*?
3. If you are wronged, what will you feel? If you know who persecutes or harms you, will you take any actions against him or her?

Questions about the Author and the Story

1. Which of the following is NOT written by Leo Tolstoy?
   A. *Anna Karenina*.   B. *The Death of Ivan Ilyich*.
   C. *Crime and Punishment*.   D. *War and Peace*.
2. Why did Aksyonof's wife ask him not to go to the market?
   A. Because she was afraid that he would drink to excess.
   B. Because she would be too busy to take care of their children.
   C. Because he would leave home for many days.
   D. Because she had a dreadful nightmare.
3. What happened to Aksyonof on his way to the market?
   A. He had his horse stolen.
   B. He was suspected of murdering.
   C. He had a fight with another merchant.
   D. He had the pleasure of making acquaintances with a police officer.
4. What do we know about Aksyonof's life in Siberia?
   A. He has never given up petitioning all those years.
   B. He was accustomed to the life there and lived happily.
   C. He won respect from both the inmates and the prison authorities.
   D. He was so heart-broken that he wanted to erase all his memory about his family.
5. Why didn't Aksyonof tell on Makar Semyonitch?
   A. Because he didn't have any evidence.
   B. Because he didn't want to destroy his image as a "saint".
   C. Because he didn't believe in revenge.
   D. Because he was afraid of Makar Semyonitch's threats.

In the town of Vladimir① lived a young merchant named Ivan Dmitrich Aksyonof. He had two shops and a house of his own.

Aksyonof was a handsome man. He was full of fun, and very fond of singing. He used to drink too much, but after he married he gave up drinking, except now and then.

One summer Aksyonof was going to the Nizhny Fair, and as he said good-bye to his family, his wife said to him, "Ivan Dmitrich, do not start today; I have had a bad dream about you."

Aksyonof laughed, and said, "You are afraid that when I get to the fair I shall go on the spree."

His wife replied: "I do not know what I am afraid of; all I know is that I had a bad dream. I dreamed you returned from the town, and when you took off your cap I saw that your hair was quite grey."

Aksyonof laughed. "That's a lucky sign," said he. "See if I don't sell out all my goods, and bring you some presents from the fair."

So he said good-bye to his family and drove away.

When he had travelled halfway, he met a merchant whom he knew, and they put up at the same inn for the night. They had some tea together, and then went to bed in adjoining rooms.

It was not Aksyonof's habit to sleep late, and wishing to travel while it was still cool, he woke up his driver before dawn, and told him to put in the horses.

Then he made his way across to the landlord of the inn (who lived in a cottage at the back), paid his bill, and continued his journey.

When he had gone about twenty-five miles, he stopped for the horses to be fed. Aksyonof rested a while in the passage of the inn, then he stepped out into the porch, and, ordering a samovar② to be heated, got out his guitar and began to play.

Suddenly a troika③ drove up with tinkling bells, and an official alighted, followed by two soldiers. He came to Aksyonof and began to question him, asking him who he was and whence he came. Aksyonof answered him fully, and said, "Won't you have some tea with me?" But the official went on cross-questioning him and asking him. "Where did you spend last night? Were you alone, or with a fellow merchant? Did you see the other merchant this morning? Why did you leave the inn before dawn?"

Aksyonof wondered why he was asked all these questions, but he described all that had happened, and then added, "Why do you cross-question me as if I were a thief or a robber? I am travelling on business of my own, and there is no need to question me."

Then the official, calling the soldiers, said, "I am the police-officer of this district,

---

① Vladimir: a Russian city; 弗拉基米尔(地名)
② samovar: a type of tea service popular in Russia; 茶炊
③ troika: also spelled as troika, refers to a carriage with three horses; 三匹马拉着的马车

and I question you because the merchant with whom you spent last night has been found with his throat cut. We must search your things."

They entered the house. The soldiers and the police officer unstrapped Aksyonof's luggage and searched it. Suddenly the officer drew a knife out of a bag, crying, "Whose knife is this?"

Aksyonof looked, and seeing a bloodstained knife taken from his bag, he was frightened.

"How is it there is blood on this knife?"

Aksyonof tried to answer, but could hardly utter a word, and only stammered: "I—I don't know—not mine."

Then the police officer said: "This morning the merchant was found in bed with his throat cut. You are the only person who could have done it. The house was locked from inside, and no one else was there. Here is this bloodstained knife in your bag, and your face and manner betray you! Tell me how you killed him, and how much money you stole?"

Aksyonof swore he had not done it; that he had not seen the merchant after they had tea together; that he had no money except eight thousand rubles of his own, and that the knife was not his. But his voice was broken, his face pale, and he shook with fear as though he were guilty.

The police officer ordered the soldiers to bind Aksyonof and to put him in the cart. As they tied his feet together and flung him into the cart, Aksyonof crossed himself and wept. His money and goods were taken from him, and he was sent to the nearest town and imprison there. Inquiries as to his character were made in Vladimir. The merchants and other inhabitants of that town said that in former days he used to drink and waste his time, but that he was a good man. Then the trial came on: he was charged with murdering a merchant from Ryaza①, and robbing him of twenty thousand rubles.

His wife was in despair, and did not know what to believe. Her children were all quite small; one was a baby at her breast. Taking them all with her, she went to the town where her husband was in jail. At first she was not allowed to see him; but after much begging, she got permission from the officials, and was taken to him. When she saw her husband in prison dress and in chains, shut up with thieves and criminals, she fell down, and did not come to her senses for a long time. Then she drew her children to her, and sat down near him. She told him of things at home, and asked about what had happened to him. He told her all, and she asked, "What can we do now?"

"We must petition the czar not to let an innocent man perish."

His wife told him that she had sent a petition to the czar, but it had not been accepted.

---

① Ryaza: a city in central Russia; 梁赞(地名)

Chapter Six

Aksyonof did not reply, but only looked downcast.

Then his wife said, "It was not for nothing I dreamed your hair had turned gray. You remember? You should not have started that day." And passing her fingers through his hair, she said: "My dearest, tell your wife the truth; was it not you who did it?"

"So you, too, suspect me!" said Aksyonof, and, hiding his face in his hands, he began to weep. Then a soldier came to say that the wife and children must go away; and Aksyonof said good-bye to his family for the last time.

When they were gone, Aksyonof recalled what had been said, and when he remembered that his wife also had suspected him, he said to himself, "It seems that only God can know the truth; it is to Him alone we must appeal, and from Him alone expect mercy."

And Aksyonof wrote no more petitions; gave up all hope, and only prayed to God.

Aksyonof was condemned to be flogged and sent to the mines. So he was flogged with a knout, and when the wounds made by the knout were healed, he was driven to Siberia with other convicts.

For twenty-six years Aksyonof lived as a convict in Siberia. His hair turned white as snow, and his beard grew long, thin, and gray. All his mirth went; he stooped; he walked slowly, spoke little, and never laughed, but he often prayed.

In prison Aksyonof learned to make boots, and earned a little money, with which he bought *The Lives of the Saints*. He read this book when there was light enough in the prison; and on Sundays in the prison church he read the lessons and sang in the choir; for his voice was still good.

The prison authorities liked Aksyonof for his meekness, and his fellow prisoners respected him: they called him "Grandfather," and "The Saint." When they wanted to petition the prison authorities about anything, they always made Aksyonof their spokesman, and when there were quarrels among the prisoners they came to him to put things right, and to judge the matter.

No news reached Aksyonof from his home, and he did not even know if his wife and children were still alive.

One day a fresh gang of convicts came to the prison. In the evening the old prisoners collected round the new ones and asked them what towns or villages they came from, and what they were sentenced for. Among the rest Aksyonof sat down near the newcomers, and listened with downcast air to what was said.

One of the new convicts, a tall, strong man of sixty, with a closely cropped gray beard, was telling the others what he had been arrested for.

"Well, friends," he said, "I only took a horse that was tied to a sledge, and I was arrested and accused of stealing. I said I had only taken it to get home quicker, and had then let it go; besides, the driver was a friend of mine. So I said, 'It's all right.' 'No,' said they, 'you stole it.' But how or where I stole it they could not say. I once really did something wrong, and ought by rights to have come here long ago, but that time I was not found out. Now I have been sent here for nothing at all. ... Eh, but it's lies I'm telling you; I've been to Siberia before, but I did not stay long."

"Where are you from?" asked some one.

"From Vladimir. My family are of that town. My name is Makar, and they also call me Semyonitch."

Aksyonof raised his head and said: "Tell me, Semyonitch, do you know anything of the merchant Aksyonof of Vladimir? Are they still alive?"

"Know them! Of course I do. The Aksyonofs are rich, though their father is in Siberia: a sinner like ourselves, it seems! As for you, Gran'dad, how did you come here?"

Aksyonof did not like to speak of his misfortune. He only sighed, and said, "For my sins I have been in prison these twenty-six years."

"What wrongs?" asked Makar Semyonitch.

But Aksyonof only said, "Well, well—I must have deserved it!" He would have said no more, but his companions told the newcomer how Aksyonof came to be in Siberia; how someone had killed a merchant, and had put the knife among Aksyonof's things, and Aksyonof had been unjustly condemned.

When Makar Semyonitch heard this, he looked at Aksyonof, slapped his own knee and exclaimed, "Well, this is wonderful! But how old you've grown, Gran'dad?"

The others asked him why he was so surprised, and where he had seen Aksyonof before; but Makar Semyonitch did not reply. He only said: "It's wonderful that we should meet here, lads!"

These words made Aksyonof wonder whether this man knew who had killed the merchant; so he said, "Perhaps, Semyonitch, you have heard of that affair, or maybe you've seen me before?"

"How could I help hearing? The world's full of rumors. But it's a long time ago, and I've forgotten what I heard."

"Perhaps you heard who killed the merchant?" asked Aksyonof.

Makar Semyonitch laughed, and replied: "It must have been him in whose bag the knife was found! If someone else hid the knife there, 'He's not a thief till he's caught,' as the saying goes. How could anyone put a knife into your bag while it was under your head? It would surely have woke you up."

When Aksyonof heard these words, he felt sure this was the man who had killed the merchant. He rose and went away. All that night Aksyonof lay awake. He felt terribly unhappy, and all sorts of images rose in his mind. There was the image of his wife as she was when he parted from her to go to the fair. He saw her as if she were present; her face and her eyes rose before him; he heard her speak and laugh. Then he saw his children, quite little, as they were at that time. And then he remembered himself as he used to be—young and merry. He remembered how he sat playing the guitar in the porch of the inn where he was arrested, and how free from care he had been. He saw, in his mind, the place where he was flogged, the executioner, and the people standing around; the chains, the convicts, all the twenty-six years of his prison life, and his premature old age. The thought of it all made him so wretched that he was ready to kill himself.

"And it's all that villain's doing!" thought Aksyonof. And his anger was so great against Makar Semyonitch that he longed for vengeance, even if he himself should perish for it. He kept repeating prayers all night, but could get no peace. During the day he did not go near Makar Semyonitch, nor even look at him.

A fortnight passed in this way. Aksyonof could not sleep at night, and was so miserable that he did not know what to do.

One night as he was walking about the prison he noticed some earth that came rolling out from under one of the shelves on which the prisoners slept. He stopped to see what it was. Suddenly Makar Semyonitch crept out from under the shelf, and looked up at Aksyonof with frightened face. Aksyonof tried to pass without looking at him, but Makar seized his hand and told him that he had dug a hole under the wall, getting rid of the earth by putting it into his high-boots, and emptying it out every day on the road when the prisoners were driven to their work.

"Just you keep quiet, old man, and you shall get out too. If you blab they'll flog the life out of me, but I will kill you first."

Aksyonof trembled with anger as he looked at his enemy. He drew his hand away, saying, "I have no wish to escape, and you have no need to kill me; you killed me long ago! As to telling of you I may do so or not, as God shall direct."

Next day, when the convicts were led out to work, the convoy soldiers noticed that one or other of the prisoners emptied some earth out of his boots. The prison was searched and the tunnel found. The Governor came and questioned all the prisoners to find out who had dug the hole. They all denied any knowledge of it. At last the Governor turned to Aksyonof, whom he knew to be a just man, and said:

"You are a truthful old man; tell me, before God, who dug the hole?"

Makar Semyonitch stood as if he were quite unconcerned, looking at the Governor and not so much as glancing at Aksyonof. Aksyonof's lips and hands trembled, and for a long time he could not utter a word. He thought, "Why should I screen him who ruined my life? Let him pay for what I have suffered. But if I tell, they will probably flog the life out of him, and maybe I suspect wrongly. And, after all, what good would it be to me?"

"Well, old man," repeated the governor, "tell us the truth: who has been digging under the wall?"

Aksyonof glanced at Makar Semyonitch, and said, "I cannot say, your honor. It is not God's will that I should tell! Do what you like with me; I am in your hands."

However much the Governor tried, Aksyonof would say no more, and so the matter had to be left.

That night, when Aksyonof was lying on his bed and just beginning to doze, some one came quietly and sat down on his bed. He peered through the darkness and recognized Makar.

"What more do you want of me?" asked Aksyonof. "Why have you come here?"

Makar Semyonitch was silent. So Aksyonof sat up and said, "What do you want? Go away, or I will call the guard!"

Makar Semyonitch bent close over Aksyonof, and whispered, "Ivan Dmitritch, forgive me!"

"What for?" asked Aksyonof.

"It was I who killed the merchant and hid the knife among your things. I meant to kill you too, but I heard a noise outside, so I hid the knife in your bag and escaped out of the window."

Aksyonof was silent, and did not know what to say. Makar Semyonitch got off the bed-shelf and knelt upon the ground. "Aksyonof," said he, "forgive me! For the love of God, forgive me! I will confess that it was I who killed the merchant, and you will be released and can go to your home."

"It is easy for you to talk," said Aksyonof, "but I have suffered for you these twenty-six years. Where could I go to now? ... My wife is dead, and my children have forgotten me. I have nowhere to go ..."

Makar Semyonitch did not rise, but beat his head on the floor. "Aksyonof, forgive me!" he cried. "When they flogged me with the knout it was not so hard to bear as it is to see you now ... yet you had pity on me, and did not tell. For Christ's sake, forgive me, wretch that I am!" And he began to sob.

When Aksyonof heard him sobbing he, too, began to weep.

"God will forgive you!" said he, "Maybe I am a hundred times worse than you." And at these words his heart grew light, and the longing for home left him. He no longer had any wish to leave the prison, but only hoped for his last hour to come.

In spite of what Aksyonof had said, Makar Semyonitch confessed his guilt. But when the order for his release came, Aksyonof was already dead.

❀ Questions for Discussion

1. What do you think about Aksyonof's life experience? Is he a sage or saint in your mind? Why or why not?
2. If you are deeply hurt, would you rather choose "eye for eye, tooth for tooth" or "render good for evil"? And explain your reasons.
3. How do you understand the title "God sees the truth, but waits"?

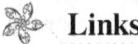 **Links**
1. https://en.wikipedia.org/wiki/Leo_Tolstoy
   关于列夫·托尔斯泰生平及创作的详细介绍。
2. http://great-authors.albertarose.org/leo_tolstoy/
   关于列夫·托尔斯泰的小说《上帝全看见,只是在等待》的细读资料。

The Christmas Tree and the Wedding

By Fyodor Dostoevsky

Fyodor Dostoevsky (1821—1881) was a Russian novelist, short story writer, essayist, journalist and philosopher whose literary works explore human psychology in the troubled political, social, and spiritual atmosphere of 19th-century Russia. His psychological penetration into the human soul had a profound influence on the 20th century novel.

Dostoyevsky was the second son of a former army doctor. Graduated as a military engineer, he resigned in 1844 to devote himself to writing. His first novel, *Poor Folk*, appeared in 1846. At the same year, he joined a group of utopian socialists. He was arrested in 1849 and sentenced to death, commuted to imprisonment in Siberia. His experience of hard labor and four years as a soldier were reflected in his three works: *The House of the Dead*, *The Insulted and Injured*, and *Winter Notes on Summer Impressions*.

Most of his well-known works got published in 1860s: From the turmoil of the 1860s emerged *Notes from the Underground*, which marked a watershed in Dostoevsky's artistic development. The novel starts with the confessions of a mentally ill narrator and continues with the promise of spiritual rebirth. It was followed by *Crime and Punishment* (1866) and it is an account of an individual's fall and redemption, *The Idiot* (1868), depicting a Christ-like figure, Prince Myshkin, and *The Possessed* (1871), an exploration of philosophical nihilism.

An epileptic all his life, Dostoevsky died in St. Petersburg on February 9, 1881. Fyodor Dostoevsky has left a legacy of literature that makes him one of the world's, not just Russia's greatest writers of the 19th century. Dostoyevsky is usually regarded as one of the finest novelists who ever lived. He explored and captured the depth of the human soul, surfacing emotions and feelings in times both dark and happy. Literary modernism, existentialism, and various schools of psychology, theology, and literary criticism have been profoundly shaped by his ideas.

Lead-in Questions

1. What will come into your mind at the mention of the Christmas tree and the wedding respectively?
2. Can you think of any connection between the Christmas tree and a wedding?

Questions about the Author and the Story

1. Which of the following is NOT the works of Fyodor Dostoevsky?
   A. *Crime and Punishment*.   B. *The Brothers Karamazov*.
   C. *The Last Leaf*.   D. *The Idiot*.
2. "The host was a well-known businessman with many connections, friends and intrigues, so you might think the children's party was a pretext for the parents to meet each other and to talk things over in an innocent, casual and inadvertent manner." According to the context, what does "inadvertent" most probably mean?
   A. formal   B. careless   C. serious   D. careful
3. What do we know about the young gentleman in the novel?
   A. He is a remote relative of the host and hostess.
   B. He enjoys the company of the guests and indulges himself in the party.
   C. He feels bored at the party the whole night.
   D. He is a merry, humoros man who is accustomed to all sorts of socializing.
4. What can be inferred about Yulian Mastakovitch according to the novel?
   A. He is a man of double personality, good at calculation.
   B. He is popular with all the people present, including the children.
   C. He is a respectable nobleman.
   D. He is more interested in innocent children than flattering adults.
5. What's TRUE about the final wedding?
   A. The marriage is a blessed one between a matching couple.
   B. The marriage ceremony is celebrated secretly.
   C. The bride looks happy and hopefully looks forward to the marriage.
   D. The marriage invites quite a lot of discussion among the crowd.

The other day I saw a wedding ... but no! Better I tell you about the Christmas tree. The wedding was nice; I enjoyed it very much, but the other thing that happened was better. I do not know why, but while looking at the wedding, I thought about that

Chapter Six

Christmas tree. This was the way it happened.

On New Year's Eve, exactly five years ago, I was invited to a children's party. The host was a well-known businessman with many connections, friends and intrigues, so you might think the children's party was a pretext for the parents to meet each other and to talk things over in an innocent, casual and inadvertent manner.

I was an outsider. I did not have anything to contribute, and therefore I spent the evening on my own. There was another gentleman present who had no special family or position, but, like myself, had dropped in on this family happiness. He was the first to catch my eye. He was a tall, lean man, very serious and very properly dressed. Actually he was not enjoying this family-type party in the least. If he withdrew into a corner, he immediately stopped smiling and knit his thick bushy black eyebrows. Except for our host, the man had not a single acquaintance at the whole party. Obviously, he was terribly bored, but he was making a gallant effort to play the role of a perfectly happy, contented man. Afterwards I learned he was a gentleman from the province, with important, puzzling business in the capital; he had brought our host a letter of introduction, from a person our host did not patronize, so this man was invited to this children's party only out of courtesy. He didn't even play cards. They offered him no cigars; no one engaged him in conversation. Perhaps we recognized the bird by its feathers from a distance; that is why my gentleman was compelled to sit out the whole evening and stroke his whiskers merely to have something to do with his hands. His whiskers really were very fine, but he stroke them so diligently, you thought the whiskers came first, and were then fixed onto his face, the better to stroke him.

Beside this man—who had five well-fed boys—my attention was caught by a second gentleman. He was an important person. His name was Yulian Mastakovitch. With one glance, you saw he was a guest of honor. He looked down on the host much as the host looked down on the gentleman who stroked his whiskers. The host and hostess spoke to the important man from across a chasm of courtesy, waited on him, give him drink, pampered him, and brought their guests to him for introductions. They did not take him to anyone.

When Yulian Mastakovitch commented, in regard to the evening, that he had seldom spent time in such a pleasant manner, I noticed tears sparkled in the host's eyes. In the presence of such a person, I was frightened, and, after admiring the children, I walked into a small deserted drawing-room and sat down beside an arbor of flowers which took up almost half of the room.

All the children were incredibly sweet. They absolutely refused to imitate their "elders", despite all the exhortations of their governesses and mothers. In an instant the children untwisted all the Christmas tree candy and broke half of the toys before they knew for whom they were intended. One small, black eyed, curly haired boy was especially nice. He kept wanting to shoot me with his wooden gun. But my attention was still more drawn to his sister, a girl of eleven, a quiet, pensive, pale little cupid with large thoughtful eyes. In some way, the children wounded her feelings, and so she came into the same room where I sat and busied herself in the corner—with her doll.

The guests respectfully pointed out one of the wealthy commissioned tax gatherers—her father. In a whisper someone said three hundred thousand roubles[①] were already set aside for her dowry.

I swung around to look at those who were curious about such circumstances; my gaze fell on Yulian Mastakovitch. With his hands behind his back, with his head cocked a little to one side, he listened with extraordinary attention to the empty talk of the guests.

Later, I marveled at the wisdom of the host and hostess in the distribution of the children's gifts. The little girl—already the owner of three hundred thousand roubles—received the most expensive doll. Then followed presents lowering in value according to the class of the parents of these happy children. Finally, the last gift: a young boy, ten years-old, slender, small, freckled, red-haired, received only a book of stories about the marvels of nature and the tears of devotion—without pictures and even without engravings. He was the son of the governess of the hosts' children, a poor widow; he was a little boy, extremely oppressed and frightened. He wore a jacket made from a wretched nankeen. After he received his book, he walked around the other toys for a long time; he wanted to play with the other children, but he did not dare; he already felt and understood his position.

I love to watch children. They are extraordinary fascinating in their first independent interests in life. I noticed the red-haired boy was so tempted by the costly toys of the other children, especially a theatre in which he certainly wanted to take some kind of part, that he decided to act differently. He smiled and began playing with the other children. He gave away his apple to a puffy little boy, who had bound up a full handkerchief of sweets. He even went as far as to carry another boy on his back, so they would not turn him away from the theatre. But a minute later, a kind of mischievous child gave him a considerable beating. The boy did not dare to cry. Here the governess, his mother, appeared and ordered him not to disturb the play of the other children. Then the boy went to the same room where the little girl was. She allowed him to join her. Very eagerly they both began to dress the expensive doll.

I had been already sitting in the ivy-covered arbour for half an hour. I was almost asleep, yet listening to the little conversations of the red-haired boy and the little beauty with the dowry of three hundred thousand fussing over her doll.

Suddenly Yulian Mastakovitch walked into the room. Under cover of the quarreling children, he had noiselessly left the drawing-room. A minute before I noticed he was

---

① rouble: currency of Russia; 卢布,货币单位

talking very fervently with the father of the future heiress, with whom he had just become acquainted. He discussed the advantages of one branch of the service over another. Now he stood deep in thought, as if he were calculating something on his fingers.

"Three hundred ... three hundred," he whispered. "Eleven, twelve, thirteen," and so forth. "Sixteen—five years! Let us assume it is at four percent—five times twelve is sixty, yes, to that sixty ... now let us assume what it will be in five years—four hundred. Yes! Well ... oh, but he won't hold to four percent, the swindler. Maybe he can get eight or ten. Well, five hundred, let us assume five hundred thousand, the final measure, that's certain. Well, say a little extra for frills. H'm ... "

He ended his reflection. He blew his nose, and intended to leave the room. Suddenly he glanced at the little girl and stopped short. He did not see me behind the pots of greenery. It seemed to me that he was really disturbed. Either his calculations had affected him, or something else. He rubbed his hands and could not stand in one place. This nervousness increased to the utmost limit. And then he stopped and threw another resolute glance at the future heiress. He was about to advance but first he looked around. On tiptoe, as if he felt guilty, he approached the children. With a half-smile, he drew near, stooped, and kissed the little girl on the head. Not expecting the attack, she cried out, frightened.

"And what are you doing here, sweet child?" he asked in a whisper, looking around and patting the girl on the cheek.

"We are playing."

"Ah, with him?" Yulian Mastakovitch looked to one side at the boy. "And you, my dear, go into the drawing-room."

The boy kept silent and stared at him with open eyes.

Yulian Mastakovitch again looked around him and again stooped to the little girl.

"And what is this you have," he asked, "A dolly, sweet child?"

"A dolly." the little girl answered, wrinkling her face, a trifle shy.

"A dolly ... and do you know, my sweet child, from what your dolly is made?"

"I don't know ... " answered the little girl in a whisper, hanging her head.

"From rags, darling. You'd better go into the drawing-room to your companions, little boy," said Yulian Mastakovitch, staring severely at the child. The little girl and boy made a wry face and held onto each other's hand. They did not want to be separated.

"And do you know why they gave you that doll?" asked Yulian Mastakovitch, lowering his voice more and more.

"I don't know."

"Because you have been a sweet, well-behaved child all week."

Here Yulian Mastakovithc, emotional as could be, looked around and lowered his voice more and more, and finally asked, inaudibly, almost standing completely still from excitement and with an impatient voice,

"And will you love me, sweet little girl? When I come to visit your parents?"

Having said that, Yulian Mastakovitch tried once again to kiss the sweet girl. The red-haired boy, seeing that she wanted to cry, gripped her hand and began to whimper from sheer sympathy for her. Yulian Mastakovitch became angry, and not in jest.

"Go away. Go away from here, go away!" he said to the little boy. "Go into the drawing-room! Go in there to your companions!"

"No, he doesn't have to, doesn't have to! You go away," said the little girl, almost crying, "Leave him alone, leave him alone!"

Someone made a noise at the door.

Yulian Mastakovitch immediately raised his majestic body and became frightened. But the red-haired boy was even more startled than Yulian Mastakovitch. He left the little girl and quietly, guided by the wall, passed from the drawing-room into the dinning-room. To avoid arousing suspicion, Yulian Mastakovitch also went into the mirror, as if he were disconcerted. He was perhaps annoyed with himself for his fervor and his impatience. At first perhaps he was so struck by the calculations on his fingers, so enticed and inspired that in spite of all his dignity and importance, he decided to act like a little boy, and directly pursue the object of his attentions even though she could not possibly be *his* object for at least five more years.

I followed the respectable gentleman into the dining-room. I beheld a strange sight. All red from vexation and anger, Yulian Mastakovitch frightened the red-haired boy, who was walking farther and farther, and in his fear did not know where to run.

"Go away. What are you doing here? Go away, you scamp, go away! You're stealing the fruits here, ah? You're stealing the fruits here? Go away, you reprobate. Go away. You snot-nosed boy, go away. Go to your companions!"

The frightened boy tried to get under the table. Then his persecutor, flushed as could be, took out his large batiste handkerchief and began to lash under the table at the child, who remained absolutely quiet.

It must be noted that Yulian Mastakovitch was a little stout. He was a man, well-filled out, red-faced, sleek, with a paunch, with thick legs; in short, what is called a fine figure of a man, round as a nut. He was sweating, puffing and turning terribly red. Finally, he was almost in a frenzy, so great was his feeling of indignation and perhaps (who knows?) jealousy.

I burst out laughing at the top of my voice. Yulian Mastakovitch turned around, and despite all his manners, he was confounded into dust. From the opposite door at that moment came the host. The little boy climbed out from under the table and wiped his elbows and knees. Yulian Mastakovitch hurriedly blew his nose on a handkerchief, which he held in his hand by a corner.

Chapter Six

Meanwhile, the host gave the three of us a puzzled look. But as with a man who knows life and looks at it with dead seriousness, he immediately availed himself of the chance to catch his guest in private.

"Here's the little boy," he said pointing to the red-haired boy, "For whom I was intending to intercede, your honor ..."

"Ah?" answered Yulian Mastakovitch, still not fully put in order.

"The son of my children's governess," the host continued with a pleading tone. "A poor woman, a widow, wife an honest official; and therefore ... Yulian Mastakovitch if it were possible ..."

"Oh, no, no," hurriedly answered Yulian Mastakovitch, "no, excuse me, Filip Alexyevitch, it's no way possible. I've asked, there are no vacancies. If there were, there are already ten candidates—all better qualified than he ... I'm very sorry. Very sorry ..."

"I'm sorry," repeated the host. "The little boy is modest, quiet ..."

"A very mischievous boy, as I've noticed," answered Yulian Mastakovitch, hysterically distorting his mouth. "Go away, little boy," he said addressing the child. "Why are you staying, go to your companions!"

It seemed he could not restrain himself. He glanced at me with one eye. In fun I could not restrain myself and burst out laughing directly in his face.

Yulian Mastakovitch immediately turned away, and clear enough for me to hear, he asked the host who was that strange young man. They whispered together and left the room. Afterwards, I saw Yulian Mastakovitch listening to the host, mistrustfully shaking his head.

After laughing to my heart's content, I returned to the drawing-room. Surrounded by the fathers and mothers of the families and the host and hostess, the great man was uttering a mating call with warmth, towards a lady to whom he had just been introduced.

The lady was holding by the hand the girl, with whom ten minutes ago Yulian Mastakovitch had had the scene in the drawing-room. Now he was showering praise and delight about the beauty, talent, grace and good manners of the sweet child. He was fawning, obviously over the mamma; the mother listened to him almost in tears from delight. The father's lips made a smile; the host rejoiced because of the general satisfaction. All the guests were the same, and even the children stopped playing in order not to disturb the conversation. The whole atmosphere was saturated with reverence.

Later, as if touched to the depth of her heart, I heard the mother of the interesting child beg Yulian Mastakovitch to do her the special honor of presenting them his precious acquaintanceship; and I heard, with his kind of unaffected delight, Yulian Mastakovitch accepting the invitation. Afterwards, the guests all dispersed in different directions, as decency demanded; they spilled out to each other touching words of praise upon the commissioned tax gatherer who worked farmers, his wife, their daughter, and especially Yulian Mastakovitch.

"Is that gentleman married?" I asked, almost aloud, of one of my acquaintances, who was standing closest to Yulian Mastakovitch.

"No!" my friend answered me, chagrined to the bottom of his heart at my awkwardness, which I had displayed deliberately.

Recently, I walked by a certain church. The crowd, the congress of people startled me. All around they talked about the wedding. The day was cloudy, and it was starting to drizzle; I made my way through the crowd around the church and saw the bridegroom. He was a small, rotund, well-fed man with a slight paunch and highly dressed. He was running about, bustling, and giving orders. Finally, the voices of the crowd said that the bride was coming. I pushed my way through the crowd and saw a wonderful beauty, who had scarcely begun her first season. But the beauty was pale and sad. She looked distracted; it even seemed to me that her eyes were red from recent crying. The classical severity of every line of her face added a certain dignity and solemnity to her beauty. Through that severity and dignity, through that sadness, still appeared the first look of childish innocence—very naive, fluid, youthful, and yet neither asking nor entreating for mercy.

They were saying she was just sixteen years old. Glancing carefully at the bridegroom, I suddenly recognized him as Yulian Mastakovitch, whom I had not seen for five years. I took a look at her. My God!

I began to push my way quickly out of the church. The voices of the crowd said the bride was rich: a dowry of five hundred thousand ... and a trousseau with ever so much ...

"It was a good calculation, though." I thought, and made my way out into the street.

Questions for Discussion

1. What is the theme of this piece of writing?
2. What do you think of the marriage between Yulian Mastakovitch and his young bride? What is the perfect marriage in your mind?
3. According to the story, how do you understand the sentence "It was a good calculation, though."?

Links

1. http://russiapedia.rt.com/prominent-russians/literature/fyodor-dostoevsky/
   关于陀思妥耶夫斯基的生平及创作的详细介绍。
2. https://en.wikipedia.org/wiki/Fyodor_Dostoyevsky
   关于陀思妥耶夫斯基的小说《圣诞树和婚礼》的细读资料。

Chapter Seven

The Bet

By Anton Pavlovich Chekhov

Anton Pavlovich Chekhov (1860—1904) is a Russian playwright and short story writer of the 19th century. Chekhov was born into a grocery store owner's family on January 29, 1860, in Taganrog, Russia. Chekhov practiced as a medical doctor throughout most of his literary career: "Medicine is my lawful wife," he once said, "and literature is my mistress."

Chekhov's best known works include the short novel *The Chameleon*, the trilogy—*The Gooseberry*, *The Man in a Case*, *A Story about Aegean*. Chekhov wrote many of his greatest works from the 1890s through the last few years of his life. In his short stories of that period, including *Ward No.6* and *The Lady with the Dog*, he revealed a profound understanding of human nature and the ways in which ordinary events can carry deeper meaning. In his plays of these years, Chekhov concentrated primarily on mood and characters, showing that they could be more important than the plots. Not much seems to happen to his lonely, often desperate characters, but their inner conflicts take on great significance. Their stories are very specific, painting a picture of pre-revolutionary Russian society, yet timeless. Chekhov died of tuberculosis on July 15, 1904, in Badenweiler, Germany.

As a supreme master of the short story, he is considered the equal of Maupassant. Like the latter, Chekhov mostly dealt with the tragedies of life in his writing. His career as a playwright produced four classics and his best short stories are held in high esteem by writers and critics. Chekhov is regarded as one of the major literary figures of his time. His plays are still staged worldwide, and his overall body of work influenced important writers of an array of genres, including James Joyce, Ernest Hemingway, Tennessee Williams and Henry Miller.

Lead-in Questions

1. Which is more humane, death penalty or lifelong imprisonment?
2. Can you imagine under what circumstances one will take the bet of spending 15 prime years in confinement?

Questions about the Author and the Story

1. Which of the following is NOT true of Anton Pavlovich Chekhov?
   A. He is enshrined as one of the best short novel writers in the world.
   B. He practiced medicine for most of his career life and died young.
   C. He once joined the army and his novel always chose war time as background.
   D. Tragedies of life, especially the life of ordinary people, are dealt with in his writings.
2. What does "capital punishment" (Para. 1) most probably mean?
   A. Life imprisonment.   B. Capital confiscation.
   C. Death penalty.   D. Money laundering.
3. According to the bet, which of the following is forbidden on the part of the lawyer?
   A. To read and write.   B. To get contact with other people.
   C. To play musical instruments. D. To drink wine and smoke.
4. According to the novel, which of the following statements is NOT true of the lawyer during his long captivity?
   A. For the first two years he suffered from severe loneliness.
   B. He read lots of classics and played musical instruments once in a while.
   C. He had a wide array of interests including language, music and philosophy.
   D. He was in despair and on the brink of a breakdown in the last year.
5. Why did the lawyer eventually choose to escape the night before?
   A. Because he lost his mind after so many years.
   B. Because the banker told him to do so.
   C. Because he regretted and couldn't stand it at the last moment.
   D. Because he realized there is something more important to him than money.

It was a dark autumn night. The old banker was walking up and down his study and remembering how, fifteen years before, he had given a party one autumn evening. There had been many clever men there, and there had been interesting conversations. Among other things they had talked of capital punishment. The majority of the guests, among whom were many journalists and intellectual men, disapproved of the death penalty. They considered that form of punishment out of date, immoral, and unsuitable for Christian States. In the opinion of some of them the death penalty ought to be replaced everywhere by imprisonment for life. "I don't agree with you," said their host the banker. "I have not tried either the death penalty or imprisonment for life, but if one may judge a priori, the death penalty is more moral and more humane than imprisonment for life. Capital punishment kills a man at once, but lifelong imprisonment kills him slowly. Which executioner is the more humane, he who kills you in a few minutes or he who drags the life out of you in the course of many years?"

"Both are equally immoral," observed one of the guests, "for they both have the same object—to take away life. The State is not God. It has not the right to take away what it cannot restore when it wants to."

Among the guests was a young lawyer, a young man of five-and-twenty. When he was asked his opinion, he said:

"The death sentence and the life sentence are equally immoral, but if I had to choose between the death penalty and imprisonment for life, I would certainly choose the second. To live anyhow is better than not at all."

A lively discussion arose. The banker, who was younger and more nervous in those days, was suddenly carried away by excitement; he struck the table with his fist and shouted at the young man:

"It's not true! I'll bet you two million you wouldn't stay in solitary confinement for five years."

"If you mean that in earnest," said the young man, "I'll take the bet, but I would stay not five but fifteen years."

"Fifteen? Done!" cried the banker. "Gentlemen, I stake two million!"

"Agreed! You stake your millions and I stake my freedom!" said the young man.

And this wild, senseless bet was carried out! The banker, spoilt and frivolous, with millions beyond his reckoning, was delighted at the bet. At supper he made fun of the young man, and said:

"Think better of it, young man, while there is still time. To me two million is a trifle, but you are losing three or four of the best years of your life. I say three or four, because you won't stay longer. Don't forget either, you unhappy man, that voluntary confinement is a great deal harder to bear than compulsory. The thought that you have the right to step out in liberty at any moment will poison your whole existence in prison. I am sorry for you."

And now the banker, walking to and fro, remembered all this, and asked himself: "What was the object of that bet? What is the good of that man's losing fifteen years of his life and my throwing away two million? Can it prove that the death penalty is better or worse than imprisonment for life? No, no. It was all nonsensical and meaningless. On my part it was the caprice of a pampered man, and on his part simple greed for money ..."

Then he remembered what followed that evening. It was decided that the young man should spend the years of his captivity under the strictest supervision in one of the lodges in the banker's garden. It was agreed that for fifteen years he should not be free to cross the threshold of the lodge, to see human beings, to hear the human voice, or to receive letters and newspapers. He was allowed to have a musical instrument and books, and was allowed to write letters, to drink wine, and to smoke. By the terms of the agreement, the only relations he could have with the outer world were by a little window made purposely for that object. He might have anything he wanted—books, music, wine, and so on—in any quantity he desired by writing an order, but could only receive them through the window. The agreement provided for every detail and every trifle that would make his imprisonment strictly solitary, and bound the young man to stay there exactly fifteen years, beginning from twelve o'clock of November 14, 1870, and ending at twelve o'clock of November 14, 1885. The slightest attempt on his part to break the conditions, if only two minutes before the end, released the banker from the obligation to pay him the two million.

For the first year of his confinement, as far as one could judge from his brief notes, the prisoner suffered severely from loneliness and depression. The sounds of the piano could be heard continually day and night from his lodge. He refused wine and tobacco. Wine, he wrote, excites the desires, and desires are the worst foes of the prisoner; and besides, nothing could be more dreary than drinking good wine and seeing no one. And tobacco spoilt the air of his room. In the first year the books he sent for were principally of a light character; novels with a complicated love plot, sensational and fantastic stories, and so on.

In the second year the piano was silent in the lodge, and the prisoner asked only for the classics. In the fifth year music was audible again, and the prisoner asked for wine. Those who watched him through the window said that all that year he spent doing nothing but eating and drinking and lying on his bed, frequently yawning and angrily talking to himself. He did not read books. Sometimes at night he would sit down to write; he would spend hours writing, and in the morning tear up all that he had written. More than once he could be heard crying.

In the second half of the sixth year the prisoner began zealously studying languages, philosophy, and history. He threw himself eagerly into these studies—so much so that the banker had enough to do to get him the books he ordered. In the course of four years some six hundred volumes were procured at his request. It was during this period that the banker received the following letter from his prisoner:

"My dear Jailer, I write you these lines in six languages. Show them to people who know the languages. Let them read them. If they find not one mistake I implore you to fire a shot in the garden. That shot will show me that my efforts have not been thrown away. The geniuses of all ages and of all lands speak different languages, but the same flame burns in them all. Oh, if you only knew what unearthly happiness my soul feels now from being able to understand them!" The prisoner's desire was fulfilled. The banker ordered two shots to be fired in the garden.

Then after the tenth year, the prisoner sat immovably at the table and read nothing but the Gospel. It seemed strange to the banker that a man who in four years had mastered six hundred learned volumes should waste nearly a year over one thin book easy of comprehension. Theology and histories of religion followed the Gospels.

In the last two years of his confinement the prisoner read an immense quantity of books quite indiscriminately. At one time he was busy with the natural sciences, then he would ask for Byron or Shakespeare. There were notes in which he demanded at the same time books on chemistry, and a manual of medicine, and a novel, and some treatise on philosophy or theology. His reading suggested a man swimming in the sea among the wreckage of his ship, and trying to save his life by greedily clutching first at one spar and then at another.

The old banker remembered all this, and thought:

"Tomorrow at twelve o'clock he will regain his freedom. By our agreement I ought to pay him two million. If I do pay him, it is all over with me: I shall be utterly ruined."

Fifteen years before, his millions had been beyond his reckoning; now he was afraid to ask himself which were greater, his debts or his assets. Desperate gambling on the Stock Exchange, wild speculation and the excitability which he could not get over even in advancing years, had by degrees led to the decline of his fortune and the proud, fearless, self-confident millionaire had become a banker of middling rank, trembling at every rise and fall in his investments. "Cursed bet!" muttered the old man, clutching his head in despair "Why didn't the man die? He is only forty now. He will take my last penny from me, he will marry, will enjoy life, will gamble on the Exchange; while I shall look at him with envy like a beggar, and hear from him every day the same sentence: 'I am indebted to you for the happiness of my life, let me help you!' No, it is too much! The one means of being saved from bankruptcy and disgrace is the death of that man!"

It struck three o'clock, the banker listened; everyone was asleep in the house and nothing could be heard outside but the rustling of the chilled trees. Trying to make no noise, he took from a fireproof safe the key of the door which had not been opened for fifteen years, put on his overcoat, and went out of the house.

It was dark and cold in the garden. Rain was falling. A damp cutting wind was racing about the garden, howling and giving the trees no rest. The banker strained his eyes, but could see neither the earth nor the white statues, nor the lodge, nor the trees. Going to the spot where the lodge stood, he twice called the watchman. No answer followed. Evidently the watchman had sought shelter from the weather, and was now asleep somewhere either in the kitchen or in the greenhouse.

"If I had the pluck to carry out my intention," thought the old man, "Suspicion would fall first upon the watchman."

He felt in the darkness for the steps and the door, and went into the entry of the lodge. Then he groped his way into a little passage and lighted a match. There was not a soul there. There was a bedstead with no bedding on it, and in the corner there was a dark cast-iron stove. The seals on the door leading to the prisoner's rooms were intact.

When the match went out the old man, trembling with emotion, peeped through the little window. A candle was burning dimly in the prisoner's room. He was sitting at the table. Nothing could be seen but his back, the hair on his head, and his hands. Open books were lying on the table, on the two easy-chairs, and on the carpet near the table.

Five minutes passed and the prisoner did not once stir. Fifteen years' imprisonment had taught him to sit still. The banker tapped at the window with his finger, and the prisoner made no movement whatever in response. Then the banker cautiously broke the seals off the door and put the key in the keyhole. The rusty lock gave a grating sound and the door creaked. The banker expected to hear at once footsteps and a cry of astonishment, but three minutes passed and it was as quiet as ever in the room. He made up his mind to go in.

At the table a man unlike ordinary people was sitting motionless. He was a skeleton with the skin drawn tight over his bones, with long curls like a woman's and a shaggy beard. His face was yellow with an earthy tint in it, his cheeks were hollow, his back long and narrow, and the hand on which his shaggy head was propped was so thin and delicate that it was dreadful to look at it. His hair was already streaked with silver, and seeing his emaciated, aged-looking face, no one would have believed that he was only forty. He was asleep ... In front of his bowed head there lay on the table a sheet of paper on which there was something written in fine handwriting.

"Poor creature!" thought the banker, "he is asleep and most likely dreaming of the millions. And I have only to take this half-dead man, throw him on the bed, stifle him a little with the pillow, and the most conscientious expert would find no sign of a violent death. But let us first read what he has written here ... "

The banker took the page from the table and read as follows:

"Tomorrow at twelve o'clock I regain my freedom and the right to associate with other men, but before I leave this room and see the sunshine, I think it necessary to say a few words to you. With a clear conscience I tell you, as before God, who beholds me, that I despise freedom and life and health, and all that in your books is called the good things of the world."

"For fifteen years I have been intently studying earthly life. It is true I have not seen the earth nor men, but in your books I have drunk fragrant wine, I have sung songs, I have hunted stags and wild boars in the forests, have loved women ... Beauties as ethereal as clouds, created by the magic of your poets and geniuses, have visited me at night, and have whispered in my ears wonderful tales that have set my brain in a whirl. In your books I have climbed to the peaks of Elburz① and Mont Blanc②, and from there I have seen the sun rise and have watched it at evening flood the sky, the ocean, and the mountain-tops with gold and crimson. I have watched from there the lightning flashing over my head and cleaving the storm-clouds. I have seen green forests, fields, rivers, lakes, towns. I have heard the singing of the sirens, and the strains of the shepherds' pipes; I have touched the wings of comely devils who flew down to converse with me of God ... In your books I have flung myself into the bottomless pit, performed miracles, slain, burned towns, preached new religions, conquered whole kingdoms ..."

"Your books have given me wisdom. All that the unresting thought of man has created in the ages is compressed into a small compass in my brain. I know that I am wiser than all of you."

"And I despise your books, I despise wisdom and the blessings of this world. It is all worthless, fleeting, illusory, and deceptive, like a mirage. You may be proud, wise, and fine, but death will wipe you off the face of the earth as though you were no more than mice burrowing under the floor, and your posterity, your history, your immortal geniuses will burn or freeze together with the earthly globe."

"You have lost your reason and taken the wrong path. You have taken lies for truth, and hideousness for beauty. You would marvel if, owing to strange events of some sorts, frogs and lizards suddenly grew on apple and orange trees instead of fruit, or if roses began to smell like a sweating horse; so I marvel at you who exchange heaven for earth. I don't want to understand you."

"To prove to you in action how I despise all that you live by, I renounce the two million of which I once dreamed as of paradise and which now I despise. To deprive myself of the right to the money I shall go out from here five hours before the time fixed, and so break the compact ..."

When the banker had read this he laid the page on the table, kissed the strange man on the head, and went out of the lodge, weeping. At no other time, even when he had lost heavily on the Stock Exchange, had he felt so great a contempt for himself. When he got home he lay on his bed, but his tears and emotion kept him for hours from sleeping.

Next morning the watchmen ran in with pale faces, and told him they had seen the man who lived in the lodge climb out of the window into the garden, go to the gate, and disappear. The banker went at once with the servants to the lodge and made sure of the flight of his prisoner. To avoid arousing unnecessary talk, he took from the table the writing in which the millions were renounced, and when he got home locked it up in the fireproof safe.

---

① Elburz: a mountain located between Iran Plateau and Caspian Sea;厄尔布士山脉
② Mont Blanc: here referring to the summit of the Alps;勃朗峰

Questions for Discussion

1. What kind of person is the banker? What changes have taken place to the lawyer during the 15-year captivity?
2. Can a man live without the interaction with others like Robinson Crusoe?
3. What is the theme of this story?

Links

1. https://en.wikipedia.org/wiki/Anton_Chekhov
   关于契科夫生平及创作的详细介绍。
2. http://www.eldritchpress.org/ac/chekhov.html
   关于契科夫的小说《打赌》的细读资料。

Part B

The Lottery Ticket

By Anton Pavlovich Chekhov

Lead-in Questions

1. Have you ever bought any lottery tickets? Did you win?
2. Does it occur to you that winning lottery tickets may bring you trouble or annoyance?
3. If you were fortunate enough to win 5 million *RMB*, would you disguise yourself in cartoon costumes to accept the prize? What would you do with this large sum of money?

Questions about the Author and the Story

1. Which of the following is NOT the short story written by Anton Chekhov?
   A. *The Dragonfly*.   B. *The Man in the Case*.
   C. *Ward No.6*.   D. *The Chameleon*.
2. Which of the following statements is NOT true about Anton Chekhov?
   A. He is a master of short stories and regarded as the equal of Maupassant.
   B. He died young of TB.
   C. He once wrote short, humorous sketches under different pseudonyms.
   D. He is a full-time short novelist.
3. What can be inferred from the novel *The Lottery Ticket*?
   A. The prize is not attractive enough.

B. The couple has won the ticket only once.
C. The wife bought the ticket.
D. The husband is very satisfied with his wife.
4. If they were lucky enough, which of the following would NOT be on the husband's agenda?
A. To buy a real estate.
B. To travel abroad with his wife.
C. To deposit some in the bank.
D. To pay debts and buy some furniture.
5. What is the author's tone in *The Lottery Ticket*?
A. Sympathetic.　B. Ironic.　　C. Indifferent.　D. Relieved.

Ivan Dmitritch, a middle-class man who lived with his family on an income of twelve hundred a year and was very well satisfied with his lot, sat down on the sofa after supper and began reading the newspaper.

"I forgot to look at the newspaper today," his wife said to him as she cleared the table. "Look and see whether the list of drawings is there."

"Yes, it is," said Ivan Dmitritch, "but hasn't your ticket lapsed?"

"No. I took the interest on Tuesday."

"What is the number?"

"Series 9,499, number 26."

"All right ... we will look ... 9,499 and 26."

Ivan Dmitritch had no faith in lottery luck, and would not, as a rule, have consented to look at the lists of winning numbers, but now, as he had nothing else to do and as the newspaper was before his eyes, he passed his finger downwards along the column of numbers. And immediately, as though in mockery of his skepticism, no further than the second line from the top, his eye was caught by the figure 9,499! Unable to believe his eyes, he hurriedly dropped the paper on his knees without looking to see the number of the ticket, and, just as though some one had given him a douche of cold water, he felt an agreeable chill in the pit of the stomach, tingling and terrible and sweet!

"Masha, 9,499 is there!" he said in a hollow voice.

His wife looked at his astonished and panic-stricken face, and realized that he was not joking.

"9,499?" she asked, turning pale and dropping the folded tablecloth on the table.

"Yes, yes ... it really is there!"

"And the number of the ticket?"

"Oh yes! There's the number of the ticket too. But stay ... wait! No, I say!

Anyway, the number of our series is there! Anyway, you understand ..."

Looking at his wife, Ivan Dmitritch gave a broad, senseless smile, like a baby when a bright object is shown it. His wife smiled too; it was as pleasant to her as to him that he only mentioned the series, and did not try to find out the number of the winning ticket. To torment and tantalize oneself with hopes of possible fortune is so sweet, so thrilling!

"It is our series," said Ivan Dmitritch, after a long silence. "So there is a probability that we have won. It's only a probability, but there it is!"

"Well, now look!"

"Wait a little. We have plenty of time to be disappointed. It's on the second line from the top, so the prize is seventy-five thousand. That's not money, but power, capital! And in a minute I shall look at the list, and there—26! Eh? I say, what if we really have won?"

The husband and wife began laughing and staring at one another in silence. The possibility of winning bewildered them; they could not have said, could not have dreamed, what they both needed that seventy-five thousand for, what they would buy, where they would go. They thought only of the figures 9,499 and 75,000 and pictured them in their imagination, while somehow they could not think of the happiness itself which was so possible.

Ivan Dmitritch, holding the paper in his hand, walked several times from corner to corner, and only when he had recovered from the first impression began dreaming a little.

"And if we have won," he said—"why, it will be a new life, it will be a transformation! The ticket is yours, but if it were mine I should, first of all, of course, spend twenty-five thousand on real property in the shape of an estate; ten thousand on immediate expenses, new furnishing ... travelling ... paying debts, and so on ... The other forty thousand I would put in the bank and get interest on it."

"Yes, an estate, that would be nice," said his wife, sitting down and dropping her hands in her lap.

"Somewhere in the Tula① or Oryol② provinces .... In the first place we shouldn't need a summer villa, and besides, it would always bring in an income."

And pictures came crowding on his imagination, each more gracious and poetical than the last. And in all these pictures he saw himself well-fed, serene, healthy, felt warm, even hot! Here, after eating a summer soup, cold as ice, he lay on his back on

---

① Tula: hometown of Leo Trotsky, about 185 km south of Moscow;图拉,又译土拉,是列夫·托尔斯泰的故乡,位于莫斯科以南185公里处。

② Oryol: hometown of many great Russian writers;奥廖尔,又译奥尔洛夫。它是莫斯科以南的一座城市,城市中有屠格涅夫、蒲宁、安德烈耶夫、列斯科夫等作家的故居。

the burning sand close to a stream or in the garden under a lime-tree ... It is hot ... His little boy and girl are crawling about near him, digging in the sand or catching ladybirds in the grass. He dozes sweetly, thinking of nothing, and feeling all over that he need not go to the office today, tomorrow, or the day after. Or, tired of lying still, he goes to the hayfield, or to the forest for mushrooms, or watches the peasants catching fish with a net. When the sun sets he takes a towel and soap and saunters to the bathing shed, where he undresses at his leisure, slowly rubs his bare chest with his hands, and goes into the water. And in the water, near the opaque soapy circles, little fish flit to and fro and green water-weeds nod their heads. After bathing there is tea with cream and milk rolls ... In the evening a walk or vint with the neighbors.

"Yes, it would be nice to buy an estate," said his wife, also dreaming, and from her face it was evident that she was enchanted by her thoughts.

Ivan Dmitritch pictured to himself autumn with its rains, its cold evenings, and its St. Martin's summer. At that season he would have to take longer walks about the garden and beside the river, so as to get thoroughly chilled, and then drink a big glass of vodka① and eat a salted mushroom or a soused cucumber, and then—drink another ... The children would come running from the kitchen-garden, bringing a carrot and a radish smelling of fresh earth ... And then, he would lie stretched full length on the sofa, and in leisurely fashion turn over the pages of some illustrated magazine, or, covering his face with it and unbuttoning his waistcoat, give himself up to slumber.

The St. Martin's summer is followed by cloudy, gloomy weather. It rains day and night, the bare trees weep, the wind is damp and cold. The dogs, the horses, the fowl—all are wet, depressed, downcast. There is nowhere to walk; one can't go out for days together; one has to pace up and down the room, looking despondently at the grey window. It is dreary!

Ivan Dmitritch stopped and looked at his wife.

"I should go abroad, you know, Masha," he said.

And he began thinking how nice it would be in late autumn to go abroad somewhere to the South of France ... to Italy ... to India!

"I should certainly go abroad too," his wife said. "But look at the number of the ticket!"

"Wait, wait! ..."

He walked about the room and went on thinking. It occurred to him: what if his wife really did go abroad? It is pleasant to travel alone, or in the society of light, careless women who live in the present, and not such as think and talk all the journey about nothing but their children, sigh, and tremble with dismay over every farthing. Ivan Dmitritch imagined his wife in the train with a multitude of parcels, baskets, and

---

① Vodka: a kind of Russian alcohol; 伏尔加酒, 俄罗斯传统烈性酒。

bags; she would be sighing over something, complaining that the train made her head ache, that she had spent so much money ... At the stations he would continually be having to run for boiling water, bread and butter. ... She wouldn't have dinner because of its being too dear ...

"She would begrudge me every farthing," he thought, with a glance at his wife. "The lottery ticket is hers, not mine! Besides, what is the use of her going abroad? What does she want there? She would shut herself up in the hotel, and not let me out of her sight ... I know!"

And for the first time in his life his mind dwelt on the fact that his wife had grown elderly and plain, and that she was saturated through and through with the smell of cooking, while he was still young, fresh, and healthy, and might well have got married again.

"Of course, all that is silly nonsense," he thought, "but ... why should she go abroad? What would she make of it? And yet she would go, of course ... I can fancy ... In reality it is all one to her, whether it is Naples or Klin①. She would only be in my way. I should be dependent upon her. I can fancy how, like a regular woman, she will lock the money up as soon as she gets it ... She will look after her relations and grudge me every farthing."

Ivan Dmitritch thought of her relations. All those wretched brothers and sisters and aunts and uncles would come crawling about as soon as they heard of the winning ticket, would begin whining like beggars, and fawning upon them with oily, hypocritical smiles. Wretched, detestable people! If they were given anything, they would ask for more; while if they were refused, they would swear at them, slander them, and wish them every kind of misfortune.

Ivan Dmitritch remembered his own relations, and their faces, at which he had looked impartially in the past, struck him now as repulsive and hateful.

"They are such reptiles!" he thought.

And his wife's face, too, struck him as repulsive and hateful. Anger surged up in his heart against her, and he thought malignantly:

"She knows nothing about money, and so she is stingy. If she won it she would give me a hundred roubles, and put the rest away under lock and key."

And he looked at his wife, not with a smile now, but with hatred. She glanced at him too, and also with hatred and anger. She had her own daydreams, her own plans, her own reflections; she understood perfectly well what her husband's dreams were. She knew who would be the first to try to grab her winnings.

"It's very nice making daydreams at other people's expense!" is what her eyes expressed. "No, don't you dare!"

---

① Klin: a city in the northwest of Moscow; 克林(地名), 位于莫斯科西北方向的一个城市。

Her husband understood her look; hatred began stirring again in his breast, and in order to annoy his wife he glanced quickly, to spite her at the fourth page on the newspaper and read out triumphantly:

"Series 9,499, number 46! Not 26!"

Hatred and hope both disappeared at once, and it began immediately to seem to Ivan Dmitritch and his wife that their rooms were dark and small and low-pitched, that the supper they had been eating was not doing them good, but lying heavy on their stomachs, that the evenings were long and wearisome ...

"What the devil's the meaning of it?" said Ivan Dmitritch, beginning to beill-humored. "Wherever one steps there are bits of paper under one's feet, crumbs, husks. The rooms are never swept! One is simply forced to go out. Damnation take my soul entirely! I shall go and hang myself on the first aspen-tree!"

Questions for Discussion

1. What does the short story intend to tell us?
2. The lottery ticket is the weaving thread of the whole story. Can you detect any change in the attitude on the part of the husband and the wife before and after the lottery incident?

Links

1. https://en.wikipedia.org/wiki/Anton_Chekhov
   关于契科夫生平及创作的详细介绍。
2. http://www.eldritchpress.org/ac/chekhov.html
   关于契科夫的小说《彩票》的细读资料。

Chapter Eight

Part A

After Twenty Years

By O. Henry

O. Henry (1862—1910), pen name of William Sydney Porter, was a famous American short story writer. An aunt who ran a small private school supervised his education which included a surprising wide reading of classic literature and influenced his life long interest in the rich variety of the English language. He worked at add jobs, and later founded a humorous magazine which eventually failed. He was charged, perhaps unfairly, with embezzlement while working in a bank. He escaped to Honduras, but eventually returned to pay the penalty. On his release from prison, he landed in New York. There he began to write distinctive short fiction that has made his name synonymous with the surprise-ending story. O. Henry's short stories are known for their surprising endings, also called "O. Henry Twist."

Wit, humor, irony, cleverness, and local color are traditional earmarks of the typical O. Henry story. In addition, his warmth of human understanding and sympathy with the "underdog" give many of his stories poignancy.

His approximately 300 stories are collected in *Cabbages and Kings* (1904), *The Four Million* (1906), *The Voice of the City* (1908), *Options* (1909), and others. Among his best known stories are "The Cop and the Anthem" (1904), "The Gift of the Magi" (1905), "The Last Leaf" (1907), "The Ransom of Red Chief" (1910), and "After Twenty Year".

O. Henry is the father of the modern American short story and is one of three leading short story writers in the world. His works are hailed as humor encyclopedia of American life by critics.

Lead-in Questions
1. How do you understand friendship and justice?
2. What do you know about the Westward Movement in America?

Questions about the Author and the Story
1. Which is NOT O. Henry's short story?
   A. *The Four Million*.   B. *The Gift of the Magi*.
   C. *The Cop and the Anthem*.   D. *The Last Leaf*.
2. O. Henry earned his fame mainly for his _____.
   A. novels   B. poems   C. dramas   D. short stories
3. O. Henry is famous for _____ in his works.
   A. stream of consciousness   B. ironic and surprising ending
   C. symbolism   D. naturalism
4. From the word "trembled", we can infer Bob's feeling at that time. Which of the following is INCORRECT?
   A. embarrassed   B. surprised   C. frightened   D. excited
5. Which one is NOT the positive significance of Westward Movement in America?
   A. It helped spur a huge immigration.
   B. It resulted in great suffering, destruction, and cultural loss for the Native Americans.
   C. It promoted the development of economy in the West.
   D. It provided ample labors and wealth for the exploration.

    𝒯he policeman on the beat moved up the avenue impressively. The impressiveness was habitual and not for show, for spectators were few. The time was barely 10 o'clock at night, but chilly gusts of wind with a taste of rain in them had well-nigh depeopled the streets.

    Trying doors as he went, twirling his club with many intricate and artful movements, turning now and then to cast his watchful eye adown the pacific thoroughfare, the officer, with his stalwart form and slight swagger, made a fine picture of a guardian of the peace. The vicinity① was one that kept early hours. Now and then you might see the lights of a cigar store or of an all-night lunch counter; but the majority of the doors belonged to business places that had long since been closed.

    When about midway of a certain block the policeman suddenly slowed his walk. In the doorway of a darkened hardware store a man leaned, with an unlighted cigar in his

---

① vicinity: 附近地区

mouth. As the policeman walked up to him the man spoke up quickly.

"It's all right, officer," he said, reassuringly. "I'm just waiting for a friend. It's an appointment made twenty years ago. Sounds a little funny to you, doesn't it? Well, I'll explain if you'd like to make certain it's all straight. About that long ago there used to be a restaurant where this store stands—Big Joe' Brady's restaurant."

"Until five years ago," said the policeman. "It was torn down then."

The man in the doorway struck a match and lit his cigar. The light showed a pale, square-jawed face with keen eyes, and a little white scar near his right eyebrow. His scarfpin was a large diamond, oddly set.

"Twenty years ago tonight," said the man, "I dined here at 'Big Joe' Brady's with Jimmy Wells, my best chum, and the finest chap in the world. He and I were raised here in New York, just like two brothers, together. I was eighteen and Jimmy was twenty. The next morning I was to start for the West to make my fortune. You couldn't have dragged Jimmy out of New York; he thought it was the only place on earth. Well, we agreed that night that we would meet here again exactly twenty years from that date and time, no matter what our conditions might be or from what distance we might have to come. We figured that in twenty years each of us ought to have our destiny worked out and our fortunes made, whatever they were going to be."

"It sounds pretty interesting," said the policeman. "Rather a long time between meets, though, it seems to me. Haven't you heard from your friend since you left?"

"Well, yes, for a time we corresponded," said the other. "But after a year or two we lost track of each other. You see, the West is a pretty big proposition, and I kept hustling around over it pretty lively. But I know Jimmy will meet me here if he's alive, for he always was the truest, stanchest old chap in the world. He'll never forget. I came a thousand miles to stand in this door tonight, and it's worth it if my old partner turns up."

The waiting man pulled out a handsome watch, the lids of it set with small diamonds.

"Three minutes to ten," he announced. "It was exactly ten o'clock when we parted here at the restaurant door."

"Did pretty well out West, didn't you?" asked the policeman.

"You bet! I hope Jimmy has done half as well. He was a kind of plodder, though, good fellow as he was. I've had to compete with some of the sharpest wits going to get my pile. A man gets in a groove in New York. It takes the West to put a razor-edge on him."

The policeman twirled his club and took a step or two.

"I'll be on my way. Hope your friend comes around all right. Going to call time on him sharp?"

"I should say not!" said the other. "I'll give him half an hour at least. If Jimmy is alive on earth he'll be here by that time. So long, officer."

"Good-night, sir," said the policeman, passing on along his beat, trying doors as he went.

There was now a fine, cold drizzle falling, and the wind had risen from its uncertain puffs into a steady blow. The few foot passengers astir in that quarter hurried dismally and silently along with coat collars turned high and pocketed hands. And in the door of the hardware store the man who had come a thousand miles to fill an appointment, uncertain almost to absurdity, with the friend of his youth, smoked his cigar and waited.

About twenty minutes he waited, and then a tall man in a long overcoat, with collar turned up to his ears, hurried across from the opposite side of the street. He went directly to the waiting man.

"Is that you, Bob?" he asked, doubtfully.

"Is that you, Jimmy Wells?" cried the man in the door.

"Bless my heart!" exclaimed the new arrival, grasping both the other's hands with his own. "It's Bob, sure as fate. I was certain I'd find you here if you were still in existence. Well, well, well! —Twenty years is a long time. The oldrestaurant's gone, Bob; I wish it had lasted, so we could have had another dinner there. How has the West treated you, old man?"

"Bully; it has given me everything I asked it for. You've changed lots, Jimmy. I never thought you were so tall by two or three inches."

"Oh, I grew a bit after I was twenty."

"Doing well in New York, Jimmy?"

"Moderately[①]. I have a position in one of the city departments. Come on, Bob; we'll go around to a place I know of, and have a good long talk about old times."

The two men started up the street, arm in arm. The man from the West, his egotism enlarged by success, was beginning to outline the history of his career. The other, submerged in his overcoat, listened with interest.

At the corner stood a drug store, brilliant with electric lights. When they came into this glare each of them turned simultaneously to gaze upon the other's face.

The man from the West stopped suddenly and released his arm.

"You're not Jimmy Wells," he snapped. "Twenty years is a long time, but not long enough to change a man's nose from a Roman to a pug."

"It sometimes changes a good man into a bad one," said the tall man. "You've been under arrest for ten minutes, 'Silky' Bob. Chicago thinks you may have dropped over our way and wires us she wants to have a chat with you. Going quietly, are you? That's sensible. Now, before we go on to the station here's a note I was asked to hand you.

---

① moderately: 适度地,普通地

You may read it here at the window. It's from Patrolman Wells."

The man from the West unfolded the little piece of paper handed him. His hand was steady when he began to read, but it trembled① a little by the time he had finished. The note was rather short.

"Bob: I was at the appointed place on time. When you struck the match to light your cigar I saw it was the face of the man wanted in Chicago. Somehow I couldn't do it myself, so I went around and got a plain clothes man to do the job. JIMMY."

 Questions for Discussion

1. What are the characteristics of Bob and Jim in the story?
2. How do you understand the surprising elements in the story?

Links

1. https://en.wikipedia.org/wiki/O._Henry
   关于欧·亨利的生平及创作的详细介绍。
2. http://www.classicreader.com/book/1745/1/
   关于欧·亨利的小说《二十年后》的细读资料。

Part B

The Cop and the Anthem②

By O. Henry

Leading-in questions

1. How do you think of American society?
2. How do you understand "the cop" and "the anthem" in the title?

Questions about the Author and the Story

1. Which one is O. Henry's work?
   A. *The Cop and the Anthem*.   B. *A Chameleon*.
   C. *Ball of Fat*.   D. *The Call of the Wild*.
2. Whose works are hailed as "American life humor encyclopedia"?
   A. Emily Dickinson's.   B. Ernest Hemingway's.

---

① tremble: 颤动
② anthem: 赞美诗, 圣歌

      C. O. Henry's.　　　　　　　D. Mark Twain's.
3. O. Henry is famous for _____ in his works.
      A. stream of consciousness　　B. ironic and surprising ending
      C. symbolism　　　　　　　　D. naturalism
4. What was Soapy's desire at the beginning of the story?
      A. Three months in prison.
      B. Getting a good meal at some expensive restaurant.
      C. Breaking shop window.
      D. Stealing an umbrella.
5. How many times did Soapy try to be arrested by a policeman and sent to prison by the judge?
      A. Four.　　　B. Five.　　　C. Six.　　　D. Seven.

    On his bench in Madison Square Soapy moved uneasily. When wild geese honk high of nights, and when women without sealskin coats grow kind to their husbands, and when Soapy moves uneasily on his bench in the park, you may know that winter is near at hand.

    A dead leaf fell in Soapy's lap. That was Jack Frost's[①] card. Jack is kind to the regular denizens of Madison Square, and gives fair warning of his annual call. At the corners of four streets he hands his pasteboard to the North Wind, footman of the mansion of All Outdoors, so that the inhabitants thereof may make ready.

    Soapy's mind became cognisant of the fact that the time had come for him to resolve himself into a singular Committee of Ways and Means to provide against the coming rigor. And therefore he moved uneasily on his bench.

    The hibernatorial ambitions of Soapy were not of the highest. In them there were no considerations of Mediterranean cruises, of soporific Southern skies drifting in the Vesuvian Bay. Three months on the Island was what his soul craved. Three months of assured board and bed and congenial company, safe from Boreas and bluecoats, seemed to Soapy the essence of things desirable.

    For years the hospitable Blackwell's had been his winter quarters. Just as his more fortunate fellow New Yorkers had bought their tickets to Palm Beach and the Riviera each winter, so Soapy had made his humble arrangements for his annual hegira to the Island. And now the time was come. On the previous night three Sabbath newspapers, distributed beneath his coat, about his ankles and over his lap, had failed to repulse the cold as he slept on his bench near the spurting fountain in the ancient square. So the

---

① Jack Frost:是英文中对"寒霜"的拟人称号

Island loomed big and timely in Soapy's mind. He scorned the provisions made in the name of charity for the city's dependents. In Soapy's opinion the Law was more benign than Philanthropy. There was an endless round of institutions, municipal and eleemosynary, on which he might set out and receive lodging and food accordant with the simple life. But to one of Soapy's proud spirit the gifts of charity are encumbered. If not in coin you must pay in humiliation of spirit for every benefit received at the hands of philanthropy. As Caesar had his Brutus, every bed of charity must have its toll of a bath, every loaf of bread its compensation of a private and personal inquisition. Wherefore it is better to be a guest of the law, which though conducted by rules, does not meddle unduly with a gentleman's private affairs.

Soapy, having decided to go to the Island, at once set about accomplishing his desire. There were many easy ways of doing this. The pleasantest was to dine luxuriously at some expensive restaurant; and then, after declaring insolvency, be handed over quietly and without uproar to a policeman. An accommodating magistrate would do the rest.

Soapy left his bench and strolled out of the square and across the level sea of asphalt, where Broadway and Fifth Avenue flow together. Up Broadway he turned, and halted at a glittering cafe, where are gathered together nightly the choicest products of the grape, the silkworm and the protoplasm.

Soapy had confidence in himself from the lowest button of his vest upward. He was shaven, and his coat was decent and his neat black, ready-tied four-in-hand had been presented to him by a lady missionary on Thanksgiving Day. If he could reach a table in the restaurant unsuspected success would be his. The portion of him that would show above the table would raise no doubt in the waiter's mind. A roasted mallard duck, thought Soapy, would be about the thing—with a bottle of Chablis, and then Camembert①, a demi-tasse and a cigar. One dollar for the cigar would be enough. The total would not be so high as to call forth any supreme manifestation of revenge from the cafe management; and yet the meat would leave him filled and happy for the journey to his winter refuge.

But as Soapy set foot inside the restaurant door the head waiter's eye fell upon his frayed trousers and decadent shoes. Strong and ready hands turned him about and conveyed him in silence and haste to the sidewalk and averted the ignoble fate of the menaced mallard.

Soapy turned off Broadway. It seemed that his route to the coveted island was not to be an epicurean one. Some other way of entering limbo must be thought of.

At a corner of Sixth Avenue electric lights and cunningly displayed wares behind plate-glass made a shop window conspicuous. Soapy took a cobblestone and dashed it

---

① Camembert:法国 Camembert 村所产的软质奶酪

Chapter Eight

through the glass. People came running around the corner, a policeman in the lead. Soapy stood still, with his hands in his pockets, and smiled at the sight of brass buttons.

"Where's the man that done that?" inquired the officer excitedly.

"Don't you figure out that I might have had something to do with it?" said Soapy, not without sarcasm, but friendly, as one greets good fortune.

The policeman's mind refused to accept Soapy even as a clue. Men who smash windows do not remain to parley with the law's minions. They take to their heels. The policeman saw a man half way down the block running to catch a car. With drawn club he joined in the pursuit. Soapy, with disgust in his heart, loafed along, twice unsuccessful.

On the opposite side of the street was a restaurant of no great pretensions. It catered to large appetites and modest purses. Its crockery and atmosphere were thick; its soup and napery thin.

Into this place Soapy took his accusive shoes and telltale trousers without challenge. At a table he sat and consumed beefsteak, flapjacks, doughnuts and pie. And then to the waiter he betrayed the fact that the minutest coin and himself were strangers.

"Now, get busy and call a cop," said Soapy. "And don't keep a gentleman waiting."

"No cop for you," said the waiter, with a voice like butter cakes and an eye like the cherry in a Manhattan cocktail. "Hey, Con!"

Neatly upon his left ear on the callous pavement two waiters pitched Soapy. He arose, joint by joint, as a carpenter's rule opens, and beat the dust from his clothes. Arrest seemed but a rosy dream. The Island seemed very far away. A policeman who stood before a drug store two doors away laughed and walked down the street.

Five blocks Soapy travelled before his courage permitted him to woo capture again. This time the opportunity presented what he fatuously termed to himself a "cinch." A young woman of a modest and pleasing guise was standing before a show window gazing with sprightly interest at its display of shaving mugs and inkstands, and two yards from the window a large policeman of severe demeanour leaned against a water plug.

It was Soapy's design to assume the role of the despicable and execrated "masher." The refined and elegant appearance of his victim and the contiguity of the conscientious cop encouraged him to believe that he would soon feel the pleasant official clutch upon his arm that would insure his winter quarters on the right little, tight little isle.

Soapy straightened the lady missionary's readymade tie, dragged his shrinking cuffs into the open, set his hat at a killing cant and sidled toward the young woman. He made eyes at her, was taken with sudden coughs and "hems," smiled, smirked and went brazenly through the impudent and contemptible litany of the "masher." With half an eye Soapy saw that the policeman was watching him fixedly. The young woman moved away a few steps, and again bestowed her absorbed attention upon the shaving mugs. Soapy followed, boldly stepping to her side, raised his hat and said:

"Ah there, Bedelia! Don't you want to come and play in my yard?"

The policeman was still looking. The persecuted young woman had but to beckon a finger and Soapy would be practically en route for his insular haven. Already he imagined he could feel the cozy warmth of the station-house. The young woman faced him and, stretching out a hand, caught Soapy's coat sleeve.

"Sure, Mike," she said joyfully, "if you'll blow me to a pail of suds. I'd have spoke to you sooner, but the cop was watching."

With the young woman playing the clinging ivy to his oak Soapy walked past the policeman overcome with gloom. He seemed doomed to liberty.

At the next corner he shook off his companion and ran. He halted in the district where by night are found the lightest streets, hearts, vows and librettos.

Women in furs and men in greatcoats moved gaily in the wintry air. A sudden fear seized Soapy that some dreadful enchantment had rendered him immune to arrest. The thought brought a little of panic upon it, and when he came upon another policeman lounging grandly in front of a transplendent theatre he caught at the immediate straw of "disorderly conduct."

On the sidewalk Soapy began to yell drunken gibberish at the top of his harsh voice. He danced, howled, raved and otherwise disturbed the welkin.

The policeman twirled his club, turned his back to Soapy and remarked to a citizen.

"'Tis one of them Yale lads celebratin' the goose egg they give to the Hartford College. Noisy; but no harm. We've instructions to lave them be."

Disconsolate, Soapy ceased his unavailing racket. Would never a policeman lay hands on him? In his fancy the Island seemed an unattainable Arcadia①. He buttoned his thin coat against the chilling wind.

In a cigar store he saw a well-dressed man lighting a cigar at a swinging light. His silk umbrella he had set by the door on entering. Soapy stepped inside, secured the umbrella and sauntered off with it slowly. The man at the cigar light followed hastily.

"My umbrella," he said, sternly.

"Oh, is it?" sneered Soapy, adding insult to petit larceny. "Well, why don't you call a policeman? I took it. Your umbrella! Why don't you call a cop? There stands one on the corner."

The umbrella owner slowed his steps. Soapy did likewise, with a presentiment that luck would again run against him. The policeman looked at the two curiously.

"Of course," said the umbrella man—"that is—well, you know how these mistakes occur—I—if it's your umbrella I hope you'll excuse me—I picked it up this morning in a restaurant—If you recognise it as yours, why—I hope you'll—"

"Of course it's mine," said Soapy, viciously.

The ex-umbrella man retreated. The policeman hurried to assist a tall blonde in an

---

① Arcadia:世外桃源

opera cloak across the street in front of a street car that was approaching two blocks away.

　　Soapy walked eastward through a street damaged by improvements. He hurled the umbrella wrathfully into an excavation. He muttered against the men who wear helmets and carry clubs. Because he wanted to fall into their clutches, they seemed to regard him as a king who could do no wrong.

　　At length Soapy reached one of the avenues to the east where the glitter and turmoil was but faint. He set his face down this toward Madison Square, for the homing instinct survives even when the home is a park bench.

　　But on an unusually quiet corner Soapy came to a standstill. Here was an old church, quaint and rambling and gabled. Through one violet-stained window a soft light glowed, where, no doubt, the organist loitered over the keys, making sure of his mastery of the coming Sabbath[①] anthem. For there drifted out to Soapy's ears sweet music that caught and held him transfixed against the convolutions of the iron fence.

　　The moon was above, lustrous and serene; vehicles and pedestrians were few; sparrows twittered sleepily in the eaves—for a little while the scene might have been a country churchyard. And the anthem that the organist played cemented Soapy to the iron fence, for he had known it well in the days when his life contained such things as mothers and roses and ambitions and friends and immaculate thoughts and collars.

　　The conjunction[②] of Soapy's receptive state of mind and the influences about the old church wrought a sudden and wonderful change in his soul. He viewed with swift horror the pit into which he had tumbled, the degraded days, unworthy desires, dead hopes, wrecked faculties and base motives that made up his existence.

　　And also in a moment his heart responded thrillingly to this novel mood. An instantaneous and strong impulse moved him to battle with his desperate fate. He would pull himself out of the mire; he would make a man of himself again; he would conquer the evil that had taken possession of him. There was time; he was comparatively young yet; he would resurrect his old eager ambitions and pursue them without faltering. Those solemn but sweet organ notes had set up a revolution in him. To-morrow he would go into the roaring downtown district and find work. A fur importer had once offered him a place as driver. He would find him to-morrow and ask for the position. He would be somebody in the world. He would—

　　Soapy felt a hand laid on his arm. He looked quickly around into the broad face of a policeman.

　　"What are you doin' here?" asked the officer.

　　"Nothin'," said Soapy.

---

① Sabbath:安息日

② conjunction:连接

"Then come along," said the policeman.

"Three months on the Island," said the Magistrate in the Police Court the next morning.

Questions for Discussion

1. What is your understanding of black humor? How will you comment on the black humor in this story?
2. According to your understanding, did Soapy realize his dream? Give your reasons.
3. Please compare the cops in *After Twenty Years* with those in *The Cop and the Anthem*.

Links

1. https://en.wikipedia.org/wiki/O._Henry
   关于欧·亨利生平及创作的详细介绍。
2. https://en.wikipedia.org/wiki/The_Cop_and_the_Anthem
   关于欧·亨利的小说《二十年后》的细读资料。

Chapter Nine

Part A

The White Silence

By Jack London

Jack London (1876—1916) was an American novelist, journalist, and social activist. A pioneer in the world of commercial magazine fiction, he was one of the first writers to become a worldwide celebrity and earn a large fortune from writing. He was also an innovator in the genre that would later become known as science fiction.

London's most famous novels are *The Call of the Wild* (1903), *White Fang* (1906), *The Sea-Wolf* (1904), *The Iron Heel* (1908), and *Martin Eden* (1903). *The Call of the Wild* and *White Fang* both set in the Klondike Gold Rush, so did the short stories "To Build a Fire", "An Odyssey of the North" (1900), and "Love of Life" (1901). He also wrote about the South Pacific in stories such as "The Pearls of Parlay" (1911) and "The Heathen" (1910), and of the San Francisco Bay area in *The Sea Wolf*.

London's "strength of utterance" is at its height in his stories, and they are painstakingly well constructed. London was part of the radical literary group "The Crowd" in San Francisco and a passionate advocate of unionization, socialism, and the rights of workers. He wrote several powerful works dealing with these topics.

Lead-in Questions

1. Have you ever suffered any severe living condition? Can you survive the frozen and snow-covered land?
2. Why did the Masons and Malemute Kid go to the north of Canada's Savannah? What did they experience?

Questions about the Author and the Story

1. Which of the following is NOT written by Jack London?
   A. *The Call of the Wild*.
   B. *The Sea-Wolf*.
   C. *Martin Eden*.
   D. *The Bear Came Over the Mountain*.
2. Who is the story's narrator?
   A. Mason.
   B. An Indian woman.
   C. Malemute Kid.
   D. An unnamed, all-knowing storyteller.
3. What is the story of *The White Silence*?
   A. The story chronicles the travels of three people across the Northland Trail on the Yukon, as they try to reach civilization before spring.
   B. The story opens with a harmonious scene between human and animal.
   C. Mason wanted to get the gold and he succeeded.
   D. They went to Yukon to make explorations.
4. Jack London's works have NOT been described as _____.
   A. vigorous stories of men and animals against the environment and survival against hardships
   B. the description of the fragile relationship between man and nature
   C. the description of relationship between man and animal
   D. the complicated experimentation in the social network
5. What happens to Mason at the end of the story?
   A. As Mason waits for Malemute Kid's death, "the White Silence seemed to sneer, and a great fear came upon him."
   B. Mason's heart stops beating.
   C. Mason is not accustomed to showing grief, kisses Ruth and blindly takes off on his sled towards civilization.
   D. They all survive and arrive at the civilization at spring.

"Carmen won't last more than a couple of days." Mason spat out a chunk of ice and surveyed the poor animal ruefully, then put her foot in his mouth and proceeded to bite out the ice which clustered cruelly between the toes.

"I never saw a dog with a highfalutin' name that ever was worth a rap," he said, as he concluded his task and shoved her aside. "They just fade away and die under the responsibility. Did ye ever see one go wrong with a sensible name like Cassiar, Siwash, or Husky? No, sir! Take a look at Shookum here, he's—"

Snap! The lean brute flashed up, the white teeth just missing Mason's throat.

"Ye will, will ye?" A shrewd clout behind the ear with the butt of the dog whip stretched the animal in the snow, quivering softly, a yellow slaver dripping from its fangs.

"As I was saying, just look at Shookum here—he's got the spirit. Bet ye he eats Carmen before the week's out."

"I'll bank another proposition against that," replied Malemute Kid, reversing the frozen bread placed before the fire to thaw. "We'll eat Shookum before the trip is over. What d'ye say, Ruth?"

The Indian woman settled the coffee with a piece of ice, glanced from Malemute Kid to her husband, then at the dogs, but vouchsafed no reply. It was such a palpable truism that none was necessary. Two hundred miles of unbroken trail in prospect, with a scant six days' grub for themselves and none for the dogs, could admit no other alternative. The two men and the woman grouped about the fire and began their meager meal. The dogs lay in their harnesses for it was a midday halt, and watched each mouthful enviously.

"No more lunches after today," said Malemute Kid. "And we've got to keep a close eye on the dogs,—they're getting vicious. They'd just as soon pull a fellow down as not, if they get a chance."

"And I was president of an Epworth once, and taught in the Sunday school." Having irrelevantly delivered himself of this, Mason fell into a dreamy contemplation of his steaming moccasins, but was aroused by Ruth filling his cup. "Thank God, we've got slathers of tea! I've seen it growing, down in Tennessee. What wouldn't I give for a hot corn pone just now! Never mind, Ruth; you won't starve much longer, nor wear moccasins either."

The woman threw off her gloom at this, and in her eyes welled up a great love for her white lord,—the first white man she had ever seen,—the first man whom she had known to treat a woman as something better than a mere animal or beast of burden.

"Yes, Ruth," continued her husband, having recourse to the macaronic① jargon② in which it was alone possible for them to understand each other; "wait till we clean up and pull for the Outside. We'll take the White Man's canoe and go to the Salt Water. Yes, bad water, rough water,—great mountains dance up and down all the time. And so big, so far, so far away—you travel ten sleep, twenty sleep, forty sleep" (he graphically enumerated the days on his fingers), "all the time water, bad water. Then you come to great village, plenty people, just the same mosquitoes next summer. Wigwams oh, so high,—ten, twenty pines. Hi-yu Shookum!"

He paused impotently, cast an appealing glance at Malemute Kid, then laboriously placed the twenty pines, end on end, by sign language. Malemute Kid smiled with cheery cynicism; but Ruth's eyes were wide with wonder, and with pleasure; for she

---

① macaronic:两种语言混合的
② jargon:行话

half believed he was joking, and such condescension pleased her poor woman's heart.

"And then you step into a—a box, and pouf! Up you go." He tossed his empty cup in the air by way of illustration and, as he deftly caught it, cried: "And biff! Down you come. Oh, great medicine-men! You go Fort Yukon, I go Arctic City,—twenty-five sleep,—big string, all the time,—I catch him string,—I say, 'Hello, Ruth! How are ye?'—and you say, 'Is that my good husband?'—and I say 'Yes'—and you say, 'No can bake good bread, no more soda,'—then I say, 'Look in cache, under flour; good-by.' You look and catch plenty soda. All the time you Fort Yukon, me Arctic City. Hi-yu medicine-man!"

Ruth smiled so ingenuously at the fairy story, that both men burst into laughter. A row among the dogs cut short the wonders of the Outside, and by the time the snarling combatants were separated, she had lashed the sleds and all was ready for the trail.

"Mush! Baldy! Hi! Mush on!" Mason worked his whip smartly, and as the dogs whined low in the traces, broke out the sled with the gee-pole. Ruth followed with the second team, leaving Malemute Kid, who had helped her start, to bring up the rear. Strong man, brute that he was, capable of felling an ox at a blow, he could not bear to beat the poor animals, but humored them as a dog driver rarely does,—nay, almost wept with them in their misery.

"Come, mush on there, you poor sore-footed brutes!" he murmured, after several ineffectual attempts to start the load. But his patience was at last rewarded, and though whimpering with pain, they hastened to join their fellows.

No more conversation; the toil of the trail will not permit such extravagance. And of all deadening labors, that of the Northland trail is the worst. Happy is the man who can weather a day's travel at the price of silence, and that on a beaten track.

And of all heartbreaking labors, that of breaking trail is the worst. At every step the great webbed shoe sinks till the snow is level with the knee. Then up, straight up, the deviation of a fraction of an inch being a certain precursor of disaster, the snowshoe must be lifted till the surface is cleared; then forward, down, and the other foot is raised perpendicularly for the matter of half a yard. He who tries this for the first time, if haply he avoids bringing his shoes in dangerous propinquity and measures not his length on the treacherous footing, will give up exhausted at the end of a hundred yards; he who can keep out of the way of the dogs for a whole day may well crawl into his sleeping bag with a clear conscience and a pride which passeth all understanding; and he who travels twenty sleeps on the Long Trail is a man whom the gods may envy.

The afternoon wore on, and with the awe, born of the White Silence, the voiceless travelers bent to their work. Nature has many tricks wherewith she convinces man of his finity,—the ceaseless flow of the tides, the fury of the storm, the shock of the earthquake, the long roll of heaven's artillery,—but the most tremendous, the most stupefying of all, is the passive phase of the White Silence. All movement ceases, the sky clears, the heavens are as brass; the slightest whisper seems sacrilege, and man becomes timid, affrighted at the sound of his own voice. Sole speck of life journeying across the ghostly wastes of a dead world, he trembles at his audacity, realizes that his is a maggot's life, nothing more. Strange thoughts arise unsummoned, and the mystery of all things strives for utterance. And the fear of death, of God, of the universe, comes over him,—the hope of the Resurrection and the Life, the yearning for immortality, the vain striving of the imprisoned essence,—it is then, if ever, man walks alone with God.

So wore the day away. The river took a great bend, and Mason headed his team for the cutoff across the narrow neck of land. But the dogs balked at the high bank. Again and again, though Ruth and Malemute Kid were shoving on the sled, they slipped back. Then came the concerted effort. The miserable creatures, weak from hunger, exerted their last strength. Up—up—the sled poised on the top of the bank; but the leader swung the string of dogs behind him to the right, fouling Mason's snow-shoes. The result was grievous. Mason was whipped off his feet; one of the dogs fell in the traces; and the sled toppled back, dragging everything to the bottom again.

Slash! The whip fell among the dogs savagely, especially upon the one which had fallen.

"Don't,—Mason," entreated Malemute Kid; "the poor devil's on its last legs. Wait and we'll put my team on."

Mason deliberately withheld the whip till the last word had fallen, then out flashed the long lash, completely curling about the offending creature's body. Carmen—for it was Carmen—cowered in the snow, cried piteously, then rolled over on her side.

It was a tragic moment, a pitiful incident of the trail,—a dying dog, two comrades in anger. Ruth glanced solicitously from man to man. But Malemute Kid restrained himself, though there was a world of reproach in his eyes, and, bending over the dog cut the traces. No word was spoken. The teams were double-spanned and the difficulty overcome; the sleds were under way again, the dying dog dragging herself along in the rear. As long as an animal can travel, it is not shot, and this last chance is accorded it,—the crawling into camp, if it can, in the hope of a moose being killed.

Already penitent for his angry action, but too stubborn to make amends, Mason toiled on at the head of the cavalcade, little dreaming that danger hovered in the air. The timber clustered thick in the sheltered bottom, and through this they threaded their way. Fifty feet or more from the trail towered a lofty pine. For generations it had stood there, and for generations destiny had had this one end in view,—perhaps the same had been decreed of Mason.

He stooped to fasten the loosened thong of his moccasin. The sleds came to a halt, and the dogs lay down in the snow without a whimper. The stillness was weird; not a breath rustled the frost-encrusted forest; the cold and silence of outer space had chilled the heart and smote the trembling lips of nature. A sigh pulsed through the air,—they did not seem to actually hear it, but rather felt it, like the premonition of movement in a motionless void. Then the great tree, burdened with its weight of years and snow, played its last part in the tragedy of life. He heard the warning crash and attempted to spring up but, almost erect, caught the blow squarely on the shoulder.

The sudden danger, the quick death,—how often had Malemute Kid faced it! The pine needles were still quivering as he gave his commands and sprang into action. Nor did the Indian girl faint or raise her voice in idle wailing, as might many of her white sisters. At his order, she threw her weight on the end of a quickly extemporized handspike, easing the pressure and listening to her husband's groans, while Malemute Kid attacked the tree with his ax. The steel rang merrily as it bit into the frozen trunk, each stroke being accompanied by a forced, audible respiration, the "Huh!" "Huh!" of the woodsman.

At last the Kid laid the pitiable thing that was once a man in the snow. But worse than his comrade's pain was the dumb anguish in the woman's face, the blended look of hopeful, hopeless query. Little was said; those of the Northland are early taught the futility of words and the inestimable value of deeds. With the temperature at sixty-five below zero, a man cannot lie many minutes in the snow and live. So the sled lashings were cut, and the sufferer, rolled in furs, laid on a couch of boughs. Before him roared a fire, built of the very wood which wrought the mishap. Behind and partially over him was stretched the primitive fly,—a piece of canvas, which caught the radiating heat and threw it back and down upon him a trick which men may know who study physics at the fount.

And men who have shared their bed with death know when the call is sounded. Mason was terribly crushed. The most cursory examination revealed it. His right arm, leg, and back were broken; his limbs were paralyzed from the hips; and the likelihood of internal injuries was large. An occasional moan was his only sign of life.

No hope; nothing to be done. The pitiless night crept slowly by,—Ruth's portion, the despairing stoicism of her race, and Malemute Kid adding new lines to his face of bronze. In fact, Mason suffered least of all, for he spent his time in eastern Tennessee, in the Great Smoky Mountains, living over the scenes of his childhood. And most pathetic was the melody of his long-forgotten Southern vernacular, as he raved of swimming holes and coon hunts and watermelon raids. It was as Greek to Ruth, but the Kid understood and felt,—felt as only one can feel who has been shut out for years from all that civilization means.

Morning brought consciousness to the stricken man, and Malemute Kid bent closer to catch his whispers.

"You remember when we foregathered on the Tanana, four years come next ice run? I didn't care so much for her then. It was more like she was pretty, and there was a smack of excitement about it, I think. But d' ye know, I've come to think a heap of her. She's been a good wife to me, always at my shoulder in the pinch. And when it comes to trading, you know there isn't her equal. D'ye recollect the time she shot the Moosehorn Rapids to pull you and me off that rock, the bullets whipping the water like hailstones? —And the time of the famine at Nuklukyeto? —Or when she raced the ice run to bring the news? Yes, she's been a good wife to me, better'n that other one. Didn't know I'd been there? Never told you, eh? Well, I tried it once, down in the States. That's why I'm here. Been raised together, too. I came away to give her a chance for divorce. She got it.

"But that's got nothing to do with Ruth. I had thought of cleaning up and pulling for the Outside next year,—her and I,—but it's too late. Don't send her back to her people, Kid. It's beastly hard for a woman to go back. Think of it! —Nearly four years on our bacon and beans and flour and dried fruit, and then to go back to her fish and caribou. It's not good for her to have tried our ways, to come to know they're better 'n' her people's, and then return to them. Take care of her, Kid,—why don't you,— but no, you always fought shy of them,—and you never told me why you came to this country. Be kind to her, and send her back to the States as soon as you can. But fix it so she can come back,—liable to get homesick, you know.

"And the youngster—it's drawn us closer, Kid. I only hope it is a boy. Think of it! —Flesh of my flesh, Kid. He mustn't stop in this country. And if it's a girl, why she can't. Sell my furs; they'll fetch at least five thousand, and I've got as much more with the company. And handle my interests with yours. I think that bench claim will show up. See that he gets a good schooling; and Kid, above all, don't let him come back. This country was not made for white men.

"I'm a gone man, Kid. Three or four sleeps at the best. You've got to go on. You must go on! Remember, it's my wife, it's my boy,—O God! I hope it's a boy! You can't stay by me,—and I charge you, a dying man, to pull on."

"Give me three days," pleaded Malemute Kid. "You may change for the better; something may turn up."

"No."

"Just three days."

"You must pull on."

"Two days."

"It's my wife and my boy, Kid. You would not ask it."

"One day."

"No, no! I charge—"

"Only one day. We can shave it through on the grub, and I might knock over a moose."

"No—all right; one day, but not a minute more. And, Kid, don't—don't leave me to face it alone. Just a shot, one pull on the trigger. You understand. Think of it! Think of it! Flesh of my flesh, and I'll never live to see him!

"Send Ruth here. I want to say goodbye and tell her that she must think of the boy and not wait till I'm dead. She might refuse to go with you if I didn't. Goodbye, old man; goodbye."

"Kid! I say—a—sink a hole above the pup, next to the slide. I panned out forty cents on my shovel there."

"And, Kid!" He stooped lower to catch the last faint words, the dying man's surrender of his pride. "I'm sorry—for—you know—Carmen."

Leaving the girl crying softly over her man, Malemute Kid slipped into his parka and snowshoes, tucked his rifle under his arm, and crept away into the forest. He was no tyro in the stern sorrows of the Northland, but never had he faced so stiff a problem as this. In the abstract, it was a plain, mathematical proposition,—three possible lives as against one doomed one. But now he hesitated. For five years, shoulder to shoulder, on the rivers and trails, in the camps and mines, facing death by field and flood and famine, had they knitted the bonds of their comradeship. So close was the tie that he had often been conscious of a vague jealousy of Ruth, from the first time she had come between. And now it must be severed by his own hand.

Though he prayed for a moose, just one moose, all game seemed to have deserted the land, and nightfall found the exhausted man crawling into camp, light-handed, heavy-hearted. An uproar from the dogs and shrill cries from Ruth hastened him.

Bursting into the camp, he saw the girl in the midst of the snarling pack, laying about her with an ax. The dogs had broken the iron rule of their masters and were rushing the grub. He joined the issue with his rifle reversed, and the hoary game of natural selection was played out with all the ruthlessness of its primeval environment. Rifle and ax went up and down, hit or missed with monotonous regularity; lithe bodies flashed, with wild eyes and dripping fangs; and man and beast fought for supremacy to the bitterest conclusion. Then the beaten brutes crept to the edge of the firelight, licking their wounds, voicing their misery to the stars.

The whole stock of dried salmon had been devoured, and perhaps five pounds of flour remained to tide them over two hundred miles of wilderness. Ruth returned to her husband, while Malemute Kid cut up the warm body of one of the dogs, the skull of which had been crushed by the ax. Every portion was carefully put away, save the hide and offal, which were cast to his fellows of the moment before.

Morning brought fresh trouble. The animals were turning on each other. Carmen, who still clung to her slender thread of life, was downed by the pack. The lash fell among them unheeded. They cringed and cried under the blows, but refused to scatter till the last wretched bit had disappeared—bones, hide, hair, everything.

Malemute Kid went about his work, listening to Mason, who was back in Tennessee, delivering tangled discourses and wild exhortations to his brethren of other days.

Taking advantage of neighboring pines, he worked rapidly, and Ruth watched him make a cache similar to those sometimes used by hunters to preserve their meat from the wolverines and dogs. One after the other, he bent the tops of two small pines toward each other and nearly to the ground, making them fast with thongs of moosehide①. Then he beat the dogs into submission and harnessed them to two of the sleds, loading the same with everything but the furs which enveloped Mason. These he wrapped and lashed tightly about him, fastening either end of the robes to the bent pines. A single stroke of his hunting knife would release them and send the body high in the air.

Ruth had received her husband's last wishes and made no struggle. Poor girl, she had learned the lesson of obedience well. From a child, she had bowed, and seen all women bow, to the lords of creation, and it did not seem in the nature of things for woman to resist. The Kid permitted her one outburst of grief, as she kissed her husband,—her own people had no such custom,—then led her to the foremost sled and helped her into her snowshoes. Blindly, instinctively, she took the gee-pole and whip, and "mushed" the dogs out on the trail. Then he returned to Mason, who had fallen into a coma, and long after she was out of sight crouched by the fire, waiting, hoping, praying for his comrade to die.

It is not pleasant to be alone with painful thoughts in the White Silence. The silence of gloom is merciful, shrouding one as with protection and breathing a thousand intangible sympathies; but the bright White Silence, clear and cold, under steely skies, is pitiless.

An hour passed,—two hours,—but the man would not die. At high noon, the sun, without raising its rim above the southern horizon, threw a suggestion of fire athwart the heavens, then quickly drew it back. Malemute Kid roused and dragged himself to his comrade's side. He cast one glance about him. The White Silence seemed to sneer, and a great fear came upon him. There was a sharp report; Mason swung into his aerial sepulcher, and Malemute Kid lashed the dogs into a wild gallop as he fled across the snow.

 Questions for Discussion
1. Will you do the same choice with Malemute Kid if you were him?
2. What's the social position of Ruth? Please give examples to support your points of view.
3. What do frozen place and the civilization stand for?

---

① moosehide: 鹿皮

Links

1. https://en.wikipedia.org/wiki/Jack_London#Short_stories
   关于杰克·伦敦的生平及创作的详细介绍。
2. http://www.jack-london.org/
   关于对杰克·伦敦的小说《寂静的雪野》的细读资料。

Part B

The Law of Life①

By Jack London

Lead-in Questions

1. What is the law of life based on your experience or some stories you have read?
2. Should human being face the death positively and take it for granted according to the law of life?

Questions about the Author and the Story

1. Which of the following is NOT the theme of Jack London?
   A. Strong and weak individuals.　　B. The irresistible natural forces.
   C. Violence.　　D. The romance.
2. Who is the story's narrator?
   A. Koskoosh.
   B. Koskoosh's son.
   C. Someone in Koskoosh's tribe.
   D. An unnamed, all-knowing storyteller.
3. What is the story of *The Law of Life*?
   A. The story chronicles the travels of Koskoosh.
   B. Koskoosh's tribe needs to travel in search of food and shelter so he is left to die because of his age and inability to see properly. Even his son has to leave him because he has a new family to feed and take care of.
   C. Koskoosh wants to disobey the law of life and he succeeded.
   D. Koskoosh's son takes good care of his father in spite of losing his life.
4. What is the conflict NOT mentioned in *The Law of Life*?

---

① *The Law of Life* is a short story by the American naturalist writer Jack London. It was first published in *McClure's Magazine*, Vol. 16, March, 1901. In 1902, it was published in a collection of Jack London's stories, *The Children of Frost*, by Macmillan Publishers.

    A. Man vs. man.   B. Body vs. mind.
    C. Man vs. nature.   D. Man vs. woman.

5. What happened to Koskoosh at the end of the story?
    A. Koskoosh killed all the enemies and survived.
    B. Koskoosh was eaten by the lions.
    C. Koskoosh's son came back and took him away.
    D. Koskoosh obeyed the law of life.

    Old Koskoosh listened greedily. Though his sight had long since faded, his hearing was still acute, and the slightest sound penetrated to the glimmering intelligence which yet abode behind the withered forehead, but which no longer gazed forth upon the things of the world. Ah! That was Sit-cum-to-ha, shrilly anathematizing the dogs as she cuffed and beat them into the harnesses. Sit-cum-to-ha was his daughter's daughter, but she was too busy to waste a thought upon her broken grandfather, sitting alone there in the snow, forlorn and helpless. Camp must be broken. The long trail waited while the short day refused to linger. Life called her, and the duties of life, not death. And he was very close to death now.

    The thought made the old man panicky for the moment, and he stretched forth a palsied hand which wandered tremblingly over the small heap of dry wood beside him. Reassured that it was indeed there, his hand returned to the shelter of his mangy furs, and he again fell to listening. The sulky crackling of half-frozen hides told him that the chief's moose-skin lodge had been struck, and even then was being rammed and jammed into portable compass. The chief was his son, stalwart and strong, head man of the tribesmen, and a mighty hunter. As the women toiled with the camp luggage, his voice rose, chiding them for their slowness. Old Koskoosh strained his ears. It was the last time he would hear that voice. There went Geehow's lodge! And Tusken's! Seven, eight, nine; only the shaman's could be still standing. There! They were at work upon it now. He could hear the shaman grunt as he piled it on the sled. A child whimpered, and a woman soothed it with soft, crooning gutturals. Little Koo-tee, the old man thought, a fretful child, and not overstrong. It would die soon, perhaps, and they would burn a hole through the frozen tundra and pile rocks above to keep the wolverines away. Well, what did it matter? A few years at best, and as many an empty belly as a full one. And in the end, Death waited, ever-hungry and hungriest of them all.

    What was that? Oh, the men lashing the sleds and drawing tight the thongs. He listened, who would listen no more. The whip-lashes snarled and bit among the dogs. Hear them whine! How they hated the work and the trail! They were off! Sled after sled churned slowly away into the silence. They were gone. They had passed out of his life, and he faced the last bitter hour alone. No. The snow crunched beneath a moccasin; a man stood beside him; upon his head a hand rested gently. His son was good to do this thing. He remembered other old men whose sons had not waited after the tribe. But his son had. He wandered away into the past, till the young man's voice brought him back.

"Is it well with you?" he asked.

And the old man answered, "It is well."

"There be wood beside you," the younger man continued, "and the fire burns bright. The morning is gray, and the cold has broken. It will snow presently. Even now is it snowing."

"My voice is become like an old woman's."

"Ay, even now is it snowing."

"The tribesmen hurry. Their bales are heavy, and their bellies flat with lack of feasting. The trail is long and they travel fast. Go now. It is well?"

"It is well. I am as a last year's leaf, clinging lightly to the stem. The first breath that blows, and I fall. My voice is become like an old woman's. My eyes no longer show me the way of my feet, and my feet are heavy, and I am tired. It is well."

He bowed his head in content till the last noise of the complaining snow had died away, and he knew his son was beyond recall. Then his hand crept out in haste to the wood. It alone stood between him and the eternity that yawned in upon him. At last the measure of his life was a handful of fagots. One by one they would go to feed the fire, and just so, step by step, death would creep upon him. When the last stick had surrendered up its heat, the frost would begin to gather strength. First his feet would yield, then his hands; and the numbness would travel, slowly, from the extremities to the body. His head would fall forward upon his knees, and he would rest. It was easy. All men must die.

He did not complain. It was the way of life, and it was just. He had been born close to the earth, close to the earth had he lived, and the law thereof was not new to him. It was the law of all flesh. Nature was not kindly to the flesh. She had no concern for that concrete thing called the individual. Her interest lay in the species, the race. This was the deepest abstraction old Koskoosh's barbaric mind was capable of, but he grasped it firmly. He saw it exemplified in all life. The rise of the sap, the bursting greenness of the willow bud, the fall of the yellow leaf—in this alone was told the whole history. But one task did Nature set the individual. Did he not perform it, he died. Did he perform it, it was all the same, he died. Nature did not care; there were plenty who were obedient, and it was only the obedience in this matter, not the obedient, which lived and lived always. The tribe of Koskoosh was very old. The old men he had known when a boy, had known old men before them. Therefore it was true that the tribe lived, that it stood for the obedience of all its members, way down into the forgotten past, whose very resting-places were unremembered. They did not count; they were episodes. They had passed away like clouds from a summer sky. He also was an episode, and would pass away. Nature did not care. To life she set one task, gave one law. To perpetuate was the task of life, its law was death. A maiden was a good creature to look upon, full-breasted and strong, with spring to her step and light in her eyes. But her task was yet before her. The light in her eyes brightened, her step quickened, she was now bold with the young men, now timid, and she gave them of her own unrest. And ever she grew fairer and yet fairer to look upon, till some hunter, able no longer to withhold himself, took her to his lodge to cook and toil for him and to become the mother of his children. And with the coming of her offspring her looks left her. Her limbs dragged and shuffled, her eyes dimmed and bleared, and only the little children found joy against the withered cheek of the old squaw by the fire. Her task was done. But a little while, on the first pinch of famine or the first long trail, and she would be left, even as he had been left, in the snow, with a little pile of wood. Such was the law. He placed a stick carefully upon the fire and resumed his meditations. It was the same everywhere, with all things. The mosquitoes vanished with the first frost. The little tree-squirrel crawled away to die. When age settled upon the rabbit it became slow and heavy, and could no longer outfoot its enemies. Even the big bald-face grew clumsy and blind and quarrelsome, in the end to be dragged down by a handful of yelping huskies. He remembered how he had abandoned his own father on an upper reach of the Klondike one winter, the winter before the missionary came with his talk-books and his box of medicines. Many a time had Koskoosh smacked his lips over the recollection of that box, though now his mouth refused to moisten. The "painkiller" had been especially good. But the missionary was a bother after all, for he brought no meat into the camp, and he ate heartily, and the hunters grumbled. But he chilled his lungs on the divide by the Mayo, and the dogs afterwards nosed the stones away and fought over his bones.

"Through the long darkness the children wailed and died."

Koskoosh placed another stick on the fire and harked back deeper into the past. There was the time of the Great Famine, when the old men crouched empty-bellied to the fire, and let fall from their lips dim traditions of the ancient day when the Yukon ran wide open for three winters, and then lay frozen for three summers. He had lost his mother in that famine. In the summer the salmon run had failed, and the tribe looked forward to the winter and the coming of the caribou. Then the winter came, but with it there were no caribou. Never had the like been known, not even in the lives of the old men. But the caribou did not come, and it was the seventh year, and the rabbits had not replenished, and the dogs were naught but bundles of bones. And through the long darkness the children wailed and died, and the women, and the old men; and not one in ten of the tribe lived to meet the sun when it came back in the spring. That was a famine!

But he had seen times of plenty, too, when the meat spoiled on their hands, and the dogs were fat and worthless with overeating—times when they let the game go unkilled, and the women were fertile, and the lodges were cluttered with sprawling men-children and women-children. Then it was the men became high-stomached, and revived ancient quarrels, and crossed the divides to the south to kill the Pellys, and to the west that they might sit by the dead fires of the Tananas. He remembered, when a boy, during a time of plenty, when he saw a moose pulled down by the wolves. Zing-ha lay with him in the snow and watched—Zing-ha, who later became the craftiest of hunters, and who, in the end, fell through an air-hole on the Yukon. They found him, a month afterward, just as he had crawled halfway out and frozen stiff to the ice.

But the moose. Zing-ha and he had gone out that day to play at hunting after the manner of their fathers. On the bed of the creek they struck the fresh track of a moose, and with it the tracks of many wolves. "An old one," Zing-ha, who was quicker at reading the sign, said—"an old one who cannot keep up with the herd. The wolves have cut him out from his brothers, and they will never leave him." And it was so. It was their way. By day and by night, never resting, snarling on his heels, snapping at his nose, they would stay by him to the end. How Zing-ha and he felt the blood-lust quicken! The finish would be a sight to see!

Eager-footed, they took the trail, and even he, Koskoosh, slow of sight and an unversed tracker, could have followed it blind, it was so wide. Hot were they on the heels of the chase, reading the grim tragedy, fresh-written, at every step. Now they came to where the moose had made a stand. Thrice the length of a grown man's body, in every direction, had the snow been stamped about and uptossed. In the midst were the deep impressions of the splay-hoofed game, and all about, everywhere, were the lighter footmarks of the wolves. Some, while their brothers harried the kill, had lain to one side and rested. The full-stretched impress of their bodies in the snow was as perfect as though made the moment before. One wolf had been caught in a wild lunge of the maddened victim and trampled to death. A few bones, well picked, bore witness.

Again, they ceased the uplift of their snowshoes at a second stand. Here the great animal had fought desperately. Twice had he been dragged down, as the snow attested, and twice had he shaken his assailants clear and gained footing once more. He had done his task long since, but none the less was life dear to him. Zing-ha said it was a strange thing, a moose once down to get free again; but this one certainly had. The shaman would see signs and wonders in this when they told him.

And yet again, they come to where the moose had made to mount the bank and gain the timber. But his foes had laid on from behind, till he reared and fell back upon them, crushing two deep into the snow. It was plain the kill was at hand, for their brothers had left them untouched. Two more stands were hurried past, brief in time-length and very close together. The trail was red now, and the clean stride of the great beast had grown short and slovenly. Then they heard the first sounds of the battle—not the full-throated chorus of the chase, but the short, snappy bark which spoke of close quarters and teeth to flesh. Crawling up the wind, Zing-ha bellied it through the snow, and with him crept he, Koskoosh, who was to be chief of the tribesmen in the years to come. Together they shoved aside the under branches of a young spruce and peered forth. It was the end they saw.

The picture, like all of youth's impressions, was still strong with him, and his dim eyes watched the end played out as vividly as in that far-off time. Koskoosh marvelled at this, for in the days which followed, when he was a leader of men and a head of councillors, he had done great deeds and made his name a curse in the mouths of the Pellys, to say naught of the strange white man he had killed, knife to knife, in open fight.

For long he pondered on the days of his youth, till the fire died down and the frost bit deeper. He replenished it with two sticks this time, and gauged his grip on life by what remained. If Sit-cum-to-ha had only remembered her grandfather, and gathered a larger armful, his hours would have been longer. It would have been easy. But she was ever a careless child, and honored not her ancestors from the time the Beaver, son of the son of Zing-ha, first cast eyes upon her. Well, what mattered it? Had he not done likewise in his own quick youth? For a while he listened to the silence. Perhaps the heart of his son might soften, and he would come back with the dogs to take his old father on with the tribe to where the caribou ran thick and the fat hung heavy upon them.

He strained his ears, his restless brain for the moment stilled. Not a stir, nothing. He alone took breath in the midst of the great silence. It was very lonely. Hark! What was that? A chill passed over his body. The familiar, long-drawn howl broke the void, and it was close at hand. Then on his darkened eyes was projected the vision of the moose—the old bull moose—the torn flanks and bloody sides, the riddled mane, and the great branching horns, down low and tossing to the last. He saw the flashing forms of gray, the gleaming eyes, the lolling tongues, the slavered fangs. And he saw the inexorable circle close in till it became a dark point in the midst of the stamped snow.

A cold muzzle thrust against his cheek, and at its touch his soul leaped back to the present. His hand shot into the fire and dragged out a burning faggot. Overcome for the nonce by his hereditary fear of man, the brute retreated, raising a prolonged call to his brothers; and greedily they answered, till a ring of crouching, jaw-slobbered gray was stretched round about. The old man listened to the drawing in of this circle. He waved his brand wildly, and sniffs turned to snarls; but the panting brutes refused to scatter. Now one wormed his chest forward, dragging his haunches after, now a second, now a third; but never a one drew back. Why should he cling to life? he asked, and dropped the blazing stick into the snow. It sizzled and went out. The circle grunted uneasily, but held its own. Again he saw the last stand of the old bull moose, and Koskoosh dropped his head wearily upon his knees. What did it matter after all? Was it not the law of life?

Questions for Discussion

1. Do you agree with the law of life illustrated in this novel? Should we follow it?
2. If Koskoosh's son takes him with the whole tribe, what will happen to Koskoosh? Is there any difference between the two kinds of ending?
3. How will you define Naturalism? What are the features of Naturalism?

 Links

http://www.jack-london.org/
关于对杰克·伦敦的小说《生命的法则》的细读资料。

Chapter Ten

The Philosopher in the Apple Orchard

By Anthony Hope

Anthony Hope (in full Sir Anthony Hope Hawkins) (1863—1933) is a British novelist and playwright.

Anthony Hope was born as the youngest child in London. His father was the headmaster of the St. Johns Foundation School for the Sons of Poor Clergy. He was educated at Marlborough School and Baliol College, Oxford, obtaining an M. A. with honors in 1885. He studied to become a lawyer, and indeed became one in 1887. He set up his own practice, but not so successful, and he spent the periods in between cases writing novels. When he couldn't find a publisher for his first novel, he published it himself. The novel became a hit, and at the same time, his law practice also began to succeed. When he had to choose between his law practice and writing, he chose writing. Although he was a prolific writer, especially of adventure novels, he is now mainly remembered for only two books: his masterpiece *The Prisoner of Zenda* (1894) and its sequel *Rupert of Hentzau* (1898). The success of the two works made him a popular and highly influential author for much of the first half of the 20th century.

He married an American woman Elizabeth Somerville Sheldon in 1903 and was knighted in 1918. He wrote more books and several plays. He died of throat cancer at his home on 8 July 1933.

❀ Lead-in Questions

1. How do you view juvenile love?
2. What kind of love should people seek?

Questions about the Author and the Story

1. What is Anthony Hope now remembered as?
   A. A playwright   B. An essayist   C. A novelist   D. A & C
2. Anthony Hope can be best described as a writer of _____.
   A. romance   B. non-fiction   C. mystery   D. adventure
3. Who is the protagonist of the story?
   A. Miss May.   B. Mr. Jerningham.
   C. "I" in the story.   D. None of the above.
4. "And—I don't know how to put it, quite—she thinks that if he ever thought about it at all he might care for her; because he doesn't care for anybody else, and she's pretty—". Who does he refer to?
   A. The philosopher.   B. The narrator.
   C. Mr. Jerningham.   D. The unknown.
5. What do you think is the story about?
   A. Friendship.   B. War.   C. Love.   D. Terror.

It was a charmingly mild and balmy① day. The sun shone beyond the orchard, and the shade was cool inside. A light breeze stirred the boughs of the old apple-tree under which the philosopher sat. None of these things did the philosopher notice, unless it might be when the wind blew about the leaves of the large volume on his knees, and he had to find his place again. Then he would exclaim against the wind, shuffle the leaves till he got the right page, and settle to his reading. The book was a treatise on ontology②; it was written by another philosopher, a friend of this philosopher's; it bristled with fallacies, and this philosopher was discovering them all, and noting them on the fly-leaf at the end. He was not going to review the book (as some might have thought from his behavior), or even to answer it in a work of his own. It was just that he found a pleasure in stripping any poor fallacy naked and crucifying it. Presently a girl in a white frock came into the orchard. She picked up an apple, bit it, and found it ripe. Holding it in her hand, she walked up to where the philosopher sat, and looked at him. He did not stir. She took a bite out of the apple, munched it, and swallowed it. The philosopher crucified a fallacy on the fly-leaf. The girl flung the apple away.

"Mr. Jerningham," said she, "are you very busy?" The philosopher, pencil in hand, looked up. "No, Miss May," said he, "not very."

"Because I want your opinion."

---

① balmy: weather etc. warm and pleasant;暖和的;温暖的

② ontology: a subject of study in philosophy that is concerned with the nature of existence;本体论,实体论

Chapter Ten

"In one moment," said the philosopher, apologetically.

He turned back to the fly-leaf and began to nail the last fallacy a little tighter to the cross. The girl regarded him, first with amused impatience, then with a vexed frown, finally with a wistful regret. He was so very old for his age, she thought; he could not be much beyond thirty; his hair was thick and full of waves, his eyes bright and clear, his complexion not yet divested of all youth's relics.

"Now, Miss May, I'm at your service," said the philosopher, with a lingering look at his impaled fallacy; and he closed the book, keeping it, however, on his knee.

The girl sat down just opposite to him.

"It's a very important thing I want to ask you," she began, tugging at a tuft of grass, "and it's very—difficult, and you mustn't tell anyone I asked you; at least, I'd rather you didn't."

"I shall not speak of it; indeed, I shall probably not remember it," said the philosopher. "And you mustn't look at me, please, while I'm asking you."

"I don't think I was looking at you, but if I was I beg your pardon," said the philosopher, apologetically. She pulled the tuft of grass right out of the ground, and flung it from her with all her force.

"Suppose a man"—she began. "No, that's not right."

"You can take any hypothesis you please," observed the philosopher, "but you must verify it afterward, of course."

"Oh, do let me go on. Suppose a girl, Mr. Jerningham—I wish you wouldn't nod."

"It was only to show that I followed you."

"Oh, of course you 'follow me,' as you call it. Suppose a girl had two lovers—you're nodding again—or, I ought to say, suppose there were two men who might be in love with a girl."

"Only two?" asked the philosopher. "You see, any number of men might be in love with—"

"Oh, we can leave the rest out," said Miss May, with a sudden dimple; "they don't matter."

"Very well," said the philosopher, "if they are irrelevant we will put them aside."

"Suppose, then, that one of these men was, oh, awfully in love with the girl, and—and proposed, you know—"

"A moment!" said the philosopher, opening a note-book. "Let me take down his proposition. What was it?"

"Why, proposed to her—asked her to marry him," said the girl, with a stare.

"Dear me! How stupid of me! I forgot that special use of the word. Yes?"

"The girl likes him pretty well, and her people approve of him, and all that, you know."

"That simplifies the problem," said the philosopher, nodding again.

"But she's not in—in love with him, you know. She doesn't really care for him—much. Do you understand?"

"Perfectly. It is a most natural state of mind."

"Well then, suppose that there's another man—what are you writing?"

"I only put down—like that," pleaded the philosopher, meekly exhibiting his notebook.

She looked at him in a sort of helpless exasperation, with just a smile somewhere in the background of it.

"Oh, you really are—" she exclaimed. "But let me go on. The other man is a friend of the girl's: he's very clever—oh, fearfully clever—and he's rather handsome. You needn't put that down."

"It is certainly not very material," admitted the philosopher, and he crossed out "handsome"; "clever" he left.

"And the girl is most awfully—she admires him tremendously; she thinks him just the greatest man that ever lived, you know. And she—she—" The girl paused.

"I'm following," said the philosopher, with pencil poised.

"She'd think it better than the whole world if—if she could be anything to him, you know."

"You mean become his wife?"

"Well, of course I do—at least, I suppose I do."

"You spoke rather vaguely, you know."

The girl cast one glance at the philosopher as she replied:

"Well, yes; I did mean become his wife."

"Yes. Well?"

"But," continued the girl, starting on another tuft of grass, "he doesn't think much about those things. He likes her. I think he likes her—"

"Well, doesn't dislike her?" suggested the philosopher. "Shall we call him indifferent?"

"I don't know. Yes, rather indifferent. I don't think he thinks about it, you know. But she—she's pretty. You needn't put that down."

"I was not about to do so," observed the philosopher.

"She thinks life with him would be just heaven; and—and she thinks she would make him awfully happy. She would—would be so proud of him, you see."

"I see. Yes?"

"And—I don't know how to put it, quite—she thinks that if he ever thought about it at all he might care for her; because he doesn't care for anybody else, and she's pretty—"

"You said that before."

"Oh dear, I dare say I did. And most men care for somebody, don't they? Some girl, I mean."

"Most men, no doubt," conceded the philosopher.

"Well then, what ought she to do? It's not a real thing, you know, Mr. Jerningham. It's in—in a novel I was reading." She said this hastily, and blushed as she spoke.

"Dear me! And it's quite an interesting case! Yes, I see. The question is, will she act most wisely in accepting the offer of the man who loves her exceedingly, but for whom she entertains only a moderate affection—"

"Yes, just a liking. He's just a friend."

"Exactly. Or in marrying the other whom she loves ex—"

"That's not it. How can she marry him? He hasn't—he hasn't asked her, you see."

"True; I forgot. Let us assume, though, for the moment, that he has asked her. She would then have to consider which marriage would probably be productive of the greater sum total of—"

"Oh, but you needn't consider that."

"But it seems the best logical order. We can afterward make allowance for the element of uncertainty caused by—"

"Oh no; I don't want it like that. I know perfectly well which she'd do if he—the other man you know—asked her."

"You apprehend that—"

"Never mind what I 'apprehend.' Take it as I told you."

"Very good. A has asked her hand,① B has not."

"Yes."

"May I take it that, but for the disturbing influence of B, A would be a satisfactory—er—candidate?"

"Ye-es; I think so."

"She therefore enjoys a certainty of considerable happiness if she marries A?"

"Ye-es; not perfect, because of—B, you know."

"Quite so, quite so; but still a fair amount of happiness. Is it not so?"

"I don't—well, perhaps."

"On the other hand, if B did ask her, we are to postulate a higher degree of happiness for her?"

"Yes, please, Mr. Jerningham—much higher."

"For both of them?"

"For her. Never mind him."

"Very well. That again simplifies the problem. But his asking her is a contingency only?"

---

① asked her hand: propose, 求婚。

"Yes, that's all."

The philosopher spread out his hands.

"My dear young lady," he said, "it becomes a question of degree. How probable or improbable is it?"

"I don't know; not very probable—unless—"

"Well?"

"Unless he did happen to notice, you know."

"Ah, yes; we supposed that, if he thought of it, he would probably take the desired step—at least, that he might be led to do so. Could she not—er—indicate her preference?"

"She might try—no, she couldn't do much. You see, he—he doesn't think about such things."

"I understand precisely. And it seems to me, Miss May, that in that very fact we find our solution."

"Do we?" she asked.

"I think so. He has evidently no natural inclination toward her—perhaps not toward marriage at all. Any feeling aroused in him would be necessarily shallow and, in a measure, artificial, and in all likelihood purely temporary. Moreover, if she took steps to arouse his attention one of two things would be likely to happen. Are you following me?"

"Yes, Mr. Jerningham."

"Either he would be repelled by her overtures,—which you must admit is not improbable,—and then the position would be unpleasant, and even degrading, for her; or, on the other hand, he might, through a misplaced feeling of gallantry①—"

"Through what?"

"Through a mistaken idea of politeness, or a mistaken view of what was kind, allow himself to be drawn into a connection for which he had no genuine liking. You agree with me that one or other of these things would be likely?"

"Yes, I suppose they would, unless he did come to care for her."

"Ah, you return to that hypothesis. I think it's an extremely fanciful one. No, she need not marry A; but she must let B alone."

The philosopher closed his book, took off his glasses, wiped them, replaced them, and leaned back against the trunk of the apple-tree. The girl picked a dandelion in pieces. After a long pause she asked:

"You think B's feelings wouldn't be at all likely to—to change?"

"That depends on the sort of man he is. But if he is an able man, with intellectual interests which engross him—a man who has chosen his path in life—a man to whom

---

① gallantry:1. courage, especially in a battle 2. polite attention given by men to women;1. 勇敢 2. (对女子)献殷勤,此处指后者。

women's society is not a necessity—"

"He's just like that," said the girl, and she bit the head off a daisy.

"Then," said the philosopher, "I see not the least reason for supposing that his feelings will change."

"And would you advise her to marry the other—A?"

"Well, on the whole, I should. A is a good fellow (I think we made A a good fellow), he is a suitable match, his love for her is true and genuine—"

"It's tremendous!"

"Yes—and—er—extreme. She likes him. There is every reason to hope that her liking will develop into a sufficiently deep and stable affection. She will get rid of her folly about B, and make a good wife. Yes, Miss May, if I were the author of your novel I should make her marry A, and I should call that a happy ending."

A silence followed. It was broken by the philosopher.

"Is that all you wanted my opinion about, Miss May?" he asked, with his finger between the leaves of the treatise on ontology.

"Yes, I think so. I hope I haven't bored you?"

"I've enjoyed the discussion extremely. I had no idea that novels raised points of such psychological interest. I must find time to read one."

The girl had shifted her position till, instead of her full face, her profile was turned toward him. Looking away toward the paddock that lay brilliant in sunshine on the skirts of the apple orchard, she asked in low slow tones, twisting her hands in her lap:

"Don't you think that perhaps if B found out afterward—when she had married A, you know—that she had cared for him so very, very much, he might be a little sorry?"

"If he were a gentleman he would regret it deeply."

"I mean—sorry on his own account; that—that he had thrown away all that, you know?"

The philosopher looked meditative.

"I think," he pronounced, "that it is very possible he would. I can well imagine it."

"He might never find anybody to love him like that again," she said, gazing on the gleaming paddock.

"He probably would not," agreed the philosopher.

"And—and most people like being loved, don't they?"

"To crave for love is an almost universal instinct, Miss May."

"Yes, almost," she said, with a dreary little smile. "You see, he'll get old, and—and have no one to look after him."

"He will."

"And no home."

"Well, in a sense, none," corrected the philosopher, smiling. "But really you'll frighten me. I'm a bachelor myself, you know, Miss May."

"Yes," she whispered, just audibly.

"And all your terrors are before me."

"Well, unless—"

"Oh, we needn't have that 'unless,'" laughed the philosopher, cheerfully. "There's no 'unless' about it, Miss May."

The girl jumped to her feet; for an instant she looked at the philosopher. She opened her lips as if to speak, and at the thought of what lay at her tongue's tip her face grew red. But the philosopher was gazing past her, and his eyes rested in calm contemplation on the gleaming paddock.

"A beautiful thing, sunshine, to be sure," said he.

Her blush faded away into paleness; her lips closed. Without speaking, she turned and walked slowly away, her head drooping. The philosopher heard the rustle of her skirt in the long grass of the orchard; he watched her for a few moments.

"A pretty, graceful creature," said he, with a smile. Then he opened his book, took his pencil in his hand, and slipped in a careful forefinger to mark the fly-leaf.

The sun had passed mid-heaven and began to decline westward before he finished the book. Then he stretched himself and looked at his watch.

"Good gracious①, two o'clock! I shall be late for lunch!" and he hurried to his feet. He was very late for lunch.

"Everything's cold," wailed his hostess. "Where have you been, Mr. Jerningham?"

"Only in the orchard-reading."

"And you've missed May!"

"Missed Miss May? How do you mean? I had a long talk with her this morning—a most interesting talk."

"But you weren't here to say good-bye. Now you don't mean to say that you forgot that she was leaving by the two-o'clock train? What a man you are!"

"Dear me! To think of my forgetting it!" said the philosopher, shamefacedly.

"She told me to say good-bye to you for her."

"She's very kind. I can't forgive myself."

His hostess looked at him for a moment; then she sighed, and smiled, and sighed again.

"Have you everything you want?" she asked.

"Everything, thank you," said he, sitting down opposite the cheese, and propping his book (he thought he would just run through the last chapter again) against the loaf; "everything in the world that I want, thanks."

His hostess did not tell him that the girl had come in from the apple orchard and run hastily upstairs, lest her friend should see what her friend did see in her eyes. So that he

---

① Goodness gracious, (old-fashioned) used to express surprise or to emphasize "yes" or "no".

had no suspicion at all that he had received an offer of marriage—and refused it. And he did not refer to anything of that sort when he paused once in his reading and exclaimed:

"I'm really sorry I missed Miss May. That was an interesting case of hers. But I gave the right answer; the girl ought to marry A."

And so the girl did.

❋ Questions for Discussion

1. What would the story unfold if it were told from the point of view of the girl Miss May?
2. What is the theme of the story? Why was the story set in an apple orchard?
3. Why is the story titled "The philosopher in the apple orchard"?

❋ Links

1. http://www.online-literature.com/anthony-hope/
   关于安东尼·霍普生平及创作的详细介绍。
2. http://www.iyangcong.com/book/detail/3308/
   关于安东尼·霍普的小说《苹果园里的哲学家》的细读资料。

Part B

The Signal-Man

By Charles Dickens

Charles Dickens (1812—1870) was an English writer and social critic. He created some of the world's best-known fictional characters and is regarded by many as the greatest novelist of the Victorian era. His works enjoyed unprecedented popularity during his lifetime, and by the 20th century critics and scholars had recognized him as a literary genius. His novels and short stories enjoy lasting popularity.

Born in Portsmouth, Dickens left school to work in a factory when his father was incarcerated in a debtors' prison. Despite his lack of formal education, he edited a weekly journal for 20 years, wrote 15 novels, five novellas, hundreds of short stories and non-fiction articles, lectured and performed extensively. He was an indefatigable letter writer, and campaigned vigorously for children's rights, education, and other social reforms. Dickens's literary success began with the 1836 serial publication of

The Pickwick Papers. Within a few years, he had become an international literary celebrity, famous for his humor, satire, and keen observation of character and society. His main works include *Oliver Twist* (1838), *David Copperfield* (1849), *Hard Times* (1854), *A Tale of Two Cities* (1854), *Great Expectations* (1860), and etc.

Dickens enjoyed a wider popularity during his lifetime than any previous author had. Dickens depicted many striking and unforgettable characters successfully, and his works reflected widely the life of common people. Dickens kept his sympathy for the poor people and exposed and condemned the greed, hypocrisy and bribery of bourgeois. Dickens' works moved the readers of one generation to another.

"The Signal-Man" is a short story by Charles Dickens. The railway signal-man of the title tells the narrator of a ghost that has been haunting him. Each spectral appearance precedes a tragic event on the railway on which the signal-man works.

Lead-in Questions

1. Why is Charles Dickens regarded by many as the greatest novelist of the Victorian era? What is the status of the Victorian era in British history?
2. Would you please list some works of Charles Dickens and talk about one of them?

Questions about the Author and the Story

1. Which of the following is NOT written by Charles Dickens?
   A. *A Tale of Two Cities*.   B. *Hard Times*.
   C. *David Copperfield*.   D. *The Old Man and the Sea*.
2. Which literary school does Dickens belong to?
   A. Romanticism.   B. Classicism.
   C. Critical realism.   D. Modernism.
3. Who sees the ghost in "The Signal-Man"?
   A. The signal-man.   B. The narrator.
   C. No one sees the ghost.   D. None of these are correct.
4. What does the appearance of the ghost indicate in "The Signal-Man"?
   A. A train is coming.   B. Bad weather.
   C. A tragedy is pending.   D. None above is correct.
5. The story begins with "Halloa". What does it mean?
   A. An informal welcome.   B. Goodbye.
   C. Thanks.   D. Sorry.

"Hallo! Below there!"

When he heard a voice thus calling to him, he was standing at the door of his box, with a flag in his hand, furled round its short pole. One would have thought, considering the nature of the ground, that he could not have doubted from what quarter the voice came; but instead of looking up to where I stood on the top of the steep cutting nearly over his head, he turned himself about, and looked down the Line. There was something remarkable in his manner of doing so, though I could not have said for my life what. But I know it was remarkable enough to attract my notice, even though his figure was foreshortened and shadowed, down in the deep trench, and mine was high above him, so steeped in the glow of an angry sunset, that I had shaded my eyes with my hand before I saw him at all.

"Hallo! Below!"

From looking down the Line, he turned himself about again, and, raising his eyes, saw my figure high above him.

"Is there any path by which I can come down and speak to you?"

He looked up at me without replying, and I looked down at him without pressing him too soon with a repetition of my idle question. Just then there came a vague vibration in the earth and air, quickly changing into a violent pulsation, and an oncoming rush that caused me to start back, as though it had force to draw me down. When such vapour as rose to my height from this rapid train had passed me, and was skimming away over the landscape, I looked down again, and saw him refurling the flag he had shown while the train went by.

I repeated my inquiry. After a pause, during which he seemed to regard me with fixed attention, he motioned with his rolled-up flag towards a point on my level, some two or three hundred yards distant. I called down to him, "All right!" and made for that point. There, by dint of① looking closely about me, I found a rough zigzag descending path notched out, which I followed.

The cutting was extremely deep, and unusually precipitate. It was made through a clammy stone, that became oozier and wetter as I went down. For these reasons, I found the way long enough to give me time to recall a singular air of reluctance or compulsion with which he had pointed out the path.

When I came down low enough upon the zigzag descent to see him again, I saw that he was standing between the rails on the way by which the train had lately passed, in an attitude as if he were waiting for me to appear. He had his left hand at his chin, and that left elbow rested on his right hand, crossed over his breast. His attitude was one of such expectation and watchfulness that I stopped a moment, wondering at it.

I resumed my downward way, and stepping out upon the level of the railroad, and drawing nearer to him, saw that he was a dark sallow man, with a dark beard and rather heavy eyebrows. His post was in as solitary and dismal a place as ever I saw. On either

---

① by dint of (doing) something: by using a particular method,借助;用;靠

side, a dripping-wet①wall of jagged stone, excluding all view but a strip of sky; the perspective one way only a crooked prolongation of this great dungeon; the shorter perspective in the other direction terminating in a gloomy red light, and the gloomier entrance to a black tunnel, in whose massive architecture there was a barbarous, depressing, and forbidding air. So little sunlight ever found its way to this spot, that it had an earthy, deadly smell; and so much cold wind rushed through it, that it struck chill to me, as if I had left the natural world.

Before he stirred, I was near enough to him to have touched him. Not even then removing his eyes from mine, he stepped back one step, and lifted his hand.

This was a lonesome post to occupy (I said), and it had riveted my attention when I looked down from up yonder. A visitor was a rarity, I should suppose; not an unwelcome rarity, I hoped? In me, he merely saw a man who had been shut up within narrow limits all his life, and who, being at last set free, had a newly-awakened interest in these great works. To such purpose I spoke to him; but I am far from sure of the terms I used; for, besides that I am not happy in opening any conversation, there was something in the man that daunted me.

He directed a most curious look towards the red light near the tunnel's mouth, and looked all about it, as if something were missing from it, and then looked it me.

That light was part of his charge? Was it not?

He answered in a low voice,—"Don't you know it is?"

The monstrous thought came into my mind, as I perused the fixed eyes and the saturnine② face, that this was a spirit, not a man. I have speculated since, whether there may have been infection in his mind.

In my turn, I stepped back. But in making the action, I detected in his eyes some latent fear of me. This put the monstrous thought to flight.

"You look at me," I said, forcing a smile, "as if you had a dread of me."

"I was doubtful," he returned, "whether I had seen you before."

"Where?" He pointed to the red light he had looked at.

"There?" I said.

Intently watchful of me, he replied (but without sound), "Yes."

"My good fellow, what should I do there? However, be that as it may, I never was there, you may swear."

"I think I may," he rejoined. "Yes; I am sure I may."

His manner cleared, like my own. He replied to my remarks with readiness, and in well-chosen words. Had he much to do there? Yes; that was to say, he had enough responsibility to bear; but exactness and watchfulness were what was required of him,

---

① dripping-wet: 湿淋淋的

② saturnine: looking sad and serious, especially in a threatening way; 表情忧郁的,阴沉的

and of actual work—manual labor—he had next to none. To change that signal, to trim those lights, and to turn this iron handle now and then, was all he had to do under that head. Regarding those many long and lonely hours of which I seemed to make so much, he could only say that the routine of his life had shaped itself into that form, and he had grown used to it. He had taught himself a language down here,—if only to know it by sight, and to have formed his own crude ideas of its pronunciation, could be called learning it. He had also worked at fractions and decimals①, and tried a little algebra②; but he was, and had been as a boy, a poor hand at figures. Was it necessary for him when on duty always to remain in that channel of damp air, and could he never rise into the sunshine from between those high stone walls? Why, that depended upon times and circumstances. Under some conditions there would be less upon the Line than under others, and the same held good as to certain hours of the day and night. In bright weather, he did choose occasions for getting a little above these lower shadows; but, being at all times liable to be called by his electric bell, and at such times listening for it with redoubled anxiety, the relief was less than I would suppose.

He took me into his box, where there was a fire, a desk for an official book in which he had to make certain entries, a telegraphic instrument with its dial, face, and needles, and the little bell of which he had spoken. On my trusting that he would excuse the remark that he had been well educated, and (I hoped I might say without offence) perhaps educated above that station, he observed that instances of slight incongruity in such wise would rarely be found wanting among large bodies of men; that he had heard it was so in workhouses, in the police force, even in that last desperate resource, the army; and that he knew it was so, more or less, in any great railway staff. He had been, when young (if I could believe it, sitting in that hut,—he scarcely could), a student of natural philosophy, and had attended lectures; but he had run wild, misused his opportunities, gone down, and never risen again. He had no complaint to offer about that. He had made his bed, and he lay upon it. It was far too late to make another.

All that I have here condensed he said in a quiet manner, with his grave dark regards divided between me and the fire. He threw in the word, "Sir," from time to time, and especially when he referred to his youth,—as though to request me to understand that he claimed to be nothing but what I found him. He was several times interrupted by the little bell, and had to read off messages, and send replies. Once he had to stand without the door, and display a flag as a train passed, and make some verbal communication to the driver. In the discharge of his duties, I observed him to be remarkably exact and vigilant, breaking off his discourse at a syllable, and remaining

---

① fractions and decimals: 分数与小数
② algebra: 代数

silent until what he had to do was done.

In a word, I should have set this man down as one of the safest of men to be employed in that capacity, but for the circumstance that while he was speaking to me he twice broke off with a fallen color, turned his face towards the little bell when it did NOT ring, opened the door of the hut (which was kept shut to exclude the unhealthy damp), and looked out towards the red light near the mouth of the tunnel. On both of those occasions, he came back to the fire with the inexplicable air upon him which I had remarked, without being able to define, when we were so far asunder.

Said I, when I rose to leave him, "You almost make me think that I have met with a contented man."

(I am afraid I must acknowledge that I said it to lead him on.)

"I believe I used to be so," he rejoined, in the low voice in which he had first spoken; "but I am troubled, sir, I am troubled."

He would have recalled the words if he could. He had said them, however, and I took them up quickly.

"With what? What is your trouble?"

"It is very difficult to impart, sir. It is very, very difficult to speak of. If ever you make me another visit, I will try to tell you."

"But I expressly intend to make you another visit. Say, when shall it be?"

"I go off early in the morning, and I shall be on again at ten tomorrow night, sir."

"I will come at eleven."

He thanked me, and went out at the door with me. "I'll show my white light, sir," he said, in his peculiar low voice, "till you have found the way up. When you have found it, don't call out! And when you are at the top, don't call out!"

His manner seemed to make the place strike colder to me, but I said no more than, "Very well."

"And when you come down tomorrow night, don't call out! Let me ask you a parting question. What made you cry, 'Halloa! Below there!' tonight?"

"Heaven knows[①]," said I. "I cried something to that effect—"

"Not to that effect, sir. Those were the very words. I know them well."

"Admit those were the very words. I said them, no doubt, because I saw you below."

"For no other reason?"

"What other reason could I possibly have?"

"You had no feeling that they were conveyed to you in any supernatural way?"

"No."

He wished me good-night, and held up his light. I walked by the side of the down

---

① Heaven knows: 天知道; 的确

Chapter Ten

Line of rails (with a very disagreeable sensation of a train coming behind me) until I found the path. It was easier to mount than to descend, and I got back to my inn without any adventure.

Punctual to my appointment, I placed my foot on the first notch of the zigzag next night, as the distant clocks were striking eleven. He was waiting for me at the bottom, with his white light on. "I have not called out," I said, when we came close together; "may I speak now?" "By all means, sir." "Good-night, then, and here's my hand." "Good-night, sir, and here's mine." With that we walked side by side to his box, entered it, closed the door, and sat down by the fire.

"I have made up my mind, sir," he began, bending forward as soon as we were seated, and speaking in a tone but a little above a whisper, "that you shall not have to ask me twice what troubles me. I took you for some one else yesterday evening. That troubles me."

"That mistake?"

"No. That some one else."

"Who is it?"

"I don't know."

"Like me?"

"I don't know. I never saw the face. The left arm is across the face, and the right arm is waved,—violently waved. This way."

I followed his action with my eyes, and it was the action of an arm gesticulating, with the utmost passion and vehemence, "For God's sake①, clear the way!"

"One moonlight night," said the man, "I was sitting here, when I heard a voice cry, 'Halloa! Below there!' I started up, looked from that door, and saw this Some one else standing by the red light near the tunnel, waving as I just now showed you. The voice seemed hoarse with shouting, and it cried, 'Look out! Look out!' And then attain, 'Halloa! Below there! Look out!' I caught up my lamp, turned it on red, and ran towards the figure, calling, 'What's wrong? What has happened? Where?' It stood just outside the blackness of the tunnel. I advanced so close upon it that I wondered at its keeping the sleeve across its eyes. I ran right up at it, and had my hand stretched out to pull the sleeve away, when it was gone."

"Into the tunnel?" said I.

"No. I ran on into the tunnel, five hundred yards. I stopped, and held my lamp above my head, and saw the figures of the measured distance, and saw the wet stains stealing down the walls and trickling through the arch. I ran out again faster than I had run in (for I had a mortal abhorrence② of the place upon me), and I looked all round the

---

① For God's sake:看在上帝分上
② abhorrence: a deep feeling of hatred towards something;厌恶;憎恨

red light with my own red light, and I went up the iron ladder to the gallery atop of it, and I came down again, and ran back here. I telegraphed both ways, 'An alarm has been given. Is anything wrong?' The answer came back, both ways, 'All well.'"

Resisting the slow touch of a frozen finger tracing out my spine, I showed him how that this figure must be a deception of his sense of sight; and how that figures, originating in disease of the delicate nerves that minister to the functions of the eye, were known to have often troubled patients, some of whom had become conscious of the nature of their affliction, and had even proved it by experiments upon themselves. "As to an imaginary cry," said I, "do but listen for a moment to the wind in this unnatural valley while we speak so low, and to the wild harp it makes of the telegraph wires."

That was all very well, he returned, after we had sat listening for a while, and he ought to know something of the wind and the wires,—he who so often passed long winter nights there, alone and watching. But he would beg to remark that he had not finished.

I asked his pardon, and he slowly added these words, touching my arm,—"Within six hours after the Appearance, the memorable accident on this Line happened, and within ten hours the dead and wounded were brought along through the tunnel over the spot where the figure had stood."

A disagreeable shudder crept over me, but I did my best against it. It was not to be denied, I rejoined, that this was a remarkable coincidence, calculated deeply to impress his mind. But it was unquestionable that remarkable coincidences did continually occur, and they must be taken into account① in dealing with such a subject. Though to be sure I must admit, I added (for I thought I saw that he was going to bring the objection to bear upon me), men of common sense did not allow much for coincidences in making the ordinary calculations of life.

He again begged to remark that he had not finished.

I again begged his pardon for being betrayed into interruptions.

"This," he said, again laying his hand upon my arm, and glancing over his shoulder with hollow eyes, "was just a year ago. Six or seven months passed, and I had recovered from the surprise and shock, when one morning, as the day was breaking, I, standing at the door, looked towards the red light, and saw the spectre again." He stopped, with a fixed look at me.

"Did it cry out?"

"No. It was silent."

"Did it wave its arm?"

"No. It leaned against the shaft of the light, with both hands before the face. Like this."

---

① taken into account: consider; 考虑

Chapter Ten

Once more I followed his action with my eyes. It was an action of mourning. I have seen such an attitude in stone figures on tombs.

"Did you go up to it?"

"I came in and sat down, partly to collect my thoughts, partly because it had turned me faint. When I went to the door again, daylight was above me, and the ghost was gone."

"But nothing followed? Nothing came of this?"

He touched me on the arm with his forefinger twice or thrice giving a ghastly nod each time:

"That very day, as a train came out of the tunnel, I noticed, at a carriage window on my side, what looked like a confusion of hands and heads, and something waved. I saw it just in time to signal the driver, stop! He shut off, and put his brake on, but the train drifted past here a hundred and fifty yards or more. I ran after it, and, as I went along, heard terrible screams and cries. A beautiful young lady had died instantaneously in one of the compartments, and was brought in here, and laid down on this floor between us."

Involuntarily I pushed my chair back, as I looked from the boards at which he pointed to himself.

"True, sir. True. Precisely as it happened, so I tell it you."

I could think of nothing to say, to any purpose, and my mouth was very dry. The wind and the wires took up the story with a long lamenting wail.

He resumed①. "Now, sir, mark this, and judge how my mind is troubled. The spectre came back a week ago. Ever since, it has been there, now and again, by fits and starts②."

"At the light?"

"At the Danger-light."

"What does it seem to do?"

He repeated, if possible with increased passion and vehemence, that former gesticulation of, "For God's sake, clear the way!"

Then he went on. "I have no peace or rest for it. It calls to me, for many minutes together, in an agonised manner, 'Below there! Look out! Look out!' It stands waving to me. It rings my little bell—"

I caught at that. "Did it ring your bell yesterday evening when I was here, and you went to the door?"

"Twice."

"Why, see," said I, "how your imagination misleads you. My eyes were on the bell, and my ears were open to the bell, and if I am a living man, it did NOT ring at those

---

① resume: start doing something again, 重新开始做, 恢复
② By (/in) fits and starts: keeps starting and stopping again; 一阵一阵地; 忽冷忽热; 忽断忽续

times. No, nor at any other time, except when it was rung in the natural course of physical things by the station communicating with you."

He shook his head. "I have never made a mistake as to that yet, sir. I have never confused the spectre's ring with the man's. The ghost's ring is a strange vibration in the bell that it derives from nothing else, and I have not asserted that the bell stirs to the eye. I don't wonder that you failed to hear it. But I heard it."

"And did the spectre seem to be there, when you looked out?"

"It WAS there."

"Both times?"

He repeated firmly: "Both times."

"Will you come to the door with me, and look for it now?"

He bit his under lip as though he were somewhat unwilling, but arose. I opened the door, and stood on the step, while he stood in the doorway. There was the Danger-light. There was the dismal mouth of the tunnel. There were the high, wet stone walls of the cutting. There were the stars above them.

"Do you see it?" I asked him, taking particular note of his face. His eyes were prominent and strained, but not very much more so, perhaps, than my own had been when I had directed them earnestly towards the same spot.

"No," he answered. "It is not there."

"Agreed," said I.

We went in again, shut the door, and resumed our seats. I was thinking how best to improve this advantage, if it might be called one, when he took up the conversation in such a matter-of-course① way, so assuming that there could be no serious question of fact between us, that I felt myself placed in the weakest of positions.

"By this time you will fully understand, sir," he said, "that what troubles me so dreadfully is the question, what does the spectre mean?"

I was not sure, I told him, that I did fully understand.

"What is its warning against?" he said, ruminating②, with his eyes on the fire, and only by times turning them on me. "What is the danger? Where is the danger? There is danger overhanging somewhere on the Line. Some dreadful calamity will happen. It is not to be doubted this third time, after what has gone before. But surely this is a cruel haunting of me. What can I do?"

He pulled out his handkerchief, and wiped the drops from his heated forehead.

"If I telegraph Danger, on either side of me, or on both, I can give no reason for it," he went on, wiping the palms of his hands. "I should get into trouble, and do no good. They would think I was mad. This is the way it would work,—Message: 'Danger!

---

① matter-of-course: 当然的,确定的
② ruminate: to think carefully and deeply about something,沉思,反复考虑

Take care!' Answer: 'What Danger? Where?' Message: 'Don't know. But, for God's sake, take care!' They would displace me. What else could they do?"

His pain of mind was most pitiable to see. It was the mental torture of a conscientious man, oppressed beyond endurance by an unintelligible responsibility involving life.

"When it first stood under the Danger-light," he went on, putting his dark hair back from his head, and drawing his hands outward across and across his temples in an extremity of feverish distress, "why not tell me where that accident was to happen,—if it must happen? Why not tell me how it could be averted,—if it could have been averted? When on its second coming it hid its face, why not tell me, instead, 'She is going to die. Let them keep her at home'? If it came, on those two occasions, only to show me that its warnings were true, and so to prepare me for the third, why not warn me plainly now? And I, Lord help me! A mere poor signal-man on this solitary station! Why not go to somebody with credit to be believed, and power to act?"

When I saw him in this state, I saw that for the poor man's sake, as well as for the public safety, what I had to do for the time was to compose his mind. Therefore, setting aside all question of reality or unreality between us, I represented to him that whoever thoroughly discharged his duty must do well, and that at least it was his comfort that he understood his duty, though he did not understand these confounding appearances. In this effort I succeeded far better than in the attempt to reason him out① of his conviction. He became calm; the occupations incidental to his post as the night advanced began to make larger demands on his attention: and I left him at two in the morning. I had offered to stay through the night, but he would not hear of it.

That I more than once looked back at the red light as I ascended the pathway, that I did not like the red light, and that I should have slept but poorly if my bed had been under it, I see no reason to conceal. Nor did I like the two sequences of the accident and the dead girl. I see no reason to conceal that either.

But what ran most in my thoughts was the consideration how ought I to act, having become the recipient of this disclosure? I had proved the man to be intelligent, vigilant, painstaking, and exact; but how long might he remain so, in his state of mind? Though in a subordinate position, still he held a most important trust, and would I (for instance) like to stake my own life on the chances of his continuing to execute it with precision?

Unable to overcome a feeling that there would be something treacherous② in my communicating what he had told me to his superiors in the Company, without first being plain with himself and proposing a middle course to him, I ultimately resolved to offer to accompany him (otherwise keeping his secret for the present) to the wisest medical

---

① reason out of: 以理说服，使其放弃
② treacherous: not loyal; 不忠的，背信弃义的

practitioner we could hear of in those parts, and to take his opinion. A change in his time of duty would come round next night, he had apprised me, and he would be off an hour or two after sunrise, and on again soon after sunset. I had appointed to return accordingly.

Next evening was a lovely evening, and I walked out early to enjoy it. The sun was not yet quite down when I traversed the field-path near the top of the deep cutting. I would extend my walk for an hour, I said to myself, half an hour on and half an hour back, and it would then be time to go to my signal-man's box.

Before pursuing my stroll, I stepped to the brink, and mechanically looked down, from the point from which I had first seen him. I cannot describe the thrill that seized upon me, when, close at the mouth of the tunnel, I saw the appearance of a man, with his left sleeve across his eyes, passionately waving his right arm.

The nameless horror that oppressed me passed in a moment, for in a moment I saw that this appearance of a man was a man indeed, and that there was a little group of other men, standing at a short distance, to whom he seemed to be rehearsing the gesture he made. The Danger-light was not yet lighted. Against its shaft, a little low hut, entirely new to me, had been made of some wooden supports and tarpaulin. It looked no bigger than a bed.

With an irresistible sense that something was wrong,—with a flashing self-reproachful fear that fatal mischief had come of my leaving the man there, and causing no one to be sent to overlook or correct what he did,—I descended the notched path with all the speed I could make.

"What is the matter?" I asked the men.

"Signal-man killed this morning, sir."

"Not the man belonging to that box?"

"Yes, sir."

"Not the man I know?"

"You will recognise him, sir, if you knew him," said the man who spoke for the others, solemnly uncovering his own head, and raising an end of the tarpaulin, "for his face is quite composed①."

"O, how did this happen, how did this happen?" I asked, turning from one to another as the hut closed in again.

"He was cut down by an engine, sir. No man in England knew his work better. But somehow he was not clear of the outer rail. It was just at broad day. He had struck the light, and had the lamp in his hand. As the engine came out of the tunnel, his back was towards her, and she cut him down. That man drove her, and was showing how it happened. Show the gentleman, Tom."

---

① composed: calm; 沉着的

The man, who wore a rough dark dress, stepped back to his former place at the mouth of the tunnel.

"Coming round the curve in the tunnel, sir," he said, "I saw him at the end, like as if I saw him down a perspective-glass. There was no time to check speed, and I knew him to be very careful. As he didn't seem to take heed of the whistle, I shut it off when we were running down upon him, and called to him as loud as I could call."

"What did you say?"

"I said, 'Below there! Look out! Look out! For God's sake, clear the way!'"

I started.

"Ah! it was a dreadful time, sir. I never left off calling to him. I put this arm before my eyes not to see, and I waved this arm to the last; but it was no use."

Without prolonging the narrative to dwell on any one of its curious circumstances more than on any other, I may, in closing it, point out the coincidence that the warning of the Engine-Driver included, not only the words which the unfortunate Signal-man had repeated to me as haunting him, but also the words which I myself—not he—had attached, and that only in my own mind, to the gesticulation① he had imitated.

❋ Questions for Discussion

1. In the story, the empty countryside and the steep zigzag pathway separates the narrator from the signal-man at the beginning of the story. Neither man is given a name. Each wonders whether the other is a ghost rather than a human being. What does the author want to imply?
2. Is there any supernatural element in the story? If yes, what is the function of the supernatural?
3. In the story, the signal-man and the narrator refer to each other as "sir". What tone does the author employ in writing this way?

❋ Links

1. http://www.helsinki.fi/kasv/nokol/dichens.html
   关于查尔斯·狄更斯生平及创作的详细介绍。
2. https://en.wikipedia.org/wiki/The_Signal-Man
   关于查尔斯·狄更斯的小说《信号员》的细读资料。

---

① gesticulation: movements with arms or hands while speaking; 做手势, 示意动作

Chapter Eleven

Part A

The Monkey's Paw

By W. W. Jacobs

William Wymark Jacobs (W. W. Jacobs) (1863—1943) was an English author of short stories and novels.

Born as the eldest son of a large and poor family, Jacobs saw a lot about the tramp steamers and their crew because his father's job was a wharf manager. His mother died when he was very young. In 1879, he became a clerk in the civil service and then worked in a bank. From about 1885, he began writing. By 1899, he resigned from his civil service post and devoted entirely to writing.

Jacobs is now remembered for his macabre tale "The Monkey's Paw" (1902), which has been filmed and adapted for the stage numerous times, and several other ghost stories, including "The Toll House" (1909) and "Jerry Bundler" (1901). However, the majority of his output was humoros in tone. His favorite subjects were marine life: "... men who go down to the sea in ships of moderate tonnage." Reviewing his first collection of stories, *Many Cargoes*, which achieved great popular success on its publication in 1896, Michael Sadleir described Jacobs' fiction thus: "... he wrote stories of three kinds: describing the misadventures of sailor-men ashore; celebrating the artful dodger of a slow-witted village; and tales of the macabre."

Lead-in Questions

1. In "The Monkey's Paw", three wishes are granted to the owner of the monkey's paw. If you were granted three wishes, what wishes will you choose and why?
2. If you were in Mr. and Mrs. White's position, would you wish for Herbert to come back to life? Why or why not?

Questions about the Author and the Story

1. Although best remembered for his macabre tales "The Monkey's Paw", the majority of Jacobs' output was _____ in tone.
   A. humoros   B. sad   C. confident   D. ironical

2. What type of story is "The Monkey's Paw"?
   A. Mystery.   B. Romance.   C. Non-fiction.   D. Supernatural.

3. Jacobs drew from a number of widely known literary sources in writing "The Monkey's Paw" to make the story both familiar and unsettling. His most recognizable influence was the tale of "Aladdin and the Magic Lamp", one of the many famous tales in _____.
   A. *Iliad*
   B. Greek mythology
   C. The Book of *One Thousand and One Nights*, or simply *Arabian Nights*
   D. *Grimm's Fairy Tales*

4. Who is the owner of the monkey's paw?
   A. Bob Pretty.   B. Sergeant-Major Morris.
   C. Herbert White.   D. Captain Rogers.

5. Why does Morris grow pale after he makes his third wish on the monkey's paw?
   A. He is ashamed of believing in the monkey's paw.
   B. He is remembering the horrible effects of his wishes.
   C. The idea of magic frightens him.
   D. He is trying not to laugh as he fools his friends.

*W*ithout, the night was cold and wet, but in the small parlour of Laburnum villa the blinds① were drawn and the fire burned brightly. Father and son were at chess; the former, who possessed ideas about the game involving radical chances, putting his king into such sharp and unnecessary perils that it even provoked comment from the white-haired old lady knitting placidly by the fire.

"Hark at the wind," said Mr. White, who, having seen a fatal mistake after it was too late, was amiably desirous of preventing his son from seeing it.

"I'm listening," said the latter grimly surveying the board as he stretched out his hand. "Check."

"I should hardly think that he's come tonight," said his father, with his hand poised over the board.

"Mate," replied the son.

---

① blinds: 窗帘

"That's the worst of living so far out," balled Mr. White with sudden and unlooked—for violence; "Of all the beastly, slushy, out of the way places to live in, this is the worst. Path's a bog, and the road's a torrent. I don't know what people are thinking about. I suppose because only two houses in the road are let, they think it doesn't matter."

"Never mind, dear," said his wife soothingly; "perhaps you'll win the next one."

Mr. White looked up sharply, just in time to intercept a knowing glance between mother and son. The words died away on his lips, and he hid a guilty grin in his thin grey beard.

"There he is," said Herbert White as the gate banged to loudly and heavy footsteps came toward the door.

The old man rose with hospitable haste and opening the door, was heard condoling with the new arrival. The new arrival also condoled with himself, so that Mrs. White said, "Tut, tut!" and coughed gently as her husband entered the room followed by a tall, burly man, beady of eye and rubicund of visage.

"Sergeant-Major① Morris," he said, introducing him.

The Sergeant-Major took hands and taking the proffered seat by the fire, watched contentedly as his host got out whiskey and tumblers and stood a small copper kettle on the fire.

At the third glass his eyes got brighter, and he began to talk, the little family circle regarding with eager interest this visitor from distant parts, as he squared his broad shoulders in the chair and spoke of wild scenes and doughty deeds; of wars and plagues and strange peoples.

"Twenty-one years of it," said Mr. White, nodding at his wife and son. "When he went away he was a slip of a youth in the warehouse. Now look at him."

"He don't look to have taken much harm." said Mrs. White politely.

"I'd like to go to India myself," said the old man, "just to look around a bit, you know."

"Better where you are," said the Sergeant-Major, shaking his head. He put down the empty glass and sighing softly, shook it again.

"I should like to see those old temples and fakirs and jugglers," said the old man. "What was that that you started telling me the other day about a monkey's paw or something, Morris?"

"Nothing." said the soldier hastily. "Leastways, nothing worth hearing."

"Monkey's paw?" said Mrs. White curiously.

"Well, it's just a bit of what you might call magic, perhaps." said the Sergeant-Major off-handedly.

---

① Sergeant—Major: 少校

His three listeners leaned forward eagerly. The visitor absent—mindedly put his empty glass to his lips and then set it down again. His host filled it for him again.

"To look at," said the Sergeant-Major, fumbling in his pocket, "it's just an ordinary little paw, dried to a mummy."

He took something out of his pocket and proffered it. Mrs. White drew back with a grimace, but her son, taking it, examined it curiously.

"And what is there special about it?" inquired Mr. White as he took it from his son, and having examined it, placed it upon the table.

"It had a spell① put on it by an old Fakir," said the Sergeant-Major, "a very holy man. He wanted to show that fate ruled people's lives, and that those who interfered with it did so to their sorrow. He put a spell on it so that three separate men could each have three wishes from it."

His manners were so impressive that his hearers were conscious that their light laughter had jarred somewhat.

"Well, why don't you have three, sir?" said Herbert White cleverly.

The soldier regarded him the way that middle age is wont to regard presumptuous youth. "I have," he said quietly, and his blotchy face whitened.

"And did you really have the three wishes granted?" asked Mrs. White.

"I did," said the Sergeant-Major, and his glass tapped against his strong teeth.

"And has anybody else wished?" persisted the old lady.

"The first man had his three wishes. Yes," was the reply, "I don't know what the first two were, but the third was for death. That's how I got the paw."

His tones were so grave that a hush fell upon the group.

"If you've had your three wishes it's no good to you now then Morris," said the old man at last. "What do you keep it for?"

The soldier shook his head. "Fancy I suppose," he said slowly. "I did have some idea of selling it, but I don't think I will. It has caused me enough mischief already. Besides, people won't buy. They think it's a fairy tale, some of them; and those who do think anything of it want to try it first and pay me afterward."

"If you could have another three wishes," said the old man, eyeing him keenly, "would you have them?"

"I don't know," said the other. "I don't know."

He took the paw, and dangling it between his forefinger and thumb, suddenly threw it upon the fire. White, with a slight cry, stooped down and snatched it off.

"Better let it burn," said the soldier solemnly.

"If you don't want it Morris," said the other, "give it to me."

"I won't." said his friend doggedly. "I threw it on the fire. If you keep it, don't

---

① put/cast a spell on somebody: do a piece of magic to change something; 对某人施展魔法

blame me for what happens. Pitch it on the fire like a sensible man."

The other shook his head and examined his possession closely. "How do you do it?" He inquired.

"Hold it up in your right hand, and wish aloud," said the Sergeant-Major, "But I warn you of the consequences."

"Sounds like the 'Arabian Nights①'," said Mrs. White, as she rose and began to set the supper. "Don't you think you might wish for four pairs of hands for me."

Her husband drew the talisman from his pocket, and all three burst into laughter as the Seargent-Major, with a look of alarm on his face, caught him by the arm.

"If you must wish," he said gruffly, "Wish for something sensible."

Mr. White dropped it back in his pocket, and placing chairs, motioned his friend to the table. In the business of supper the talisman was partly forgotten, and afterward the three sat listening in an enthralled fashion to a second installment of the soldier's adventures in India.

"If the tale about the monkey's paw is not more truthful than those he has been telling us," said Herbert, as the door closed behind their guest, just in time to catch the last train, "we shan't make much out of it."

"Did you give anything for it, father?" inquired Mrs. White, regarding her husband closely.

"A trifle," said he, coloring slightly, "He didn't want it, but I made him take it. And he pressed me again to throw it away."

"Likely," said Herbert, with pretended horror. "Why, we're going to be rich, and famous, and happy. Wish to be an emperor, father, to begin with; then you can't be henpecked."

He darted around the table, pursued by the maligned Mrs. White armed with an antimacassar②.

Mr. White took the paw from his pocket and eyed it dubiously. "I don't know what to wish for, and that's a fact," he said slowly. "It seems to me I've got all I want."

"If you only cleared the house, you'd be quite happy, wouldn't you!" said Herbert, with his hand on his shoulder. "Well, wish for two hundred pounds, then; that'll just do it."

His father, smiling shamefacedly at his own credulity, held up the talisman, as his son, with a solemn face, somewhat marred by a wink at his mother, sat down and struck a few impressive chords.

"I wish for two hundred pounds," said the old man distinctly.

A fine crash from the piano greeted his words, interrupted by a shuddering cry from

---

① Arabian Nights:《天方夜谭》又译《一千零一夜》

② antimacassar: a piece of ornamented cloth that protects the back of chair from hair oils; 椅子罩子

Chapter Eleven

the old man. His wife and son ran toward him.

"It moved," he cried, with a glance of disgust at the object as it lay on the floor. "As I wished, it twisted in my hand like a snake."

"Well, I don't see the money," said his son, as he picked it up and placed it on the table, "and I bet I never shall."

"It must have been your fancy, father," said his wife, regarding him anxiously.

He shook his head. "Never mind, though; there's no harm done, but it gave me a shock all the same."

They sat down by the fire again while the two men finished their pipes. Outside, the wind was higher than ever, the old man started nervously at the sound of a door banging upstairs. A silence unusual and depressing settled on all three, which lasted until the old couple rose to retire for the rest of the night.

"I expect you'll find the cash tied up in a big bag in the middle of your bed," said Herbert, as he bade them good night, "and something horrible squatting on top of your wardrobe watching you as you pocket your ill-gotten gains."

He sat alone in the darkness, gazing at the dying fire, and seeing faces in it. The last was so horrible and so simian that he gazed at it in amazement. It got so vivid that, with a little uneasy laugh, he felt on the table for a glass containing a little water to throw over it. His hand grasped the monkey's paw, and with a little shiver he wiped his hand on his coat and went up to bed.

In the brightness of the wintry sun next morning as it streamed over the breakfast table he laughed at his fears. There was an air of prosaic wholesomeness about the room which it had lacked on the previous night, and the dirty, shriveled little paw was pitched on the side-board with a carelessness which betokened no great belief in its virtues.

"I suppose all old soldiers are the same," said Mrs. White. "The idea of our listening to such nonsense! How could wishes be granted in these days? And if they could, how could two hundred pounds hurt you, father?"

"Might drop on his head from the sky," said the frivolous Herbert.

"Morris said the things happened so naturally," said his father, "that you might if you so wished attribute it to coincidence."

"Well don't break into the money before I come back," said Herbert as he rose from the table. "I'm afraid it'll turn you into a mean, avaricious man, and we shall have to disown you."

His mother laughed, and following him to the door, watched him down the road; and returning to the breakfast table, was very happy at the expense of her husband's credulity. All of which did not prevent her from scurrying to the door at the postman's knock, nor prevent her from referring somewhat shortly to retired Sergeant-Majors of bibulous habits when she found that the post brought a tailor's bill.

"Herbert will have some more of his funny remarks, I expect, when he comes home," she said as they sat at dinner.

"I dare say," said Mr. White, pouring himself out some beer; "but for all that①, the thing moved in my hand; that I'll swear to."

"You thought it did," said the old lady soothingly.

"I say it did," replied the other. "There was no thought about it; I had just—What's the matter?"

His wife made no reply. She was watching the mysterious movements of a man outside, who, peering in an undecided fashion at the house, appeared to be trying to make up his mind to enter. In mental connexion with the two hundred pounds, she noticed that the stranger was well dressed, and wore a silk hat of glossy newness. Three times he paused at the gate, and then walked on again. The fourth time he stood with his hand upon it, and then with sudden resolution flung it open and walked up the path. Mrs. White at the same moment placed her hands behind her, and hurriedly unfastening the strings of her apron, put that useful article of apparel beneath the cushion of her chair.

She brought the stranger, who seemed ill at ease, into the room. He gazed at her furtively, and listened in a preoccupied fashion as the old lady apologized for the appearance of the room, and her husband's coat, a garment which he usually reserved for the garden. She then waited as patiently as her sex would permit for him to broach his business, but he was at first strangely silent.

"I—was asked to call," he said at last, and stooped and picked a piece of cotton from his trousers. "I come from 'Maw and Meggins.'"

The old lady started. "Is anything the matter?" she asked breathlessly. "Has anything happened to Herbert? What is it? What is it?"

Her husband interposed. "There there mother," he said hastily. "Sit down, and don't jump to conclusions②. You've not brought bad news, I'm sure sir," and eyed the other wistfully.

"I'm sorry—"began the visitor.

"Is he hurt?" demanded the mother wildly.

The visitor bowed in assent. "Badly hurt," he said quietly, "but he is not in any pain."

"Oh thank God!" said the old woman, clasping her hands. "Thank God for that! Thank—"

She broke off as the sinister meaning of the assurance dawned on her and she saw the awful confirmation of her fears in the others averted face. She caught her breath, and turning to her slower-witted husband, laid her trembling hand on his. There was a

---

① but for all that:但即便如此

② jump to conclusions:草率下结论

long silence.

"He was caught in the machinery," said the visitor at length in a low voice.

"Caught in the machinery," repeated Mr. White, in a dazed fashion, "yes."

He sat staring out the window, and taking his wife's hand between his own, pressed it as he had been wont to do in their old courting days nearly forty years before.

"He was the only one left to us," he said, turning gently to the visitor. "It is hard."

The other coughed, and rising, walked slowly to the window. "The firm wishes me to convey their sincere sympathy with you in your great loss," he said, without looking round. "I beg that you will understand I am only their servant and merely obeying orders."

There was no reply; the old woman's face was white, her eyes staring, and her breath inaudible; on the husband's face was a look such as his friend the Sergeant might have carried into his first action.

"I was to say that Maw and Meggins disclaim all responsibility," continued the other. "They admit no liability at all, but in consideration of your son's services, they wish to present you with a certain sum as compensation."

Mr. White dropped his wife's hand, and rising to his feet, gazed with a look of horror at his visitor. His dry lips shaped the words, "How much?"

"Two hundred pounds," was the answer.

Unconscious of his wife's shriek, the old man smiled faintly, put out his hands like a sightless man, and dropped, a senseless heap, to the floor.

In the huge new cemetery, some① two miles distant, the old people buried their dead, and came back to the house steeped in shadows and silence. It was all over so quickly that at first they could hardly realize it, and remained in a state of expectation as though of something else to happen—something else which was to lighten this load, too heavy for old hearts to bear.

But the days passed, and expectations gave way to resignation—the hopeless resignation of the old, sometimes mis—called apathy. Sometimes they hardly exchanged a word, for now they had nothing to talk about, and their days were long to weariness.

It was about a week after that the old man, waking suddenly in the night, stretched out his hand and found himself alone. The room was in darkness, and the sound of subdued weeping came from the window. He raised himself in bed and listened.

"Come back," he said tenderly. "You will be cold."

"It is colder for my son," said the old woman, and wept afresh.

The sounds of her sobs died away on his ears. The bed was warm, and his eyes heavy with sleep. He dozed fitfully, and then slept until a sudden wild cry from his wife awoke him with a start.

---

① some: about;大约

"THE PAW!" she cried wildly. "THE MONKEY'S PAW!"

He started up in alarm. "Where? Where is it? What's the matter?"

She came stumbling across the room toward him. "I want it," she said quietly. "You've not destroyed it?"

"It's in the parlour, on the bracket," he replied, marveling. "Why?"

She cried and laughed together, and bending over, kissed his cheek.

"I only just thought of it," she said hysterically. "Why didn't I think of it before? Why didn't you think of it?"

"Think of what?" he questioned.

"The other two wishes," she replied rapidly. "We've only had one."

"Was not that enough?" he demanded fiercely.

"No," she cried triumphantly; "We'll have one more. Go down and get it quickly, and wish our boy alive again."

The man sat in bed and flung the bedclothes from his quaking limbs. "Good God, you are mad!" he cried aghast. "Get it," she panted; "get it quickly, and wish—Oh my boy, my boy!"

Her husband struck a match and lit the candle. "Get back to bed," he said unsteadily. "You don't know what you are saying."

"We had the first wish granted," said the old woman, feverishly; "why not the second?"

"A coincidence," stammered the old man.

"Go get it and wish," cried his wife, quivering with excitement.

The old man turned and regarded her, and his voice shook. "He has been dead ten days, and besides he—I would not tell you else, but—I could only recognize him by his clothing. If he was too terrible for you to see then, how now?"

"Bring him back," cried the old woman, and dragged him towards the door. "Do you think I fear the child I have nursed?"

He went down in the darkness, and felt his way to the parlour, and then to the mantelpiece. The talisman was in its place, and a horrible fear that the unspoken wish might bring his mutilated son before him ere he could escape from the room seized up on him, and he caught his breath as he found that he had lost the direction of the door. His brow cold with sweat, he felt his way round the table, and groped along the wall until he found himself in the small passage with the unwholesome thing in his hand.

Even his wife's face seemed changed as he entered the room. It was white and expectant, and to his fears seemed to have an unnatural look upon it. He was afraid of her.

"WISH!" she cried in a strong voice.

"It is foolish and wicked," he faltered.

"WISH!" repeated his wife.

Chapter Eleven

He raised his hand. "I wish my son alive again."

The talisman fell to the floor, and he regarded it fearfully. Then he sank trembling into a chair as the old woman, with burning eyes, walked to the window and raised the blind.

He sat until he was chilled with the cold, glancing occasionally at the figure of the old woman peering through the window. The candle-end, which had burned below the rim of the china candlestick, was throwing pulsating shadows on the ceiling and walls, until with a flicker larger than the rest, it expired. The old man, with an unspeakable sense of relief at the failure of the talisman, crept back to his bed, and a minute afterward the old woman came silently and apathetically beside him.

Neither spoke, but sat silently listening to the ticking of the clock. A stair creaked, and a squeaky mouse scurried noisily through the wall. The darkness was oppressive, and after lying for some time screwing up his courage, he took the box of matches, and striking one, went downstairs for a candle.

At the foot of the stairs the match went out, and he paused to strike another; and at the same moment a knock came so quiet and stealthy as to be scarcely audible, sounded on the front door.

The matches fell from his hand and spilled in the passage. He stood motionless, his breath suspended until the knock was repeated. Then he turned and fled swiftly back to his room, and closed the door behind him. A third knock sounded through the house.

"WHAT'S THAT?" cried the old woman, starting up.

"A rat," said the old man in shaking tones—"a rat. It passed me on the stairs."

His wife sat up in bed listening. A loud knock resounded through the house.

"It's Herbert!"

She ran to the door, but her husband was before her, and catching her by the arm, held her tightly.

"What are you going to do?" he whispered hoarsely.

"It's my boy; it's Herbert!" she cried, struggling mechanically. "I forgot it was two miles away. What are you holding me for? Let go. I must open the door."

"For God's sake don't let it in," cried the old man, trembling.

"You're afraid of your own son," she cried struggling. "Let me go. I'm coming, Herbert; I'm coming."

There was another knock, and another. The old woman with a sudden wrench broke free and ran from the room. Her husband followed to the landing, and called after her appealingly as she hurried downstairs. He heard the chain rattle back and the bolt drawn slowly and stiffly from the socket. Then the old woman's voice, strained and panting.

"The bolt," she cried loudly. "Come down. I can't reach it."

But her husband was on his hands and knees groping wildly on the floor in search of the paw. If only he could find it before the thing outside got in. A perfect fusillade of knocks reverberated through the house, and he heard the scraping of a chair as his wife put it down in the passage against the door. He heard the creaking of the bolt as it came slowly back, and at the same moment he found the monkey's paw, and frantically[1] breathed his third and last wish.

The knocking ceased suddenly, although the echoes of it were still in the house. He heard the chair drawn back, and the door opened. A cold wind rushed up the staircase, and a long loud wail of disappointment and misery from his wife gave him the courage to run down to her side, and then to the gate beyond. The street lamp flickering opposite shone on a quiet and deserted road.

 Questions for Discussion

1. "The Monkey's Paw" is usually considered a supernatural fiction? Do you agree with this classification? Why or why not?
2. Why does the story begin with the father and son's playing chess? Does the father's strategy at the chess game reveal anything about his personality? If so, what is it?
3. What do you think happens at the end of the story? Why does Mr. White beg his wife not to let "it" into the house? What is the meaning of his words? What is he afraid of? Who or what was outside the house?
4. What makes Jacobs' writing style unique?
5. How does Jacobs set the tone of the story? How does he build the suspense?

 Links

1. https://en.wikipedia.org/wiki/W._W._Jacobs
   关于雅各布斯生平及创作的详细介绍。
2. http://www.sparknotes.com/short-stories/the-monkeys-paw/summary.html
   关于雅各布斯的小说《猴爪》的细读资料。

---

① frantically: in an uncontrolled manner; 疯狂地, 狂热地

Part B

A Cup of Tea

By Katherine Mansfield

Katherine Mansfield (1888—1923) was a prominent New Zealand modernist short story writer who was widely regarded as one of the best short story writers of her period. She was born and brought up in colonial New Zealand. At 19, Mansfield left New Zealand and settled in the United Kingdom, where she became a friend of modernist writers D. H. Lawrence and Virginia Woolf. At 29, she was diagnosed with extrapulmonary tuberculosis, which led to her death at the age of 34.

Her first printed stories appeared in the *High School Reporter* and the *Wellington Girls' High School* magazine in 1898 and 1899. Mansfield's stories were the first of significance in English to be written without a conventional plot. Supplanting the strictly structured plots of her predecessors in the genre, Mansfield concentrated on one moment, a crisis or a turning point, rather than on a sequence of events. The plot is secondary to mood and characters. Mansfield also proved ahead of her time in her adoration of Russian playwright and short story writer Anton Chekhov, and incorporated some of his themes and techniques into her writing. Themes, too, are universal: human isolation, the questioning of traditional roles of men and women in society, the conflict between love and disillusionment, idealism and reality, beauty and ugliness, joy and suffering and the inevitability of these paradoxes.

Lead-in Questions

1. What would you respond if you met a poor but beautiful girl who asks you for some money in the street?
2. Can you list some other famous short stories written by Mansfield?

Questions about the Author and the Story

1. Who influenced Katherine Mansfield most in writing?
   A. Rudyard Kipling.　　　　　　B. H. G. Wells.
   C. Anton Chekhov.　　　　　　D. Edgar Allan Poe.
2. Which is NOT the main feature of Katherine Mansfield's short stories?
   A. Having a conventional plot.　　B. Concentrating on one moment.

C. Concentrating on mood. D. Describing detailed psychology.
3. Which word CANNOT be used to describe Rosemary Fell in this story?
   A. Wealthy.   B. Dominant.   C. Kind-hearted.   D. Hypocritical.
4. Rosemary Fell decides to take the girl to home because _____.
   A. she is a kind woman
   B. the girl begs her to do so
   C. she is sympathetic to the girl
   D. she wants to experience something adventurous just like written in books
5. What is the author's attitude in this story?
   A. Indifferent.   B. Satiric.   C. Sympathetic.   D. Complimentary.

Rosemary Fell was not exactly beautiful. No, you couldn't have called her beautiful. Pretty? Well, if you took her to pieces ... But why be so cruel as to take anyone to pieces? She was young, brilliant, extremely modern, exquisitely well dressed, amazingly well read in the newest of the new books, and her parties were the most delicious mixture of the really important people and ... artists—quaint creatures, discoveries of hers, some of them too terrifying for words, but others quite presentable and amusing.

Rosemary had been married two years. She had a duck of a boy. No, not Peter—Michael. And her husband absolutely adored her. They were rich, really rich, not just comfortably well off, which is odious and stuffy and sounds like one's grandparents. But if Rosemary wanted to shop she would go to Paris as you and I would go to Bond Street. If she wanted to buy flowers, the car pulled up at that perfect shop in Regent Street, and Rosemary inside the shop just gazed in her dazzled, rather exotic way, and said: "I want those and those and those. Give me four bunches of those. And that jar of roses. Yes, I'll have all the roses in the jar. No, no lilac. I hate lilac. It's got no shape." The attendant bowed and put the lilac out of sight, as though this was only too true; lilac was dreadfully shapeless. "Give me those stumpy little tulips. Those red and white ones." And she was followed to the car by a thin shopgirl staggering under an immense white paper armful that looked like a baby in long clothes ...

One winter afternoon she had been buying something in a little antique shop in Curzon Street. It was a shop she liked. For one thing, one usually had it to oneself. And then the man who kept it was ridiculously fond of serving her. He beamed whenever she came in. He clasped his hands; he was so gratified he could scarcely speak. Flattery, of course. All the same, there was something ...

"You see, madam," he would explain in his low respectful tones, "I love my things. I would rather not part with them than sell them to someone who does not appreciate

Chapter Eleven

them, who has not that fine feeling which is so rare ... " And, breathing deeply he unrolled a tiny square of blue velvet and pressed it on the glass counter with his pale finger-tips.

Today it was a little box. He had been keeping it for her. He had shown it to nobody as yet. An exquisite little enamel box with a glaze so fine it looked as though it had been baked in cream. On the lid a minute creature stood under a flowery tree, and a more minute creature still had her arms round his neck. Her hat, really no bigger than a geranium petal, hung from a branch; it had green ribbons. And there was a pink cloud like a watchful cherub floating above their heads. Rosemary took her hands out of her long gloves. She always took off her gloves to examine such things. Yes, she liked it very much. She loved it; it was a great duck. She must have it. And, turning the creamy box, opening and shutting it, she couldn't help noticing how charming her hands were against the blue velvet. The shopman, in some dim cavern of his mind, may have dared to think so too. For he took a pencil, leant over the counter, and his pale bloodless fingers crept timidly towards those rosy, flashing ones, as he murmured gently: "If I may venture to point out to madam, the flowers on the little lady's bodice."

"Charming!" Rosemary admired the flowers. But what was the price? For a moment the shopman did not seem to hear. Then a murmur reached her. "Twenty-eight guineas, madam."

"Twenty-eight guineas." Rosemary gave no sign. She laid the little box down; she buttoned her gloves again. Twenty-eight guineas. Even if one is rich ... She looked vague. She stared at a plump tea-kettle like a plump hen above the shopman's head, and her voice was dreamy as she answered: "Well, keep it for me—will you? I'll ... "

But the shopman had already bowed as though keeping it for her was all any human being could ask. He would be willing, of course, to keep it for her forever.

The discreet door shut with a click. She was outside on the step, gazing at the winter afternoon. Rain was falling, and with the rain it seemed the dark came too, spinning down like ashes. There was a cold bitter taste in the air, and the new-lighted lamps looked sad. Sad were the lights in the houses opposite. Dimly they burned as if regretting something. And people hurried by, hidden under their hateful umbrellas. Rosemary felt a strange pang. She pressed her muff against her breast; she wished she had the little box, too, to cling to. Of course, the car was there. She'd only to cross the pavement. But still she waited. There are moments, horrible moments in life, when one emerges from shelter and looks out, and it's awful. One oughtn't to give way to them. One ought to go home and have an extra-special tea. But at the very instant of thinking that, a young girl, thin, dark, shadowy—where had she come from? —was standing at Rosemary's elbow and a voice like a sigh, almost like a sob, breathed: "Madam, may I speak to you a moment?"

"Speak to me?" Rosemary turned. She saw a little battered creature with enormous eyes, someone quite young, no older than herself, who clutched at her coat-collar with reddened hands, and shivered as though she had just come out of the water.

"M-madam," stammered the voice. "Would you let me have the price of a cup of tea?"

"A cup of tea?" There was something simple, sincere in that voice; it wasn't in the least the voice of a beggar. "Then have you no money at all?" asked Rosemary.

"None, madam," came the answer.

"How extraordinary!" Rosemary peered through the dusk, and the girl gazed back at her. How more than extraordinary! And suddenly it seemed to Rosemary such an adventure. It was like something out of a novel by Dostoevsky, this meeting in the dusk. Supposing she took the girl home? Supposing she did do one of those things she was always reading about or seeing on the stage, what would happen? It would be thrilling. And she heard herself saying afterwards to the amazement of her friends: "I simply took her home with me," as she stepped forward and said to that dim person beside her: "Come home to tea with me."

The girl drew back startled. She even stopped shivering for a moment. Rosemary put out a hand and touched her arm. "I mean it," she said, smiling. And she felt how simple and kind her smile was. "Why won't you? Do. Come home with me now in my car and have tea."

"You—you don't mean it, madam," said the girl, and there was pain in her voice.

"But I do," cried Rosemary. "I want you to. To please me. Come along."

The girl put her fingers to her lips and her eyes devoured Rosemary. "You're—you're not taking me to the police station?" she stammered.

"The police station!" Rosemary laughed out. "Why should I be so cruel? No, I only want to make you warm and to hear—anything you care to tell me."

Hungry people are easily led. The footman held the door of the car open, and a moment later they were skimming through the dusk.

"There!" said Rosemary. She had a feeling of triumph as she slipped her hand through the velvet strap. She could have said, "Now I've got you," as she gazed at the little captive she had netted. But of course she meant it kindly. Oh, more than kindly. She was going to prove to this girl that—wonderful things did happen in life, that—fairy godmothers were real, that—rich people had hearts, and that women were sisters. She turned impulsively, saying: "Don't be frightened. After all, why shouldn't you come back with me? We're both women. If I'm the more fortunate, you ought to expect ..."

But happily at that moment, for she didn't know how the sentence was going to end, the car stopped. The bell was rung, the door opened, and with a charming, protecting, almost embracing movement, Rosemary drew the other into the hall. Warmth, softness, light, a sweet scent, all those things so familiar to her she never even thought about them, she watched that other receive. It was fascinating. She was like the

Chapter Eleven

rich little girl in her nursery with all the cupboards to open, all the boxes to unpack.

"Come, come upstairs," said Rosemary, longing to begin to be generous. "Come up to my room." And, besides, she wanted to spare this poor little thing from being stared at by the servants; she decided as they mounted the stairs she would not even ring for Jeanne, but take off her things by herself. The great thing was to be natural!

And "There!" cried Rosemary again, as they reached her beautiful big bedroom with the curtains drawn, the fire leaping on her wonderful lacquer furniture, her gold cushions and the primrose and blue rugs.

The girl stood just inside the door; she seemed dazed. But Rosemary didn't mind that.

"Come and sit down," she cried, dragging her big chair up to the fire, "in this comfy chair. Come and get warm. You look so dreadfully cold."

"I daren't, madam," said the girl, and she edged backwards.

"Oh, please,"—Rosemary ran forward—"you mustn't be frightened, you mustn't, really. Sit down, and when I've taken off my things we shall go into the next room and have tea and be cosy. Why are you afraid?" And gently she half pushed the thin figure into its deep cradle.

But there was no answer. The girl stayed just as she had been put, with her hands by her sides and her mouth slightly open. To be quite sincere, she looked rather stupid. But Rosemary wouldn't acknowledge it. She leant over her, saying: "Won't you take off your hat? Your pretty hair is all wet. And one is so much more comfortable without a hat, isn't one?"

There was a whisper that sounded like "Very good, madam," and the crushed hat was taken off.

"And let me help you off with your coat, too," said Rosemary.

The girl stood up. But she held on to the chair with one hand and let Rosemary pull. It was quite an effort. The other scarcely helped her at all. She seemed to stagger like a child, and the thought came and went through Rosemary's mind, that if people wanted helping they must respond a little, just a little, otherwise it became very difficult indeed. And what was she to do with the coat now? She left it on the floor, and the hat too. She was just going to take a cigarette off the mantelpiece when the girl said quickly, but so lightly and strangely: "I'm very sorry, madam, but I'm going to faint. I shall go off, madam, if I don't have something."

"Good heavens, how thoughtless I am!" Rosemary rushed to the bell.

"Tea! Tea at once! And some brandy immediately!"

The maid was gone again, but the girl almost cried out. "No, I don't want no brandy. I never drink brandy. It's a cup of tea I want, madam." And she burst into tears.

It was a terrible and fascinating moment. Rosemary knelt beside her chair.

"Don't cry, poor little thing," she said. "Don't cry." And she gave the other her lace handkerchief. She really was touched beyond words. She put her arm round those thin, bird-like shoulders.

Now at last the other forgot to be shy, forgot everything except that they were both women, and gasped out: "I can't go on no longer like this. I can't bear it. I can't bear it. I shall do away with myself. I can't bear no more."

"You shan't have to. I'll look after you. Don't cry any more. Don't you see what a good thing it was that you met me? We'll have tea and you'll tell me everything. And I shall arrange something. I promise. Do stop crying. It's so exhausting. Please!"

The other did stop just in time for Rosemary to get up before the tea came. She had the table placed between them. She plied the poor little creature with everything, all the sandwiches, all the bread and butter, and every time her cup was empty she filled it with tea, cream and sugar. People always said sugar was so nourishing. As for herself she didn't eat; she smoked and looked away tactfully so that the other should not be shy.

And really the effect of that slight meal was marvellous. When the tea-table was carried away a new being, a light, frail creature with tangled hair, dark lips, deep, lighted eyes, lay back in the big chair in a kind of sweet languor, looking at the blaze. Rosemary lit a fresh cigarette; it was time to begin.

"And when did you have your last meal?" she asked softly.

But at that moment the door-handle turned.

"Rosemary, may I come in?" It was Philip.

"Of course."

He came in. "Oh, I'm so sorry," he said, and stopped and stared.

"It's quite all right," said Rosemary smiling. "This is my friend, Miss—"

"Smith, madam," said the languid figure, who was strangely still and unafraid.

"Smith," said Rosemary. "We are going to have a little talk."

"Oh, yes," said Philip. "Quite," and his eye caught sight of the coat and hat on the floor. He came over to the fire and turned his back to it. "It's a beastly afternoon," he said curiously, still looking at that listless figure, looking at its hands and boots, and then at Rosemary again.

"Yes, isn't it?" said Rosemary enthusiastically. "Vile."

Philip smiled his charming smile. "As a matter of fact," said he, "I wanted you to come into the library for a moment. Would you? Will Miss Smith excuse us?"

The big eyes were raised to him, but Rosemary answered for her. "Of course she will." And they went out of the room together.

"I say," said Philip, when they were alone. "Explain. Who is she? What does it all mean?"

Rosemary, laughing, leaned against the door and said: "I picked her up in Curzon Street. Really. She's a real pick-up. She asked me for the price of a cup of tea, and I brought her home with me."

"But what on earth are you going to do with her?" cried Philip.

"Be nice to her," said Rosemary quickly. "Be frightfully nice to her. Look after her. I don't know how. We haven't talked yet. But show her—treat her—make her feel—"

"My darling girl," said Philip, "you're quite mad, you know. It simply can't be done."

"I knew you'd say that," retorted Rosemary. "Why not? I want to. Isn't that a reason? And besides, one's always reading about these things. I decided—"

"But," said Philip slowly, and he cut the end of a cigar, "she's so astonishingly pretty."

"Pretty?" Rosemary was so surprised that she blushed. "Do you think so? I—I hadn't thought about it."

"Good Lord!" Philip struck a match. "She's absolutely lovely. Look again, my child. I was bowled over when I came into your room just now. However ... I think you're making a ghastly mistake. Sorry, darling, if I'm crude and all that. But let me know if Miss Smith is going to dine with us in time for me to look up The Milliner's Gazette."

"You absurd creature!" said Rosemary, and she went out of the library, but not back to her bedroom. She went to her writing-room and sat down at her desk. Pretty! Absolutely lovely! Bowled over! Her heart beat like a heavy bell. Pretty! Lovely! She drew her cheque-book towards her. But no, cheques would be no use, of course. She opened a drawer and took out five pound notes, looked at them, put two back, and holding the three squeezed in her hand; she went back to her bedroom.

Half an hour later Philip was still in the library, when Rosemary came in.

"I only wanted to tell you," said she, and she leaned against the door again and looked at him with her dazzled exotic gaze, "Miss Smith won't dine with us tonight."

Philip put down the paper. "Oh, what's happened? Previous engagement?"

Rosemary came over and sat down on his knee. "She insisted on going," said she, "so I gave the poor little thing a present of money. I couldn't keep her against her will, could I?" she added softly.

Rosemary had just done her hair, darkened her eyes a little, and put on her pearls. She put up her hands and touched Philip's cheeks.

"Do you like me?" said she, and her tone, sweet, husky, troubled him.

"I like you awfully," he said, and he held her tighter. "Kiss me."

There was a pause.

Then Rosemary said dreamily. "I saw a fascinating little box today. It cost twenty-eight guineas. May I have it?"

Philip jumped her on his knee. "You may, little wasteful one," said he.

But that was not really what Rosemary wanted to say.

"Philip," she whispered, and she pressed his head against her bosom, "am I pretty?"

Questions for Discussion

1. What are the details listed in the story that show the luxurious life of Rosemary?
2. Does Philip really think the poor girl is very beautiful? What is his purpose by saying so?
3. What does Katherine Mansfield intend to express with the image of Rosemary?

Links

1. https://en.wikipedia.org/wiki/Katherine_Mansfield
   关于凯瑟琳·曼斯菲尔德生平及创作的详细介绍。
2. http://nzetc.victoria.ac.nz/tm/scholarly/tei-ManDove-t1-body1-d4.html
   关于凯瑟琳·曼斯菲尔德的小说《一杯茶》的细读资料。

Chapter Twelve

Part A

Is He Living or Is He Dead?

By Mark Twain

Mark Twain (1835—1910), pen name for Samuel Longhorne Clemens, was an American writer, humorist, entrepreneur, publisher and lecturer.

Mark Twain took his pen name from his days as a riverboat pilot on the Mississippi River where the cry "mark twain" signaled the depth of water—about 12 feet was required for the safe passage of riverboats. He started his career as a typesetter at a newspaper, worked as a printer, then riverboat pilot and then turned to gold mining. When he failed at gold mining, he turned to journalism and it was during that time that he wrote the short story that launched his career.

Twain grew up in Hannibal, Missouri and would later use that location as the setting for two of his most famous works, *The Adventures of Tom Sawyer* (1876) and its sequel *Adventures of Huckleberry Finn* (1885), the latter has been called the greatest novel in American literature. His humorous story *The Celebrated Jumping Frog of Calaveras County* was published in 1865. His wit and satire, in prose and in speech, earned him praise from critics and peers.

Twain was born shortly after a visit by Halley's Comet, and he predicted that he would "go out with it" too; he died the day after the comet returned. Mark Twain was lauded as "the greatest American humorist this country has produced", and William Faulkner called him "the father of American literature".

❀ Lead-in Questions

1. Do you know any famous people who were very poor when they were alive but became famous after their death?

2. Would you please retell some classic plots in *The Adventures of Tom Sawyer* by Mark Twain?

Questions about the Author and the Story

1. What is the main feature of Mark Twain's writing?
   A. Humorous.   B. Adventurous.   C. Nostalgic.   D. Pessimistic.
2. What's the rhetorical method of the description of the caged bird in the story?
   A. Metaphor.   B. Simile.   C. Symbolism.   D. Exaggeration.
3. Whois chosen by the painter as the one to pretend death?
   A. Smith.   B. Millet.   C. Carl.   D. Claude.
4. Which word can NOT be used to describe the life of Millet after he gets rich?
   A. Happy.   B. Wealthy.   C. Lonely.   D. Dreamy.
5. Millet's painting "Angelus" is sold at last at the price of _____.
   A. 5 francs   B. 8 francs   C. 2200 francs   D. 55000 francs

    I was spending the month of March 1892 at Mentone, in the Riviera. At this retired spot one has all the advantages, privately, which are to be had publicly at Monte Carlo and Nice, a few miles farther along. That is to say, one has the flooding sunshine, the balmy air and the brilliant blue sea, without the marring additions of human pow-wow and fuss and feathers and display. Mentone is quiet, simple, restful, unpretentious; the rich and the gaudy do not come there. As a rule, I mean, the rich do not come there. Now and then a rich man comes, and I presently got acquainted with one of these. Partially to disguise him I will call him Smith. One day, in the Hotel des Anglais, at the second breakfast, he exclaimed:

"Quick! Cast your eye on the man going out at the door. Take in every detail of him."

"Why?"

"Do you know who he is?"

"Yes. He spent several days here before you came. He is an old, retired, and very rich silk manufacturer from Lyons, they say, and I guess he is alone in the world, for he always looks sad and dreamy, and doesn't talk with anybody. His name is Theophile Magnan."

I supposed that Smith would now proceed to justify the large interest which he had shown in Monsieur Magnan, but, instead, he dropped into a brown study, and was apparently lost to me and to the rest of the world during some minutes. Now and then he passed his fingers through his flossy white hair, to assist his thinking, and meantime he allowed his breakfast to go on cooling. At last he said:

"No, it's gone; I can't call it back."

"Can't call what back?"

"It's one of Hans Andersen's beautiful little stories. But it's gone from me. Part of it is like this: A child has a caged bird, which it loves but thoughtlessly neglects. The bird pours out its song unheard and unheeded; but, in time, hunger and thirst assail the creature, and its song grows plaintive and feeble and finally ceases—the bird dies. The child comes, and is smitten to the heart with remorse: then, with bitter tears and lamentations, it calls its mates, and they bury the bird with elaborate pomp and the tenderest grief, without knowing, poor things, that it isn't children only who starve poets to death and then spend enough on their funerals and monuments to have kept them alive and made them easy and comfortable. Now—"

But here we were interrupted. About ten that evening I ran across Smith, and he asked me up to his parlour to help him smoke and drink hot Scotch. It was a cozy place, with its comfortable chairs, its cheerful lamps, and its friendly open fire of seasoned olive-wood. To make everything perfect, there was a muffled booming of the surf outside. After the second Scotch and much lazy and contented chat, Smith said:

"Now we are properly primed—I to tell a curious history and you to listen to it. It has been a secret for many years—a secret between me and three others; but I am going to break the seal now. Are you comfortable?"

"Perfectly. Go on."

Here follows what he told me:

"A long time ago I was a young artist—a very young artist, in fact—and I wandered about the country parts of France, sketching here and sketching there, and was presently joined by a couple of darling young Frenchmen who were at the same kind of thing that I was doing. We were as happy as we were poor, or as poor as we were happy—phrase it to suit yourself. Claude Frere and Carl Boulanger—these are the names of those boys; dear, dear fellows, and the sunniest spirits that ever laughed at poverty and had a noble good time in all weathers."

"At last we ran hard aground in a Breton village, and an artist as poor as ourselves took us in and literally saved us from starving—Francois Millet—"

"What! The great Francois Millet?"

"Great? He wasn't any greater than we were, then. He hadn't any fame, even in his own village; and he was so poor that he hadn't anything to feed us on but turnips, and even the turnips failed us sometimes. We four became fast friends, doting friends, inseparables. We painted away together with all our might, piling up stock, but very seldom getting rid of any of it. We had lovely times together; but, O my soul! How we were pinched now and then!"

"For a little over two years this went on. At last, one day," Claude said:

"Boys, we've come to the end. Do you understand that? —absolutely to the end.

Everybody has struck—there's a league formed against us. I've been all around the village and it's just as I tell you. They refuse to credit us for another centime until all the odds and ends are paid up."

This struck us as cold. Every face was blank with dismay. We realized that our circumstances were desperate, now. There was a long silence. Finally, Millet said with a sigh:

"Nothing occurs to me—nothing. Suggest something, lads."

There was no response, unless a mournful silence may be called a response. Carl got up, and walked nervously up and down a while, then said:

"It's a shame! Look at these canvases: stacks and stacks of as good pictures as anybody in Europe paints—I don't care who he is. Yes, and plenty of lounging strangers have said the same—or nearly that, anyway."

"But didn't buy," Millet said.

"No matter, they said it; and it's true, too. Look at your 'Angelus' there! Will anybody tell me—"

"Pah, Carl—My 'Angelus!' I was offered five francs for it."

"When?"

"Who offered it?"

"Where is he?"

"Why didn't you take it?"

"Come—don't all speak at once. I thought he would give more—I was sure of it—he looked it—so I asked him eight."

"Well—and then?"

"He said he would call again."

"Thunder and lightning! Why, Francois—"

"Oh, I know—I know! It was a mistake, and I was a fool. Boys, I meant for the best; you'll grant me that, and I—"

"Why, certainly, we know that, bless your dear heart; but don't you be a fool again."

"I? I wish somebody would come along and offer us a cabbage for it—you'd see!"

"A cabbage! Oh, don't name it—it makes my mouth water. Talk of things less trying."

"Boys," said Carl, "do these pictures lack merit? Answer me that."

"No!"

"Aren't they of very great and high merit? Answer me that."

"Yes."

"Of such great and high merit that, if an illustrious name were attached to them they would sell at splendid prices. Isn't it so?"

"Certainly it is. Nobody doubts that."

"But—I'm not joking—isn't it so?"

"Why, of course it's so—and we are not joking. But what of it. What of it? How does that concern us?"

"In this way, comrades—we'll attach an illustrious name to them!"

The lively conversation stopped. The faces were turned inquiringly upon Carl. What sort of riddle might this be? Where was an illustrious name to be borrowed? And who was to borrow it?

Carl sat down, and said:

"Now, I have a perfectly serious thing to propose. I think it is the only way to keep us out of the almshouse, and I believe it to be a perfectly sure way. I base this opinion upon certain multitudinous and long-established facts in human history. I believe my project will make us all rich."

"Rich! You've lost your mind."

"No, I haven't."

"Yes, you have—you've lost your mind. What do you call rich?"

"A hundred thousand francs apiece."

"He has lost his mind. I knew it."

"Yes, he has. Carl, privation has been too much for you, and—"

"Carl, you want to take a pill and get right to bed."

"Bandage him first—bandage his head, and then—"

"No, bandage his heels; his brains have been settling for weeks—I've noticed it."

"Shut up!" said Millet, with ostensible severity, "and let the boy have his say. Now, then—come out with your project, Carl. What is it?"

"Well, then, by way of preamble I will ask you to note this fact in human history: that the merit of many a great artist has never been acknowledged until after he was starved and dead. This has happened so often that I make bold to found a law upon it. This law: that the merit of every great unknown and neglected artist must and will be recognized and his pictures climb to high prices after his death. My project is this: we must cast lots—one of us must die."

The remark fell so calmly and so unexpectedly that we almost forgot to jump. Then there was a wild chorus of advice again—medical advice—for the help of Carl's brain; but he waited patiently for the hilarity to calm down, and then went on again with his project:

"Yes, one of us must die, to save the others—and himself. We will cast lots. The one chosen shall be illustrious, all of us shall be rich. Hold still, now—hold still; don't interrupt—I tell you I know what I am talking about. Here is the idea. During the next three months the one who is to die shall paint with all his might, enlarge his stock all he can—not pictures, no! Skeleton sketches, studies, parts of studies, fragments of studies, a dozen dabs of the brush on each—meaningless, of course, but his, with his cipher on them; turn out fifty a day, each to contain some peculiarity or mannerism easily detectable as his—they're the things that sell, you know, and are collected at fabulous prices for the world's museums, after the great man is gone; we'll have a ton of them ready—a ton! And all that time the rest of us will be busy supporting the moribund, and working Paris and the dealers—preparations for the coming event, you know; and when everything is hot and just right, we'll spring the death on them and have the notorious funeral. You get the idea?"

"No; at least, not qu—"

"Not quite? Don't you see? The man doesn't really die; he changes his name and vanishes; we bury a dummy, and cry over it, with all the world to help. And I—"

But he wasn't allowed to finish. Everybody broke out into a rousing hurrah of applause; and all jumped up and capered about the room and fell on each other's necks in transports of gratitude and joy. For hours we talked over the great plan, without ever feeling hungry; and at last, when all the details had been arranged satisfactorily, we cast lots and Millet was elected—elected to die, as we called it. Then we scraped together those things which one never parts with until he is betting them against future wealth—keepsake trinkets and suchlike—and these we pawned for enough to furnish us a frugal farewell supper and breakfast, and leave us a few francs over for travel, and a stake of turnips and such for Millet to live on for a few days.

Next morning, early, the three of us cleared out, straightway after breakfast—on foot, of course. Each of us carried a dozen of Millet's small pictures, purposing to market them. Carl struck for Paris, where he would start the work of building up Millet's name against the coming great day. Claude and I were to separate, and scatter abroad over France.

Now, it will surprise you to know what an easy and comfortable thing we had. I walked two days before I began business. Then I began to sketch a villa in the outskirts of a big town—because I saw the proprietor standing on an upper veranda. He came down to look on—I thought he would. I worked swiftly, intending to keep him interested. Occasionally he fired off a little ejaculation of approbation, and by-and-by he spoke up with enthusiasm, and said I was a master!

I put down my brush, reached into my satchel, fetched out a Millet, and pointed to the cipher in the corner. I said, proudly:

"I suppose you recognize that? Well, he taught me! I should think I ought to know my trade!"

The man looked guiltily embarrassed, and was silent. I said sorrowfully:

"You don't mean to intimate that you don't know the cipher of Francois Millet!"

Of course he didn't know that cipher; but he was the gratefullest man you ever saw, just the same, for being let out of an uncomfortable place on such easy terms. He said:

"No! Why, it is Millet's, sure enough! I don't know what I could have been

Chapter Twelve

thinking of. Of course I recognize it now."

Next, he wanted to buy it; but I said that although I wasn't rich I wasn't that poor. However, at last, I let him have it for eight hundred francs.

Eight hundred!

Yes. Millet would have sold it for a pork chop. Yes, I got eight hundred francs for that little thing. I wish I could get it back for eighty thousand. But that time's gone by. I made a very nice picture of that man's house and I wanted to offer it to him for ten francs, but that wouldn't answer, seeing I was the pupil of such a master, so I sold it to him for a hundred. I sent the eight hundred francs straight to Millet from that town and struck out again next day.

But I didn't walk—no. I rode. I have ridden ever since. I sold one picture every day, and never tried to sell two. I always said to my customer:

"I am a fool to sell a picture of Francois Millet's at all, for that man is not going to live three months, and when he dies his pictures can't be had for love or money."

I took care to spread that little fact as far as I could, and prepare the world for the event.

I take credit to myself for our plan of selling the pictures—it was mine. I suggested it that last evening when we were laying out our campaign, and all three of us agreed to give it a good fair trial before giving it up for some other. It succeeded with all of us. I walked only two days, Claude walked two—both of afraid to make Millet celebrated too close to home—but Carl walked only half a day, the bright, conscienceless rascal, and after that he travelled like a duke.

Every now and then we got in with a country editor and started an item around through the press; not an item announcing that a new painter had been discovered, but an item which let on that everybody knew Francois Millet; not an item praising him in any way, but merely a word concerning the present condition of the "master"—sometimes hopeful, sometimes despondent, but always tinged with fears for the worst. We always marked these paragraphs, and sent the papers to all the people who had bought pictures of us.

Carl was soon in Paris and he worked things with a high hand. He made friends with the correspondents, and got Millet's condition reported to England and all over the continent, and America, and everywhere.

At the end of six weeks from the start, we three met in Paris and called a halt, and stopped sending back to Millet for additional pictures. The boom was so high, and everything so ripe, that we saw that it would be a mistake not to strike now, right away, without waiting any longer. So we wrote Millet to go to bed and begin to waste away pretty fast, for we should like him to die in ten days if he could get ready.

Then we figured up and found that among us we had sold eighty-five small pictures and studies, and had sixty-nine thousand francs to show for it. Carl had made the last sale and the most brilliant one of all. He sold the "Angelus" for twenty-two hundred francs. How we did glorify him! —Not foreseeing that a day was coming by-and-by when France would struggle to own it and a stranger would capture it for five hundred and fifty thousand, cash.

We had a wind-up champagne supper that night, and next day Claude and I packed up and went off to nurse Millet through his last days and keep busybodies out of the house and send daily bulletins to Carl in Paris for publication in the papers of several continents for the information of a waiting world. The sad end came at last, and Carl was there in time to help in the final mournful rites.

You remember that great funeral, and what a stir it made all over the globe, and how the illustrious of two worlds came to attend it and testify their sorrow. We four—still inseparable—carried the coffin, and would allow none to help. And we were right about that, because it hadn't anything in it but a wax figure, and any other coffin-bearers would have found fault with the weight. Yes, we same old four, who had lovingly shared privation together in the old hard times now gone forever, carried the cof—"

"Which four?"

"We four—for Millet helped to carry his own coffin. In disguise, you know. Disguised as a relative—distant relative."

"Astonishing!"

"But true just the same. Well, you remember how the pictures went up. Money? We didn't know what to do with it. There's a man in Paris today who owns seventy Millet pictures. He paid us two million francs for them. And as for the bushels of sketches and studies which Millet shovelled out during the six weeks that we were on the road, well, it would astonish you to know the figure we sell them at nowadays—that is, when we consent to let one go!"

"It is a wonderful history, perfectly wonderful!"

"Yes—it amounts to that."

"Whatever became of Millet?"

"Can you keep a secret?"

"I can."

"Do you remember the man I called your attention to in the dining room today? That was Francois Millet."

"Great—"

"Scott! Yes. For once they didn't starve a genius to death and then put into other pockets the rewards he should have had himself. This song-bird was not allowed to pipe out its heart unheard and then be paid with the cold pomp of a big funeral. We looked out for that."

Questions for Discussion

1. What kind of place is Mentone like? What's the purpose of the author to describe it in this way?
2. What's the theme of this story? Does the phenomenon still exist in today's society?
3. How is Mark Twain's humor embodied in the story?

 Links

1. https://en.wikipedia.org/wiki/Mark_Twain
   提供马克·吐温生平及创作的详细介绍。
2. https://americanliterature.com/author/mark-twain/short-story/is-he-living-or-is-he-dead
   提供马克·吐温的小说《他是活着还是死了》细读资料。

The Mark on the Wall

By Virginia Woolf

Virginia Woolf（1882—1941）was the daughter of Sir Leslie Stephen（1832- 1904）, the biographer, critic and editor of the *Dictionary of National Biography*. She was educated at home and in frequent contact with her father's literary and political friends, all "high-brows."[①] She began her literary career in youth as a book reviewer for *The Times Literary Supplement*. She later wrote: "I made one pound ten and six by my first review; and I bought a persian cat with the proceeds. Then I grew ambitious ... I must have a motorcar. And thus it was that I became a novelist." After her father's death, her house in the Bloomsbury district of London became the center for the Bloomsbury Group, which was a coterie of talented intellectuals including the novelist E. M. Foster（1879—1970）, the biographer Lytton Strachey（1880—1932）, the philosopher G.E. Moore, the economist J. M. Keynes, and T.S. Eliot were also associated with the group. These artists, thinkers and writers

---

① high-brows: refer to people with superior culture and learning

achieved considerable distinction in their various fields. In 1912, Virginia married Leonard Woolf, who was her brother's classmate at Cambridge. He encouraged her to write novels.

From childhood she suffered from fits of nervous breakdown. In order that she might have some normal occupation with a curative effect, she and her husband learned typesetting and printing with a hand press installed in their dining-room. Then, in 1917, they founded the Hogarth Press, which published her books and those by other promising young writers of the time.

Woolf is considered a major innovator in the English language. In her works, she experimented with stream of consciousness and the underlying psychological as well as emotional motives of characters. She is also in many ways an icon for the study of feminist jurisprudence. Although Woolf never aligned herself with any of the women's political movements of her time, her works "waged a spirited campaign in favor of the moral emancipation of women". Her 1925 novel, *Mrs. Dalloway*, encompasses the full range of Woolf's feminist views. In Woolf's best-known nonfiction works, *A Room of One's Own* (1929), she demonstrates "women should have a room of their own" to show economic power is the first element women should have to free themselves. Therefore, in *The Second Sex* (1949), Simone de Beauvoir counts, of all women who ever lived, only three female writers—Emily Bront, Woolf and "sometimes" Katherine Mansfield—who have explored "the given".

Throughout her life, Woolf, who was plagued by periodic mood swings and associated illnesses, committed suicide by drowning in 1941 at the age of 59.

Lead-in Questions

1. Could you list a few famous writers in the field of Stream of Consciousness in the western literature history?
2. Have you ever experienced a stream of consciousness in your daily life? If yes, what is it like?

Questions about the Author and This Story

1. Which of the following is NOT written by Woolf?
   A. *The Voyage Out*. B. *To the Lighthouse*.
   C. *The Second Sex*. D. *The Waves*.
2. How many times, throughout the whole story, does the heroine try to figure out what the mark is?
   A. Five times. B. Six times.
   C. Four times. D. Seven times.
3. From which sentence can we draw her thinking of equality between human beings, between man and woman? Which is her repeated theme in her literature

works?

    A. "This train of thought, she perceives, is threatening mere waste of energy, even some collision with reality, for who will ever be able to lift a finger against Whitaker's Table of Precedency?"

    B. "To steady myself, let me catch hold of the first idea that passes ... Shakespeare ... Well, he will do as well as another."

    C. "In certain lights that mark on the wall seems actually to project from the wall."

    D. "I must jump up and see for myself what that mark on the wall really is—a nail, a rose-leaf, a crack in the wood?"

3. Which sentence gives an exhaustive view of Woolf's philosophical thinking?

    A. "I looked up through the smoke of my cigarette and my eye lodged for a moment upon the burning coals, and that old fancy of the crimson flag flapping from the castle tower came into my mind, and I thought of the cavalcade of red knights riding up the side of the black rock."

    B. "I don't believe it was made by a nail after all; it's too big, too round, for that."

    C. "In certain lights that mark on the wall seems actually to project from the wall."

    D. "How readily our thoughts swarm upon a new object, lifting it a little way, as ants carry a blade of straw so feverishly, and then leave it."

5. At last the heroin finds out that the mark is _____.

    A. a petal of rose   B. a hole of a nail

    C. a nail   D. a snail

    Perhaps it was the middle of January in the present that I first looked up and saw the mark on the wall. In order to fix a date it is necessary to remember what one saw. So now I think of the fire; the steady film of yellow light upon the page of my book; the three chrysanthemums in the round glass bowl on the mantelpiece. Yes, it must have been the winter time, and we had just finished our tea, for I remember that I was smoking a cigarette when I looked up and saw the mark on the wall for the first time. I looked up through the smoke of my cigarette and my eye lodged for a moment upon the burning coals, and that old fancy of the crimson flag flapping from the castle tower came into my mind, and I thought of the cavalcade of red knights riding up the side of the black rock. Rather to my relief the sight of the mark interrupted the fancy, for it is an old fancy, an automatic fancy, made as a child perhaps. The mark was a small round mark, black upon the white wall, about six or seven inches above the mantelpiece.

    How readily our thoughts swarm upon a new object, lifting it a little way, as ants carry a blade of straw so feverishly, and then leave it ... If that mark was made by a nail, it can't have been for a picture, it must have been for a miniature—the miniature of a lady with white powdered curls, powder-dusted cheeks, and lips like red carnations. A fraud of course, for the people who had this house before us would have chosen pictures in that way—an old picture for an old room. That is the sort of people they were—very interesting people, and I think of them so often, in such queer places, because one will never see them again, never know what happened next. They wanted to leave this house because they wanted to change their style of furniture, so he said, and he was in process of saying that in his opinion art should have ideas behind it when we were torn asunder, as one is torn from the old lady about to pour out tea and the young man about to hit the tennis ball in the back garden of the suburban villa as one rushes past in the train.

But as for that mark, I'm not sure about it; I don't believe it was made by a nail after all; it's too big, too round, for that. I might get up, but if I got up and looked at it, ten to one I shouldn't be able to say for certain; because once a thing's done, no one ever knows how it happened. Oh! dear me, the mystery of life; the inaccuracy of thought! The ignorance of humanity! To show how very little control of our possessions we have—what an accidental affair this living is after all our civilization—let me just count over a few of the things lost in one lifetime, beginning, for that seems always the most mysterious of losses—what cat would gnaw, what rat would nibble—three pale blue canisters of book-binding tools? Then there were the bird cages, the iron hoops, the steel skates, the Queen Anne coal-scuttle, the bagatelle board, the hand organ—all gone, and jewels, too. Opals and emeralds, they lie about the roots of turnips. What a scraping paring affair it is to be sure! The wonder is that I've any clothes on my back, that I sit surrounded by solid furniture at this moment. Why, if one wants to compare life to anything, one must liken it to being blown through the Tube at fifty miles an hour—landing at the other end without a single hairpin in one's hair! Shot out at the feet of God entirely naked! Tumbling head over heels in the asphodel meadows like brown paper parcels pitched down a shoot in the post office! With one's hair flying back like the tail of a race-horse. Yes, that seems to express the rapidity of life, the perpetual waste and repair; all so casual, all so haphazard ...

But after life. The slow pulling down of thick green stalks so that the cup of the flower, as it turns over, deluges one with purple and red light. Why, after all, should one not be born there as one is born here, helpless, speechless, unable to focus one's eyesight, groping at the roots of the grass, at the toes of the Giants? As for saying which are trees, and which are men and women, or whether there are such things, that one won't be in a condition to do for fifty years or so. There will be nothing but spaces of light and dark, intersected by thick stalks, and rather higher up perhaps, rose-shaped blots of an indistinct color—dim pinks and blues—which will, as time goes on, become more definite, become—I don't know what ...

Chapter Twelve

And yet that mark on the wall is not a hole at all. It may even be caused by some round black substance, such as a small rose leaf, left over from the summer, and I, not being a very vigilant housekeeper—look at the dust on the mantelpiece, for example, the dust which, so they say, buried Troy three times over, only fragments of pots utterly refusing annihilation, as one can believe.

The tree outside the window taps very gently on the pane ... I want to think quietly, calmly, spaciously, never to be interrupted, never to have to rise from my chair, to slip easily from one thing to another, without any sense of hostility, or obstacle. I want to sink deeper and deeper, away from the surface, with its hard separate facts. To steady myself, let me catch hold of the first idea that passes ... Shakespeare ... Well, he will do as well as another. A man who sat himself solidly in an arm-chair, and looked into the fire, so—a shower of ideas fell perpetually from some very high Heaven down through his mind. He leant his forehead on his hand, and people, looking in through the open door,—for this scene is supposed to take place on a summer's evening—But how dull this is, this historical fiction! It doesn't interest me at all. I wish I could hit upon a pleasant track of thought, a track indirectly reflecting credit upon myself, for those are the pleasantest thoughts, and very frequent even in the minds of modest mouse-colored people, who believe genuinely that they dislike to hear their own praises. They are not thoughts directly praising oneself; that is the beauty of them; they are thoughts like this:

"And then I came into the room. They were discussing botany. I said how I'd seen a flower growing on a dust heap on the site of an old house in Kingsway. The seed, I said, must have been sown in the reign of Charles the First. What flowers grew in the reign of Charles the First?" I asked—(but, I don't remember the answer). Tall flowers with purple tassels to them perhaps. And so it goes on. All the time I'm dressing up the figure of myself in my own mind, lovingly, stealthily, not openly adoring it, for if I did that, I should catch myself out, and stretch my hand at once for a book in self-protection. Indeed, it is curious how instinctively one protects the image of oneself from idolatry or any other handling that could make it ridiculous, or too unlike the original to be believed in any longer. Or is it not so very curious after all? It is a matter of great importance. Suppose the looking glass smashes, the image disappears, and the romantic figure with the green of forest depths all about it is there no longer, but only that shell of a person which is seen by other people—what an airless, shallow, bald, prominent world it becomes! A world not to be lived in. As we face each other in omnibuses and underground railways we are looking into the mirror that accounts for the vagueness, the gleam of glassiness, in our eyes. And the novelists in future will realize more and more the importance of these reflections, for of course there is not one reflection but an almost infinite number; those are the depths they will explore, those the phantoms they will pursue, leaving the description of reality more and more out of their stories, taking a knowledge of it for granted, as the Greeks did and Shakespeare perhaps—but these generalizations are very worthless. The military sound of the word is enough. It recalls leading articles, cabinet ministers—a whole class of things indeed which as a child one thought the thing itself, the standard thing, the real thing, from which one could not depart save at the risk of nameless damnation. Generalizations bring back somehow Sunday in London, Sunday afternoon walks, Sunday luncheons, and also ways of speaking of the dead, clothes, and habits—like the habit of sitting all together in one room until a certain hour, although nobody liked it. There was a rule for everything. The rule for tablecloths at that particular period was that they should be made of tapestry with little yellow compartments marked upon them, such as you may see in photographs of the carpets in the corridors of the royal palaces. Tablecloths of a different kind were not real tablecloths. How shocking, and yet how wonderful it was to discover that these real things, Sunday luncheons, Sunday walks, country houses, and tablecloths were not entirely real, were indeed half phantoms, and the damnation which visited the disbeliever in them was only a sense of illegitimate freedom. What now takes the place of those things I wonder, those real standard things? Men perhaps, should you be a woman; the masculine point of view which governs our lives, which sets the standard, which establishes Whitaker's Table of Precedency, which has become, I suppose, since the war half a phantom to many men and women, which soon—one may hope, will be laughed into the dustbin where the phantoms go, the mahogany sideboards and the Landseer prints, Gods and Devils, Hell and so forth, leaving us all with an intoxicating sense of illegitimate freedom—if freedom exists ...

In certain lights that mark on the wall seems actually to project from the wall. Nor is it entirely circular. I cannot be sure, but it seems to cast a perceptible shadow, suggesting that if I ran my finger down that strip of the wall it would, at a certain point, mount and descend a small tumulus, a smooth tumulus like those barrows on the South Downs which are, they say, either tombs or camps. Of the two I should prefer them to be tombs, desiring melancholy like most English people, and finding it natural at the end of a walk to think of the bones stretched beneath the turf ... There must be some book about it. Some antiquary must have dug up those bones and given them a name ... What sort of a man is an antiquary, I wonder? Retired Colonels for the most part, I dare say, leading parties of aged labourers to the top here, examining clods of earth and stone, and getting into correspondence with the neighboring clergy, which, being opened at breakfast time, gives them a feeling of importance, and the comparison of arrow-heads necessitates cross-country journeys to the county towns, an agreeable necessity both to them and to their elderly wives, who wish to make plum jam or to clean out the study, and have every reason for keeping that great question of the camp or the tomb in perpetual suspension, while the Colonel himself feels agreeably philosophic in accumulating evidence on both sides of the question. It is true that he does finally incline to believe in the camp; and, being opposed, indicates a pamphlet which he is about to read at the quarterly meeting of the local society when a stroke lays him low, and his last conscious thoughts are not of wife or child, but of the camp and that arrowhead there, which is now in the case at the local museum, together with the foot of a Chinese murderess, a handful of Elizabethan nails, a great many Tudor clay pipes, a piece of Roman pottery, and the wine-glass that Nelson drank out of—proving I really don't know what.

No, no, nothing is proved, nothing is known. And if I were to get up at this very moment and ascertain that the mark on the wall is really—what shall we say? —the head of a gigantic old nail, driven in two hundred years ago, which has now, owing to the patient attrition of many generations of housemaids, revealed its head above the coat of paint, and is taking its first view of modern life in the sight of a white-walled fire-lit room, what should I gain? —Knowledge? Matter for further speculation? I can think sitting still as well as standing up. And what is knowledge? What are our learned men save the descendants of witches and hermits who crouched in caves and in woods brewing herbs, interrogating shrew-mice and writing down the language of the stars? And the less we honour them as our superstitions dwindle and our respect for beauty and health of mind increases ... Yes, one could imagine a very pleasant world. A quiet, spacious world, with the flowers so red and blue in the open fields. A world without professors or specialists or house-keepers with the profiles of policemen, a world which one could slice with one's thought as a fish slices the water with his fin, grazing the stems of the water-lilies, hanging suspended over nests of white sea eggs ... How peaceful it is drown here, rooted in the centre of the world and gazing up through the grey waters, with their sudden gleams of light, and their reflections—if it were not for Whitaker's Almanack—if it were not for the Table of Precedency!

I must jump up and see for myself what that mark on the wall really is—a nail, a rose-leaf, a crack in the wood?

Here is nature once more at her old game of self-preservation. This train of thought, she perceives, is threatening mere waste of energy, even some collision with reality, for who will ever be able to lift a finger against Whitaker's Table of Precedency? The Archbishop of Canterbury is followed by the Lord High Chancellor; the Lord High Chancellor is followed by the Archbishop of York. Everybody follows somebody, such is the philosophy of Whitaker; and the great thing is to know who follows whom. Whitaker knows, and let that, so Nature counsels, comfort you, instead of enraging you; and if you can't be comforted, if you must shatter this hour of peace, think of the mark on the wall.

I understand Nature's game—her prompting to take action as a way of ending any thought that threatens to excite or to pain. Hence, I suppose, comes our slight contempt for men of action—men, we assume, who don't think. Still, there's no harm in putting a full stop to one's disagreeable thoughts by looking at a mark on the wall.

Indeed, now that I have fixed my eyes upon it, I feel that I have grasped a plank in the sea; I feel a satisfying sense of reality which at once turns the two Archbishops and the Lord High Chancellor to the shadows of shades. Here is something definite, something real. Thus, waking from a midnight dream of horror, one hastily turns on the light and lies quiescent, worshiping the chest of drawers, worshiping solidity, worshiping reality, worshiping the impersonal world which is a proof of some existence other than ours. That is what one wants to be sure of ... Wood is a pleasant thing to think about. It comes from a tree; and trees grow, and we don't know how they grow. For years and years they grow, without paying any attention to us, in meadows, in forests, and by the side of rivers—all things one likes to think about. The cows swish their tails beneath them on hot afternoons; they paint rivers so green that when a moorhen dives one expects to see its feathers all green when it comes up again. I like to think of the fish balanced against the stream like flags blown out; and of water-beetles slowly raiding domes of mud upon the bed of the river. I like to think of the tree itself:—first the close dry sensation of being wood; then the grinding of the storm; then the slow, delicious ooze of sap. I like to think of it, too, on winter's nights standing in the empty field with all leaves close-furled, nothing tender exposed to the iron bullets of the moon, a naked mast upon an earth that goes tumbling, tumbling, all night long. The song of birds must sound very loud and strange in June; and how cold the feet of insects must feel upon it, as they make laborious progresses up the creases of the bark, or sun themselves upon the thin green awning of the leaves, and look straight in front of them with diamond-cut red eyes ... One by one the fibres snap beneath the immense cold pressure of the earth, then the last storm comes and, falling, the highest branches drive deep into the ground again. Even so, life isn't done with; there are a million patient, watchful lives still for a tree, all over the world, in bedrooms, in ships, on the pavement, lining rooms, where men and women sit after tea, smoking cigarettes. It is full of peaceful thoughts, happy thoughts, this tree. I should like to take each one separately—but something is getting in the way ... Where was I? What has it all been about? A tree? A river? The Downs? Whitaker's Almanack? The fields of asphodel? I can't remember a thing. Everything's moving, falling, slipping, vanishing ... There is a vast upheaval of matter. Someone is standing over me and saying—

"I'm going out to buy a newspaper."

"Yes?"

"Though it's no good buying newspapers ... Nothing ever happens. Curse this war; God damn this war! ... All the same, I don't see why we should have a snail on our wall."

Ah, the mark on the wall! It was a snail.

Questions for Discussion

1. What are the images seen as the mark in the story? Why does the author think of these images?
2. What do you think of the ending? Do you think it is surprising? What kind of conclusion can you draw from this ending?
3. Some experts said that Woolf's short story *The Mark on the Wall* was of great significance, and it was a start, from which she began to voice a female's thinking out loud. Do you agree with this idea? Justify yourself.

Links

1. https://en.wikipedia.org/wiki/Virginia_Woolf#Works_by_Virginia_Woolf
   提供弗吉尼亚·伍尔夫生平及创作的详细介绍。
2. http://yingyu.xdf.cn/201211/9161635.html
   提供弗吉尼亚·伍尔夫的小说《墙上的斑点》细读资料。

Chapter Thirteen

Part A

The End of the Flight

By William Somerset Maugham

William Somerset Maugham (1874—1965), better known as W. Somerset Maugham, was a British playwright, novelist and short story writer. He was among the most popular writers of his era and reputedly the highest-paid author during the 1930s.

By 1914, Maugham was famous, with 10 plays produced and 10 novels published. Commercial success with high book sales, successful theatre productions and a string of film adaptations, backed by astute stock market investments, allowed Maugham to live a very comfortable life. Yet, despite his triumphs, he never attracted the highest respect from the critics or his peers. Maugham attributed this to his lack of "lyrical quality", his small vocabulary, and failure to make expert use of metaphor in his work.

Maugham's masterpiece is *Of Human Bondage*, a semiautobiographical novel that deals with the life of the main character Philip Carey. Two of his later novels were based on historical people: *The Moon and Sixpence* is about the life of Paul Gauguin; and *Cakes and Ale* contains what were taken as thinly veiled and unflattering characterizations of the authors Thomas Hardy (who had died two years previously) and Hugh Walpole.

Among his short stories, the most memorable ones deal with the lives of Western, mostly British, colonists in the Far East. They typically express the emotional toll the colonists bear by their isolation. "Rain", "Footprints in the Jungle", and "The Outstation" are considered especially notable.

In 1947, Maugham instituted the Somerset Maugham Award to award the best British writer or writers under the age of thirty-five for a work of fiction published in the past year.

Chapter Thirteen

🌸 Lead-in Questions

1. Why is William Somerset Maugham regarded as the best storyteller in 20th century? Would you please list some of Maugham's best stories?
2. Maugham explains his philosophy of life as a resigned atheism and a certain skepticism about the extent of man's innate goodness and intelligence. How do you understand it?

🌸 Questions about the Author and the Story

1. *Of Human Bondage* is a novel by _____.
   A. Herbert George Wells   B. Arnold Bennett
   C. William Somerset Maugham   D. John Galsworthy
2. _____ described himself as "in the very first row of the second-raters".
   A. T. S. Eliot   B. George Bernard Shaw
   C. James Joyce   D. William Somerset Maugham
3. Who is the narrator of the story about the Dutchman?
   A. The skipper.   B. A boy.   C. The host.   D. I.
4. Why were "I" unwilling to listen to the story at the beginning?
   A. Because I was tired and wanted to go to bed.
   B. Because I am not interested in the story.
   C. Because the story is too horrible.
   D. Because the story is too boring.
5. Which one is NOT the reaction of the Dutchman when the host's clerk opened the door a bit suddenly?
   A. He gave a shout.
   B. He jumped about two feet into the air.
   C. He whipped out a revolver.
   D. He was indifferent.

  I shook hands with the skipper① and he wished me luck. Then I went down to the lower deck crowded with passengers, Malays, Chinese and Dyaks, and made my way to the ladder. Looking over the ship's side I saw that my luggage was already in the boat. It was a large, clumsy-looking craft, with a great square sail of bamboo matting, and it was crammed full of gesticulating natives. I scrambled in and a place was made for me. We were about three miles from the shore and a stiff breeze was blowing. As we drew near I saw that the coconut trees in a green abundance grew to the water's edge,

---

① skipper: 船长

and among them I saw the brown roofs of the village. A Chinese who spoke English pointed out to me a white bungalow as the residence of the District Officer. Though he did not know it, it was with him that I was going to stay. I had a letter of introduction to him in my pocket.

I felt somewhat forlorn when I landed and my bags were set down beside me on the glistening beach. This was a remote spot to find myself in, this little town on the north coast of Borneo, and I felt a trifle shy at the thought of presenting myself to a total stranger with the announcement that I was going to sleep under his roof, eat his food and drink his whisky, till another boat came in to take me to the port for which I was bound.

But I might have spared myself these misgivings, for the moment I reached the bungalow and sent in my letter he came out, a sturdy, ruddy, jovial man, of thirty-five perhaps, and greeted me with heartiness. While he held my hand he shouted to a boy to bring drinks and to another to look after my luggage. He cut short my apologies.

"Good God, man, you have no idea how glad I am to see you. Don't think I'm doing anything for you in putting you up. The boot's on the other leg. And stay as long as you damned well like. Stay a year."

I laughed. He put away his day's work, assuring me that he had nothing to do that could not wait till the morrow, and threw himself into a long chair. We talked and drank and talked. When the heat of the day wore off we went for a long tramp in the jungle and came back wet to the skin. A bath and a change were very grateful, and then we dined. I was tired out and though my host was plainly willing to go on talking straight through the night I was obliged to beg him to allow me to go to bed.

"All right, I'll just come along to your room and see everything's all right."

It was a large room with verandahs on two sides of it, sparsely furnished, but with a huge bed protected by mosquito netting①.

"The bed is rather hard. Do you mind?"

"Not a bit. I shall sleep without rocking tonight."

My host looked at the bed reflectively.

"It was a Dutchman② who slept in it last. Do you want to hear a funny story?"

I wanted chiefly to go to bed, but he was my host, and being at times somewhat of a humorist myself I know that it is hard to have an amusing story to tell and find no listener.

"He came on the boat that brought you, on its last journey along the coast, he came into my office and asked where the dak bungalow③ was. I told him there wasn't one, but

---

① mosquito netting：蚊帐
② Dutchman：荷兰人
③ dak bungalow：(旧时印度的)驿站旅馆(或客栈)

Chapter Thirteen

if he hadn't anywhere to go I didn't mind putting him up. He jumped at the invitation. I told him to have his kit sent along."

"This is all I've got," he said.

He held out a little shiny black grip. It seemed a bit scanty, but it was no business of mine, so I told him to go along to the bungalow and I'd come as soon as I was through with my work. While I was speaking the door of my office was opened and my clerk came in. The Dutchman had his back to the door and it may be that my clerk opened it a bit suddenly. Anyhow, the Dutchman gave a shout, he jumped about two feet into the air and whipped out a revolver.

"What the hell are you doing?" I said.

When he saw it was the clerk he collapsed. He leaned against the desk, panting, and upon my word he was shaking as though he'd got fever.

"I beg your pardon," he said. "It's my nerves. My nerves are terrible."

"It looks like it," I said.

I was rather short with him. To tell you the truth I wished I hadn't asked him to stop with me. He didn't look as though he'd been drinking a lot and I wondered if he was some fellow the police were after. If he were, I said to myself, he could hardly be such a fool as to walk right into the lion's den.

"You'd better go and lie down," I said.

He took himself off, and when I got back to my bungalow I found him sitting quite quietly, but bolt upright, on the verandah. He'd had a bath and shaved and put on clean things and he looked fairly presentable.

"Why are you sitting in the middle of the place like that?" I asked him. 'You'll be much more comfortable in one of the long chairs."

"I prefer to sit up," he said.

Queer, I thought. But if a man in this heat would rather sit up than lie down it's his own lookout. He wasn't much to look at, tallish and heavily built, with a square head and close cropped bristly hair. I should think he was about forty. The thing that chiefly struck me about him was his expression. There was a look in his eyes, blue eyes they were and rather small, that beat me altogether; and his face sagged as it were; it gave you the feeling he was going to cry. He had a way of looking quickly over his left shoulder as though he thought he heard something. By God, he was nervous. But we had a couple of drinks and he began to talk. He spoke English very well; except for a slight accent you'd never have known that he was a foreigner, and I'm bound to admit he was a good talker. He'd been everywhere and he'd read any amount. It was a treat to listen to him.

We had three or four whiskies in the afternoon and a lot of gin pahits later on, so that when dinner came along we were by way of being rather hilarious and I'd come to the conclusion that he was a damned good fellow. Of course we had a lot of whisky at dinner and I happened to have a bottle of Benedictine, so we had some liqueurs afterwards. I can't help thinking we both got very tight.

And at last he told me why he'd come. It was a rum story.

My host stopped and looked at me with his mouth slightly open as though, remembering it now, he was struck again with its rumness.

He came from Sumatra, the Dutchman, and he'd done something to an Achinese① and the Achinese had sworn to kill him. At first, he made light of it, but the fellow tried two or three times and it began to be rather a nuisance, so he thought he'd better go away for a bit. He went over to Batavia and made up his mind to have a good time. But when he'd been there a week he saw the fellow slinking along a wall. By God, he'd followed him. It looked as though he meant business. The Dutchman began to think it was getting beyond a joke and he thought the best thing he could do would be to skip off to Soerabaya. Well, he was strolling about there one day, you know how crowded the streets are, when he happened to turn round and saw the Achinese walking quite quietly just behind him. It gave him a turn. It would give anyone a turn.

The Dutchman went straight back to his hotel, packed his things, and took the next boat to Singapore. Of course he put up at the Van Wyck, all the Dutch stay there, and one day when he was having a drink in the courtyard in front of the hotel, the Achinese walked in as bold as brass, looked at him for a minute, and walked out again. The Dutchman told me he was just paralysed. The fellow could have stuck his kris into him there and then and he wouldn't have been able to move a hand to defend himself. The Dutchman knew he was just biding his time, that damned native was going to kill him, he saw it in his eyes; and he went all to pieces.

"But why didn't he go to the police?" I asked.

"I don't know. I expect it wasn't a thing he wanted the police to be mixed up in."

"But what had he done to the man?"

"I don't know that either. He wouldn't tell me. But by the look he gave when I asked him, I expect it was something pretty rotten. I have an idea he knew he deserved whatever the Achinese could do."

My host lit a cigarette.

"Go on," I said.

The skipper of the boat that runs between Singapore and Kuching lives at the Van Wyck between trips and the boat was starting at dawn. The Dutchman thought it a grand chance to give the fellow the slip; he left his luggage at the hotel and walked down to the ship with the skipper, as if he were just going to see him off, and stayed on her when she sailed. His nerves were all anyhow by then. He didn't care about anything but getting rid of the Achinese. He felt pretty safe at Kuching. He got a room at the rest-house and

---

① Achinese：（印度尼西亚苏门答腊岛北部的）亚齐族,亚齐人[语]

Chapter Thirteen

bought himself a couple of suits and some shirts in the Chinese shops. But he told me he couldn't sleep. He dreamt of that man and half a dozen times he awakened just as he thought a kris was being drawn across his throat. By God, I felt quite sorry for him. He just shook as he talked to me and his voice was hoarse with terror. That was the meaning of the look I had noticed. You remember, I told you he had a funny look on his face and I couldn't tell what it meant. Well, it was fear.

And one day when he was in the club at Kuching he looked out of the window and saw the Achinese sitting there. Their eyes met. The Dutchman just crumpled up and fainted. When he came to, his first idea was to get out. Well, you know, there's not a hell of a lot of traffic at Kuching and this boat that brought you was the only one that gave him a chance to get away quickly. He got on her. He was positive the man was not on board.

"But what made him come here?"

"Well, the old tramp stops at a dozen places on the coast and the Achinese couldn't possibly guess he'd chosen this one because he only made up his mind to get off when he saw there was only one boat to take the passengers ashore, and there weren't more than a dozen people in it."

"I'm safe here for a bit at all events," he said, "and if I can only be quiet for a while I shall get my nerve back."

"Stay as long as you like," I said. "You're all right here, at all events till the boat comes along next month, and if you like we'll watch the people who come off."

He was all over me. I could see what a relief it was to him.

It was pretty late and I suggested to him that we should turn in. I took him to his room to see that it was all right. He locked the door of the bath-house and bolted the shutters, though I told him there was no risk, and when I left I heard him lock the door I had just gone out of.

Next morning when the boy brought me my tea I asked him if he'd called the Dutchman. He said he was just going to. I heard him knock and knock again. Funny, I thought. The boy hammered on the door, but there was no answer. I felt a little nervous, so I got up. I knocked too. We made enough noise to rouse the dead, but the Dutchman slept on. Then I broke down the door. The mosquito curtains were neatly tucked in round the bed. I pulled them apart. He was lying there on his back with his eyes wide open. He was as dead as mutton①. A kris lay across his throat, and say I'm a liar if you like, but I swear to God it's true, there wasn't a wound about him anywhere. The room was empty.

"Funny, wasn't it?"

"Well, that all depends on your idea of humour," I replied.

---

① as dead as mutton: 肯定死了

My host looked at me quickly.

"You don't mind sleeping in that bed, do you?"

"N-no. But I'd just as soon you'd told me the story tomorrow morning."

Questions for Discussion

1. Can the story told by the host attract your attention? Why or why not?
2. Who killed the Dutchman according to your understanding?
3. What is the theme of the story?

Links

1. https://en.wikipedia.org/wiki/W._Somerset_Maugham
   提供毛姆生平及创作的详细介绍。
2. https://en.wikipedia.org/wiki/Of_Human_Bondage
   提供毛姆的小说《飞行之末》细读资料。

Part B

The Necklace

By Guy de Maupassant

Guy de Maupassant (1850—1893) was a French writer and a master of short story. He depicted human lives, destinies and social forces in disillusioned and often pessimistic terms. And he was a representative of the naturalist school of writers.

Maupassant's stories are characterized by economy of style and efficient, effortless outcome. Many are set during the Franco-Prussian War[①] of the 1870s, describing the futility of war and the innocent civilians who, caught up in events beyond their control, are permanently changed by their experiences. He wrote about 300 short stories, six novels, three travel books, and one volume of verse. His first published story, *Ball of Fat* (1880), is

---

① the Franco-Prussian War: 普法战争(由法国挑起,结果普鲁士大获全胜,以建立"德意志帝国"而告终)。

often considered his masterpiece. In 1881 he published his first volume of short stories under the title of *La Maison Tellier*. In 1883 he finished his first novel, *A Woman's Life*, 25,000 copies of which were sold in less than a year.

Maupassant is regarded as one of the fathers of the modern short story. He delighted in clever plotting and wrote comfortably in both realistic and fantastic modes. His stories and novels aim to recreate Third Republic France① in a realistic way, whereas many of the short stories describe apparently supernatural phenomena. The supernatural in Maupassant, however, is often implicitly a symptom of the protagonists' troubled minds.

Lead-in Questions

1. How do you define vanity? What kind of mistake have you made because of your vanity?
2. Who is Mathilde? What's relationship of Mathilde and Madame Forestier? Why is the necklace so important in Mathilde's life?

Questions about the Author and the Story

1. Which of the following is NOT written by Maupassant?
   A. *Ball of Fat*. B. *La Maison Tellier*.
   C. *A Woman's Life*. D. *The Gift of the Magi*.
2. Who is the story's narrator?
   A. Madame Ramponncau. B. Madame Forestier.
   C. Madame Loisel. D. An unnamed, all-knowing storyteller.
3. _____ was a hallmark of de Maupassant's style.
   A. Twist ending B. Irony
   C. Psychological time D. Symbol
4. Maupassant's work has been described as _____.
   A. plain plotting
   B. writing comfortably in both realistic and fantastic modes
   C. implicating the positive aspect of the life
   D. having revolutionized the theme of short stories, especially in its tendency to move forward and backward in time
5. What's the theme of Maupassant's story "The Necklace"?
   A. The dichotomy of reality vs. appearance.
   B. Material wealth will bring joy.
   C. The contradiction between beauty and vanity.

---

① Third Republic France: 法兰西第三共和国

D. Pride and self-esteem.

She was one of those pretty and charming girls born, as though fate had blundered over her, into a family of artisans. She had no marriage portion, no expectations, no means of getting known, understood, loved, and wedded by a man of wealth and distinction; and she let herself be married off to a little clerk in the Ministry of Education. Her tastes were simple because she had never been able to afford any other, but she was as unhappy as though she had married beneath her; for women have no caste or class, their beauty, grace, and charm serving them for birth or family, their natural delicacy, their instinctive elegance, their nimbleness of wit, are their only mark of rank, and put the slum girl on a level with the highest lady in the land.

She suffered endlessly, feeling herself born for every delicacy and luxury. She suffered from the poorness of her house, from its mean walls, worn chairs, and ugly curtains. All these things, of which other women of her class would not even have been aware, tormented and insulted her. The sight of the little Breton girl who came to do the work in her little house aroused heart-broken regrets and hopeless dreams in her mind. She imagined silent antechambers, heavy with Oriental tapestries, lit by torches in lofty bronze sockets, with two tall footmen in knee-breeches sleeping in large arm-chairs, overcome by the heavy warmth of the stove. She imagined vast saloons hung with antique silks, exquisite pieces of furniture supporting priceless ornaments, and small, charming, perfumed rooms, created just for little parties of intimate friends, men who were famous and sought after, whose homage roused every other woman's envious longings.

When she sat down for dinner at the round table covered with a three-day-old cloth, opposite her husband, who took the cover off the soup-tureen, exclaiming delightedly: "Aha! Scotch broth! What could be better?" she imagined delicate meals, gleaming silver, tapestries peopling the walls with folk of a past age and strange birds in faery forests; she imagined delicate food served in marvellous dishes, murmured gallantries, listened to with an inscrutable smile as one trifled with the rosy flesh of trout or wings of asparagus chicken.

She had no clothes, no jewels, nothing. And these were the only things she loved; she felt that she was made for them. She had longed so eagerly to charm, to be desired, to be wildly attractive and sought after.

She had a rich friend, an old school friend whom she refused to visit, because she suffered so keenly when she returned home. She would weep whole days, with grief, regret, despair, and misery.

One evening her husband came home with an exultant air, holding a large envelope in his hand.

Chapter Thirteen

"Here's something for you," he said.

Swiftly she tore the paper and drew out a printed card on which were these words:

"The Minister of Education and Madame Ramponneau request the pleasure of the company of Monsieur and Madame Loisel at the Ministry on the evening of Monday, January the 18th."

Instead of being delighted, as her husband hoped, she flung the invitation petulantly across the table, murmuring:

"What do you want me to do with this?"

"Why, darling, I thought you'd be pleased. You never go out, and this is a great occasion. I had tremendous trouble to get it. Every one wants one; it's very select, and very few go to the clerks. You'll see all the really big people there."

She looked at him out of furious eyes, and said impatiently: "And what do you suppose I am to wear at such an affair?"

He had not thought about it; he stammered: "Why, the dress you go to the theatre in. It looks very nice, to me ..."

He stopped, stupefied and utterly at a loss when he saw that his wife was beginning to cry. Two large tears ran slowly down from the corners of her eyes towards the corners of her mouth.

"What's the matter with you? What's the matter with you?" he faltered.

But with a violent effort she overcame her grief and replied in a calm voice, wiping her wet cheeks:

"Nothing. Only I haven't a dress and so I can't go to this party. Give your invitation to some friend of yours whose wife will be turned out better than I shall."

He was heart-broken.

"Look here, Mathilde," he persisted. "What would be the cost of a suitable dress, which you could use on other occasions as well, something very simple?"

She thought for several seconds, reckoning up prices and also wondering for how large a sum she could ask without bringing upon herself an immediate refusal and an exclamation of horror from the careful-minded clerk.

At last she replied with some hesitation: "I don't know exactly, but I think I could do it on four hundred francs."

He grew slightly pale, for this was exactly the amount he had been saving for a gun, intending to get a little shooting next summer on the plain of Nanterre with some friends who went lark-shooting there on Sundays.

Nevertheless he said: "Very well. I'll give you four hundred francs. But try and get a really nice dress with the money."

The day of the party drew near, and Madame Loisel seemed sad, uneasy and anxious. Her dress was ready, however. One evening her husband said to her:

"What's the matter with you? You've been very odd for the last three days."

"I'm utterly miserable at not having any jewels, not a single stone, to wear," she replied. "I shall look absolutely no one. I would almost rather not go to the party."

"Wear flowers," he said. "They're very smart at this time of the year. For ten francs you could get two or three gorgeous roses."

She was not convinced.

"No ... there's nothing so humiliating as looking poor in the middle of a lot of rich women."

"How stupid you are!" exclaimed her husband. "Go and see Madame Forestier and ask her to lend you some jewels. You know her quite well enough for that."

She uttered a cry of delight.

"That's true. I never thought of it."

Next day she went to see her friend and told her her trouble.

Madame Forestier went to her dressing-table, took up a large box, brought it to Madame Loisel, opened it, and said: "Choose, my dear."

First she saw some bracelets, then a pearl necklace, then a Venetian cross in gold and gems, of exquisite workmanship. She tried the effect of the jewels before the mirror, hesitating, unable to make up her mind to leave them, to give them up. She kept on asking:

"Haven't you anything else?"

"Yes. Look for yourself. I don't know what you would like best."

Suddenly she discovered, in a black satin case, a superb diamond necklace; her heart began to beat covetously. Her hands trembled as she lifted it. She fastened it round her neck, upon her high dress, and remained in ecstasy at sight of herself.

Then, with hesitation, she asked in anguish:

"Could you lend me this, just this alone?"

"Yes, of course."

She flung herself on her friend's breast, embraced her frenziedly, and went away with her treasure. The day of the party arrived. Madame Loisel was a success. She was the prettiest woman present, elegant, graceful, smiling, and quite above herself with happiness. All the men stared at her, inquired her name, and asked to be introduced to her. All the Under-Secretaries of State were eager to waltz with her. The Minister noticed her.

She danced madly, ecstatically, drunk with pleasure, with no thought for anything, in the triumph of her beauty, in the pride of her success, in a cloud of happiness made up of this universal homage and admiration, of the desires she had aroused, of the completeness of a victory so dear to her feminine heart.

She left about four o'clock in the morning. Since midnight her husband had been dozing in a deserted little room, in company with three other men whose wives were having a good time. He threw over her shoulders the garments he had brought for them

Chapter Thirteen

to go home in, modest everyday clothes, whose poverty clashed with the beauty of the ball-dress. She was conscious of this and was anxious to hurry away, so that she should not be noticed by the other women putting on their costly furs.

Loisel restrained her.

"Wait a little. You'll catch cold in the open. I'm going to fetch a cab."

But she did not listen to him and rapidly descended the staircase. When they were out in the street they could not find a cab; they began to look for one, shouting at the drivers whom they saw passing in the distance.

They walked down towards the Seine, desperate and shivering. At last they found on the quay one of those old nightprowling carriages which are only to be seen in Paris after dark, as though they were ashamed of their shabbiness in the daylight.

It brought them to their door in the Rue des Martyrs, and sadly they walked up to their own apartment. It was the end, for her. As for him, he was thinking that he must be at the office at ten.

She took off the garments in which she had wrapped her shoulders, so as to see herself in all her glory before the mirror. But suddenly she uttered a cry. The necklace was no longer round her neck!

"What's the matter with you?" asked her husband, already half undressed.

She turned towards him in the utmost distress.

"I ... I ... I've no longer got Madame Forestier's necklace. ..."

He started with astonishment.

"What! ... Impossible!"

They searched in the folds of her dress, in the folds of the coat, in the pockets, everywhere. They could not find it.

"Are you sure that you still had it on when you came away from the ball?" he asked.

"Yes, I touched it in the hall at the Ministry."

"But if you had lost it in the street, we should have heard it fall."

"Yes. Probably we should. Did you take the number of the cab?"

"No. You didn't notice it, did you?"

"No."

They stared at one another, dumbfounded. At last Loisel put on his clothes again.

"I'll go over all the ground we walked," he said, "and see if I can't find it."

And he went out. She remained in her evening clothes, lacking strength to get into bed, huddled on a chair, without volition or power of thought.

Her husband returned about seven. He had found nothing.

He went to the police station, to the newspapers, to offer a reward, to the cab companies, everywhere that a ray of hope impelled him.

She waited all day long, in the same state of bewilderment at this fearful catastrophe.

Loisel came home at night, his face lined and pale; he had discovered nothing.

"You must write to your friend," he said, "and tell her that you've broken the clasp of her necklace and are getting it mended. That will give us time to look about us."

She wrote at his dictation.

By the end of a week they had lost all hope.

Loisel, who had aged five years, declared: "We must see about replacing the diamonds."

Next day they took the box which had held the necklace and went to the jewellers whose name was inside. He consulted his books.

"It was not I who sold this necklace, Madame; I must have merely supplied the clasp."

Then they went from jeweller to jeweller, searching for another necklace like the first, consulting their memories, both ill with remorse and anguish of mind.

In a shop at the Palais-Royal they found a string of diamonds which seemed to them exactly like the one they were looking for. It was worth forty thousand francs. They were allowed to have it for thirty-six thousand.

They begged the jeweller not to sell it for three days. And they arranged matters on the understanding that it would be taken back for thirty-four thousand francs, if the first one were found before the end of February.

Loisel possessed eighteen thousand francs left to him by his father. He intended to borrow the rest.

He did borrow it, getting a thousand from one man, five hundred from another, five louis here, three louis there. He gave notes of hand, entered into ruinous agreements, did business with usurers and the whole tribe of money-lenders. He mortgaged the whole remaining years of his existence, risked his signature without even knowing if he could honor it, and, appalled at the agonising face of the future, at the black misery about to fall upon him, at the prospect of every possible physical privation and moral torture, he went to get the new necklace and put down upon the jeweller's counter thirty-six thousand francs.

When Madame Loisel took back the necklace to Madame Forestier, the latter said to her in a chilly voice:

"You ought to have brought it back sooner; I might have needed it."

She did not, as her friend had feared, open the case. If she had noticed the substitution, what would she have thought? What would she have said? Would she not have taken her for a thief?

Madame Loisel came to know the ghastly life of abject poverty. From the very first she played her part heroically. This fearful debt must be paid off. She would pay it. The servant was dismissed. They changed their flat; they took a garret under the roof.

She came to know the heavy work of the house, the hateful duties of the kitchen.

Chapter Thirteen

She washed the plates, wearing out her pink nails on the coarse pottery and the bottoms of pans. She washed the dirty linen, the shirts and dish-cloths, and hung them out to dry on a string; every morning she took the dustbin down into the street and carried up the water, stopping on each landing to get her breath. And, clad like a poor woman, she went to the fruiterer, to the grocer, to the butcher, a basket on her arm, haggling, insulted, fighting for every wretched halfpenny of her money.

Every month notes had to be paid off, others renewed, time gained.

Her husband worked in the evenings at putting straight a merchant's accounts, and often at night he did copying at twopence-halfpenny a page.

And this life lasted ten years.

At the end of ten years everything was paid off, everything, the usurer's charges and the accumulation of superimposed interest.

Madame Loisel looked old now. She had become like all the other strong, hard, coarse women of poor households. Her hair was badly done, her skirts were awry, her hands were red. She spoke in a shrill voice, and the water slopped all over the floor when she scrubbed it. But sometimes, when her husband was at the office, she sat down by the window and thought of that evening long ago, of the ball at which she had been so beautiful and so much admired.

What would have happened if she had never lost those jewels. Who knows? Who knows? How strange life is, how fickle! How little is needed to ruin or to save!

One Sunday, as she had gone for a walk along the Champs-Elysees to freshen herself after the labours of the week, she caught sight suddenly of a woman who was taking a child out for a walk. It was Madame Forestier, still young, still beautiful, still attractive.

Madame Loisel was conscious of some emotion. Should she speak to her? Yes, certainly. And now that she had paid, she would tell her all. Why not?

She went up to her.

"Good morning, Jeanne."

The other did not recognize her, and was surprised at being thus familiarly addressed by a poor woman.

"But ... Madame ... " she stammered. "I don't know ... you must be making a mistake."

"No ... I am Mathilde Loisel."

Her friend uttered a cry.

"Oh! ... my poor Mathilde, how you have changed! ..."

"Yes, I've had some hard times since I saw you last; and many sorrows ... and all on your account."

"On my account! ... How was that?"

"You remember the diamond necklace you lent me for the ball at the Ministry?"

"Yes. Well?"

"Well, I lost it."

"How could you? Why, you brought it back."

"I brought you another one just like it. And for the last ten years we have been paying for it. You realise it wasn't easy for us; we had no money. ... Well, it's paid for at last, and I'm glad indeed."

Madame Forestier had halted.

"You say you bought a diamond necklace to replace mine?"

"Yes. You hadn't noticed it? They were very much alike."

And she smiled in proud and innocent happiness.

Madame Forestier, deeply moved, took her two hands.

"Oh, my poor Mathilde! But mine was imitation. It was worth at the very most five hundred francs! ..."

Questions for Discussion

1. Why did Mathilde borrow a necklace from her friend? How did the author employ irony in the story?
2. What happened on their way home after the ball? What did they do in order to pay for the necklace?
3. Should Mathilde tell the truth to her friend earlier? If she did so, what kind of result would the story have?

Links

1. https://en.wikipedia.org/wiki/Guy_de_Maupassant#Short_stories
   提供莫泊桑生平及创作的详细介绍。
2. http://www.maupassantiana.fr/
   提供莫泊桑的小说《项链》的细读资料。

Chapter Fourteen

Letter from an Unknown Woman

By Stephan Zweig

Stephan Zweig (1881—1943), German biographer, essayist, short story writer, and cosmopolitan, was a prolific writer whose vivid portrayals of his characters, whether fictional or factual, were emphatically probing and believable. In the 1930s, Zweig was one of the most widely translated authors of the world. His extensive travels led him to India, Africa, North and Central America, and Russia.

Born in Vienna into a family of wealthy industrialist, Zweig studied in Austria, France, and Germany. By 1904 he had earned a doctorate from Vienna University, and he traveled widely before settling in Salzburg in 1913. In 1914, he married Friderike von Winternitz, who had started to send him fan mail in 1901, when his first work, a collection of poems, appeared. He was interested in the teachings of Sigmund Freud, which influenced his biographies as well as his fiction. Several of Zweig's stories have been filmed, the best-known of which is *Letter From an Unknown Woman*, directed by Max Ophüls (1948).

During the years at Salzburg, Zweig began to suspect that Hitler's persecution of Jews was directed at him personally, and he never recovered from this paranoia. His work was banned by the Nazis and Zweig was driven into exile. In 1938, he became a British citizen, and in 1940, after a successful lecture tour in South America, he settled in Brazil. Disillusioned and isolated, Zweig committed suicide with his second wife near Rio de Janeiro on February 23, 1942. Zweig's autobiography, *The World of Yesterday*, was published posthumously the following year, in which he wrote that "my main interest in writing has always been the psychological representation of persons and their lives."

Classical Western Short Stories

 Lead-in Questions

1. Do you know anything about Sigmund Freud's theory of psychological analysis?
2. Have you read any Stephan Zweig's works? Is there anything in common in his works?
3. What kind of a woman occurred to you while you read the title of the story *Letter from an Unknown woman*?

 Questions about the Author and the Story

1. In the story, who does "My boy" refer to?
    A. The son of the woman and the novelist's.
    B. The woman's son but not the novelist's.
    C. The Duke and the woman's son.
    D. The boy's identification is not revealed in the novel.
2. What does "Unknown" in the title imply according to the story?
    A. The man and the woman have never met with each other.
    B. To the man, the woman's whole life is unknown to him even they have been so "close" physically.
    C. The woman wrote the letter without her signature, even when the man have read the letter, he still couldn't recall who the woman was.
    D. None of the above.
3. How long had it been before the woman returned to the place where the man was still living?
    A. Four years.   B. Five years.   C. Three years.   D. Two years.
4. At the end of letter, the woman request the man to buy the white rose for himself on his birthday. Why?
    A. Because she believes the man loves white roses.
    B. Because she wants the man to celebrate his birthday by himself.
    C. Because she wants the man to remember her and live in the man' life at least one day.
5. What's the tone of the woman in the letter?
    A. Hateful.   B. Complaining.   C. Affectionately.   D. Cheerful.

R., the famous novelist, had been away on a brief holiday in the mountains. Reaching Vienna early in the morning, he bought a newspaper at the station, and when he glanced at the date was reminded that it was his birthday. "Forty-one!"—the thought came like a flash. He was neither glad nor sorry at the realization. He hailed a taxi, and skimmed the newspaper as he drove home. His man reported that there had been a few

Chapter Fourteen

callers during the master's absence, besides one or two telephone messages. A bundle of letters was awaiting him. Looking indifferently at these, he opened one or two because he was interested in the senders, but laid aside for the time a bulky packet addressed in a strange handwriting. At ease in an armchair, he drank his morning tea, finished the newspaper, and read a few circulars. Then, having lighted a cigar, he turned to the remaining letter.

It was a manuscript rather than an ordinary letter, comprising a couple of dozen hastily penned sheets in a feminine handwriting. Involuntarily he examined the envelope once more, in case he might have overlooked a covering letter. But there was nothing of the kind, no signature, and no sender's address on either envelope or contents. "Strange," he thought, as he began to read the manuscript. The first words were a superscription: "To you, who have never known me." He was perplexed. Was this addressed to him, or to some imaginary being? His curiosity suddenly awakened, he read as follows:

My boy died yesterday. For three days and three nights I have been wrestling with Death for this frail little life. During forty consecutive hours, while the fever of influenza was shaking his poor burning body, I sat beside his bed. I put cold compresses on his forehead; day and night, night and day, I held his restless little hands. The third evening, my strength gave out. My eyes closed without my being aware of it, and for three or four hours I must have slept on the hard stool. Meanwhile, Death took him. There he lies, my darling boy, in his narrow cot, just as he died. Only his eyes have been closed, his wise, dark eyes; and his hands have been crossed over his breast. Four candles are burning, one at each corner of the bed. I cannot bear to look, I cannot bear to move; for when the candles flicker, shadows chase one another over his face and his closed lips. It looks as if his features stirred, and I could almost fancy that he is not dead after all, that he will wake up, and with his clear voice will say something childishly loving. But I know that he is dead; and I will not look again, to hope once more, and once more to be disappointed. I know, I know, my boy died yesterday. Now I have only you left in the world; only you, who do not know me; you, who are enjoying yourself all unheeding, sporting with men and things. Only you, who have never known me, and whom I have never ceased to love.

I have lighted a fifth candle, and am sitting at the table writing to you. I cannot stay alone with my dead child without pouring my heart out to someone and to whom should I do that in this dreadful hour if not to You, who have been and still are all in all to me? Perhaps I shall not be able to make myself plain to you. Perhaps you will not be able to understand me. My head feels so heavy; my temples are throbbing; my limbs are aching. I think I must be feverish. Influenza is raging in this quarter, and probably I have caught the infection. I should not be sorry if I could join my child in that way, instead of making short work of myself. Sometimes it seems dark before my eyes, and perhaps I shall not be able to finish this letter; but I shall try with all my strength, this one and only time, to speak to you, my beloved, to you who have never known me. To you only do I want to speak, that I may tell you everything for the first time. I should like you to know the whole of my life, of that life which has always been yours, and of which you have known nothing. But you shall only know my secret after I am dead, when there will be no one whom you will have to answer; you shall only know it if that which is now shaking my limbs with cold and with heat should really prove, for me, the end. If I have to go on living, I shall tear up this letter and shall keep the silence I have always kept. If you ever hold it in your hands, you may know that a dead woman is telling you her life story; the story of a life which was yours from its first to its last fully conscious hour. You need have no fear of my words. A dead woman wants nothing; neither love, nor compassion, nor consolation. I have only one thing to ask of you, that you believe to the full what the pain in me forces me to disclose to you. Believe my words, for I ask nothing more of you; a mother will not speak falsely beside the deathbed of her only child.

I am going to tell you my whole life, the life which did not really begin until the day I first saw you. What I can recall before that day is gloomy and confused, a memory as of a cellar filled with dusty, dull, and cob-webbed things and people—a place with which my heart has no concern. When you came into my life, I was thirteen, and I lived in the house where you live today, in the very house in which you are reading this letter, the last breath of my life. I lived on the same floor, for the door of our flat was just opposite the door of yours. You will certainly have forgotten us. You will long ago have forgotten the accountant's widow in her threadbare mourning, and the thin, half-grown girl. We were always so quiet; characteristic examples of shabby gentility. It is unlikely that you ever heard our name, for we had no plate on our front door, and no one ever came to see us. Besides, it is so long ago, fifteen or sixteen years. Impossible that you should remember. But I, how passionately I remember every detail. As if it had just happened, I recall the day, the hour, when I first heard of you, first saw you. How could it be otherwise, seeing that it was then the world began for me? Have patience awhile, and let me tell you everything from first to last. Do not grow weary of listening to me for a brief space, since I have not been weary of loving you my whole life long.

Before you came, the people who lived in your flat were horrid folk, always quarrelling. Though they were wretchedly poor themselves, they hated us for our poverty because we held aloof from them. The man was given to drink, and used to beat his wife. We were often wakened in the night by the clatter of falling chairs and breaking plates. Once, when he had beaten her till the blood came, she ran out on the landing with her hair streaming, followed by her drunken husband abusing her, until all the people came out onto the staircase and threatened to send for the police. My mother would have nothing to do with them. She forbade me to play with the children, who took every opportunity of venting their spleen on me for this refusal. When they met me in the street, they would call me names; and once they threw a snowball at me which was so hard that it cut my forehead. Everyone in the house detested them, and we all breathed more freely when something happened and they had to leave—I think the man had been arrested for theft. For a few days there was a "To Let" notice at the main door. Then it was taken down, and the caretaker told us that the flat had been rented by an author, who was a bachelor, and was sure to be quiet. That was the first time I heard your name.

A few days later, the flat was thoroughly cleaned, and the painters and decorators came. Of course they made a lot of noise, but my mother was glad, for she said that would be the end of the disorder next door. I did not see you during the move. The decorations and furnishings were supervised by your servant, the little grey-haired man with such a serious demeanour, who had obviously been used to service in good families. He managed everything in a most businesslike way, and impressed us all very much. A high-class domestic of this kind was something quite new in our suburban flats. Besides, he was extremely civil, but was never hail-fellow-well-met with the ordinary servants. From the outset he treated my mother respectfully, as a lady; and he was always courteous even to little me. When he had occasion to mention your name, he did so in a way which showed that his feeling towards you was that of a family retainer. I used to love good, old John for this, though I envied him at the same time because it was his privilege to see you constantly and to serve you.

Do you know why I am telling you these trifles? I want you to understand how it was that from the very beginning your personality came to exercise so much power over me when I was still a shy and timid child. Before I had actually seen you, there was a halo round your head. You were enveloped in an atmosphere of wealth, marvel, and mystery. People whose lives are narrow, are avid of novelty; and in this little suburban house we were all impatiently awaiting your arrival. In my own case, curiosity rose to fever point when I came home from school one afternoon and found the furniture van in front of the house. Most of the heavy things had gone up, and the furniture removers were dealing with the smaller articles. I stood at the door to watch and admire, for everything belonging to you was so different from what I had been used to. There were Indian idols, Italian sculptures, and great, brightly colored pictures. Last of all came books, such lovely books, many more than I should have thought possible. They were piled by the door. The manservant stood there carefully dusting them one by one. I greedily watched the pile as it grew. Your servant did not send me away, but he did not encourage me either, so I was afraid to touch any of them, though I should have so liked to stroke the smooth leather bindings. I did glance timidly at some of the titles; many of them were in French and in English, and in languages of which I did not know a single word. I should have liked to stand there watching for hours, but my mother called me and I had to go in.

I thought about you the whole evening, although I had not seen you yet. I had only about a dozen cheap books, bound in worn cardboard. I loved them more than anything else in the world, and was continually reading and rereading them. Now I was wondering what the man could be like who had such a lot of books, who had read so much, who knew so many languages, who was rich and at the same time so learned. The idea of so many books aroused a kind of unearthly veneration. I tried to picture you in my mind. You must be an old man with spectacles and a long, white beard, like our geography master, but much kinder, nicer-looking, and gentler. I don't know why I was sure that you must be handsome, for I fancied you to be an elderly man. That very night, I dreamed of you for the first time.

Next day you moved in; but though I was on the watch I could not get a glimpse of your face, and my failure inflamed my curiosity. At length I saw you, on the third day. How astounded I was to find that you were quite different from the ancient godfather conjured up by my childish imagination. A bespectacled, good-natured old fellow was what I had expected to see; and you came, looking just as you still look, for you are one on whom the years leave little mark. You were wearing a beautiful suit of light-brown tweeds, and you ran upstairs two steps at a time with the boyish ease that always characterizes your movements. You were hat in hand, so that, with indescribable amazement, I could see your bright and lively face and your youthful hair. Your handsome, slim, and spruce figure was a positive shock to me. How strange it was that in this first moment I should have plainly realized that which I and all others are continually surprised at in you. I realized that you are two people rolled into one: that you are an ardent, light-hearted youth, devoted to sport and adventure; and at the same time, in your art, a deeply read and highly cultured man, grave, and with a keen sense of responsibility. Unconsciously I perceived what everyone who knew you came to perceive, that you led two lives. One of these was known to all, it was the life open to the whole world; the other was turned away from the world, and was fully known only to yourself. I, a girl of thirteen, coming under the spell of your attraction, grasped this secret of your existence, this profound cleavage of your two lives, at the first glance.

Can you understand, now, what a miracle, what an alluring enigma, you must have seemed to me, the child? Here was a man whom everyone spoke of with respect because he wrote books, and because he was famous in the great world. Of a sudden he had revealed himself to me as a boyish, cheerful young man of five-and-twenty! I need hardly tell you that henceforward, in my restricted world, you were the only thing that interested me; that my life revolved round yours with the fidelity proper to a girl of

Chapter Fourteen

thirteen. I watched you, watched your habits, watched the people who came to see you—and all this increased instead of diminishing my interest in your personality, for the two-sidedness of your nature was reflected in the diversity of your visitors. Some of them were young men, comrades of yours, carelessly dressed students with whom you laughed and larked. Some of them were ladies who came in motors. Once the conductor of the opera—the great man whom before this I had seen only from a distance, baton in hand—called on you. Some of them were girls, young girls still attending the commercial school, who shyly glided in at the door. A great many of your visitors were women. I thought nothing of this, not even when, one morning, as I was on my way to school, I saw a closely veiled lady coming away from your flat. I was only just thirteen, and in my immaturity I did not in the least realize that the eager curiosity with which I scanned all your doings was already love.

But I know the very day and hour when I consciously gave my whole heart to you. I had been for a walk with a schoolfellow, and we were standing at the door chattering. A motor drove up. You jumped out, in the impatient, springy fashion which has never ceased to charm me, and were about to go in. An impulse made me open the door for you, and this brought me in your path, so that we almost collided. You looked at me with a cordial, gracious, all-embracing glance, which was almost a caress. You smiled at me tenderly—yes, tenderly is the word—and said gently, nay, confidentially: "Thanks so much."

That was all you said. But from this moment, from the time when you looked at me so gently, so tenderly, I was yours. Later, before long indeed, I was to learn that this was a way you had of looking at all women with whom you came in contact. It was a caressing and alluring glance, at once enfolding and disclothing, the glance of the born seducer. Involuntarily, you looked in this way at every showgirl who served you, at every maidservant who opened the door to you. It was not that you consciously longed to possess all these women, but your impulse towards the sex unconsciously made your eyes melting and warm whenever they rested on a woman. At thirteen, I had no thought of this; and I felt as if I had been bathed in fire. I believed that the tenderness was for me, for me only; and in this one instant the woman was awakened in the half-grown girl, the woman who was to be yours for all future time.

"Who was that?" asked my friend. At first, I could not answer. I found it impossible to utter your name. It had suddenly become sacred to me, had become my secret. "Oh, it's just someone who lives in the house," I said awkwardly. "Then why did you blush so fiery red when he looked at you?" enquired my schoolfellow with the malice of an inquisitive child. I felt that she was making fun of me, and was reaching out towards my secret, and this colored my cheeks more than ever. I was deliberately rude to her: "You silly idiot," I said angrily—I should have liked to throttle her. She laughed mockingly, until the tears came into my eyes from impotent rage. I left her at the door and ran upstairs.

I have loved you ever since. I know full well that you are used to hearing women say that they love you. But I am sure that no one else has ever loved you so slavishly, with such doglike fidelity, with such devotion, as I did and do. Nothing can equal the unnoticed love of a child. It is hopeless and subservient; it is patient and passionate; it is something which the covetous love of a grown woman, the love that is unconsciously exacting, can never be. None but lonely children can cherish such a passion. The others will squander their feelings in companionship, will dissipate them in confidential talks. They have heard and read much of love, and they know that it comes to all. They play with it like a toy; they flaunt it as a boy flaunts his first cigarette. But I had no confidant; I had been neither taught nor warned; I was inexperienced and unsuspecting. I rushed to meet my fate. Everything that stirred in me, all that happened to me, seemed to be centred upon you, upon my imaginings of you. My father had died long before. My mother could think of nothing but her troubles, of the difficulties of making ends meet upon her narrow pension, so that she had little in common with the growing girl. My schoolfellows, half-enlightened and half-corrupted, were uncongenial to me because of their frivolous outlook upon that which to me was a supreme passion. The upshot was that everything which surged up in me, all which in other girls of my age is usually scattered, was focused upon you. You became for me—what simile can do justice to my feelings? You became for me the whole of my life. Nothing existed for me except in so far as it related to you. Nothing had meaning for me unless it bore upon you in some way. You had changed everything for me. Hitherto I had been indifferent at school, and undistinguished. Now, of a sudden, I was the first. I read book upon book, far into the night, for I knew that you were a book-lover. To my mother's astonishment, I began, almost stubbornly, to practise the piano, for I fancied that you were fond of music. I stitched and mended my clothes, to make them neat for your eyes. It was a torment to me that there was a square patch in my old school-apron (cut down from one of my mother's overalls). I was afraid you might notice it and would despise me, so I used to cover the patch with my satchel when I was on the staircase. I was terrified lest you should catch sight of it. What a fool I was! You hardly ever looked at me again.

Yet my whole day was spent in waiting for you and watching you. There was a judas① in our front door, and through this a glimpse of your door could be had. Don't laugh at me, dear. Even now, I am not ashamed of the hours I spent at this spy-hole. The hall was icy cold, and I was always afraid of exciting my mother's suspicions. But there I would watch through the long afternoons, during those months and years, book in hand, tense as a violin string, and vibrating at the touch of your nearness. I was ever near you, and ever tense; but you were no more aware of it than you were aware of the

---

① judas：窥视孔。

Chapter Fourteen

tension of the mainspring of the watch in your pocket, faithfully recording the hours for you, accompanying your footsteps with its unheard ticking, and vouchsafed only a hasty glance for one second among millions. I knew all about you, your habits, the neckties you wore; I knew each one of your suits. Soon I was familiar with your regular visitors, and had my likes and dislikes among them. From my thirteenth to my sixteenth year, my every hour was yours. What follies did I not commit? I kissed the door-handle you had touched; I picked up a cigarette end you had thrown away, and it was sacred to me because your lips had pressed it. A hundred times, in the evening, on one pretext or another, I ran out into the street in order to see in which room your light was burning, that I might be more fully conscious of your invisible presence. During the weeks when you were away (my heart always seemed to stop beating when I saw John carry your portmanteau downstairs), life was devoid of meaning. Out of sorts, bored to death, and in an ill-humor, I wandered about not knowing what to do, and had to take precautions lest my tear-stained eyes should betray my despair to my mother.

I know that what I am writing here is a record of grotesque absurdities, of a girl's extravagant fantasies. I ought to be ashamed of them; but I am not ashamed, for never was my love purer and more passionate than at this time. I could spend hours, days, in telling you how I lived with you though you hardly knew me by sight. Of course you hardly knew me, for if I met you on the stairs and could not avoid the encounter, I would hasten by with lowered head, afraid of your burning glance, hasten like one who is jumping into the water to avoid being singed. For hours, days, I could tell you of those years you have long since forgotten; could unroll all the calendar of your life; but I will not weary you with details. Only one more thing I should like to tell you dating from this time, the most splendid experience of my childhood. You must not laugh at it, for, trifle though you may deem it, to me it was of infinite significance.

It must have been a Sunday. You were away, and your man was dragging back the heavy rugs, which he had been beating, through the open door of the flat. They were rather too much for his strength, and I summoned up courage to ask whether he would let me help him. He was surprised, but did not refuse. Can I ever make you understand the awe, the pious veneration, with which I set foot in your dwelling, with which I saw your world—the writing-table at which you were accustomed to sit (there were some flowers on it in a blue crystal vase), the pictures, the books? I had no more than a stolen glance, though the good John would no doubt have let me see more had I ventured to ask him. But it was enough for me to absorb the atmosphere, and to provide fresh nourishment for my endless dreams of you in waking and sleeping. This swift minute was the happiest of my childhood. I wanted to tell you of it, so that you who do not know me might at length begin to understand how my life hung upon yours. I wanted to tell you of that minute, and also of the dreadful hour which so soon followed. As I have explained, my thoughts of you had made me oblivious to all else. I paid no attention to my mother's doings, or to those of any of our visitors. I failed to notice that an elderly gentleman, an Innsbruck merchant, a distant family connection of my mother, came often and stayed for a long time. I was glad that he took Mother to the theatre sometimes, for this left me alone, undisturbed in my thoughts of you, undisturbed in the watching which was my chief, my only pleasure. But one day my mother summoned me with a certain formality, saying that she had something serious to talk to me about. I turned pale, and felt my heart throb. Did she suspect anything? Had I betrayed myself in some way? My first thought was of you, of my secret, of that which linked me with life. But my mother was herself embarrassed. It had never been her way to kiss me. Now she kissed me affectionately more than once, drew me to her on the sofa, and began hesitatingly and rather shamefacedly to tell me that her relative, who was a widower, had made her a proposal of marriage, and that, mainly for my sake, she had decided to accept. I palpitated with anxiety, having only one thought, that of you. "We shall stay here, shan't we?" I stammered out. "No, we are going to Innsbruck, where Ferdinand has a fine villa." I heard no more. Everything seemed to turn black before my eyes. I learned afterwards that I had fainted. I clasped my hands convulsively, and fell like a lump of lead. I cannot tell you all that happened in the next few days; how I, a powerless child, vainly revolted against the mighty elders. Even now, as I think of it, my hand shakes so that I can hardly write. I could not disclose the real secret, and therefore my opposition seemed ill-tempered obstinacy. No one told me anything more. All the arrangements were made behind my back. The hours when I was at school were turned to account. Each time I came home some new article had been removed or sold. My life seemed falling to pieces; and at last one day, when I returned to dinner, the furniture removers had cleared the flat. In the empty rooms there were some packed trunks, and two camp-beds for Mother and myself. We were to sleep there one night more, and were then to go to Innsbruck①.

On this last day I suddenly made up my mind that I could not live without being near you. You were all the world to me. I can hardly say what I was thinking of, and whether in this hour of despair I was able to think at all. My mother was out of the house. I stood up, just as I was, in my school dress, and went over to your door. Yet I can hardly say that I went. With stiff limbs and trembling joints, I seemed to be drawn towards your door as by a magnet. It was in my mind to throw myself at your feet, and to beg you to keep me as a maid, as a slave. I cannot help feeling afraid that you will laugh at this infatuation of a girl of fifteen. But you would not laugh if you could realize how I stood there on the chilly landing, rigid with apprehension, and yet drawn onward by an irresistible force; how my arm seemed to lift itself in spite of me. The struggle appeared to last for endless, terrible seconds; and then I rang the bell. The shrill noise

---

① Innsbruck:因斯布鲁克,奥地利西部城市。

still sounds in my ears. It was followed by a silence in which my heart well-nigh stopped beating, and my blood stagnated, while I listened for your coming.

But you did not come. No one came. You must have been out that afternoon, and John must have been away too. With the dead note of the bell still sounding in my ears, I stole back into our empty dwelling, and threw myself exhausted upon a rug, tired out by the four steps as if I had been wading through deep snow for hours. Yet beneath this exhaustion there still glowed the determination to see you, to speak to you, before they carried me away. I can assure you that there were no sensual longings in my mind; I was still ignorant, just because I never thought of anything but you. All I wanted was to see you once more, to cling to you. Throughout that dreadful night I waited for you. Directly my mother had gone to sleep, I crept into the hall to listen for your return. It was a bitterly cold night in January. I was tired, my limbs ached, and there was no longer a chair on which I could sit; so I lay upon the floor, scourged by the draught that came under the door. In my thin dress I lay there, without any covering. I did not want to be warm, lest I should fall asleep and miss your footstep. Cramps seized me, so cold was it in the horrible darkness; again and again I had to stand up. But I waited, waited, waited for you, as for my fate.

At length (it must have been two or three in the morning) I heard the house-door open, and footsteps on the stair. The sense of cold vanished, and a rush of heat passed over me. I softly opened the door, meaning to run out, to throw myself at your feet ... I cannot tell what I should have done in my frenzy. The steps drew nearer. A candle flickered. Tremblingly, I held the door-handle. Was it you coming up the stairs?

Yes, it was you, beloved; but you were not alone. I heard a gentle laugh, the rustle of silk, and your voice, speaking in low tones. There was a woman with you ...

I cannot tell how I lived through the rest of the night. At eight next morning, they took me with them to Innsbruck. I had no strength left to resist.

My boy died last night. I shall be alone once more, if I really have to go on living. Tomorrow, strange men will come, black-clad and uncouth, bringing with them a coffin for the body of my only child. Perhaps friends will come as well, with wreaths but what is the use of flowers on a coffin? They will offer consolation in one phrase or another. Words, words, words! What can words help? All I know is that I shall be alone again. There is nothing more terrible than to be alone among human beings. That is what I came to realize during those interminable two years in Innsbruck, from my sixteenth to my eighteenth year, when I lived with my people as a prisoner and an outcast. My stepfather, a quiet, taciturn man, was kind to me. My mother, as if eager to atone for an unwitting injustice, seemed ready to meet all my wishes. Those of my own age would have been glad to befriend me. But I repelled their advances with angry defiance. I did not wish to be happy, I did not wish to live content away from you; so I buried myself in a gloomy world of self-torment and solitude. I would not wear the new and gay dresses they bought for me. I refused to go to concerts or to the theatre, and I would not take part in cheerful excursions. I rarely left the house. Can you believe me when I tell you that I hardly got to know a dozen streets in this little town where I lived for two years? Mourning was my joy; I renounced society and every pleasure, and was intoxicated with delight at the mortifications I thus superadded to the lack of seeing you. Moreover, I would let nothing divert me from my passionate longing to live only for you.

Sitting alone at home, hour after hour and day after day, I did nothing but think of you, turning over in my mind unceasingly my hundred petty memories of you, renewing every movement and every time of waiting, rehearsing these episodes in the theatre of my mind. The countless repetitions of the years of my childhood from the day in which you came into my life have so branded the details on my memory that I can recall every minute of those long-passed years as if they had been but yesterday. Thus my life was still entirely centred in you. I bought all your books. If your name was mentioned in the newspaper, the day was a red-letter day ... Will you believe me when I tell you that I have read your books so often that I know them by heart? Were anyone to wake me in the night and quote a detached sentence, I could continue the passage unfalteringly even to-day, after thirteen years. Your every word was Holy Writ① to me. The world existed for me only in relationship to you. In the Viennese newspapers I read the reports of concerts and first nights, wondering which would interest you most. When evening came, I accompanied you in imagination, saying to myself: "Now he is entering the hall; now he is taking his seat." Such were my fancies a thousand times, simply because I had once seen you at a concert.

Why should I recount these things? Why recount the tragic hopelessness of a forsaken child? Why tell it to you, who have never dreamed of my admiration or of my sorrow? But was I still a child? I was seventeen; I was eighteen; young fellows would turn to look after me in the street, but they only made me angry. To love anyone but you, even to play with the thought of loving anyone but you, would have been so utterly impossible to me, that the mere tender of affection on the part of another man seemed to me a crime. My passion for you remained just as intense, but it changed in character as my body grew and my senses awakened, becoming more ardent, more physical, more unmistakably the love of a grown woman. What had been hidden from the thoughts of the uninstructed child, of the girl who had rung your door bell, was now my only longing. I wanted to give myself to you.

My associates believed me to be shy and timid. But I had an absolute fixity of purpose. My whole being was directed towards one end—back to Vienna, back to you. I fought successfully to get my own way, unreasonable, incomprehensible, though it

---

① Holy Writ: 圣经, 神圣经典

seemed to others. My stepfather was well-to-do, and looked upon me as his daughter. I insisted, however, that I would earn my own living, and at length got him to agree to my returning to Vienna as employee in a dressmaking establishment belonging to a relative of his.

Need I tell you whither my steps first led me that foggy autumn evening when, at last, at last, I found myself back in Vienna? I left my trunk in the cloakroom, and hurried to a tram. How slowly it moved! Every stop was a renewed vexation to me. In the end, I reached the house. My heart leapt when I saw a light in your window. The town, which had seemed so alien, so dreary, grew suddenly alive for me. I myself lived once more, now that I was near you, you who were my unending dream. When nothing but the thin, shining pane of glass was between you and my uplifted eyes, I could ignore the fact that in reality I was as far from your mind as if I had been separated by mountains and valleys and rivers. Enough that I could go on looking at your window. There was a light in it; that was your dwelling; you were there; that was my world. For two years I had dreamed of this hour, and now it had come. Throughout that warm and cloudy evening I stood in front of your windows, until the light was extinguished. Not until then did I seek my own quarters.

Evening after evening I returned to the same spot. Up to six o'clock I was at work. The work was hard, and yet I liked it, for the turmoil of the show-room masked the turmoil in my heart. The instant the shutters were rolled down, I flew to the beloved spot. To see you once more, to meet you just once, was all I wanted; simply from a distance to devour your face with my eyes. At length, after a week, I did meet you, and then the meeting took me by surprise. I was watching your window, when you came across the street. In an instant, I was a child once more, the girl of thirteen. My cheeks flushed. Although I was longing to meet your eyes, I hung my head and hurried past you as if someone had been in pursuit. Afterwards I was ashamed of having fled like a schoolgirl, for now I knew what I really wanted. I wanted to meet you; I wanted you to recognize me after all these weary years, to notice me, to love me.

For a long time you failed to notice me, although I took up my post outside your house every night, even when it was snowing, or when the keen wind of the Viennese winter was blowing. Sometimes I waited for hours in vain. Often, in the end, you would leave the house in the company of friends. Twice I saw you with a woman, and the fact that I was now awakened, that there was something new and different in my feeling towards you, was disclosed by the sudden heart-pang when I saw a strange woman walking confidently with you arm-in-arm. It was no surprise to me, for I had known since childhood how many such visitors came to your house; but now the sight aroused in me a definite bodily pain. I had a mingled feeling of enmity and desire when I witnessed this open manifestation of fleshly intimacy with another woman. For a day, animated by the youthful pride from which, perhaps, I am not yet free, I abstained from my usual visit; but how horrible was this empty evening of defiance and renunciation! The next night I was standing, as usual, in all humility, in front of your window; waiting, as I have ever waited, in front of your closed life.

At length came the hour when you noticed me. I marked your coming from a distance, and collected all my forces to prevent myself shrinking out of your path. As chance would have it, a loaded dray filled the street, so that you had to pass quite close to me. Involuntarily your eyes encountered my figure, and immediately, though you had hardly noticed the attentiveness in my gaze, there came into your face that expression with which you were wont to look at women. The memory of it darted through me like an electric shock—that caressing and alluring glance, at once enfolding and disclothing, with which, years before, you had awakened the girl to become the woman and the lover. For a moment or two your eyes thus rested on me, for a space during which I could not turn my own eyes away, and then you had passed. My heart was beating so furiously that I had to slacken my pace; and when, moved by irresistible curiosity, I turned to look back, I saw that you were standing and watching me. The inquisitive interest of your expression convinced me that you had not recognized me. You did not recognize me, either then or later. How can I describe my disappointment?

This was the first of such disappointments; the first time I had to endure what has always been my fate; that you have never recognized me. I must die, unrecognized. Ah, how can I make you understand my disappointment? During the years at Innsbruck I had never ceased to think of you. Our next meeting in Vienna was always in my thoughts. My fancies varied with my mood, ranging from the wildest possibilities to the most delightful. Every conceivable variation had passed through my mind. In gloomy moments it had seemed to me that you would repulse me, would despise me, for being of no account, for being plain, or importunate. I had had a vision of every possible form of disfavour, coldness, or indifference. But never, in the extremity of depression, in the utmost realization of my own unimportance, had I conceived this most abhorrent of possibilities—that you had never become aware of my existence. I understand now (you have taught me!) that a girl's or a woman's face must be for a man something extraordinarily mutable. It is usually nothing more than the reflection of moods which pass as readily as an image vanishes from a mirror. A man can readily forget a woman's face, because she modifies its lights and shades, and because at different times the dress gives it so different a setting. Resignation comes to a woman as her knowledge grows. But I, who was still a girl, was unable to understand your forgetfulness. My whole mind had been full of you ever since I had first known you, and this had produced in me the illusion that you must have often thought of me and waited for me. How could I have borne to go on living had I realized that I was nothing to you, that I had no place in your memory? Your glance that evening, showing me as it did that on your side there was not even a gossamer thread connecting your life with mine, meant for me a first plunge into

Chapter Fourteen

reality, conveyed to me the first intimation of my destiny.

You did not recognize me. Two days later, when our paths again crossed, and you looked at me with an approach to intimacy, it was not in recognition of the girl who had loved you so long and whom you had awakened to womanhood; it was simply that you knew the face of the pretty lass of eighteen whom you had encountered at the same spot two evenings before. Your expression was one of friendly surprise, and a smile fluttered about your lips. You passed me as before, and as before you promptly slackened your pace. I trembled, I exulted, I longed for you to speak to me. I felt that for the first time I had become alive for you; I, too, walked slowly, and did not attempt to evade you. Suddenly, I heard your step behind me. Without turning round, I knew that I was about to hear your beloved voice directly addressing me. I was almost paralysed by the expectation, and my heart beat so violently that I thought I should have to stand still. You were at my side. You greeted me cordially, as if we were old acquaintances—though you did not really know me, though you have never known anything about my life. So simple and charming was your manner that I was able to answer you without hesitation. We walked along the street, and you asked me whether we could not have supper together. I agreed. What was there I could have refused you?

We supped in a little restaurant. You will not remember where it was. To you it will be one of many such. For what was I? One among hundreds; one adventure, one link in an endless chain. What happened that evening to keep me in your memory? I said very little, for I was so intensely happy to have you near me and to hear you speak to me. I did not wish to waste a moment upon questions or foolish words. I shall never cease to be thankful to you for that hour, for the way in which you justified my ardent admiration. I shall never forget the gentle tact you displayed. There was no undue eagerness, no hasty offer of a caress. Yet from the first moment you displayed so much friendly confidence that you would have won me even if my whole being had not long ere this been yours. Can I make you understand how much it meant to me that my five years of expectation were so perfectly fulfilled?

The hour grew late, and we came away from the restaurant. At the door you asked me whether I was in any hurry, or still had time to spare. How could I hide from you that I was yours? I said I had plenty of time. With a momentary hesitation, you asked me whether I would not come to your rooms for a talk. "I shall be delighted," I answered with alacrity, thus giving frank expression to my feelings. I could not fail to notice that my ready assent surprised you. I am not sure whether your feeling was one of vexation or pleasure, but it was obvious to me that you were surprised. Today, of course, I understand your astonishment. I know now that it is usual for a woman, even though she may ardently desire to give herself to a man, to feign reluctance, to simulate alarm or indignation. She must be brought to consent by urgent pleading, by lies, adjurations, and promises. I know that only professional prostitutes are accustomed to answer such an invitation with a perfectly frank assent—prostitutes, or simple-minded, immature girls. How could you know that, in my case, the frank assent was but the voicing of an eternity of desire, the uprush of yearnings that bad endured for a thousand days and more?

In any case, my manner aroused your attention; I had become interesting to you. As we were walking along together, I felt that during our conversation you were trying to sample me in some way. Your perceptions, your assured touch in the whole gamut of human emotions, made you realize instantly that there was something unusual here; that this pretty, complaisant girl carried a secret about with her.

Your curiosity had been awakened, and your discreet questions showed that you were trying to pluck the heart out of my mystery. But my replies were evasive. I would rather seem a fool than disclose my secret to you.

We went up to your flat. Forgive me, beloved, for saying that you cannot possibly understand all that it meant to me to go up those stairs with you—how I was mad, tortured, almost suffocated with happiness. Even now I can hardly think of it without tears, but I have no tears left. Everything in that house had been steeped in my passion; everything was a symbol of my childhood and its longing. There was the door behind which a thousand times I had awaited your coming; the stairs on which I had heard your footstep, and where I had first seen you through the judas, which I had watched your comings and goings; the door-mat on which I had once knelt; the sound of a key in the lock, which had always been a signal to me. My childhood and its passions were nested within these few yards of space. Here was my whole life, and it surged around me like a great storm, for all was being fulfilled, and I was going with you, I with you, into your, into our house. Think (the way I am phrasing it sounds trivial, but I know no better words) that up to your door was the world of reality, the dull everyday world which had been that of all my previous life. At this door began the magic world of my childish imaginings, Aladdin's realm. Think how, a thousand times, I had had my burning eyes fixed upon this door through which I was now passing, my head in a whirl, and you will have an inkling—no more—of all that this tremendous minute meant to me.

I stayed with you that night. You did not dream that before you no man had ever touched or seen my body. How could you fancy it, when I made no resistance, and when I suppressed every trace of shame, fearing lest I might betray the secret of my love? That would certainly have alarmed you; you care only for what comes and goes easily, for that which is light of touch, is imponderable. You dread being involved in anyone else's destiny. You like to give yourself freely to all the world—but not to make any sacrifices. When I tell you that I gave myself to you as a maiden, do not misunderstand me. I am not making any charge against you. You did not entice me, deceive me, seduce me. I threw myself into your arms; went out to meet my fate. I have nothing but thankfulness towards you for the blessedness of that night. When I opened my eyes in the darkness

Chapter Fourteen

and you were beside me, I felt that I must be in heaven, and I was amazed that the stars were not shining on me. Never, beloved, have I repented giving myself to you that night. When you were sleeping beside me, when I listened to your breathing, touched your body, and felt myself so near you, I shed tears for very happiness.

I went away early in the morning. I had to go to my work, and I wanted to leave before your servant came. When I was ready to go, you put your arm round me and looked at me for a very long time. Was some obscure memory stirring in your mind; or was it simply that my radiant happiness made me seem beautiful to you? You kissed me on the lips, and I moved to go. You asked me: "Would you not like to take a few flowers with you?" There were four white roses in the blue crystal vase on the writing-table (I knew it of old from that stolen glance of childhood), and you gave them to me. For days they were mine to kiss.

We had arranged to meet on a second evening. Again it was full of wonder and delight. You gave me a third night. Then you said that you were called away from Vienna for a time—oh, how I had always hated those journeys of yours! —and promised that I should hear from you as soon as you came back. I would only give you a *poste-restante* address[①], and did not tell you my real name. I guarded my secret. Once more you gave me roses at parting—at parting.

Day after day for two months I asked myself ... No, I will not describe the anguish of my expectation and despair. I make no complaint. I love you just as you are, ardent and forgetful, generous and unfaithful. I love you just as you have always been. You were back long before the two months were up. The light in your windows showed me that, but you did not write to me. In my last hours I have not a line in your handwriting, not a line from you to whom my life was given. I waited, waited despairingly. You did not call me to you, did not write a word, not a word ...

My boy who died yesterday was yours too. He was your son, the child of one of those three nights. I was yours, and yours only from that time until the hour of his birth. I felt myself sanctified by your touch, and it would not have been possible for me then to accept any other man's caresses. He was our boy, dear; the child of my fully conscious love and of your careless, spendthrift, almost unwitting tenderness. Our child, our son, our only child. Perhaps you will be startled, perhaps merely surprised. You will wonder why I never told you of this boy; and why, having kept silence throughout the long years, I only tell you of him now, when he lies in his last sleep, about to leave me

---

① *poste-restante* address: 留存邮件地址。French pronunciation: [pʊst ʀɛtāt], "remainder post" or general delivery is a service where the post office holds the mail until the recipient calls for it. It is a common destination for mail for people who are visiting a particular location and have no need, or no way, of having mail delivered directly to their place of residence at that time.

for all time—never, never to return. How could I have told you? I was a stranger, a girl who had shown herself only too eager to spend those three nights with you. Never would you have believed that I, the nameless partner in a chance encounter, had been faithful to you, the unfaithful. You would never, without misgivings, have accepted the boy as your own. Even if, to all appearance, you had trusted my word, you would still have cherished the secret suspicion that I had seized an opportunity of fathering upon you, a man of means, the child of another lover. You would have been suspicious. There would always have been a shadow of mistrust between you and me. I could not have borne it. Besides, I know you. Perhaps I know you better than you know yourself. You love to be carefree, light of heart, perfectly at ease; and that is what you understand by love. It would have been repugnant to you to find yourself suddenly in the position of father; to be made responsible, all at once, for a child's destiny. The breath of freedom is the breath of life to you, and you would have felt me to be a tie. Inwardly, even in defiance of your conscious will, you would have hated me as an embodied claim. Perhaps only now and again, for an hour or for a fleeting minute, should I have seemed a burden to you, should I have been hated by you. But it was my pride that I should never be a trouble or a care to you all my life long. I would rather take the whole burden on myself than be a burden to you; I wanted to be the one among all the women you had intimately known of whom you would never think except with love and thankfulness. In actual fact, you never thought of me at all. You forgot me.

 I am not accusing you. Believe me, I am not complaining. You must forgive me if for a moment, now and again, it seems as if my pen had been dipped in gall. You must forgive me; for my boy, our boy, lies dead there beneath the flickering candles. I have clenched my fists against God, and have called him a murderer, for I have been almost beside myself with grief. Forgive me for complaining. I know that you are kindhearted, and always ready to help. You will help the merest stranger at a word. But your kindliness is peculiar. It is unbounded. Anyone may have of yours as much as lie can grasp with both hands. And yet, I must say it, your kindliness works sluggishly. You need to be asked. You help those who call for help; you help from shame, from weakness, and not from sheer joy in helping. Let me tell you openly that those who are in affliction and torment are not dearer to you than your brothers in happiness. Now, it is hard, very hard, to ask anything of such as you, even of the kindest among you. Once, when I was still a child, I watched through the judas in our door how you gave something to a beggar who had rung your bell. You gave quickly and freely, almost before he spoke. But there was a certain nervousness and haste in your manner, as if your chief anxiety were to be speedily rid of him; you seemed to be afraid to meet his eye. I have never forgotten this uneasy and timid way of giving help, this shunning of a word of thanks.

 That is why I never turned to you in my difficulty. Oh, I know that you would have given me all the help I needed, in spite of your doubt that my child was yours. You would have offered me comfort, and have given me money, an ample supply of money; but always with a masked impatience, a secret desire to shake off trouble. I even believe that you would have advised me to rid myself of the coming child. This was what I dreaded above all, for I knew that I should do whatever you wanted. But the child was all in all to me. It was yours; it was you reborn—not the happy and carefree you, whom I could never hope to keep; but you, given to me for my very own, flesh of my flesh, intimately intertwined with my own life. At length I held you fast; I could feel your life-blood flowing through my veins; I could nourish you, caress you, kiss you, as often as my soul yearned. That was why I was so happy when I knew that I was with child by you, and that is why I kept the secret from you. Henceforward you could not escape me; you were mine.

But you must not suppose that the months of waiting passed so happily as I had dreamed in my first transports. They were full of sorrow and care, full of loathing for the baseness of mankind. Things went hard with me. I could not stay at work during the later months, for my stepfather's relatives would have noticed my condition, and would have sent the news home. Nor would I ask my mother for money; so until my time came I managed to live by the sale of some trinkets. A week before my confinement, the few crown pieces that remained to me were stolen by my laundress, so I had to go to the maternity hospital. The child, your son, was born there, in that asylum of wretchedness, among the very poor, the outcast, and the abandoned. It was a deadly place. Everything was strange, was alien. We were all alien to one another, as we lay there in our loneliness, filled with mutual hatred, thrust together only by our kinship of poverty and distress into this crowded ward, reeking of chloroform and blood, filled with cries and moaning. A patient in these wards loses all individuality, except such as remains in the name at the head of the clinical record. What lies in the bed is merely a piece of quivering flesh, an object of study ...

I ask your forgiveness for speaking of these things. I shall never speak of them again. For eleven years I have kept silence, and shall soon be dumb for evermore. Once, at least, I had to cry aloud, to let you know how dearly bought was this child, this boy who was my delight, and who now lies dead. I had forgotten those dreadful hours, forgotten them in his smiles and his voice, forgotten them in my happiness. Now, when he is dead, the torment has come to life again; and I had, this once, to give it utterance. But I do not accuse you; only God, only God who is the author of such purposeless affliction. Never have I cherished an angry thought of you. Not even in the utmost agony of giving birth did I feel any resentment against you; never did I repent the nights when I enjoyed your love; never did I cease to love you, or to bless the hour when you came into my life. Were it necessary for me, fully aware of what was coming, to relive that time in hell, I would do it gladly, not once, but many times.

Our boy died yesterday, and you never knew him. His bright little personality has never come into the most fugitive contact with you, and your eyes have never rested on him. For a long time after our son was born, I kept myself hidden from you. My longing for you had become less overpowering. Indeed, I believe I loved you less passionately. Certainly, my love for you did not hurt so much, now that I had the boy. I did not wish to divide myself between you and him, and so I did not give myself to you, who were happy and independent of me, but to the boy who needed me, whom I had to nourish, whom I could kiss and fondle. I seemed to have been healed of my restless yearning for you. The doom seemed to have been lifted from me by the birth of this other you, who was truly my own. Rarely, now, did my feelings reach out towards you in your dwelling. One thing only—on your birthday I have always sent you a bunch of white roses, like the roses you gave me after our first night of love. Has it ever occurred to you, during these ten or eleven years, to ask yourself who sent them? Have you ever recalled having given such roses to a girl? I do not know, and never shall know. For me it was enough to send them to you out of the darkness; enough, once a year, to revive my own memory of that hour.

You never knew our boy. I blame myself today for having hidden him from you, for you would have loved him. You have never seen him smile when he first opened his eyes after sleep, his dark eyes that were your eyes, the eyes with which he looked merrily forth at me and the world. He was so bright, so lovable. All your light-heartedness, and your mobile imagination were his likewise—in the form in which these qualities can show themselves in a child. He would spend entranced hours playing with things as you play with life; and then, grown serious, would sit long over his books. He was you, reborn. The mingling of sport and earnest, which is so characteristic of you, was becoming plain in him; and the more he resembled you, the more I loved him. He was good at his lessons, so that he could chatter in French like a magpie. His exercise books were the tidiest in the class. And what a fine, upstanding little man he was! When I took him to the seaside in the summer, at Grado①, women used to stop and stroke his fair hair. At Semmering, when he was tobogganing, people would turn round to gaze after him. He was so handsome, so gentle, so appealing. Last year, when he went to college as a boarder, he began to wear the collegiates' uniform of an eighteenth-century page, with a little dagger stuck in his belt—now he lies here in his shift, with pallid lips and crossed hands.

You will wonder how I could manage to give the boy so costly an upbringing, how it was possible for me to provide for him an entry into this bright and cheerful life of the well-to-do. Dear one, I am speaking to you from the darkness. Unashamed, I will tell you. Do not shrink from me. I sold myself. I did not become a street-walker, a common

---

① Grado：格拉多海滨

prostitute, but I sold myself. My friends, my lovers, were wealthy men. At first I sought them out, but soon they sought me, for I was (did you ever notice it?) a beautiful woman. Everyone to whom I gave myself was devoted to me. They all became my grateful admirers. They all loved me—except you, except you whom I loved.

Will you despise me now that I have told you what I did? I am sure you will not. I know you will understand everything, will understand that what I did was done only for you, for your other self, for your boy. In the lying-in hospital I had tasted the full horror of poverty. I knew that, in the world of the poor, those who are downtrodden are always the victims. I could not bear to think that your son, your lovely boy, was to grow up in that abyss, amid the corruptions of the street, in the poisoned air of a slum. His delicate lips must not learn the speech of the gutter; his fine, white skin must not be chafed by the harsh and sordid underclothing of the poor. Your son must have the best of everything, all the wealth and all the lightheartedness of the world. He must follow your footsteps through life, must dwell in the sphere in which you had lived.

That is why I sold myself. It was no sacrifice to me, for what are conventionally termed "honour" and "disgrace" were unmeaning words to me. You were the only one to whom my body could belong, and you did not love me, so what did it matter what I did with that body? My companions' caresses, even their most ardent passion, never sounded my depths, although many of them were persons I could not but respect, and although the thought of my own fate made me sympathize with them in their unrequited love. All these men were kind to me; they all petted and spoiled me; they all paid me every deference. One of them, a widower, an elderly man of title, used his utmost influence until he secured your boy's nomination to the college. This man loved me like a daughter. Three or four times he urged me to marry him. I could have been a Countess today, mistress of a lovely castle in Tyrol. I could have been free from care, for the boy would have had a most affectionate father, and I should have had a sedate, distinguished, and kindhearted husband. But I persisted in my refusal, though I knew it gave him pain. It may have been foolish of me. Had I yielded, I should have been living a safe and retired life somewhere, and my child would still have been with me. Why should I hide from you the reason for my refusal? I did not want to bind myself. I wanted to remain free—for you. In my innermost self, in the unconscious, I continued to dream the dream of my childhood. Some day, perhaps, you would call me to your side, were it only for an hour. For the possibility of this one hour I rejected everything else, simply that I might be free to answer your call. Since my first awakening to womanhood, what had my life been but waiting, a waiting upon your will?

In the end, the expected hour came. And still you never knew that it had come! When it came, you did not recognize me. You have never recognized me, never, never. I met you often enough, in theatres, at concerts, in the Prater, and else-where. Always my heart leapt, but always you passed me by, unheeding. In outward appearance I had become a different person. The timid girl was a woman now; beautiful, it was said; decked out in fine clothes; surrounded by admirers. How could you recognize in me one whom you had known as a shy girl in the subdued light of your bedroom? Sometimes my companion would greet you, and you would acknowledge the greeting as you glanced at me. But your look was always that of a courteous stranger, a look of deference, but not of recognition—distant, hopelessly distant. Once, I remember, this non-recognition, familiar as it had become, was a torture to me. I was in a box at the opera with a friend, and you were in the next box. The lights were lowered when the Overture began. I could no longer see your face, but I could feel your breathing quite close to me, just as when I was with you in your room; and on the velvet-covered partition between the boxes your slender hand was resting. I was filled with an infinite longing to bend down and kiss this hand, whose loving touch I had once known. Amid the turmoil of sound from the orchestra, the craving grew even more intense. I had to hold myself back convulsively, to keep my lips away from your dear hand. At the end of the first act, I told my friend I wanted to leave. It was intolerable to me to have you sitting there beside me in the darkness, so near, and so estranged.

But the hour came once more, only once more. It was all but a year ago, on the day after your birthday. My thoughts had been dwelling on you more than ever, for I used to keep your birthday as a festival. Early in the morning I had gone to buy the white roses which I sent you every year in commemoration of an hour you had forgotten. In the afternoon I took my boy for a drive and we had tea together. In the evening we went to the theatre. I wanted him to look upon this day as a sort of mystical anniversary of his youth, though he could not know the reason. The next day I spent with my intimate of that epoch, a young and wealthy manufacturer of Brunn, with whom I had been living for two years. He was passionately fond of me, and he, too, wanted me to marry him. I refused, for no reason he could understand although he loaded me and the child with presents, and was lovable enough in his rather stupid and slavish devotion. We went together to a concert, where we met a lively company. We all had supper at a restaurant in the Ringstrasse. Amid talk and laughter, I proposed that we should move on to a dancing-hall. In general, such places, where the cheerfulness is always an expression of partial intoxication, are repulsive to me, and I would seldom go to them. But on this occasion some elemental force seemed at work in me, leading me to make the proposal, which was hailed with acclamation by the others. I was animated by an inexplicable longing, as if some extraordinary experience were awaiting me. As usual, everyone was eager to accede to my whims. We went to the dancing-hall, drank some champagne, and I had a sudden access of almost frenzied cheerfulness such as I had never known. I drank one glass of wine after another, joined in the chorus of a suggestive song, and was in a mood to dance with glee. Then, all in a moment, I felt as if my heart had been seized by an icy or a burning hand. You were sitting with some friends at the next table, regarding me with an admiring and covetous glance, that glance which had always thrilled me beyond expression. For the first time in ten years you were looking at me again under the stress of all the unconscious passion in your nature. I trembled, and my hand shook so violently that I nearly let my wineglass fall. Fortunately my companions did not notice my condition, for their perceptions were confused by the noise of laughter and music.

Your look became continually more ardent, and touched my own senses to fire. I could not be sure whether you had at last recognized me, or whether your desires had been aroused by one whom you believed to be a stranger. My cheeks were flushed, and I talked at random. You could not help noticing the effect your glance had on me. You made an inconspicuous movement of the head, to suggest my coming into the anteroom for a moment. Then, having settled your bill, you took leave of your associates, and left the table, after giving me a further sign that you intended to wait for me outside. I shook like one in the cold stage of a fever. I could no longer answer when spoken to, could no longer control the tumult of my blood.

At this moment, as chance would have it, a couple of Negroes with clattering heels began a barbaric dance, to the accompaniment of their own shrill cries. Everyone turned to look at them, and I seized my opportunity. Standing up, I told my friend that I would be back in a moment, and followed you.

You were waiting for me in the lobby, and your face lighted up when I came. With a smile on your lips, you hastened to meet me. It was plain that you did not recognize me, neither the child, nor the girl of old days. Again, to you, I was a new acquaintance.

"Have you really got an hour to spare for me?" you asked in a confident tone, which showed that you took me for one of the women whom anyone can buy for a night. "Yes," I answered; the same tremulous but perfectly acquiescent "Yes" that you had heard from me in my girlhood, more than ten years earlier, in the darkling street. "Tell me when we can meet," you said. "Whenever you like," I replied, for I knew nothing of shame where you were concerned. You looked at me with a little surprise, with a surprise which had in it the same flavour of doubt mingled with curiosity which you had shown before when you were astonished at the readiness of my acceptance. "Now?" you enquired, after a moment's hesitation. "Yes," I replied," let us go."

I was about to fetch my wrap from the cloakroom, when I remembered that my Brunn friend had handed in our things together, and that he had the ticket. It was impossible to go back and ask him for it, and it seemed to me even more impossible to renounce this hour with you to which I had been looking forward for years. My choice was instantly made. I gathered my shawl around me, and went forth into the misty night, regardless not only of my cloak, but regardless, likewise, of the kindhearted man with whom I had been living for years—regardless of the fact that in this public way, before his friends, I was putting him into the ludicrous position of one whose mistress abandons him at the first nod of a stranger. Inwardly, I was well aware how basely and ungratefully I was behaving towards a good friend. I knew that my outrageous folly would alienate him from me forever, and that I was playing havoc with my life. But what was his friendship, what was my own life, to me when compared with the chance of again feeling your lips on mine, of again listening to the tones of your voice. Now that all is over and done with I can tell you this, can let you know how I loved you. I believe that were you to summon me from my death-bed, I should find strength to rise in answer to your call.

There was a taxi at the door, and we drove to your rooms. Once more I could listen to your voice, once more I felt the ecstasy of being near you, and was almost as intoxicated with joy and confusion as I had been so long before. But I cannot describe it all to you, how what I had felt ten years earlier was now renewed as we went up the well-known stairs together; how I lived simultaneously in the past and in the present, my whole being fused as it were with yours. In your rooms, little was changed. There were a few more pictures, a great many more books, one or two additions to your furniture—but the whole had the friendly look of an old acquaintance. On the writing-table was the vase with the roses—my roses, the ones I had sent you the day before as a memento of the woman whom you did not remember, whom you did not recognize, not even now when she was close to you, when you were holding her hand and your lips were pressed on hers. But it comforted me to see my flowers there, to know that you had cherished something that was an emanation from me, was the breath of my love for you.

You took me in your arms. Again I stayed with you for the whole of one glorious night. But even then you did not recognize me. While I thrilled to your caresses, it was plain to me that your passion knew no difference between a loving mistress and a harlot, that your spend-thrift affections were wholly concentrated in their own expression. To me, the stranger picked up at a dancing-hall, you were at once affectionate and courteous. You would not treat me lightly, and yet you were full of an enthralling ardour. Dizzy with the old happiness, I was again aware of the two-sidedness of your nature, of that strange mingling of intellectual passion with sensual, which had already enslaved me to you in my childhood. In no other man have I ever known such complete surrender to the sweetness of the moment. No other has for the time being given himself so utterly as did you who, when the hour was past, were to relapse into an interminable and almost inhuman forgetfulness. But I, too, forgot myself. Who was I, lying in the darkness beside you? Was I the impassioned child of former days; was I the mother of your son; was I a stranger? Everything in this wonderful night was at one and the same time entrancingly familiar and entrancingly new. I prayed that the joy might last forever.

But morning came. It was late when we rose, and you asked me to stay to breakfast. Over the tea, which an unseen hand had discreetly served in the dining-room, we talked quietly. As of old, you displayed a cordial frankness; and, as of old, there were no tactless questions, there was no curiosity about myself. You did not ask my name, nor where I lived. To you I was, as before, a casual adventure, a nameless woman, an ardent hour which leaves no trace when it is over. You told me that you were about to start on a long journey, that you were going to spend two or three months in Northern Africa. The words broke in upon my happiness like a knell: "Past, past, past and forgotten!" I longed to throw myself at your feet, crying: "Take me with you, that you may at length come to know me, at length after all these years!" But I was timid, cowardly, slavish, weak. All I could say was: "What a pity!" You looked at me with a smile: "Are you really sorry?"

For a moment I was as if frenzied. I stood up and looked at you fixedly. Then I said: "The man I love has always gone on a journey." I looked you straight in the eyes. "Now, now," I thought, "now he will recognize me!" You only smiled, and said consolingly: "One comes back after a time." I answered: "Yes, one comes back? But one has forgotten by then."

I must have spoken with strong feeling, for my tone moved you. You, too, rose, and looked at me wonderingly and tenderly. You put your hands on my shoulders: "Good things are not forgotten, and I shall not forget you." Your eyes studied me attentively, as if you wished to form an enduring image of me in your mind. When I felt this penetrating glance, this exploration of my whole being, I could not but fancy that the spell of your blindness would at last be broken. "He will recognize me! He will recognize me!" My soul trembled with expectation.

But you did not recognize me. No, you did not recognize me. Never had I been more of a stranger to you than I was at that moment, for had it been otherwise you could not possibly have done what you did a few minutes later. You had kissed me again, had kissed me passionately. My hair had been ruffled, and I had to tidy it once more. Standing at the glass, I saw in it—and as I saw, I was overcome with shame and horror—that you were surreptitiously slipping a couple of banknotes into my muff. I could hardly refrain from crying out; I could hardly refrain from slapping your face. You were paying me for the night I had spent with you, me who had loved you since childhood, me the mother of your son. To you I was only a prostitute picked up at a dancing-hall. It was not enough that you should forget me; you had to pay me, and to debase me by doing so.

I hastily gathered up my belongings, that I might escape as quickly as possible; the pain was too great. I looked round for my hat. There it was, on the writing-table, beside the vase with the white roses, my roses. I had an irresistible desire to make a last effort to awaken your memory. "Will you give me one of your white roses?"—"Of course," you answered, lifting them all out of the vase. "But perhaps they were given you by a woman, a woman who loves you?"—"Maybe," you replied, "I don't know. They were a present, but I don't know who sent them; that's why I'm so fond of them."

I looked at you intently: "Perhaps they were sent you by a woman whom you have forgotten!"

You were surprised. I looked at you yet more intently. "Recognize me, only recognize me at last!" was the clamour of my eyes. But your smile, though cordial, had no recognition in it. You kissed me yet again, but you did not recognize me.

I hurried away, for my eyes were filling with tears, and I did not want you to see. In the entry, as I precipitated myself from the room, I almost cannoned into John, your servant. Embarrassed but zealous, he got out of my way, and opened the front door for me. Then, in this fugitive instant, as I looked at him through my tears, a light suddenly flooded the old man's face. In this fugitive instant, I tell you, he recognized me, the man who had never seen me since my childhood. I was so grateful, that I could have knelt before him and kissed his hands. I tore from my muff the banknotes with which you had scourged me, and thrust them upon him. He glanced at me in alarm—for in this instant I think he understood more of me than you have understood in your whole life. Everyone, everyone, has been eager to spoil me; everyone has loaded me with kindness. But you, only you, forgot me. You, only you, never recognized me.

My boy, our boy, is dead. I have no one left to love; no one in the world, except you. But what can you be to me—you who have never, never recognized me; you who stepped across me as you might step across a stream, you who trod on me as you might tread on a stone; you who went on your way unheeding, while you left me to wait for all eternity? Once I fancied that I could hold you for my own; that I held you, the elusive, in the child. But he was your son. In the night, he cruelly slipped away from me on a journey; he has forgotten me, and will never return. I am alone once more, more utterly alone than ever. I have nothing, nothing from you. No child, no word, no line of writing, no place in your memory. If anyone were to mention my name in your presence, to you it would be the name of a stranger. Shall I not be glad to die, since I am dead to you? Glad to go away, since you have gone away from me?

Beloved, I am not blaming you. I do not wish to intrude my sorrows into your joyful life. Do not fear that I shall ever trouble you further. Bear with me for giving way to the longing to cry out my heart to you this once, in the bitter hour when the boy lies dead. Only this once I must talk to you. Then I shall slip back into obscurity, and be dumb towards you as I have ever been. You will not even hear my cry so long as I continue to live. Only when I am dead will this heritage come to you from one who has loved you more fondly than any other has loved you, from one whom you have never recognized, from one who has always been awaiting your summons and whom you have never summoned. Perhaps, perhaps, when you receive this legacy you will call to me; and for the first time I shall be unfaithful to you, for I shall not hear you in the sleep of death. Neither picture nor token do I leave you, just as you left me nothing, for never will you recognize me now. That was my fate in life, and it shall be my fate in death likewise. I shall not summon you in my last hour; I shall go my way leaving you ignorant of my name and my appearance. Death will be easy to me, for you will not feel it from afar. I could not die if my death were going to give you pain.

I cannot write any more. My head is so heavy; my limbs ache; I am feverish. I must lie down. Perhaps all will soon be over. Perhaps, this once, fate will be kind to me, and I shall not have to see them take away my boy ... I cannot write any more. Farewell, dear one, farewell. All my thanks go out to you. What happened was good, in spite of everything. I shall be thankful to you till my last breath. I am so glad that I have told you all. Now you will know, though you can never fully understand, how much I have loved you; and yet my love will never be a burden to you. It is my solace that I shall not fail you. Nothing will be changed in your bright and lovely life. Beloved, my death will not harm you. This comforts me.

But who, ah who, will now send you white roses on your birthday? The vase will be empty. No longer will come that breath, that aroma, from my life, which once a year was breathed into your room. I have one last request—the first, and the last. Do it for my sake. Always on your birthday—a day when one thinks of oneself—get some roses and put them in the vase. Do it just as others, once a year, have a Mass said for the beloved dead. I no longer believe in God, and therefore I do not want a Mass said for me. I believe in you alone. I love none but you. Only in you do I wish to go on living—just one day in the year, softly, quietly, as I have always lived near you. Please do this, my darling, please do it ... My first request, and my last ... Thanks, thanks ... I love you, I love you ... Farewell ...

The letter fell from his nerveless hands. He thought long and deeply. Yes, he had vague memories of a neighbour's child, of a girl, of a woman in a dancing hall, all was dim and confused, like the flickering and shapeless view of a stone in the bed of a swiftly running stream. Shadows chased one another across his mind, but would not fuse into a picture. There were stirrings of memory in the realm of feeling, and still he could not remember. It seemed to him that he must have dreamed of all these figures, must have dreamed often and vividly and yet they had only been the phantoms of a dream. His eyes wandered to the blue vase on the writing-table. It was empty. For years it had not been empty on his birthday. He shuddered, feeling as if an invisible door had been suddenly opened, a door through which a chill breeze from another world was blowing into his sheltered room. An intimation of death came to him, and an intimation of deathless love. Something welled up within him; and the thought of the dead woman stirred in his mind, bodiless and passionate, like the sound of distant music.

Questions for Discussion

1. Do you think the man really did not remember who the woman was? Why or why

not?
2. What do the white flowers represent symbolically?
3. What touch you most in the story?

Links

1. https://de.wikipedia.org/wiki/Stefan_Zweig
   提供作者斯蒂芬·茨威格生平及创作的详细介绍。
2. http://www.spectator.co.uk/2013/03/faithful-to-the-last/
   提供斯蒂芬·茨威格的小说《一封陌生女人的来信》细读资料。

Part B

The Bear Came Over the Mountain

By Alice Munro

Alice Munro（1931—   ）is a Canadian short story writer and Nobel Prize winner. Munro's work has been described as having revolutionized the architecture of short stories, especially in its tendency to move forward and backward in time. Her stories have been said to embed more than announce, reveal more than parade. Munro's fiction is often set in her native Huron County in southwestern Ontario. Her stories explore human complexities in an uncomplicated prose style. Munro's writing has established her as one of our greatest contemporary writers of fiction.

Munro's first highly acclaimed collection of stories, *Dance of Happy Shades* (1968), won the Governor Genral's Award for English fiction and Canada's highest literary prize. That success was followed by *Lives of Girls and Women* (1971), a collection of interlinked stories. *Runaway* (2004) was awarded Giller Prize and Rogers Writers' Trust Fiction Prize in 2004. In 2006, Munro's story "The Bear Came Over the Mountain" was adapted for the screen and directed by Sarah Polley as *Away from Her*. Since the 1980s, Munro has published a short-story collection at least once every four years, most recently in 2001, 2004, 2006, 2009, and 2012. Her collections have been translated into thirteen languages. On 10 October 2013, Munro was awarded the Nobel Prize in Literature, cited as a master of the contemporary short story. She is the first Canadian and the 13th woman to receive the Nobel Prize in Literature.

Munro's strong regional focus is one of the features of her fiction. Another is the omniscient narrator who serves to make sense of the world. Many critics compare Munro's small-town settings to writers from the rural South of the United States. As in the works of William Faulkner and Flannery O'Connor, the characters often confront deep-rooted customs and traditions, but the reaction of Munro's characters is generally less intense than their Southern counterparts'. Her male characters tend to capture the essence of the everyman, while her female characters are more complex. Much of Munro's work exemplifies the literary genre known as Southern Ontario Gothic.

❀ Lead-in Questions

1. What kind of life would you like to live when you are aging?
2. What is the relationship of Fiona and Grant at the beginning of the story? What change has happened to their relationship when they are old?

❀ Questions about the Author and the Story

1. Which of the following is NOT written by Alice Munro?
   A. *Dance of the Happy Shades*.
   B. *Lives of Girls and Women*.
   C. *Moon Tiger*.
   D. *The Bear Came Over the Mountain*.
2. Who is the narrator in the story?
   A. Fiona.
   B. Grant.
   C. Alice Munro.
   D. An unnamed, all-knowing storyteller.
3. What is the beginning scene of "The Bear Came Over the Mountain?"
   A. The story opens with a scene of a young, vivacious Fiona proposing marriage to Grant.
   B. The story opens with a scene of Grant and Fiona having been married for almost fifty years when she begins displaying signs of dementia.
   C. Fiona, now seventy, preparing to enter Meadowlake, a new assisted-living facility.
   D. Fiona leaves notes about her daily schedule, but then the notes start identifying the contents of the kitchen drawers.
4. Munro's work has been described as _____.
   A. having revolutionized the content of short stories
   B. having revolutionized the structure of short stories, especially in its tendency to move forward and backward in time
   C. having revolutionized the structure of short stories, especially in its tendency to mix reality and imagination
   D. having revolutionized the theme of short stories, especially in its tendency to move forward and backward in time
5. What kind of distinctive literary device was employed by Alice Munro in "The

Bear Came Over the Mountain"?

A. Nonlinear chronology. B. Metaphor.
C. Simile. D. Intertextuality.

Fiona lived in her parents' house, in the town where she and Grant went to university. It was a big, bay-windowed house that seemed to Grant both luxurious and disorderly, with rugs crooked on the floors and cup rings bitten into the table varnish. Her mother was Icelandic—a powerful woman with a froth of white hair and indignant far-left politics. The father was an important cardiologist, revered around the hospital but happily subservient at home, where he would listen to his wife's strange tirades with an absentminded smile. Fiona had her own little car and a pile of cashmere sweaters, but she wasn't in a sorority, and her mother's political activity was probably the reason. Not that she cared. Sororities were a joke to her, and so was politics—though she liked to play "The Four Insurgent Generals①" on the phonograph, and sometimes also the "Internationale,"② very loud, if there was a guest she thought she could make nervous. A curly-haired gloomy-looking foreigner was courting her—she said he was a Visigoth—and so were two or three quite respectable and uneasy young interns. She made fun of them all and of Grant as well. She would drolly repeat some of his small-town phrases. He thought maybe she was joking when she proposed to him, on a cold bright day on the beach at Port Stanley. Sand was stinging their faces and the waves delivered crashing loads of gravel at their feet.

"Do you think it would be fun—" Fiona shouted. "Do you think it would be fun if we got married?"

He took her up on it, he shouted yes. He wanted never to be away from her. She had the spark of life.

Just before they left their house Fiona noticed a mark on the kitchen floor. It came from the cheap black house shoes she had been wearing earlier in the day.

"I thought they'd quit doing that," she said in a tone of ordinary annoyance and perplexity, rubbing at the gray smear that looked as if it had been made by a greasy crayon.

She remarked that she'd never have to do this again, since she wasn't taking those shoes with her.

"I guess I'll be dressed up all the time," she said. "Or semi-dressed up. It'll be sort of like in a hotel."

---

① The Four Insurgent Generals：四个叛乱的将军(歌曲名字)
② Internationale：国际歌

Chapter Fourteen

She rinsed out the rag she'd been using and hung it on the rack inside the door under the sink. Then she put on her golden-brown, fur-collared ski jacket, over a white turtleneck sweater and tailored fawn slacks. She was a tall, narrow-shouldered woman, seventy years old but still upright and trim, with long legs and long feet, delicate wrists and ankles, and tiny, almost comical-looking ears. Her hair that was as light as milkweed fluff had gone from pale blond to white somehow without Grant's noticing exactly when, and she still wore it down to her shoulders, as her mother had done. (That was the thing that had alarmed Grant's own mother, a small-town widow who worked as a doctor's receptionist. The long white hair on Fiona's mother, even more than the state of the house, had told her all she needed to know about attitudes and politics.) But otherwise Fiona, with her fine bones and small sapphire eyes, was nothing like her mother. She had a slightly crooked mouth, which she emphasized now with red lipstick—usually the last thing she did before she left the house.

She looked just like herself on this day—direct and vague as in fact she was, sweet and ironic.

Over a year ago, Grant had started noticing so many little yellow notes stuck up all over the house. That was not entirely new. Fiona had always written things down—the title of a book she'd heard mentioned on the radio or the jobs she wanted to make sure she got done that day. Even her morning schedule was written down. He found it mystifying and touching in its precision: "7 a.m. yoga. 7:30—7:45 teeth face hair. 7:45—8:15 walk. 8:15 Grant and breakfast."

The new notes were different. Stuck onto the kitchen drawers—Cutlery, Dishtowels, Knives. Couldn't she just open the drawers and see what was inside?

Worse things were coming. She went to town and phoned Grant from a booth to ask him how to drive home. She went for her usual walk across the field into the woods and came home by the fence line—a very long way round. She said that she'd counted on fences always taking you somewhere.

It was hard to figure out. She'd said that about fences as if it were a joke, and she had remembered the phone number without any trouble.

"I don't think it's anything to worry about," she said. "I expect I'm just losing my mind."

He asked if she had been taking sleeping pills.

"If I am I don't remember," she said. Then she said she was sorry to sound so flippant. "I'm sure I haven't been taking anything. Maybe I should be. Maybe vitamins."

Vitamins didn't help. She would stand in doorways trying to figure out where she was going. She forgot to turn on the burner under the vegetables or put water in the coffeemaker. She asked Grant when they'd moved to this house.

"Was it last year or the year before?"

"It was twelve years ago," he said.

"That's shocking."

"She's always been a bit like this," Grant said to the doctor. He tried without success to explain how Fiona's surprise and apologies now seemed somehow like routine courtesy, not quite concealing a private amusement. As if she'd stumbled on some unexpected adventure. Or begun playing a game that she hoped he would catch on to.

"Yes, well," the doctor said. "It might be selective at first. We don't know, do we? Till we see the pattern of the deterioration, we really can't say."

In a while it hardly mattered what label was put on it. Fiona, who no longer went shopping alone, disappeared from the supermarket while Grant had his back turned. A policeman picked her up as she was walking down the middle of the road, blocks away. He asked her name and she answered readily. Then he asked her the name of the Prime Minister.

"If you don't know that, young man, you really shouldn't be in such a responsible job."

He laughed. But then she made the mistake of asking if he'd seen Boris and Natasha. These were the now dead Russian wolfhounds she had adopted many years ago, as a favor to a friend, then devoted herself to for the rest of their lives. Her taking them over might have coincided with the discovery that she was not likely to have children. Something about her tubes being blocked, or twisted—Grant could not remember now. He had always avoided thinking about all that female apparatus. Or it might have been after her mother died. The dogs' long legs and silky hair, their narrow, gentle, intransigent faces made a fine match for her when she took them out for walks. And Grant himself, in those days, landing his first job at the university (his father-in-law's money welcome there in spite of the political taint), might have seemed to some people to have been picked up on another of Fiona's eccentric whims, and groomed and tended and favored—though, fortunately, he didn't understand this until much later.

There was a rule that nobody could be admitted to Meadowlake during the month of December. The holiday season had so many emotional pitfalls. So they made the twenty-minute drive in January. Before they reached the highway the country road dipped through a swampy hollow now completely frozen over.

Fiona said, "Oh, remember."

Grant said, "I was thinking about that, too."

"Only it was in the moonlight," she said.

She was talking about the time that they had gone out skiing at night under the full moon and over the black-striped snow, in this place that you could get into only in the depths of winter. They had heard the branches cracking in the cold.

If she could remember that, so vividly and correctly, could there really be so much the matter with her? It was all he could do not to turn around and drive home.

Chapter Fourteen

There was another rule that the supervisor explained to him. New residents were not to be visited during the first thirty days. Most people needed that time to get settled in. Before the rule had been put in place, there had been pleas and tears and tantrums, even from those who had come in willingly. Around the third or fourth day they would start lamenting and begging to be taken home. And some relatives could be susceptible to that, so you would have people being carted home who would not get on there any better than they had before. Six months or sometimes only a few weeks later, the whole upsetting hassle would have to be gone through again.

"Whereas we find," the supervisor said, "we find that if they're left on their own the first month they usually end up happy as clams."

They had in fact gone over to Meadowlake a few times several years ago to visit Mr. Farquhar, the old bachelor farmer who had been their neighbor. He had lived by himself in a drafty brick house unaltered since the early years of the century, except for the addition of a refrigerator and a television set. Now, just as Mr. Farquhar's house was gone, replaced by a gimcrack sort of castle that was the weekend home of some people from Toronto, the old Meadow-lake was gone, though it had dated only from the fifties. The new building was a spacious, vaulted place, whose air was faintly, pleasantly pine-scented. Profuse and genuine greenery sprouted out of giant crocks in the hallways.

Nevertheless, it was the old Meadowlake that Grant found himself picturing Fiona in, during the long month he had to get through without seeing her. He phoned every day and hoped to get the nurse whose name was Kristy. She seemed a little amused at his constancy, but she would give him a fuller report than any other nurse he got stuck with.

Fiona had caught a cold the first week, she said, but that was not unusual for newcomers. "Like when your kids start school," Kristy said. "There's a whole bunch of new germs they're exposed to and for a while they just catch everything."

Then the cold got better. She was off the antibiotics and she didn't seem as confused as she had been when she came in. (This was the first Grant had heard about either the antibiotics or the confusion.) Her appetite was pretty good and she seemed to enjoy sitting in the sunroom. And she was making some friends, Kristy said.

If anybody phoned, he let the machine pick up. The people they saw socially, occasionally, were not close neighbors but people who lived around the country, who were retired, as they were, and who often went away without notice. They would imagine that he and Fiona were away on some such trip at present.

Grant skied for exercise. He skied around and around in the field behind the house as the sun went down and left the sky pink over a countryside that seemed to be bound by waves of blue-edged ice. Then he came back to the darkening house, turning the television news on while he made his supper. They had usually prepared supper together. One of them made the drinks and the other the fire, and they talked about his work (he was writing a study of legendary Norse wolves and particularly of the great wolf Fenrir, which swallows up Odin at the end of the world) and about whatever Fiona was reading and what they had been thinking during their close but separate day. This was their time of liveliest intimacy, though there was also, of course, the five or ten minutes of physical sweetness just after they got into bed—something that did not often end in sex but reassured them that sex was not over yet.

In a dream he showed a letter to one of his colleagues. The letter was from the roommate of a girl he had not thought of for a while and was sanctimonious and hostile, threatening in a whining way. The girl herself was someone he had parted from decently and it seemed unlikely that she would want to make a fuss, let alone try to kill herself, which was what the letter was elaborately trying to tell him she had done.

He had thought of the colleague as a friend. He was one of those husbands who had been among the first to throw away their neckties and leave home to spend every night on a floor mattress with a bewitching young mistress—coming to their offices, their classes, bedraggled and smelling of dope and incense. But now he took a dim view.

"I wouldn't laugh," he said to Grant—who did not think he had been laughing. "And if I were you I'd try to prepare Fiona."

So Grant went off to find Fiona in Meadowlake—the old Meadowlake—and got into a lecture hall instead. Everybody was waiting there for him to teach his class. And sitting in the last, highest row was a flock of cold-eyed young women all in black robes, all in mourning, who never took their bitter stares off him, and pointedly did not write down, or care about, anything he was saying.

Fiona was in the first row, untroubled. "Oh phooey," she said. "Girls that age are always going around talking about how they'll kill themselves."

He hauled himself out of the dream, took pills, and set about separating what was real from what was not.

There had been a letter, and the word "rat" had appeared in black paint on his office door, and Fiona, on being told that a girl had suffered from a bad crush on him, had said pretty much what she said in the dream. The colleague hadn't come into it, and nobody had committed suicide. Grant hadn't been disgraced. In fact, he had got off easy when you thought of what might have happened just a couple of years later. But word got around. Cold shoulders became conspicuous. They had few Christmas invitations and spent New Year's Eve alone. Grant got drunk, and without its being required of him—also, thank God, without making the error of a confession—he promised Fiona a new life.

Nowhere had there been any acknowledgment that the life of a philanderer (if that was what Grant had to call himself—he who had not had half as many conquests as the man who had reproached him in his dream) involved acts of generosity, and even sacrifice. Many times he had catered to a woman's pride, to her fragility, by offering

Chapter Fourteen

more affection—or a rougher passion—than anything he really felt. All so that he could now find himself accused of wounding and exploiting and destroying self-esteem. And of deceiving Fiona—as, of course, he had. But would it have been better if he had done as others had done with their wives, and left her? He had never thought of such a thing. He had never stopped making love to Fiona. He had not stayed away from her for a single night. No making up elaborate stories in order to spend a weekend in San Francisco or in a tent on Manitoulin Island. He had gone easy on the dope and the drink, and he had continued to publish papers, serve on committees, make progress in his career. He had never had any intention of throwing over work and marriage and taking to the country to practice carpentry or keep bees.

But something like that had happened, after all. He had taken early retirement with a reduced pension. Fiona's father had died, after some be-wildered and stoical time alone in the big house, and Fiona had inherited both that property and the farmhouse where her father had grown up, in the country near Georgian Bay.

It was a new life. He and Fiona worked on the house. They got cross-country skis. They were not very sociable but they gradually made some friends. There were no more hectic flirtations. No bare female toes creeping up under a man's pants leg at a dinner party. No more loose wives.

Just in time, Grant was able to think, when the sense of injustice had worn down. The feminists and perhaps the sad silly girl herself and his cowardly so-called friends had pushed him out just in time. Out of a life that was in fact getting to be more trouble than it was worth. And that might eventually have cost him Fiona.

On the morning of the day when he was to go back to Meadowlake, for the first visit, Grant woke early. He was full of a solemn tingling, as in the old days on the morning of his first planned meeting with a new woman. The feeling was not precisely sexual. (Later, when the meetings had become routine, that was all it was.) There was an expectation of discovery, almost a spiritual expansion. Also timidity, humility, alarm.

There had been a thaw. Plenty of snow was left, but the dazzling hard landscape of earlier winter had crumbled. These pocked heaps under a gray sky looked like refuse in the fields. In the town near Meadowlake he found a florist's shop and bought a large bouquet. He had never presented flowers to Fiona before. Or to anyone else. He entered the building feeling like a hopeless lover or a guilty husband in a cartoon.

"Wow. Narcissus this early," Kristy said. "You must've spent a fortune." She went along the hall ahead of him and snapped on the light in a sort of pantry, where she searched for a vase. She was a heavy young woman who looked as if she had given up on her looks in every department except her hair. That was blond and voluminous. All the puffed-up luxury of a cocktail waitress's style, or a stripper's, on top of such a workaday face and body.

"There now," she said, and nodded him down the hall. "Name's right on the door."

So it was, on a nameplate decorated with bluebirds. He wondered whether to knock, and did, then opened the door and called her name.

She wasn't there. The closet door was closed, the bed smoothed. Nothing on the bedside table, except a box of Kleenex and a glass of water. Not a single photograph or picture of any kind, not a book or a magazine. Perhaps you had to keep those in a cupboard.

He went back to the nurses' station. Kristy said, "No?" with a surprise that he thought perfunctory. He hesitated, holding the flowers. She said, "O.K., O.K.—let's set the bouquet down here." Sighing, as if he were a backward child on his first day at school, she led him down the hall toward a large central space with skylights which seemed to be a general meeting area. Some people were sitting along the walls, in easy chairs, others at tables in the middle of the carpeted floor. None of them looked too bad. Old—some of them incapacitated enough to need wheelchairs—but decent. There had been some unnerving sights when he and Fiona visited Mr. Farquhar. Whiskers on old women's chins, somebody with a bulged-out eye like a rotted plum. Dribblers, head wagglers, mad chatterers. Now it looked as if there'd been some weeding out of the worst cases.

"See?" said Kristy in a softer voice. "You just go up and say hello and try not to startle her. Just go ahead."

He saw Fiona in profile, sitting close up to one of the card tables, but not playing. She looked a little puffy in the face, the flab on one cheek hiding the corner of her mouth, in a way it hadn't done before. She was watching the play of the man she sat closest to. He held his cards tilted so that she could see them. When Grant got near the table she looked up. They all looked up—all the players at the table looked up, with displeasure. Then they immediately looked down at their cards, as if to ward off any intrusion.

But Fiona smiled her lopsided, abashed, sly, and charming smile and pushed back her chair and came round to him, putting her fingers to her mouth.

"Bridge," she whispered. "Deadly serious. They're quite rabid about it." She drew him toward the coffee table, chatting. "I can remember being like that for a while at college. My friends and I would cut class and sit in the common room and smoke and play like cutthroats. Can I get you anything? A cup of tea? I'm afraid the coffee isn't up to much here."

Grant never drank tea.

He could not throw his arms around her. Something about her voice and smile, familiar as they were, something about the way she seemed to be guarding the players from him—as well as him from their displeasure—made that impossible.

Chapter Fourteen

"I brought you some flowers," he said. "I thought they'd do to brighten up your room. I went to your room but you weren't there."

"Well, no," she said. "I'm here." She glanced back at the table.

Grant said, "You've made a new friend." He nodded toward the man she'd been sitting next to. At this moment that man looked up at Fiona and she turned, either because of what Grant had said or because she felt the look at her back.

"It's just Aubrey," she said. "The funny thing is I knew him years and years ago. He worked in the store. The hardware store where my grandpa used to shop. He and I were always kidding around and he couldn't get up the nerve to ask me out. Till the very last weekend and he took me to a ballgame. But when it was over my grandpa showed up to drive me home. I was up visiting for the summer. Visiting my grandparents—they lived on a farm."

"Fiona. I know where your grandparents lived. It's where we live. Lived."

"Really?" she said, not paying her full attention because the cardplayer was sending her his look, which was one not of supplication but of command. He was a man of about Grant's age, or a little older. Thick coarse white hair fell over his forehead and his skin was leathery but pale, yellowish-white like an old wrinkled-up kid glove. His long face was dignified and melancholy and he had something of the beauty of a powerful, discouraged, elderly horse. But where Fiona was concerned he was not discouraged.

"I better go back," Fiona said, a blush spotting her newly fattened face. "He thinks he can't play without me sitting there. It's silly, I hardly know the game anymore. If I leave you now, you can entertain yourself? It must all seem strange to you but you'll be surprised how soon you get used to it. You'll get to know who everybody is. Except that some of them are pretty well off in the clouds, you know—you can't expect them all to get to know who you are."

She slipped back into her chair and said something into Aubrey's ear. She tapped her fingers across the back of his hand.

Grant went in search of Kristy and met her in the hall. She was pushing a cart with pitchers of apple juice and grape juice.

"Well?" she said.

Grant said, "Does she even know who I am?" He could not decide. She could have been playing a joke. It would not be unlike her. She had given herself away by that little pretense at the end, talking to him as if she thought perhaps he was a new resident. If it was a pretense.

Kristy said, "You just caught her at sort of a bad moment. Involved in the game."

"She's not even playing," he said.

"Well, but her friend's playing. Aubrey."

"So who is Aubrey?"

"That's who he is. Aubrey. Her friend. Would you like a juice?" Grant shook his head. "Oh look," said Kristy. "They get these attachments. That takes over for a while. Best buddy sort of thing. It's kind of a phase."

"You mean she really might not know who I am?"

（本篇完整版请扫描扉页二维码获取）

 Questions for Discussion

1. What is the meaning of the title? Who is the bear in the story? What is the mountain?
2. Is Grant loyal to his marriage? Please support your views with examples.
3. What happened when Fiona were sent into the nursing home?

 Links

1. https：//en.wikipedia.org/wiki/Alice_Munro
   提供爱丽丝·门罗生平及创作的详细介绍。
2. http：//www.newyorker.com/magazine/2013/10/21/the-bear-came-over-the-mountain-2
   提供爱丽丝·门罗的小说《熊从山上走过》细读资料。